VAMPIRE FEUD

BOOK TWO OF THE CANDACE MARSHALL CHRONICLES

Vampire Feud

BOOK TWO OF THE CANDACE MARSHALL CHRONICLES

MICHELE ISRAEL HARPER

Love2ReadLove2Write Publishing, LLC
Indianapolis, Indiana

Copyright © 2024 by Michele Israel Harper

Published by Love2ReadLove2Write Publishing, LLC

Indianapolis, Indiana

love2readlove2writepublishing.com

All rights reserved.

No part of this book may be reproduced in any form or by any electronic or mechanical means, including information storage and retrieval systems, without written permission from the author, except for the use of brief quotations in a book review.

Library of Congress Cataloging-in-Publication Data is on file at the Library of Congress, Washington, DC.

Paperback ISBN: 978-1-943788-75-0

Ebook ISBN: 978-1-943788-76-7

This is a work of fiction. Names, characters, incidents, and dialogues are products of the author's imagination and are not to be construed as real. Any resemblance to actual events or persons, living or dead, is entirely coincidental.

No generative artificial intelligence (AI) whatsoever was used in this work. The author expressly prohibits any entity from using any part of this publication to train AI technologies of any kind. 100% author-created content; real artists and editors hired for their skill.

Cover Design by Sara Helwe Digital Arts (sara-helwe.com)

Model and Photography by Jessica "Faestock" Truscott

Additional models and stock photography: DepositPhotos.com

ALSO BY MICHELE ISRAEL HARPER

Candace Marshall Chronicles:
Ghostly Vendetta

Zombie Takeover

Vampire Feud

(Coming Soon)

Mummy Resurrection

Beast Hunters Series:
Beast Hunter: A Prequel Novella

The Lost Slipper: Cosette's Story

Kill the Beast

Silence the Siren

Quell the Nightingale

(Coming Soon)

Slay the Wolf

Stop the Snow Queen

End the Fey

Standalones:
Wisdom & Folly Sisters:

Part One

Part Two

Wisdom & Folly Sisters:

The Complete Story

Coming Soon:

Elvish Duology:
The Elvish Queen
The Mortal King

Standalones:
Queen of the Moon
Dreamworld
Stars Collide
The Ravens

Altered Time Saga:
The Lady Bodyguard
The Lady Spy
The Lady Assassin

Altered Time Novellas:
Lady in Hiding
Making of a Lady
Lady Out of Time

Tales of the Cousin Kingdoms:
Ruby Dragon Kingdom
Diamond Unicorn Kingdom
Sapphire Griffin Kingdom
Emerald Pegasus Kingdom
Time of the Dragons

To those who kept asking for this book:
Here you go!
I hope you love Candace's new misadventure.

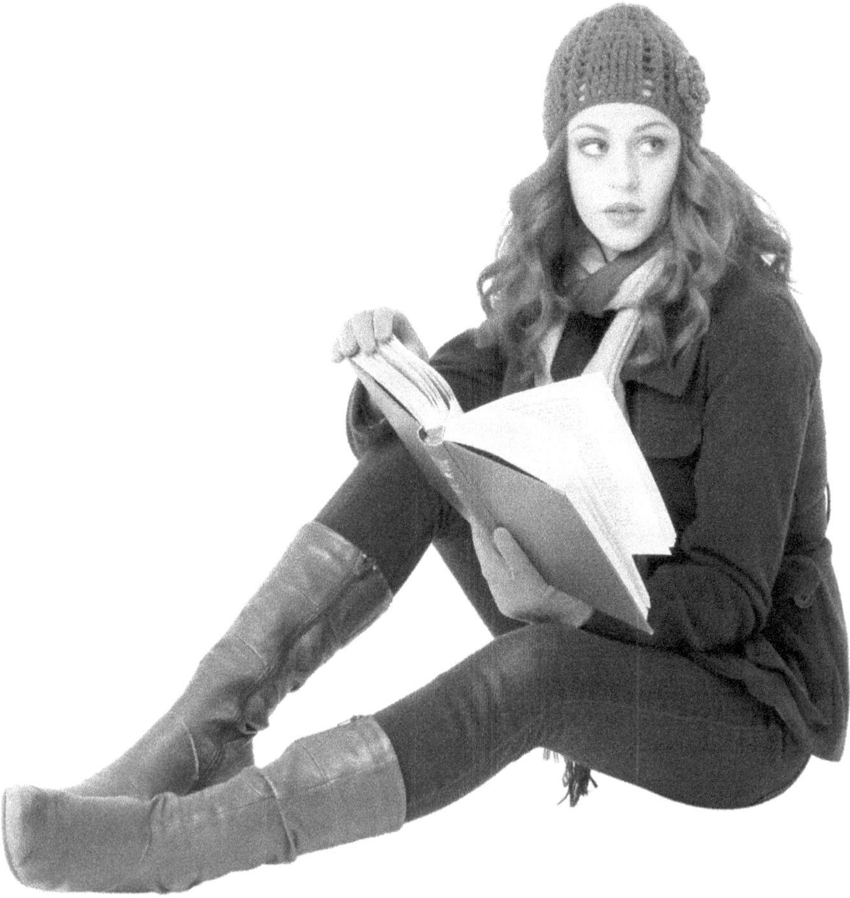

CHAPTER ONE

"Blood. Red eyes. Fangs." I felt so stupid saying the words aloud.

The detective's pen hovered midair, not even dipping toward the flip pad he held. Pretty sure he was supposed to be writing these things down.

I nodded at the paper in his hands, silently encouraging him to do his job.

"Riiiiiiight…" He made some obligatory slashes of ink.

I crossed my arms. "I'm not kidding. Some guy with red eyes—"

"And fangs." His deadpan voice didn't give away his disbelief. Not at all.

"And fangs," I repeated, trying to hurry this agony of a confession along. "He was bent over the guy's neck, drinking his blood just like a real v—"

I stumbled over the word. I couldn't say it. I just couldn't. It might make it real.

It also might make me sound like a real idiot.

The detective's voice interrupted the argument I was having with myself. "A vampire. Really."

The man's dry, unbelieving tone ignited my temper.

1

"Yes, a *vampire*. Or, well, what looked like a vampire, anyway. He was standing over there"—I pointed—"right over the body, drinking the victim's blood—"

"You know what a vampire looks like, do you, Miss Marshall?"

Not a speck of emotion graced the man's portly face, but I knew what he was thinking. *Miss cray-cray over here thinks she saw a vampire. Lock her up, boys!*

It felt like all the air was being crushed out of my lungs as the scene burned in my memory. "I wish I didn't. He was hissing, covered in the man's blood, and he disappeared the moment we shined our flashlight on him…"

My voice trailed off at the look on his face.

He didn't believe me. At all. And I couldn't blame him.

But I *knew* what I saw!

Red and blue lights flashed off the bored yet incredulous officer stuck interviewing me, the crazed witness. He was sketching instead of taking notes. Seriously. Perfect replicas of SpongeBob, Patrick, and Gary covered his page. Instead of my statement.

Which was totally, absolutely, 100% true.

I'd seen a vampire.

As outlandish as that sounded, I wanted *somebody* to explain what I'd just seen.

Coming off my stint in a zombie movie in which I was completely unaware that the zombies were actors—don't ask, I have no idea how that got past me—I couldn't blame the guy for not believing me. But at least the studio had explanations and let me ask questions to my heart's content.

This dude was having none of that.

I straightened. Was it just me, or was he edging toward the other officers? Was he going to call for backup? Was I going to go to *jail*? My heart rate spiked, and my eyes darted around the scene.

Police tape. Flashing lights. A gurney with a body. A no-longer-alive body. That had died right before my eyes in that alley right over there.

I shivered.

Where was Gavin?

My gaze landed on him. His detective laughed at something he said and clapped his shoulder. Gavin smiled in response.

Of course he'd get nice cop.

The tall, good-looking, and handsome officer interviewed the only other witness—my date, Gavin Bailey, world's greatest actor. What he saw in me I'd never know, but I was just the slightest bit smitten.

The Scottish brogue he could turn on at whim didn't help, either.

Also tall, good-looking, and handsome, with short-cropped dark hair and premature silver at his temples and chiseled features—Gavin was not only gorgeous, but a true gentleman as well. He was constantly being praised for his kindness to fans and coworkers alike.

I may have sighed aloud, but I would admit that to no one.

Nice cop listened intently to Gavin, jotted down brief notes, and had a respectful, interested look on his face.

My own officer, on the other hand, was staring at the duo with a sour expression. Short, pudgy, balding. Envy poured off the detective, directed at his fellow officer.

I was going to make a wild guess here that he hated being the guy's partner. And was taking that out on me.

I rolled my eyes. Great. How did this always happen to me? It wasn't my fault this officer had an inferiority complex. I tried to finish my story.

"And, um, well, the moment we shined our flashlight on the dude—the vampire dude, not the dead dude—he up and vanishes. Like, nowhere to be seen. We rushed over, felt for a pulse—on the dead guy, not the vampire. There wasn't one, obviously, so we called you guys right away. Well, not *you guys*, you guys. 911. Dispatch. Whatever."

Would I shut up already? I tended to ramble when nervous.

The last time I'd spent so much time with a cop, he'd been overseeing the peaceful transfer of all my worldly goods to a collections agency. Hence why I refused to go into debt. Once was enough. Even though it was my parents' fault, not mine.

Anyway.

Apparently my thoughts rambled, too.

I cleared my throat. "So, um, yes, is there anything else you want to know?"

The officer sighed and tore his gaze from the other policeman. He flipped through his notes. Sandy, Mr. Krabs, and Plankton flashed by.

My less-than-friendly detective interrupted my perusal of his notes. "Is there anything else you would like to add to your statement?"

I blinked. Hadn't I pretty much just asked that?

I opened my mouth, but the guy was already putting away his notepad. Seriously? My officer wasn't even looking at me, his gaze now on the dead dude, clearly preferring his empty presence to mine.

"What are you going to do about it?" I demanded.

His gaze focused on me. Briefly.

I nodded at the still-blank-of-any-relevant-information pages tucked away in his pocket. "How are you going to find this guy? What's your plan?"

The first hint of a smile touched his face. "We've got it under control, ma'am. I assure you."

"Sure you do," I grumbled. He couldn't even take real notes. I was just a little bit salty about that.

He glanced past me, then straightened and snapped his jacket closed. "I'll call you if I have more questions."

He turned and lumbered away.

"But…" My mouth hung open.

Not sure how he was gonna do that since he hadn't asked for contact info. Maybe he was leaving that to one of the uniformed officers?

I crossed my arms and grumbled. If I never saw detective what's-his-name again, it would be too soon.

A hand dropped on my shoulder, and I shrieked and slapped at it. Gavin jerked away and rubbed his ear.

I gasped. "What did you do that for? Trying to get me to join him?"

I pointed at the still white sheet. I immediately regretted my insensitivity and snatched my hand back.

The humor in Gavin's eyes dimmed. "I still can't believe that happened, right in front of us. If I would've been faster, acted sooner, maybe I could've saved him…"

His voice trailed off, and I eyed him suspiciously. The remorse seemed real enough, but he wasn't the world's greatest actor for nothing.

I started spiraling as questions pelted my mind. So of course they all tumbled free. Without my consent.

"Why? What happened? What did they say? Is this another movie trick? Why in the world did your statement take so long?" I gasped. "Do they suspect you? Are you going to jail? Am *I* going to jail? Gavin, I swear to God if this is another movie trick, setup, shenanigan, thing, I will walk out of here so fast…I won't react to a single, blasted vampire! Your studio won't make another red cent off me…"

The utter stillness and gaping faces of crime-scene workers slowly penetrated my totally freaked-out self. My detective squinted at me in what could only be suspicion. I flushed and tried to pretend I hadn't just been losing it for all the world to see.

"Mr. Bailey! Might I have another word?"

Good cop was back. Dark skin, warm brown eyes, and easy smile, he was far too handsome for this job. He could've easily been a movie star himself. I stared up, up, up and wondered how on earth a person got their teeth that brilliant white.

"Of course," Gavin said affably, flashing his own movie-star smile.

The nice detective smiled at me, showing off even more of those pearly whites, and ushered Gavin away. "I'm sorry, I know I said you could go, but I was wondering…"

Their voices dipped too low for me to hear, and I sighed. Looked around. Wondered how such a wonderful night had gone so horribly wrong.

A date. With *the* Gavin Bailey, only the world's best, most famous, most devastatingly handsome movie star. The man won awards like he was the only actor in Hollywood. And he'd taken me to the newest play on Broadway. Me! I actually looked gorgeous for once. He looked better, of course. Way better.

And then this.

A dead guy. A vampire lookalike sucking greedily from his neck. Then lots and lots of officers and questions.

I sighed again and leaned against a cop car, wanting nothing more than to leave. But gorgeous Gavin and gorgeous cop settled in like they were enjoying their conversation. Pretty sure that meant we would be here forever.

I fidgeted. Could it possibly be real?

Could they have—? Would Gavin have—? Was this another movie trick?

It had only happened before. I could walk into most stores and find my face silently screaming back at me from a movie poster or a Blu-ray cover. *Zombie Takeover.* My first and last film. Ever.

They wouldn't dupe me into another starring role, would

they? I hadn't signed anything legal-ish lately, had I? Surely I wouldn't make *that* same mistake twice.

I gasped. Had there been a sequel clause in the contract?

I groaned and rubbed my hands down my face, stretching my skin to garish proportions. I could probably say "Boo!" right now and scare small children.

But if this was another setup…

No. I refused to believe it. Gavin would never, ever trick me to star in a vampire movie. He'd promised.

The lovely—lots of sarcasm right there—zombie movie may have debuted months ago, it may have met with raving success and bolstered my emergency fund to epic proportions, but he would never…

Or I'd kill him.

CHAPTER TWO

I yawned and glanced up in time to see Gavin end his conversation with a firm handshake. He made his way to me, taking time to shake a few more officers' hands.

He was nice and famous like that.

I just wanted to bark at everyone like a yappy terrier to leave us alone if they weren't going to believe a word we said. Or rather, what I said.

I tilted my head. What had Gavin told them? His officer didn't look like he was going to fall over laughing, *or* like he was getting ready to lock Gavin in the loony bin.

Gavin's eyes held concern when they met mine. "You okay?"

I nodded and rubbed my bare arms, gooseflesh prickling my skin. That bloody body would be etched in my memory for a lifetime.

Gavin wrapped me in his arms, and I sighed and leaned against him.

"Move along, folks," a voice barked. "This is a murder investigation."

I turned and came face-to-face with Mr. Surly Detective Dude.

He glowered at me, then glanced at Gavin. "Please."

At least the man was taking a stab at civility.

Gavin dropped his hand to my lower back and guided me through the maze of police cars and under yellow tape, far away from any snooping reporters.

"What did your officer say?" It came out way poutier than I intended, but hey, blame it on Mr. Surly. Or not being believed. Or my perfect night being ruined.

Or all three.

Gavin tucked my freezing-cold hand into his warm one and waved down a taxi before answering in a low voice. "Said we'd most likely stumbled upon the murderer, or perhaps someone trying to resuscitate the victim, and we scared him off."

I snorted. "Right."

With a puzzled look, Gavin helped me into the taxi. He gave his address to the cabbie—well, an address close by—before pulling me close and dropping his voice to make sure our private conversation stayed, well, private. "You really think what we saw was real?"

I glared at him. "You don't? You were there, Gavin."

"Whoa, hold on there, lassie, I'm not that officer." Apparently his Scottish brogue was coming out to play.

I was so here for it.

I tried not to melt into goo, but it had a devastating effect on me, every time. I was pretty much helpless against it.

I scrubbed at my face and took several deep breaths. "You're right. You're not. And for that, I'm both grateful and sorry." I peeked at him from between my fingers. "Forgive me?"

He tugged my hands away and kissed my nose. "Always."

I gave him a shaky smile.

Streetlights flashed like strobe lights in the dark interior of the grungy cab, and I turned to watch the nightlife of New York City fly by.

"What do you think happened?" I asked, still staring out my window.

"Honestly? I'm calling the studio tomorrow."

My head whipped around, eyes wide. "You think *they* did this?" I said with way too much volume, forgetting our too quiet audience.

Gavin glanced at the driver, who was staring intently in his rearview mirror at us, not the road. "Our turn's the next one."

The driver slammed on his brakes and pulled in front of two oncoming cars as he screeched around the corner.

We slid from one side of the cab to the other. I put on my seatbelt.

Gavin winced and removed my fingernails from his tux-clad leg.

"Sorry," I mumbled. "Seriously, Gavin, you think they did this?"

"Gavin! Gavin Bailey!" boomed the cabbie, whipping around to look my date full in the face. "I knew it. I knew you looked familiar! I loved your movie, *Living Days*. How do they come up with stuff like that nowadays? Pure garbage. But sure does beat a night of listening to the missus's yammering, am I right?"

He turned back to the stopped traffic we'd only by God's great mercy and miracles not plowed into.

"Just wait'll I tell the guys who's in my cab tonight."

He dug out his phone, and the screen lit up. He wrenched the steering wheel and drove down a length of wide-open sidewalk to get past the jam. Horns blared, and he stuck his hand out the window with a rude gesture, the other still furiously tapping away on his phone while barely holding on to the steering wheel with a few spare fingers.

I thought I'd gotten used to New York City driving.

Nope.

Though someone actually driving down the sidewalk was new.

To be fair, it was more of a loading area, but there was a curb, and people were walking on it. It counted.

"Watch the road!" I yelled, unable to look away. My fingers may have been clawing Gavin's leg again.

The driver slammed on the brakes, and I clung to the seat in front of me just in time to keep from faceplanting.

"Don't get your panties in a twist, lady. Here y'are, safe and sound."

He dangled his hands over the seat, turning conversational with Gavin. I wished we'd gotten a cab with those prison-like divider thingies.

"If I was you, I'd trade her in for a dame a little less uptight, if you know what I mean. Believe me, I know from personal experience."

I gasped, and he leered at me.

"Not bad to look at, I'll give you that."

Gavin gave the guy a tight smile, paid him—tip much lower than normal, I couldn't help but notice—and ushered me out of the car.

I marched up to the sidewalk, fuming, wondering if this night could get any worse.

"Hey!"

We both turned back to the cabbie—Gavin tense, and me? Ready to snap.

"You need me to wait for ya?"

"Absolutely not." Gavin wrapped his arm around my waist and ushered me around the corner and into his apartment building, though "dragging me away" totally applied. "Next time I'm calling my driver," he muttered.

I knew he wouldn't. Gavin had given the guy the night off, and he didn't go back on his word. Gavin was pretty much the nicest guy ever.

How did I end up with him again?

And now I felt like crying. Great. Stress and I did not mix well together.

His flat was near the top of the towering structure, and stepping into the elevator was like stepping into a compression chamber, with sound and light dampened, plush carpet soothing aching feet, and music that was actually relaxing.

I kinda was in love with his building.

Built in an old-world style, everything was repurposed wood gray with age, and decorations were simple and made to look effortless, all with the intent of making you relax, take a deep breath, and feel like you'd come home.

I could totally see why Gavin had chosen this place.

That and it was secure and he didn't have to worry about neighbors.

Like mine. Whom I'd happily trade in for just about anyone else.

Anyway.

We reached Gavin's floor while I was lost in my thoughts, and I jumped when his hand touched my lower back as he ushered me off the elevator.

Gavin unlocked his door, and we didn't say a word to each other until we were safely in his apartment.

We'd planned to come back here, change, and watch a movie with snacks, but the police questioning had shaved hours off our time together.

I tried not to be resentful of that, I really did, but *come on*.

We only had one day off a week together, and both our jobs were not respectful of that fact. And although our normal shared day off was Monday, we'd both taken Sunday off this week to watch church together and then to catch my first Broadway play ever.

It had been awesome. Until it had not.

We both changed out of our Broadway finery—me in

the guest room exchanging my shimmering princess dress for a tank top and comfy pajama pants I'd left at his apartment for this evening specifically, and Gavin from his tux into a pair of jeans and a T-shirt.

How did he make normal clothes look so good? It wasn't even a little fair.

But I most definitely was enjoying the view.

I laid my hoodie across the back of the couch for when I inevitably turned instantly freezing later, for no reason whatsoever, and then hung up my Broadway finery on a hook by the door for whenever I left tonight.

I glanced at the clock. Though it was technically morning now.

Gavin moved into the kitchen, and I started casually rummaging through plants and moving mirrors.

"There aren't any cameras in there, love."

"Oh. Um, yeah, I know. Just…fluffing the plants, and, uh, cleaning the mirrors…"

He quirked an eyebrow at me as he pulled two ice-cold root beers from the fridge. I didn't often drink soda in my never-ending quest for a healthier me, but tonight definitely screamed for a few. Maybe five.

"You were cleaning my mirrors without cleaner? Or a rag?"

I crossed my arms. "Wait a minute. If the cameras aren't there, then where are they?"

The gourmet sodas clinked on the granite-topped island as Gavin left them sweating beads of water on the countertop and made his way toward me.

I backed up a step.

"Candace, I swear to you, as far as I know, this has nothing to do with a movie. And if it were, I wouldn't let them put cameras in my apartment."

I swallowed back tears, but they still made my throat

sound thick and clogged and weepy. "How do I know I can trust you?"

He wrapped two warm, heavy hands around the back of my neck, fanning his fingers into my hair. Leaning forward, he rested his forehead against mine and let out a resigned puff of air. He waited a moment before speaking. His voice sounded weary, sad.

"Candace, I would give anything to take back what I did to you for that movie. I gave you my word that I won't do anything like it again, and I meant it. Not for all the money, fame, or connections in the world. You mean more to me than any of that. I treasure you, lass, and I am so sorry for my part in it."

"I know," I whispered. "Me too."

That was me. Miss Eloquent.

He gently kissed my forehead, then tugged me into his broad arms. I nestled into his firm chest and took a deep breath. The man's cologne could turn me to mush in the middle of any argument. I think he knew that and wore it on purpose to win every fight.

Not that we fought often.

"But Gavin? I'm still scared. If it wasn't a movie, then that means a person really died. And if it is a movie, well, I can't go through that again." I pulled back. "Do you think a different studio is trying to trick me this time?"

"Candace." Gavin gently pushed me down on his white suede sofa, then sat on the rich black coffee table across from me, our knees touching. "You saw the body yourself when they asked you to identify him."

I shivered and wrapped my arms around my middle. That was an image I wanted to block for the rest of my life.

"Dan assured me it really was a dead body, killed around the time we found him. No tricks, no gimmicks, no movie props involved. If it were a studio, I'd like to see them try to win that lawsuit."

"Dan?"

"Dan Lawson. The detective who interviewed me?"

"Oh. Right." Leaning forward, I sighed and rested my forehead on his shoulder. "I'm so confused. I don't want it to be a movie, but I don't want anyone to have died either."

"I know, lass, I know."

He scooted next to me on the couch, and we sank into the plush folds together, my head nestled in the crook of his arm. After a moment of sheer, blissful cuddling, my stomach gave an angry growl.

Gavin chuckled. "You hungry?"

"Hate to say it, but amazing as the food was, those measly portions aren't enough to feed a toad."

Gavin shook his head sorrowfully. "And to think I'm dating someone so uncultured."

I faux-punched him in the stomach. He flexed, and my fist met solid muscle.

"Ow! Hey, now. Watch it, buddy, or you'll get worse than that."

Gavin groaned and clutched his stomach, gliding smoothly off the couch and offering me his hand. "I don't think I can handle any more. Truce?"

Laughing, I took his outstretched hand. "Okay. But only because you asked so nicely."

He pulled me off the couch and into him, giving me a sweet, heady kiss. "Sandwich?"

I gasped in mock horror. "You kiss me and all you can think of is food?"

I lunged for the nearest pillow. He shoved me before I could slam it into his head, and I sprawled on the couch. He used the pillow to pin me down, then tickled me mercilessly. I shrieked, giggled, laughed, howled…then snorted.

Satisfied that he'd humiliated me enough, he got up and sauntered toward the kitchen. "How about that sandwich?"

His smug grin did all kinds of things to my stomach that

had me wondering why we were even talking about food and he wasn't over here kissing me senseless.

I sat up, half my hair standing on end. "Yes dear, but do include the caviar and anchovies, just how I like it." I added in a snooty tone, "You know how picky I am about that. Must be culinary perfection!"

"Aye, my bonnie lass."

I tried not to get derailed by the low timbre of his accented voice. I was so here for the Scottish brogue. "Good. I'm off to powder my nose!"

I rose as gracefully as I could and pranced toward his luxurious bathroom. Pausing in front of a monstrous picture frame, I glanced behind me. Gavin had his back to me, assembling sandwiches that actually did border on culinary art.

I adjusted the frame, pulling it forward slightly and peeking behind it.

"There's not a camera back there either."

My hand dropped as I mock-yelled, "Well, just…fine then! See if I straighten your pictures ever again."

Gavin's chuckle floated after me as I headed for the bathroom.

✣

I surveyed the girl in the mirror and wished for the hundredth time that she was prettier. More composed. More suave.

But I was just me.

Cute-ish, klutzy-ish, and a whole lot of crazy.

I tried to tame my reddish-brown hair. It had begun to frizz the moment humidity had dared touch it, and now it was rising from its sleek locks to halo around my head like a wild lion's mane. I sighed. This was a battle I fought daily.

Rich brown eyes stood out from a creamy-pale face.

What can I say? Tanning was not an option in autumn-infested New York, not with my crazy work schedule, and not with clothing covering me from head to toe.

I was still getting used to frigid temps instead of balmy California weather or muggy Florida air or sweltering New Mexico desert temps.

But when I tanned, I turned a warm chestnut brown, and I missed the look. It was way better than this pale, frizzy, overtired blob.

I ran my fingers through my hair, enjoying the last vestiges of my styled hair I'd straightened before the Broadway play. Working at a prestigious fashion company had taught me hair and makeup lessons I'd cared nothing about before. Now I had reason to care. And that reason was Gavin Bailey.

Oh, yeah, and my job. Couldn't forget that little detail.

I leaned against the frosty marble vanity with cream snaking through its veins.

A part of me was so sick from what had happened tonight. Gavin and I had left our Broadway play to find blood all over his car—and what appeared to be a vampire sucking greedily from its victim's neck in an alleyway close by.

After spending a couple of weeks on the world's largest movie set while I thought a zombie infestation had killed everyone I knew and loved, I was understandably wary about the whole vampire thing. Except, the officers who took our statements onsite seemed real enough. And they'd said vampires were impossible.

As much as I completely agreed, I knew what I'd seen. And being belittled or shrugged off by anyone was enough to make me want to look further into the matter.

Which was, of course, exactly what those stupid movie people wanted me to do.

I bit my lip. Unless…it wasn't a studio…

I threw some water on my face and dried it, frowning at the smeared makeup on the towel. Oops.

I searched for makeup wipes in my bag. Guess I was done with the cloying stuff anyway.

As I set to work un-makeup-ing my face, my internal debate team continued to score points on either side of the argument.

I wanted to believe Gavin, I really did, but how could I? Especially after last time. Maybe I'd just have to look into it. Just a little. Make sure it wasn't another setup.

And find justice for that poor victim.

Unless he was in on it and popped up and went on his merry way after pretending to be dead. Then I was going to strangle him.

My hands stilled. But if I did any of this, I would be walking into exactly the kind of situation they wanted me to.

What was that saying? Fool me once, shame on you. Fool me twice…

I dropped my makeup-free face in my hands and groaned. What was the right thing to do here?

The doorbell rang, and I jumped and hurried to finish.

I opened the door in time to see Gavin signing for a late-night delivery. I smirked. Only in New York City, right? He tossed the packet on the stand by the door and went back into the kitchen.

Probably the revised portion of his script he'd been telling me about at some time or other.

I really should try harder to keep all the stuff he told me about his movie-star life straight.

But even if I didn't want to forget something, all I had to do was see something shiny, and "poof!" Memory fled my brain like rats from a sinking ship.

It was awesome. (As in, not.)

I eased out of the bathroom and padded into the open kitchen in Gavin's spacious two-bedroom apartment. My mouth watered as Gavin gave me an innocent grin and slid my sandwich over to me.

"Oh my goodness, thank you. I think I live for your sandwiches…" I lifted it to my mouth and, thankfully, took a deep breath. Nasty, sour fish smell and something pickled and other grossness met my nose with a vengeance. "What the—?"

I slammed the sandwich onto the plate and ripped off the bread. Little pickled dead fish and black seedy globs of goo met my gaze and stung my nose. My eyes sought Gavin's. His face was calm, far too innocent looking.

That should've tipped me off in the first place.

"What is this?" I demanded.

"Exactly what you ordered, my lady. Care for a pickle to go with it?" He brandished a green spear in my direction, further pickling the air.

"Ugh, no way! That is so nasty! You know I was just joking, right?" I eyed him, the glint in his eyes betraying his otherwise expressionless face. "No, no, no. You get the nasty, gnarly sandwich, and I get this."

I reached for his plate, but he held it out of reach. I sat back, dejected. Eyed the gloop on my plate. I was starving, but no way could I choke that down.

Gavin rounded the island and made a noise in his throat that people reserve for kittens or babies or something too pathetic for words. Like me.

"I'm sorry, lass, but you're just so darn bonnie I couldn't resist." He brushed his knuckles across my jaw.

I rolled my eyes and huffed. "Thanks a lot."

He chuckled and rounded the island once more, lifting a new plate with a different sandwich from where he'd hidden it. "Here's yours."

"For real this time?" I lifted the bread and suspiciously sifted through its layers. It looked normal. I sniffed it to be sure.

Gavin laughed. "I promise! That one is perfectly safe."

"If you say so," I muttered and risked a bite.

Flavors exploded on my tongue, and I moaned.

What can I say? Sandwiches are my love language.

Gavin smiled and crossed his arms. "That good, huh?"

I nodded and kept stuffing my face, then licked my fingers after every last crumb was gone.

Gavin waited until I'd finished to settle beside me. Not that he had to wait long. I pretty much inhaled the thing.

"Glad you enjoyed it."

"Mm." Words were not an option at the moment. How could he make a sandwich of all things taste like it deserved a Michelin Star?

He bit into his and closed his eyes briefly in appreciation.

He didn't finish his sandwich nearly as quickly as I did, but soon we were eyeing the clock, then each other, clearly thinking the same thing.

It didn't matter that it was past two in the morning. Neither of us felt like sleeping.

"Movie?" Gavin asked at the same time I asked, "Uno?"

He smiled as I laughed. "Your idea was better. Definitely," I said.

He put something mindless on while I wrapped myself in my hoodie, and I settled next to him on his plush sofa and cuddled close.

It only took a few seconds for me to start nodding off as food rested warm and satisfying in my belly and the peaceful atmosphere in the apartment took its toll.

Gavin shifted so I'd be more comfortable. "Why don't you lie down in the guest bedroom?"

"Mm-hmm." I didn't move.

He chuckled and pulled me closer.

I was just about gone to the world when his phone started buzzing.

Seriously? At this ungodly hour? It had to be, what, three, four in the morning by now?

I sat up, feeling like a sledgehammer had knocked me partway unconscious, as he smiled apologetically and mumbled, "I have to get this."

He was halfway to his room before my brain deciphered all the syllables.

I groaned, faceplanted on the sofa, and covered my head with a pillow. I did not handle being woken up well. I needed to ease into it.

For hours.

And preferably not so early.

Soon he was removing the pillow and kissing me goodbye.

"I'm sorry. It was the studio, and I need to go in early for some pick-up shots. Make yourself at home, please. I'll send a car to take you home in the morning."

I knew he went in early, like at five, when he wasn't filming at night, but this was ridiculous. I was pretty certain we were both supposed to go in late tomorrow.

I groped for words but ended up just mumbling something unintelligible.

He laughed, and the last thing I remembered before dropping off to sleep was Gavin wrapping me in a blanket and kissing my forehead.

He really was the most amazing man I'd met in my life.

CHAPTER THREE

I stumbled into the office elevator the next day, feeling like a vampire had visited in the middle of the night and drained me of all my blood too.

Or maybe that was the nightmare on repeat the few times I'd dozed?

Unable to stay on Gavin's couch after the third or fourth time I'd jolted awake from a vampire looming over me, about to attach itself to my neck (thank *goodness* it wasn't there when I opened my eyes), I'd finally given up and called a rideshare to take me home.

I'd crawled into bed and stared at the ceiling, willing sleep to find me again, but nuh-uh. Flashing red eyes and dripping blood and sharp fangs invaded my brain, and I started obsessing.

I got up, paced a mile or two into my carpet, then researched vampires on my phone until it felt like my eyes were bleeding. Even though I *knew* I had to come into work.

I shoved anything that could possibly be important in my notes app, then I went down the rabbit hole of morgues, what autopsies were like, and hundreds of "true" stories of vampire encounters.

My alarm had let me know in no uncertain terms that I had made a horrible decision choosing to obsess over vamps instead of sleeping so I could be awake *for my job*.

I stifled a yawn—didn't work, and my cheeks hurt from the effort—and wished for darker sunglasses.

The elevator pinged at my floor, and I stumbled off, thankful I'd worn flats.

I froze. I had found that matching shoe, right?

I peeked down at my feet, even though I really didn't want to if I hadn't. Both burnt orange. Thank goodness.

I sagged against thick textured wallpaper and almost took a nap right there. The elevator pinged behind me, announcing someone else's arrival. I forced myself away from the only thing keeping me upright and marched toward my office. This was ridiculous! I did accidental overnighters all the time. Why was this one any different?

Because I was drained: emotionally, physically, mentally —yet had been too revved up to sleep. I hoped nothing important was happening today.

I snorted. Since when was every moment at work not treated as life-or-death important?

I rounded the corner and came upon my office. Even now, months later, it still pulled a smile out of me.

Enclosed in glass on three sides, lit with the most brilliant lights on the entire floor, and just a few steps away from the president of the company, my office was the most beautiful working space I'd ever been in.

Well, okay, so it wasn't that close to the president's office. You had to make it past her two assistants, a hallway, and a last-defense assistant to get anywhere near her, but I was beyond thrilled to be here.

My assistant, Lola, was already hard at work.

With straight jet-black hair cut just under her jawline, pale crystal eyes, and an exquisite sense of fashion, she fit right in.

Me, on the other hand? Okay, so although I fit in better than before, my eclectic (as in, "I don't know what I'm doing") fashion sense still got a few strange looks.

At least my burnt-orange flats and burnt-orange handbag and burnt-orange headband (all crushed silk, thank you very much) accentuated the rest of my all-black outfit. It was October, after all.

I paused. Wait, was I only supposed to wear two accentuating pieces? Or were three okay? I never knew the right thing to do here.

My assistant eyed me through the glass. Probably because I was just standing there, with a vague "help me, I'm lost" expression. Or so she'd told me, once.

With her stoic expression, I could never tell what she was thinking. I offered her a bright smile as I opened the door, then promptly stumbled on nothing.

She lifted an eyebrow, but I pretended nothing had happened.

"Good morning!" I called in a singsong voice, trying to ease a smile from that cold yet beautiful face.

She just looked at me, waiting as usual for me to quit acting like a person and get down to business.

I still felt guilty every time I was around her, and I tried to make up for it in leaps and bounds. She never took advantage of it, though she totally could have.

We'd been up for the same job after a successful internship, and I'd gotten the job.

Lola had given me such a "this is your fault" look, and I'd been so sure she'd win the coveted position, I'd begged to have her as my assistant.

She was grossly overqualified, and although I'd more than earned the job as head of layout at *Voilà Magazine*, part of me still couldn't believe it. Why would anyone pick me when they could pick someone else?

"What's on our schedule for today?" I continued, bending to look at the layouts already on our lighted table.

As she went over our agenda, I tried not to detest the glaring lights I'd just been so proud of, tried so hard to focus on her voice, but I just couldn't.

"Uh-huh. That's nice," I totally interrupted.

She paused, as if she knew I hadn't been listening. Lola hated to repeat herself. And as a perpetually scattered person, I often missed a lot of what she said and just hoped it wasn't of "lose my job" importance.

How did I get this job again?

Well hello there, imposter syndrome. Nice of you to show up right on time, as always.

The glass door eased open, the noise so slight, I only heard it now because I knew what to listen for. Our office was mostly soundproof, since everything came through us before it went on Vera's desk, and she didn't want us distracted.

But she apparently *did* want to keep an eye on us, what with the glass display case and all. Even though she was rarely seen outside of her office.

And there my mind went, wandering again.

I looked up with a smile, which brightened as soon as I saw who it was. "Stan!"

"Uh-huh." The short, impeccably dressed man came right up to me and held his chin in his hand. An odd move, and I'd only seen him do it, but it fit him so well. "Sunglasses. A bit wobbly on our feet. Smile too bright. All right, girl, spill. How many drinks did you have last night?"

My mouth fell open as he moved closer, right into my personal bubble, and peered past the glasses, probably trying to see how bloodshot my eyes were.

His wiry, slate-gray hair curled all around his head, giving him a perpetually lightbulb-moment look, and his indoor-pale skin and beakish nose pretty much matched mine from working such long hours. (The skin, not the nose.)

When my brain caught up with his words, I snapped my mouth closed. "Stan! You know I don't drink."

Lola rolled her eyes and went back to our spreads.

Stan tisked and shook his head, waving his hands around as he did. "Do you want to get fired? Is that what you want to do? Get fired? Because believe me, if the boss finds out you came in here like this, that's exactly what would happen." A pause for dramatic effect. "Get fired."

I said the last two words with him, my smile easing back in place.

Stan always teased the employees he liked most with getting fired. He said it so often, in fact, it no longer held the same punch.

Apparently if he *didn't* say something about getting fired, they had cause for concern.

Believe me, I'd spent the first few days at this job hyperventilating in a janitor's closet, until someone took pity on me and explained how things worked around here.

Thank God for that random stranger, who actually *had* been fired the same day she'd comforted me. Just one more thing to feel guilty about, even though I was pretty sure it had nothing to do with me.

"Come on. What happened?" Stan pressed. "You know you want to tell me."

Once again, I stared at Stan blankly until his words caught up with my brain. I groaned and dropped my head into my hands. "You won't believe me. *I* don't even believe me, and I was there."

A standing chair that could be perfectly silent when pulled squealed across the floor, and I winced. He knew just how to make the most racket, to be the biggest nuisance until he got what he wanted.

That being said, Stan was pretty much my favorite person ever.

He had to hop a little to plant himself on my chair, but plant himself he did. Propping both elbows on the lighted table, he made a shooing motion. "Well then. Go on. I can't be here all day."

He could and he would if he thought there was even the slightest hint of office gossip.

I rolled my eyes and wanted to laugh but didn't. He would only pretend great offense, and I just didn't have it in me to pretend a great apology.

"Okay, so you know how Gavin took me to see *From Dust to Ashes* last night?"

Lola tensed. She always tensed when I talked about Gavin, so honestly, I tried not to. Around her, anyway. I was self-conscious enough that he was dating me. Maybe she thought that was the only reason I'd snagged her job?

Stan clapped his hands. "I told you that you would love it. Didn't you love it?"

I couldn't help my foolish grin. "I loved it."

He made an "Mm" sound. "And the company wasn't half bad, I suspect."

Before I could swoon or act ridiculous about my boyfriend, I slid a glance Lola's way. Her mouth was as tight as an accordion. If that even made sense. But that's what I was reminded of, I swear.

I didn't gush like I wanted to, but I'm pretty sure my smile was on the giddy side of things. "The company wasn't half bad."

Stan settled his chin on both closed fists and leaned forward. "But what happened after that?"

I frowned. Perceptive, wasn't he? "Like I said, you won't believe me."

"Try me."

I hesitated, then shrugged. What could it hurt? As long

as it didn't lead to a padded room—or a jail cell—maybe they could talk some sense into me.

So I told them everything.

About how I'd messed up, forgetting to reserve parking. How Gavin had chosen to drive instead of call a service. How we'd miraculously found a spot smack-dab closest to an alley. And though my throat burned, details about the body, the blood, and the...v-vampire...came tumbling out.

And then I held my breath. No one reacted. Lola and Stan held perfectly still. I knew it. Worst idea ever.

The silence stretched on, and I started to panic. Sweat popped up in gross places, and I wondered if design would mind if I snagged a change of clothes. And body spray.

If they even had anything that fit me.

I groaned and dropped my head into my hands. "I knew I shouldn't have said anything! The cops didn't believe me. Why should you?" I groaned some more. "I spent a sleepless night worrying for no reason. How could I have possibly seen that?"

"Now, I wouldn't say that," Stan said. "Candace"—he took my hands in his, dragging them away from my face—"I commend you for telling that detective what you saw, even though he didn't believe you."

"You mean, even though it couldn't possibly be real?"

At a soft snort from Lola, we both turned to her, but she quickly bent over her task in extreme concentration, her face expressionless.

Stan tugged my attention back to him. "I love that you care as fiercely as you do. There aren't many people like you, my dear, and I don't want you to change. I'm proud of you."

I soaked it in. Not many people had ever said such words to me, and I had to admit, I loved when Stan got serious and let his kind side show.

"Yeah, but I feel like I should do *something*, you know?

The cops didn't believe me, and what good is my testimony if they can't find who murdered that guy? I feel like I should be doing more to help that poor old man find justice."

Before he could respond, a secretary popped her head in. "Stan, Vera would like to see you, please."

He huffed and rolled his eyes, oozing himself out of the chair in the same fashion as he'd oozed himself in. "That woman just can't get any work done without me. What can I say? I'm invaluable, I guess." He shrugged.

I stifled a laugh. Even though that was exactly what he was looking for, he was also looking to scold someone for thinking he didn't do important work.

The man would've been at home on a Broadway stage.

He waggled a finger at me. "You heed my words, young miss. Nothing good can come from your snooping in this matter. Do what the good detective suggested: Stay out of it and let the professionals do their jobs."

My smile dimmed, and I ducked my head. "Okay, Stan. Thanks."

But I just couldn't get that dead man's glassy, staring eyes out of my head. Did the man have family? Did anyone care that he was gone? If someone had murdered me, wouldn't I be thankful someone tried to find the murderer?

"Coming, dearest!" he called, nice and loud, even though only the office girls could hear him, and Vera was sequestered in her plush office, past all the assistants and that eons-long hallway, where she most certainly could not.

A few of the girls tittered, just as Stan was fishing for, and he happily went to his wife's office.

Oh, did I not mention Vera was Stan's wife?

Stan was harmless, upbeat, and kept us all in terror of his wife, our boss and head of the company. He should've been an actor, for he loved to entertain and make people laugh more than anything.

I pretty much adored him.

CHAPTER FOUR

I crammed myself into an elevator loaded with people and bounced on my toes.

I had a design pickup I was almost late for, but if I didn't eat something, I was going to grab the nearest person's arm and gnaw it off.

Images of zombies immediately sprang to mind, and I smacked my forehead. Would I ever get that show out of my head?

My stomach tried to eat itself, so I made a detour to the company's cafeteria after checking my phone a million, bajillion times. I could still make it. Maybe. Probably.

My job description should've read: "Head of layout and the most random, odd jobs we can possibly find." Not that I minded one bit. I loved being busy.

And although my scattered personality could bounce from one thing to the next, perfect for my job, I could also hyper-focus when necessary. Like now.

All I could think about was that pickup and how dead I'd be if I missed it.

Did I remember what I was picking up? No. Did I

remember where and when? Nope. But did I have all that info on my phone this time?

For once in my life, yes, thank goodness.

I kept all the details pulled up on my screen, staring at it as if I did so long enough, I would remember it. But nope. The moment I glanced away, *poof*, it would all be gone, deleted from my brain as unimportant.

But dinner last night was ages ago, lunch had flown past without sustenance in sight, and my stomach was starting to greet each person we walked by. Or threaten them. I wasn't sure which.

I *had* to make time for myself.

The cafeteria was stuffed today. I shoved my phone in my pocket, snagged a flatbread sandwich, and barely had room to squeeze in at the edge of the shared seating spaces. I offered the model-gorgeous guy I accidentally brushed up against an apologetic smile. His frown wasn't enough to displace me, though.

I had seconds to eat before I needed to be on my way across town.

The lightly toasted flatbread folded gently around fresh mozzarella, tomato slices, and basil couldn't get in my mouth fast enough.

Stuffing about half the sandwich in my face, I desperately hoped none of my colleagues saw me. They would surround me, body shame me, and snap a few pictures for the bulletin board so I would be constantly reminded of what eating did to me.

Couldn't have curves and size four hips. Oh no. Size zero all the way or starve for the rest of your life. I didn't care. I liked to eat and was happy with my body.

You know, on days when my coworkers weren't telling me I looked like the green giant's obese cousin. That's what I got for working at a New York fashion magazine.

They may *say* they were accepting of all body types, but they didn't *act* like they were.

Even if Vera was curvy and on the size eight side of things (which I knew from deliveries to her office), which I loved. No body shaming around her, thank you very much.

My phone rang, and I dove for it, a tomato landing with a *splat* on the marble floor.

Life continued around me as I tried to tug my phone free from my tight overcoat pocket and not lose the rest of my sandwich.

A wide gap of people opened in front of me, and I glanced up.

And froze. Mouth open. Food just sitting in there. Phone half out of my pocket.

He was walking toward me.

The pale man with long stringy hair and dark eyes never broke eye contact. People gave him a wide berth without realizing they'd done so. And this was New York City. Personal space wasn't a thing here.

The phone rang a second time.

As he got closer, my pounding heart slowed with a sickening realization. His eyes were a murky red. Just like they'd been in that alleyway.

Murdery vampire dude was back, and this time, I was in his sights.

Candace Marshall, a voice said *inside my head*.

I squeaked, jumped, dropped the rest of my sandwich's warm insides all over my lap, and swiveled to see if anyone was whispering in my ear. Nope. I swung back around to track his movements.

My phone rang again. I ignored it.

Look into your John Doe at the 26th Street morgue. His voice was smooth, dapper, and hinted at a British accent. *The old man is a Mr. John Withers, and you don't know the whole story, love. I didn't kill anyone.*

My mouth dropped open further, and he winked. His eyes flashed bright red right before he passed me.

I squeaked and jumped again, squeezing the life out of what was left of my flatbread.

His parting smile, seconds before the crowd consumed him, chilled me to my bones.

The moment the mass of people swallowed him, I shot to my feet. Jumping up on my bench—sending my sandwich innards splatting from my lap onto my shoes and then to the floor—I wildly scanned the crowded room, but he was nowhere in sight.

A thin line of sweat beaded at my hairline, and tremors snaked through my body.

There was something wrong with that man, creature, thing, dude, yet no one had paid him any mind.

Besides not to get anywhere near him.

I looked up at the skylight. Clouds obscured direct sunlight. Perfect for a vampire. Of course, I thought they couldn't be in any sunlight—UV rays did get through clouds, right?—but what did I know about vampire lore? Pretty much nothing.

Right now, I needed to do…something. I needed to act.

Jumping off the bench, I nearly faceplanted from the pile of warm food at my feet—and on top of my favorite burnt-orange shoes—and I frantically wiped my hands and gathered my stuff.

I hurled my empty flatbread into the nearest trashcan, left everything that had fallen where it landed, and raced toward a couple of security guards.

"Please, call the police! I just saw a murderer!"

✗

Apparently I couldn't talk clearly with a giant wad of food in my mouth.

It took a little while to iron out, but the security guards eventually made me spit out my bite—"You'll thank us later, I promise you"—was everyone in on this "make Candace look like a skeleton" thing?—and I finally convinced them I hadn't just seen a *burger*, I'd seen a *murderer*.

Go, me.

While I was wasting time speaking illegibly, murderer dude was back in his murdery hidey-hole getting ready to murder some more old people.

But at least they called the cops.

With a pat to my shoulder, they returned to their posts, leaving me to the guy in charge while his boss was out. It was difficult, but I managed to convince him to let me review the footage before the police arrived.

Vampire dude wasn't on the security feeds.

"But…but, I was sitting right there."

I pointed at my grainy self, my head slowly moving as if tracking someone, but No. One. Was. There.

"See my head moving? I was watching him. See this huge gap of people? Does that ever happen in the cafeteria?"

Skepticism marred the face of the kind guard who'd been so helpful only moments before.

"Miss Marshall," said a decidedly grumpy voice behind me. "Why am I not surprised?"

Oh no. Not him. Anyone but him.

I slowly pivoted, only to meet the glower of my arch nemesis. Bad cop.

Freaking fantastic.

Frustration burned the back of my throat. I'd missed my fashion pickup for this? Stan would be furious. Already was, from how often my phone rumbled in my pocket.

A nervous chuckle escaped my mouth. "Oh, uh, hi, Officer…?"

Was it bad I'd forgotten his name already?

He scowled harder. "Detective Sawyer."

I laughed even more nervously. "Your first name wouldn't happen to be Tom, would it?"

His glare took on new depths of hatred, and the security guard who'd been so nice to me only moments before gave me a look that said, "Why would you even ask that?"

I was wondering that myself.

"My first name is none of your business," he growled.

Pretty sure that meant it was Tom.

I nodded, tucked a strand of hair behind my ear, and twiddled my thumbs, trying to look anywhere but at him.

"Miss Marshall, I will ask for your statement after I review the security footage. Please wait outside."

Those words in and of themselves should've been professional, pleasant even, but not from him. I would've felt safer with goth vampire dude out there.

I was only too happy to flee.

I stood hunched over in the hallway, texting as fast as my fingers could fly.

I didn't want to hang up on my boss when the detective came out, so I was attempting to text everyone losing their minds about the pickup I'd missed and tell them what was going on.

I was pretty much misspelling everything and sending out hundreds of unreadable texts, which was just embarrassing.

I'd been an editor at my last job, for heaven's sake! Vera even said she'd never received such clean rough-draft copy before me, or so Stan had passed on.

Detective Sawyer came out of the office.

I snapped upright, jumped forward, managed to trip on nothing, and barely kept from barreling into his generously padded chest. "Did you see him? Was he there? Could you see anything on the feed? I swear it was the same guy from that alley, and this time, he *spoke inside my head*."

I pointed at my skull for emphasis.

He snorted at me and strode past.

Uh, maybe I shouldn't have mentioned that part…

"Seriously, aren't you going to check this out?" I demanded.

He just kept walking.

I didn't have much of a temper—I really didn't—but I hated to be ignored, and if I could help someone, then by mad King George III, I was going to help.

A murderer was on the loose out there. And I was going to make sure he was locked up nice and tight, unable to hurt anyone else ever again.

I ran after him. "Detective, wait! Have you figured out who the victim was yet?"

My phone buzzed in my pocket for the millionth time.

He kept walking.

"Please, if you'll just…"

He rounded on me. "You do realize when you waste my time, someone in my city gets shot, stabbed, perhaps even murdered. Again. If you're wasting resources, I'm not there to prevent bad things from happening. Is that what you want, Miss Marshall?"

"B-b-but I am. I mean! I didn't. I haven't. I don't…"

That was me, smooth and suave. I pretty much never said what I meant to say.

"For your information, our John Doe is none of your business."

My mouth fell open. He really was a John Doe, then. Vampire dude was right.

"Mr. Withers."

Detective Sawyer raised an eyebrow. "What now?"

"His name is Mr. John Withers. That's what the vampire

told me." I pointed at my skull again. "Inside my head. At lunch. While he was walking by me. But somehow *not* on the security feeds. How is that even possible?"

I wanted to grab him and shake him for emphasis, but I kept my hands firmly planted at my sides.

Let me tell you, it was one of the hardest things I've ever done. But jail.

He was still scowling at me, but now there was something else to his eyes. Like he definitely didn't believe me, but also he just might look into what I said.

I must've gotten that wide-eyed, hopeful look to my face Gavin liked to tease me about, because he made a chuffing sound—like when a dog sneezes—and started walking again. I loped after him.

"Did you see anything on the tapes? I saw someone, I swear! I mean, he was there while I was in the cafeteria, but not on the security feed…"

I still wasn't talking sense, but it was *much* easier to talk to his back.

"It was the same guy I saw in that alley!"

He held up a square-ish something over his shoulder and kept walking. "I have the feeds, and considering there isn't a thing on here you claim, I don't have any questions for you. But if I do, *I'll* call *you*."

Which meant he wouldn't.

"B-but, wait! I have to…"

He rounded the corner, heedless of my protests.

"…do *something*."

I'd never admit this to another living soul, but I may have stomped my foot and stuck out my tongue after he'd rounded the corner.

I turned around, saw the security camera, and groaned.

At least the detective didn't have *that* on his copy of the security feed. Though chances were, he'd somehow get to see it anyway.

CHAPTER FIVE

I stood in Vera's office, shivering and leaving a sizeable puddle under my soaking-wet self. Stan immediately handed me a towel, but I was still concerned for Vera's carpet.

I'd missed the pickup, huddling outside the designer's home in sleeting rain while he threatened to pull his line from our magazine.

I couldn't even smooth things over. I'd just stood in his entryway and dripped while he railed at me. Then the man I swore didn't contain a heart in that barrel chest of his finally took pity on me and let me come in and dry off in order to touch his precious designs, which he did *not* trust to any other courier in New York City.

He didn't trust me either, but I was someone directly from Vera's office, and therefore exactly what he'd asked for. More or less.

I still couldn't feel my hands, hours later.

And I'd gotten whatever was in those bags to Vera well after dark.

Stan, who no doubt had gone down to interrogate the security guards himself and had already seen the footage, gave me a look and wouldn't let me leave as models rushed

Vera's office for whatever bold new designs no one else in the fashion industry had even seen yet. Someone up and coming from this past Fashion Week circuit, no doubt.

Which I was not salty about missing, thank you very much.

Even if I did keep pictures of the Eiffel Tower up all over my office and sigh whenever I looked at them. New York, London, and Milan were all well and good, but *Paris*.

Someone else rushed past me, cloth draped over their arms, and guilt immediately swarmed me again.

I swallowed back the burn in my throat. The designer had threatened to send them to someone else while I was shivering on his stoop—probably after he'd told the same thing to Vera—and I'd almost made that happen.

I would *not* sob or otherwise implode in front of all these people.

We were the most prestigious fashion magazine in New York City. Even though I secretly thought these people were far more crazy about their clothes than was good for them, I highly doubted he would've followed through on his threats.

And now I was back, somehow included on this side of things.

A late-night fashion shoot in Vera's office.

Lighting came in, props and backdrops were set up all over, and *the* photographer and his gaggle of assistants came in.

A little of my stress eased at the sight of him.

A friend from college, he'd given me the heads-up about this job. Well, he'd actually told me about *his* job—photographer intern—but now he was head photographer of *Voilà Magazine* and won awards for his photography and was featured everywhere important on a regular basis. And even though I'd chosen to move to Acción with my then-jerk of a boyfriend, when another spot opened, he'd fought for me.

He was probably the only person on earth who knew about my dream to be a photographer and urged me to make it happen.

He scanned the room, quietly directing the madness, a calm in the middle of a fashion storm, and caught sight of me. His face brightened.

I gave a little wave. "Hey, Jackson. I mean, Jack."

I was terrible with names, and he'd changed his since college.

I mean, *why*?

His smile morphed into concern, and he made a moment for me he didn't have. "Candace, are you okay?"

I chuckled awkwardly. I knew I looked like a drowned rat.

"Oh, this?" I pretended to fluff my scraggly hair glued to my head in the most unflattering way possible. It had not dried well. "It's the latest fashion, dahling."

"Jack! We need you," someone called.

He took a moment to squeeze my hand. "Take care of yourself."

And then he was gone, positioning the models to his liking and snapping pictures.

I sighed. I loved photography.

Of course, "loved" was too mild a word.

It was my dream. Everything I wanted in life. My hands missed my camera so much—somewhere in storage—it was all I could do not to walk over there, grab his backup, and just start snapping pics.

I sighed again, thinking of all the images I'd captured while living in Florida. Gorgeous beach, stunning sunrises and sunsets, pristine turquoise water that lapped so soothingly—

Stan dropped a steaming mug of hot chocolate in my hands, and after yelping and performing a juggling act that somehow didn't end in melted skin, I pretty much wrapped my whole body around its warmth.

"Th-thank you."

He crossed his arms in that unique way of his, like he was giving himself a hug, and tisked, shaking his head.

Once more, guilt imploded in my belly like a bomb. "I'm so sorry about the pickup, Stan."

He obviously looked at Jackson, then at me, and walked away, tisking like a boiling teakettle.

I studied Jackson, frowning, until my face reached new records in the shades-of-red department.

He thought I was swooning over Jackson? I had a boyfriend! I wasn't the two-timing type of girl. I was swooning over his *camera*.

Stan got his own hot chocolate and brought it over to me, standing next to me as we watched the shoot unfold.

I didn't try to explain myself. Gavin had nothing to worry about.

Even though Stan had the wrong idea, we watched in companionable silence, jumping in wherever asked and mostly staying out of Vera's way.

I couldn't remember the last time I'd had so much fun at work.

✝

I was nodding off holding silky material draped over my arms when Stan nudged me. I jerked awake.

Vera was just ending some kind of speech. She waved dismissively to a pile of boxes in the corner. "Several companies sent in samples. You are welcome to them. Thank you again for coming in this evening and giving of your valuable time."

Had I mentioned how much I loved Vera? She made each person feel like a cherished, valued human being, and just about everyone who worked for her gave their all, just because she brought out their best.

"And that's a wrap. See you tomorrow."

The models and assistants clapped for Vera, she waved off their thanks, and then they all went over and rummaged through the boxes.

After handing off whatever luxury item I was holding, I edged my way over, certain she hadn't meant me, and craned my neck, trying to see what goodies the boxes contained.

Designer clothing, makeup samples, fragrances, purses, and shoes were all passed around and snatched up, but something else entirely caught my eye.

A book.

As I moved a little closer, Stan bumped me with his elbow. I promptly turned and apologized to him.

He rolled his eyes. "Better get in there before all the good stuff's gone."

I pointed at myself, not sure that I was allowed in there, really. I mean, I'd caused this whole mess, made everyone work late, just because I was off telling the police I'd seen a vampire. *Again.*

Vampire or not, how could anyone talk in other people's heads?

He huffed and gently placed me directly in front of a box, then made his way to Vera's desk, shaking his head at me the whole time.

I stood there for a moment, unsure if I should assert myself or sort of ooze away.

I was ignored, so I grew a little bolder. The book was picked up, passed around—my heart dropped to my toes—then someone looked at the cover and tossed it away with a laugh.

It landed near me, so I dove for it and smoothed its

glossy back cover, silently apologizing for its rough treatment, poor book. Then I turned it over. And froze.

A female shadowed vampire graced the front, blood-red lips and fangs the only things in sharp relief, with the words *Tell me your deepest, darkest secrets* splashed underneath in a drippy, bloody font.

I almost threw it across the room. But it was so beautiful, so well designed, and of such great quality, I just couldn't do that to a book.

One of the models glanced over my shoulder and spoke to her companion. "Wasn't that from the fall line of Thorn Fragrances?" She had a decidedly French accent.

I tried to pretend I was invisible. Maybe they wouldn't notice me standing right there, holding what they were talking about?

Her companion nodded. "Yes, the fragrance didn't do well, but the artist was picked up by a major publisher. Do you remember which one?"

Kenyan, perhaps? I adored all the accents I got to hear here, but of course I was always too scared to ask if I'd gotten it right.

They moved away, and I wilted a little. It was just a fragrance? I didn't usually wear those. Not because I didn't have enough samples from work already, but most of the time, they were cloying, too strong, smelled like a vat of chemicals, and gave me a headache.

I almost set it down, but I turned it over again. Its gilded silver pages looked just like a real book, not a fragrance box.

I flipped it open—it opened at the top like a reporter's flip notebook—and sure enough, lined, gloriously blank pages flashed by. A real notebook. Score! Each line was a thorny vine that looped back and forth over the entire page. Even better, a perfect red rose was at the top left and bottom right of each page.

It was a masterpiece of a notebook.

I hypothetically drooled all over the thing. Hopefully I didn't croon over it out loud and make a fool of myself, but that's just how I felt about notebooks, okay? And pens. And office supplies. And books.

And this one was perfect. Even if it did have a vampire on the front.

I tucked it under my arm and moved to help break down. Then I could go home and place it lovingly on my shelves where, honestly, it might never be used. It was too pretty.

About thirty minutes later, my final yawn in a series of yawns nearly split my face and was most likely super attractive. Not.

Jackson gave me a tired smile but, as he was moving past me, hesitated.

Stan, standing where Jackson couldn't see him—but I most definitely could—glared at us both.

A model, more drop-dead gorgeous than I had any hope of being in my lifetime, paused next to Jackson. "Are you coming, Jack?"

Her accent was thick, sultry, and completely foreign. Russian? Slovakian? Moldavian? Whatever it was, I loved it.

He smiled at me and made his way to the elevator with her.

I watched them go, genuinely happy for him. He'd done so well for himself, in all aspects. I was proud of him.

As soon as he exited Vera's office, I turned and jumped a mile when Stan was once again in my personal bubble. "Stan!"

He was eyeing me. "Are you going to be safe on your way home?"

I laughed and waved off his concern as I gathered my things. "I'll be fine, thank you."

He still looked suspicious. After I'd started to squirm

under his direct stare, he lowered his voice under the general noise of everyone else packing up. "Don't throw away a good thing for something you think may be better." He frowned. "It might not be."

It sounded like he was speaking from personal experience, and I didn't know how to handle serious, direct, somewhat sad Stan. But I loved that he went all protective dad all of a sudden.

Impulsively, I kissed his cheek. "Goodnight, Stan." I called over my shoulder, "Goodnight, Vera!"

She waved without looking up from her desk, where she was still working.

And I made my way to the elevator, riding it down alone, looking forward to *sleep* more than anything else on this planet.

✗

I shivered as I hurried to my subway stop. I didn't care if fur wasn't in fashion this season—I was getting myself a fake-fur parka and wearing it with pride.

And although the last time I'd glanced at a clock, it was three-ish in the morning, I still wanted to catch a few hours in my bed, not in some cubicle somewhere, as I'd done before. On accident. Several times.

I squinted up at the bright buildings. What day was it, anyway?

We may have only published once a month, but we were running like mad that entire month until we went to production. And although technically I had one day off a week, Monday, I actually only had days off when we weren't in production. Which was still three weeks out, thank goodness.

And thinking of work made me think of being late and

the reason for that—vampire dude showing up and derailing my already frazzled day. Totally not cool.

As soon as I was on the subway, I pulled out my phone and texted Gavin, being casual and vague, of course, my hands shaking a little. How to make this *not* sound like it came from a nut job…

So…hey…you. Let's say, hypothetically, that a vampire can speak inside your head. Have you ever heard of that before? You know, like in any lore or movies or anything?

I bit my lip. That didn't sound too crazy, right?

And oh my gosh, I'd forgotten how late it was. Although, his film often had him up all hours of the night, shooting in random places all over NYC…

He didn't text back, and I kept darting nervous glances at the few people on the subway this late with me. My apartment was only a few stops away, but one thought occurred to me while I was waiting on Gavin.

If vampire dude had found out where I worked, did that apply to where I lived, too? How hard would it be to follow me home from work, really, especially since I traveled the same route each day?

My phone pinged, and I was so startled, I almost threw it. I caught myself and glanced down.

A text. Not from Gavin.

Have you looked into the 26th Street morgue yet?

My mouth fell open. Vampire dude had my number now? I shoved my phone away. No way was I even answering creepy stalker guy.

And no way was I calling the morgue.

I was going to leave this alone, just like everyone and their cousin half removed wanted me to.

CHAPTER SIX

What could one little phone call hurt?

I mean, it wasn't like I was committing to anything. I'd just call, ask my questions, and make sure the detective had followed up on my tip and notified the old guy's family. Easy peasy, right?

So I was absolutely, 100% going to let this go.

Right after I called the morgue.

First thing in the morning, I called while I ran around, getting ready for work.

I set my bag next to the door, ready to leave in an instant, and ran my finger over the vampire notebook I'd left there last night, apparently.

I opened it and scribbled "Mr. John Withers. 26th Street morgue" in my new vampire notebook and pulled back to admire it. See? I did have something important to write in this one!

The line cut off, and my mouth popped open. Were they not open yet or something? I dialed again.

It took a while, but someone finally picked up.

"26th Street morgue. Matilda speaking."

"Hello, this is Candace Marshall"—too late I realized I

should've used a pseudonym—"and I'm calling about a body brought in a few nights ago?"

"Name, date, and time of death?"

"Oh, um…" I scrambled for a new sheet of paper in my notebook, then quickly worked out when the play had been over. I gave her the date and the closest estimate of a time I could.

"And your relation to the deceased?"

I bit my lip. "Oh, um, I'm not."

"I'm sorry, but unless you have a court order…"

"I'm a witness. I was asked to…identify the body?"

I mean, I wasn't, not really, unless you counted while at the murder scene, but it was almost the truth, right? Then I could see if he were really dead or just some actor looking to make a fool of Candace Marshall. Again.

"Ma'am, due to the nature of this case, I'm afraid you'll need to speak to the chief medical examiner, Dr. Greenley."

"Oh, that's great! If you could just…"

"In person. He'll be in tomorrow."

"Perfect. If I could just…"

She hung up.

I stared at my phone, huffy that I'd gone to all that trouble and she'd just hung up on me. I mean, really.

Didn't matter. Guess if I was going to have a free minute to pop by the morgue, I'd have to block out some time in my schedule tomorrow to get there before closing.

Like that would even be possible.

✗

To my delight, this was the one night of the week the morgue was open late. To the public, anyway.

I raced to the morgue the second I got off work, but the clock was steadily ticking toward closing time. I risked a cab ride, and when the driver pulled up in front of loading docks in the plain brick and concrete building, I had second thoughts.

Old, rundown, crumbling—this place was creep-tastic. I wondered if I could get mugged via osmosis if I stayed in the car.

I could always walk away from this, tell my driver to keep going, make my way home…but then this thing would continue to bother me.

I'd just view the body, prove the vampire dude was lying to me, then leave. How hard could it be?

I straightened my jacket, gathered my newly made credentials from my purse, and asked the driver to wait.

He barked a laugh. "In this neighborhood? Lady, are you crazy?"

And he drove off.

I, in an extremely dignified manner, squeaked and raced as fast as I could to the door and pounded on it.

Someone yelled on the other side to knock it off, but I didn't stop until the metal door with a small reinforced square window was pulled open.

I practically fell on the night-duty guard and profusely thanked him as I tried not to look like a mess.

I did not do well in scary situations.

He eyed me suspiciously. "Office hours are over."

I waved around my business card, fighting to find an ounce of professionalism I knew was in there somewhere. "I have an appointment," I said breathlessly. "With the chief medical examiner?"

"He's out," said a new voice, which sounded familiar. "Doesn't work this late. And Harry's right. We're already closed."

We both turned to the middle-aged woman, hands in the pockets of her white doctor's jacket over her scrubs. Margaret, was it? Something that started with an M.

What hit me first was the high-pitched buzzing sound

from the overhead lights, almost painful in my exhausted state. Then how everything was the same puke-green color (oh, excuse me, except for a few snot-yellow accents), and how there was this...absence of smell.

Like, super sterile, but with something weird underneath. I shallowed my breathing, considering where I was. Didn't want to get a big whiff.

She eyed me. "Miss Marshall?"

"Yes!" I wilted in relief and hurried forward, showing her my card. Thank goodness for one-hour corner drugstore printing services.

She glanced at it briefly but didn't touch it.

"I'm here about that body?"

"I'm sorry, but the chief medical examiner—"

"Isn't here right now," I finished for her, "but I am. I'm sorry, but I can't tell you how important this is. I came as soon as I could. May I see him? The body? Please?"

I held my breath—for more reasons than one. She had no idea how difficult it was for me to get away from work to do anything during normal-people hours.

Good grief, even this late had been almost impossible.

But I should've realized the chief medical examiner would go home at a decent time.

She still looked like she didn't know how to take me. Believe me, I got that look from most people.

"I'm sorry, not while Dr. Greenley is out."

I blew out a dejected huff of air. Just my luck. "Perhaps you could answer a few questions for me, then? Until I can speak with Dr. Greenley, of course."

I offered her what I hoped was a pleasant smile and not the start of a yawn.

Then I repeated his name a million times in my head. I'd still probably call him Dr. Greenburg or Greenhart or "Hey, you..." when I met him, but it wouldn't be for lack of trying to memorize his name.

"Well, I can't tell you any personal information…"

She was weakening. I was sure of it. Besides, how many people came in here just to chat? Bet I could get her to talk.

I smiled far too brightly than was good for my face. "That's no problem at all!"

In a power move I'd seen Vera do—*please, dear Lord, may it work for me too*—I started walking, in a way kind of ushering her toward where I wanted her to go while making it seem like her idea.

She turned and moved with me.

Score one for Candace Marshall! Even in my sleep-deprived state, I was a rock star.

"Now, I heard this man was a John Doe. Has he been identified yet?" I asked.

She let out a long breath, as if resigned to her fate, and began to talk. "Yes, actually. His name is Mr. Withers, and he has no living family. Not that we can find."

I stifled my surprise just in time. How was that not personal information? Also, I was not thinking about how vampire dude had already told me this right now.

I wanted to dig out my vampire journal and scribble notes like mad, but I wasn't sure a witness dropping by to identify a body would do such a thing. "And if no one claims the body, what happens to it?"

"If no one claims the body in fifteen days, then he will be laid to rest in a burial ground reserved for unknowns."

I frowned. "Oh, that's so sad."

She nodded once, her voice quieting. "It is." She gave me an intense look. "But we do right by them."

I didn't know why, except maybe because I'd been up for most of two nights in a row by now—three if I didn't get some major sleep tonight—but tears immediately filled my eyes. I went in search of a tissue somewhere on my person.

"Oh my goodness, thank you for doing that. I mean, that's just so kind…"

She handed me a tissue. I blew my nose loudly, then tried to get my weepy self under control. I mean, sheesh.

I dabbed at my eyes and asked through a stuffy nose, "Now, rumor has it that the man had—and I'm so sorry to say this—vampire bites on his neck? Has a cause of death been determined?"

Any sympathy in her eyes vanished, and she now had a hard set to her mouth.

"That's a rumor, all right," she said flatly, neither confirming nor denying it.

Oh my gosh, why on earth had I said the word *vampire*?

I tried for a smile, but it was watery and wobbly and all I wanted to do was *sleep*. For a million years. "Is there any truth to it?"

Using my own power move against me, suddenly I found myself being hustled back to the door. "That's a question for the chief medical examiner. Now, if you want to return when he's available…"

I dug in my heels. "Hold it!"

She and the security guard, who'd apparently joined us at some point—or hadn't left us at all, for that matter—paused.

"Have you seen this neighborhood? At this time of night?" I dug in my purse for my phone, but I couldn't find it. I sighed. Must've left it at work. Or maybe at my apartment? "Can I trouble you to call a cab? Or a rideshare? Any of them will do. I'll wait quietly until they get here, I promise."

She and the security guard exchanged glances, and at her nod, he stepped over to a desk and made a phone call. She went to a little reception area and started working on paperwork, where she could keep an eye on me, I noted.

She needn't have bothered. I wasn't going to be a lick of trouble.

I slouched into the nearest sticky puke-green chair,

stretched my tight neck, and was out before the guard finished calling me a cab.

✗

I gasped and jerked away from the hand on my shoulder. A complete stranger offered me a sheepish grin.

"Sorry, ma'am, but your rideshare is here."

I stared at him with wide eyes, trying to place him, as my brain—apparently still deeply asleep with how slowly it was working—tried to process who he was, where I was, what day it was.

I staggered to my feet, clutching my bag, as he took my elbow and helped me to the door.

"You get a good night's rest now, you hear? I think you're more tired than you think."

He offered me a grin, which made him look kind of young-ish and adorable—not like a security guard at all—and he waved to the driver before closing the door behind me.

The blast of freezing air woke me up fully, and I took a deep breath as I processed the last few moments. There, I'd done what spooky vampire dude had asked of me, found nothing, and now could let this whole thing rest, just like Gavin wanted me to.

Well, technically, I still needed to speak to Dr. Greenley, but that was beside the point.

As I moved toward the car, my mind fixated on that one word: rest. I needed lots of it and now.

✗

My driver took the long route back to my apartment.

Just as I was debating saying anything, he turned on a

street that meant he would have to circle the block to get to my apartment's entrance, thanks to one-way streets.

It would be faster to walk from here. Not to mention less expensive.

I double-tapped the door. "Let me out here, please."

For a moment, I thought he was going to ignore me, but he stopped at a red light and I popped out. I tossed enough cash to cover the ride and a thank-you over my shoulder, kinda wishing I'd booked the ride through an app so I could warn people away from his money-milking schemes.

Not that I'd ever do such a thing. I always chickened out. There was a real person on the other end of that review, okay?

Even though this one was a scumbag.

My path to my apartment was wide open and well lit, and I felt perfectly safe.

Which is why I barely had time for a squeak when someone shoved a firm hand over my nose and mouth and yanked me straight back.

In less than a second, the city lights winked out as I was hauled into the dark recesses of an alley and held against a firm and somewhat musky chest.

"Let me make something clear, Miss Marshall," said a low voice in a deep timbre. "Stay out of this. You are messing with things you ought not."

Ought not? Who talked like that?

I nodded a bunch of times.

"Good. You tell anyone about this, and people you love will start having little accidents. A car crash there. A heart attack here. You get me?"

My whole body went cold, and not from the weather.

"Now, I'm going to let go. Run, and don't look back. Understand?"

I nodded some more to let him know that I did, that I wasn't going to make a fuss, that he didn't need to tell me twice, and please for the love of doughnuts, just let me go. He released me.

I shot out of that alley like a bolt of lightning and ran the whole way to my apartment building without looking back once.

My hands were shaking so hard, I barely made it past the keyless entry, but once I did, I watched the street for a while to see if anyone was following me.

Which was just awesome with the backlit lobby area making it nearly impossible to see. Dude could be watching me right now and I'd have no idea.

Oh my gosh, was he talking about the morgue? Mr. Withers? Taking a cab ride so late at night?

Sincerely doubted it was that last one, but I wanted to cover all my bases here.

Someone didn't like that I was meddling with that murder investigation, and they'd sent someone to grab me, to threaten me—to violate my personal space and scare the living daylights out of me.

No amount of curiosity was worth this.

Scary guy said to stay away? I was going to stay away.

CHAPTER SEVEN

I mean, the rational thing to do was to get far away from this and stay there, but could I, really, after being threatened like that?

"Gah!" I spun on my heel and stomped back across my apartment.

Hours after being grabbed, I was still pacing a hole in my gorgeous carpet.

And with how tired I was, there happened to be a ridiculous amount of tripping involved. But could anyone sleep after that? Not me.

My phone had been right where I'd left it, on the floor next to my nightstand, useful to no one. No wonder I'd gotten so much done at work today.

My hands were shaking too hard to text Gavin. I couldn't call the cops—they didn't believe a word I said anyway. Gavin would know what to do.

Except…

It had been 18 hours, 37 minutes, and 23 seconds since I'd texted Gavin, not that I was counting, and he hadn't bothered to text back.

And no way was I texting vampire dude who *shouldn't* have my number.

I bit my lip. Gavin didn't want me to get involved. He wasn't interested in discussing lore, probably didn't have time for it anyway, not in the middle of this shoot. But this was important, wasn't it? I mean, some rando had threatened me. Grabbed me. Covered my face with his filthy hands.

Ew, right?

I looked at the screen one more time, then tossed the phone away in disgust. I really needed to stop obsessing. Gavin was just busy.

Thankfully, my phone landed safely on my blood-red couch.

Ugh! Would I stop thinking of blood already? It was rose red. Vibrant red. Apple red. *Not* blood red.

I groaned and threw myself across my couch, next to my phone, staring at the ceiling.

Where was he? Why wasn't he calling? Was he dead?

Had he found someone a thousand times better than me and was having such a great time he hadn't even remembered to let me know it was off? I swallowed.

Replaced. By some gorgeous model-worthy blonde or brunette or redhead.

This was why I worked nonstop. I couldn't stand being alone with my thoughts.

My phone pinged, and I dove for it.

I got a single line from Gavin: *I thought you weren't going to pursue this?*

I whipped back a text. *I'm not. I mean, wasn't. I mean... maybe? I was hoping you could tell me if you've ever heard of any lore like that. For reasons. Have you heard back from the studio?*

I debated typing more, my thumbs hovering over the phone's keyboard. How to say, *Btw, was totally grabbed and threatened tonight and now I'm scared of everything and can you come hold me please?*

He answered before I could make up my mind.

Not them. Let the police handle it. I miss you. Then silence.

Okay. He was right. Of course.

But that vampire had come into my place of work. Some dude had threatened me. I couldn't let them get away with that. Right?

I shoved my phone on the coffee table—it balanced on the edge for a precarious moment before gravity tossed it on the rug. I didn't bother to pick it up. I rubbed my face, hard. What was the right thing to do here?

Bouncing to my feet, I began to pace blindly.

Unfortunately, that meant I tripped over the rug, banged my shin on the coffee table, and stepped on my phone. Stepped on my phone!

I gasped and dove for the device, snatching it up and crooning to it lovingly.

Yep, a nice, long crack snaked down the center of the screen, spider-webbing out in several places. I turned it back on, and whatever I'd done had damaged behind the screen as well. A wash of colors obscured everything, making texts impossible to read, apps impossible to see, and phone calls just barely able to happen only because I knew where the buttons were.

Plus, glass shards were going to start falling out any minute. I just knew it.

Did I even have a screen protector on this thing?

Oh my gosh, I didn't! I'd forgotten to replace it!

"Argh! I don't have time to get a new phone right now!" I told nobody.

I threw myself back on the couch again, missed, and ended up wedged between the sofa and my coffee table.

Maybe it was time to take my pity party to bed. It was probably far less dangerous in there.

What felt like hours later, I was staring at my bedroom ceiling, obsessing, my thoughts circling like buzzards.

Gavin was right. I didn't want to get involved in this, especially if vampire dude had shown up *at my work*. And now *had my number*.

Everyone and their cousin had told me to stay away, to let the cops handle it. They were most likely right, but there was just one teensy-weensy problem.

I didn't like bullies.

And the dude who'd grabbed me had just changed this from "Should I look into this?" and "Whatever you say, scary sir!" to "Oh no he didn't!" status.

Someone didn't want me to find out something at the morgue. So I wouldn't go back there…yet.

I just needed to research Mr. John Withers. Talk to someone who knew him. How many could there be?

I grabbed my phone, growled at the cracked screen, and threw the useless thing aside. Then I spent a few minutes digging through the piles of junk in my room.

I was a neat freak in my former life.

My parents were hoarders, collectors of all things useless, so in college, my side of the dorm had always been the neatest, the most sparse, the most organized.

And when I'd moved to Acción with Peter, our apartments side by side, I'd taken pride in it. I may have only lived there a few weeks, what with the fake zombie apocalypse and all, but I'd made the space mine.

Unlike here. I still had unpacked boxes stacked around my room and in my closet.

I knocked over a pile of clothes—were those clean or dirty?—and blew a strand of hair out of my eyes. It just fell back into place, doing its best to annoy me.

My frizzy hair never liked to cooperate, either.

"Aha!" I seized my computer bag with joy, inspected the crusty old machine I hadn't cracked open since college, and then tried to turn it on.

It wouldn't. I had to dig around for the charger, but eventually I found it and plugged it in.

Of course I had to wait a lifetime for it to charge, thanks to never using the darn thing anymore.

I took the time to look around my room and be depressed.

I'd been so proud of this place at first. Everything was super clean lines with chic décor and red accents, including the *pièce de résistance*: my red sofa, in the middle of the main room, facing the most gorgeous bookshelves ever. And it had a bedroom!

A one-bedroom apartment at this price was unheard of, but I was a bargain shopper. I only bought what I needed, and it had better be on sale or else I didn't need it.

Gavin had even been impressed at the deal I'd wrangled for myself.

But now it looked like a tornado had taken up residence as my roommate.

I'd rather have Gavin around.

Before he'd started filming, we'd been together nonstop. Enjoying the city, seeing the sights, getting to know each other—for real this time. We still liked each other off set, thank God.

But then I'd moved from intern to head of layout, filling a spot that took others years to climb into. And I'd just snatched it up.

Most days I had time to fly into my apartment, shower, fall into bed, climb back out what felt like a few seconds later, rummage around for something clean, and run back out again.

I loved the busyness, I did, but I needed to make my

living space livable. And I wanted to see my boyfriend every once in a while.

Once filming on Gavin's new gangsta flick had begun, we pretty much never saw each other anymore, even though we'd fought hard to have the same day off each week.

I tilted my head. It seemed like both of our jobs conspired to have "Monday emergencies" at least once a week.

Hence why we'd grabbed a Sunday Broadway date, whether we had the next day off or not.

My computer booted up just then, and I squealed and bounced upright, snagging it.

My internet was fine, but my computer didn't know that, so it just sat there, thinking about connecting.

I stared at my dinosaur-level-of-extinct computer dejectedly. It would take more time off than I had to look up anything on that monstrosity.

Then my face brightened. I knew what to do!

I called Stan.

He picked up on the second ring. "What's this? Do my eyes deceive me or is Candace Marshall calling me outside work hours. Hello? Is Candace there? Has she been kidnapped or forced to call me at knifepoint? If it's a ransom you're after, I'm afraid you'll have to leave a message."

I was laughing too hard to interrupt.

"Well, spit it out, girl. I'm having dinner with my wife."

I choked and started profusely apologizing. Pretty sure if he'd let me go on much longer, I would've started crying. "Oh my gosh, Stan! I'm so sorry. I didn't mean to—"

"Oh, please, it's not like I've ever called you into work at ungodly hours." He said, in an aside, "Excuse me, dear," and I heard a faint kiss in the background.

People didn't interrupt Vera at home having dinner with Stan. I was done for.

"Stan, really, I can call back later."

"It's done. Dinner interrupted. Life, ruined. Now, tell me why you called so I can get back to my beautiful wife."

I word vomited a streaming run-on sentence. "I was just calling about that computer you were going to trade in—do you remember the one?—and I was wondering if you still had it and if you did if you could wipe it and sell it to me and I'm so sorry I need it tonight—or tomorrow's fine too! Or whenever—mine's a dinosaur and I haven't used it since college and it's slower than New York traffic and if you don't have it that's fine and I'm so sorry I interrupted your dinner—"

"I have it and it's yours if you will get off this phone and meet me at my door in one hour, and for the love, woman, let me eat first. Can you do that?"

"Y-yes, sir. Thank you, s-sir…"

"Now that's enough of that. Bring cash, all new bills in a locked briefcase"—it sounded like he held the phone close to his mouth and whispered—"and don't tell anyone or the deal's off. I'll be expecting the secret handshake."

Then he hung up. I sagged against the wall.

Vera was going to kill me.

If my anxiety and humiliation didn't finish me off first.

CHAPTER EIGHT

An hour later, I stood on Vera and Stan's doorstep, sweating bullets. I'd found an old briefcase from my "does this make me look professional?" phase, grabbed a bunch of cash I'd squirreled away all over the apartment because I never got a chance to go to the bank—seriously, *how* did I end up with all this cash?—and wished for the millionth time I'd remembered to ask *how much I owed*.

But, hey, without a way to look it up, I'd brought enough for the base model. I hoped.

When I did nothing but save my money, I might as well treat myself every once in a while, right?

The thing was just over a year old, was the most advanced model with all the bells and whistles for that year, and Stan already wanted to replace it since the newer model had debuted.

Hey, we liked our tech.

And since all designs were proprietary property of the company, the rest of us were not allowed to take our work laptops home.

I timidly knocked, but when that got no response, I held my breath and rang the doorbell.

Immediately little yappy dogs announced my presence.

I cringed and stepped away, seriously considering doorbell ditching.

Stan opened the door, his arms full of wagging fur, and waved me in.

I closed the door behind me and stood as close as possible to it, ready to flee the moment he told me to go. Or before that, if possible.

After baby-talking to the dogs, then kissing them all, he set them free. They ran in such a whirlwind around me, I couldn't count how many there were.

"Well hello there." I bent to let them sniff my hand, which they immediately started licking, then yapping some more as their tails wagged in a flurry.

Vera came through in a robe, slippers—they looked like they cost more than my yearly salary—and a green face mask—pretty sure I couldn't afford that either—a tumbler of whiskey in one hand and a long, Cruella-de-Vil cigarette thingy in the other.

Her hair changed monthly from ice-blue to burning yellow to vibrant turquoise to any other color under the sun to complement her stunning dark-brown skin, and right now the violent purple was gone, a soft snowy white in its place.

I sighed a little. I so wish I could pull off her sense of fashion. *Any* sense of fashion, really.

I was nowhere near as cool or as gorgeous as she was. Then again, I wasn't running a multi-billion dollar international company either, was I?

I snapped upright. Oh my gosh. I'd just seen my boss, in her house, *in a green face mask*—I was going to get fired for real, wasn't I?

She waved the hand with the cigarette—I knew she was trying to quit, and she only allowed herself one a day at home in the evenings, but still, I was pretty sure she didn't want *me* of all people witnessing that—and I died a little inside with how elegant it looked.

She spoke on her way across the foyer. "Good evening, Candace Marshall."

I half returned the wave, my mouth stuck open, mind whirring and trying to boot, just as my computer had done.

Stan nudged me and said in an aside, "The polite thing to do is to say hello back."

I jumped. "Oh, um, *bonsoir*, Vera."

But she was already gone, and my French was dismal.

Just one more thing I didn't have time to do—practice French for Paris Fashion Week this spring for the fall/winter line. Which I was hoping to go to. For the first time ever.

If I was one of the lucky ones asked to go this season.

Only Stan and Vera got invites for the exclusive Haute Couture Fashion Week in Paris in January and July, which they treated as their bi-yearly vacation, but they needed an army for the Fashion Week circuit every spring and fall.

And I was planning to be a soldier in that army.

I'd been drooling over all the photos from the Paris Fashion Week that had wrapped a few weeks ago, vowing to do whatever it took to make myself invaluable enough to get there at least once in my lifetime.

I mean, there were also fashion weeks in New York, London, and Milan twice every year—but come on. Paris? I was so there in a heartbeat.

Stan clapped. "Oh good, you brought the briefcase."

I immediately shot upright and shoved it his way. "I hope it's enough…"

He waved off my words and set it aside. Then he rounded the corner and came back with a top-of-the-line, brand-new 16-inch laptop. It had everything, and I do mean everything, you could add to a computer without slowing it down.

The exact same one I'd been drooling over at work.

And it was the brand I adored and wasn't ashamed of adoring, even if Gavin teased me for being a computer snob.

But they didn't get viruses. And they were fast. And pretty.

So pretty.

"B-b-but…" I eloquently tried to point out.

He frowned. "Oh, did I forget to open it?"

He slit open the plastic wrap—no taking it back now—and opened the box to show me the silver computer.

I pointed at it. "But th-that's…"

He wrinkled his nose. "Old and boring and so last year?"

No, it was new and exquisite and so *this* year. But I couldn't seem to get that out.

He replaced the lid, waved a warranty around—"I have no idea if this thing's still good, but call that number if you have questions and so on and so forth"—and slid it all into a logo-splashed bag.

I took it from him in a daze as he ushered me out the door. At some point, the little yappers had all scampered after Vera, I was assuming, since I'd been too dazzled and distracted to pay attention.

"Ah-ha! You forgot a hug."

I tensed and braced myself. Stan hugged or air-kissed most everyone he saw, depending on the person's comfort level, and when he went in for a hug, I'd learned the hard way to be prepared.

Stan practiced the catch-and-release hug: a tug in, a firm, brief squeeze, then a release somewhat like a dance move and somewhat like being gently flung away from him.

People sometimes fell over if released too quickly.

Fine, it was only me, okay? I hadn't been prepared the first time.

I successfully didn't fall over, and he shut the door

gently in my still-speechless face, brand-new computer clutched in my hands.

I may have professed my undying love to it at some point on the way home, but I would deny it until my last breath.

✟

I spent the rest of the night guzzling coffee and setting up my account, making the gorgeous thing mine. There were legit so many wonderful new things to play with.

I knew computers, because of my job, but this was the first time I'd made one *mine*. (Besides that old hand-me-down we are not talking about and are pretending doesn't exist.)

I also researched more vampire lore, because I could.

When my bedside alarm went off for work, I jumped, screamed, threw my empty coffee mug at the dinosaur alarm—both broke—and dropped my head in my hands.

No! I needed sleep! Why did I keep pulling all-nighters when I didn't mean to?

I checked my watch—now the only working clock I owned, another oldie but goodie from my college days—decided I had time for a quick shower, and wondered what was on my agenda. Since we couldn't bring work home, I couldn't check much more than my schedule until I got to the office. I looked at my cracked phone.

Not that I could've checked it anyway.

My phone was only good for calls right now, and that was only because I knew where the numbers should be. I really needed to get that fixed.

And get a new alarm. Maybe one that played music or wasn't so shrill or wasn't one million years old?

My phone used to work as an alarm, of course, but I needed backups for my backups. The passage of time didn't exist for me. Hence the watch, old-school alarm clock, *and* phone. I was always surprised when I saw what time it was.

Thank goodness my job didn't revolve around a strict schedule or anything. (Just kidding. It totally did.)

I jumped up and got ready for my day, intense weariness slugging me upside the head as I stood in the shower.

Maybe I'd use my lunch break to sneak in a quick nap?

After jumping into something I sincerely hoped was fashionable and grabbing all my gear, I headed to my fave coffee and pastry shop, then on to the place at which I spent more time than any other: *Voilà Magazine*.

I was too tired for a happy dance, but I squealed on the inside.

How lucky was I? I really, *really* loved what I did.

Now to make that energy last through my shift.

CHAPTER NINE

"Girl." I looked up to find Stan staring at me over his glasses, arms crossed and wrists dangling over my standing layout desk. "You paid me waaay"—he rolled his eyes with the word—"too much for that computer last night."

I raised an eyebrow and minimized the layout I was working on with a swipe of my fingers. I loved my digital layout desk a little too much.

No one set coffee on this thing, or they answered to me.

"But Stan, that thing was brand new." At his stern look, I amended, "I mean, practically…"

He huffed. "Can I be faulted if I forgot to unwrap the thing?"

"But—"

He was already on his way out, waving away my words. "There's been a credit applied to your account." He paused at the glass door and offered me an exasperated look. "Next time, save me the trouble?"

I nodded, too dumbfounded to reply.

When he was out of sight, off to terrorize someone else, I grabbed my company laptop—since we weren't allowed personal devices in the office—and pulled up my account.

My mouth fell open. He'd only charged me five hundred? For a computer easily ten times that?

I blinked back tears, reminded one more time why I adored that man. He was kind, generous, and went above and beyond for anyone he called friend.

I was lucky to know him.

✗

The second shock of the day, right after Lola had grabbed her bag and left, was no less disconcerting.

"Candace? Candace Marshall?"

My head came up, and I dropped the physical layouts I'd switched to for a more hands-on approach all over my desk, giving myself another good hour of work.

But I didn't care.

Vera was at my door. Vera! My boss.

She didn't come in here. Stan was her go-between, and few were allowed within the sacred inner sanctum of her office. Pretty sure this was the first time I'd seen her outside my office. Ever.

She had the shiniest, darkest skin ever, the purest, whitest hair, the short strands swept into a curvy updo, and a regalness that scared everyone who talked to her.

Okay, me. She scared only me. She put everyone else (who had themselves together) at ease.

She was poised, confident, and the owner of one of the largest fashion empires in the world. She intimidated the heck out of me. I could barely string four words together near her. And for some reason she'd hired me anyway.

I jumped when I realized I still hadn't said anything. "Yes, um, that's me?"

Of course I would ask it like a question. But four words, score!

She nodded, unfazed. "Your boyfriend is Gavin Bailey, correct?"

I flushed, a deep, dark, angry red. "That's right."

And now my hiring was oh so very clear. Seriously? Had Gavin made sure I got this job? Or had that happened when the gossip rags said we'd gotten back together after our breakup after our movie?

Even I couldn't keep all that straight.

Certain my thoughts were transparent on my face, as everyone I'd ever met read me like a book, I tried to smooth my expression.

It wasn't that I wasn't grateful, I was, but I'd tried so very hard to make it on my own. Not use Gavin's position and connections. Not use Gavin. Had he done it anyway? Behind my back?

I didn't know how to feel about that.

"I haven't had the pleasure of meeting Gavin Bailey."

Thank goodness! I was hoping she'd interrupt my inner tirade.

I nodded, unsure of what to say. Did she want me to invite her and Stan to Gavin's? To invite myself to her place with Gavin? I never knew the right thing to do in these situations. For the first time in my life, I wisely stayed quiet.

"I realize this is all very untoward, but we've been trying to get him to model for our new line of men's fragrances for several months now, and we're getting close to launch."

I nodded again, completely tongue-tied.

"It is my understanding that he is in New York City for a film?"

I nodded, the only thing I seemed to be able to manage in her presence. Where in the blazes was Stan? I needed him to interpret Candace body language for me. Unfreeze the deer-in-headlights look. If such an uncouth saying were even allowed in this office.

"Would you be a dear and mention our proposal to him?

I realize such things can get lost with his agent amid the flurry of filming, and it was my understanding he was excited about the venture when we first approached him."

I laughed. Dear. Deer. She had no idea what she'd just said. Or why I'd laughed. I sobered instantly.

"Yes, ma'am. Absolutely, ma'am. Right away, ma'am."

She gave me a long look. "Call me Vera. My mother insisted I call her ma'am." She gave an elegant shudder.

Again, deer-in-headlights look. I'd learned to recognize it when it came over me and froze me solid. "Yes, ma —Vvvvvvv—"

I couldn't get past the V. I just couldn't. It was too familiar. Too disrespectful.

I nodded again, certain I resembled a bobblehead. "Yes. I will ask him. Tonight."

She gave me her blazing white smile I'd seen more often on Fortune 500 magazines than directed at me.

Because I'd seen her so rarely, not because she didn't smile. I have no idea how much she smiled.

"Thank you, Miss Marshall. I can't tell you how grateful I am."

She let the clear door close behind her, and I watched her go, all the way to her office.

I didn't know how long I stared at her door after it shut her within, but I do know at some point I looked down and realized my hands were shaking.

Sometimes that happened when I forgot to eat or had too much caffeine, but I didn't think that's what was happening this time.

Because my boss had placed me in a sticky situation.

And now I had to ask Gavin for a favor. Something I swore I'd never do: let anyone use him through me.

But this was my boss. Stan's wife. Head of the company.

And I wasn't going to use Gavin, not even for her.

Which meant I might get fired.

I turned back to my work, trying to get the elements straight with shaking hands. I finally gave up and gave them all different tilts. Might as well go for a crazy, offset look.

I would go to his place, ask him, and let him and his agent deal with my boss. I didn't need to stress about it a moment longer.

Or so I told myself as I finished up my work.

I just wished my stomach believed me as it tied itself into knots the entire way to Gavin's apartment.

✝

Gavin yanked open his door as my hand was poised to knock. How did he *do* that?

His excited face took in my startled look. "Candace! I wasn't expecting you."

He wrapped me in a warm hug, then pulled me inside. He took off my coat and hung it next to the door.

Thank goodness. Because I did not know how to proceed here.

"I'm so glad you caught me. I'm rarely home anymore," he said.

I attempted a laugh as he gave me another hug then pulled back, still keeping one arm around me. "Don't I know it."

"Come on in. I was just having some warm tea before bed. Man, it's good to see you! I was shocked when the doorman said you were on your way up."

Ah, that explained so many things.

"But shocked in a good way! Can you believe we're both off at the same time for once?"

He left me to grab a second mug. Oh my gosh, he was talking as much as I usually did.

I folded my arms and leaned against the counter. "That's actually why I'm here. Work stuff."

He poured steaming water over loose-leaf tea.

And that's when I noticed I could see his chest. And that he was wearing a bathrobe. And that his hair was damp, giving him a freshly showered look.

I froze, everything I'd been planning to say snuffed out. Or turned to static. Because that's what came spilling out instead. A low hum as if I'd been put on pause. Or maybe my mouth was hanging open in utter silence.

It was sometimes hard to tell what I was doing when my brain fritzed out like that.

He glanced down at himself, chuckled a little self-consciously, and gave me a kiss on his way past. "Maybe I'll go put on some pajamas real quick."

Yes, well, maybe he should.

Before I died on the spot.

He was back before I was functioning, straining my tea and adding honey and smiling in a way that let me know he was too polite to laugh at me outright.

And maybe enjoying what he did to me just a little bit.

"So you're here for work?"

"Uh…" I said.

He came around the countertop, laughing aloud as he wrapped me in another warm hug. "Oh, Candace, I love you. You know that, right?"

I nodded and buried my face in his T-shirt, too embarrassed for words. Would I ever grow up around this man?

He just held me. "I'm sorry."

I pulled back, instantly concerned as a thousand scenarios invaded my mind. "For what?"

"I should've asked if you wanted honey."

And that most definitely wasn't one of them. "Um, what?"

His smile was delicious. "I leave out the honey if I'm going right to bed. I should've asked if you were planning to be up late tonight. Working, perhaps?"

That got me back on track. "Work, right!"

He pulled away to hand me the warm mug wafting delightful aromas.

"My boss wants you for a photo shoot."

A slight wrinkle touched his forehead.

"I know that usually goes through your agent, but she says they haven't gotten a response, and they're close to launching a new men's fragrance."

He now studied his mug, his expression unreadable.

I sighed. "I realize I've never asked you about work stuff before, probably shouldn't, but before I knew it, I was telling Vera I would."

He still didn't look up, slowly stirring his tea.

Oh my word, he was mad at me. I knew it! I knew I shouldn't have asked.

"I'm so sorry, Gavin. I shouldn't have said anything. But there she was, talking to me for the first time since my interview—well, saying more than 'hi,' anyway—then I was agreeing like an idiot and...I'm so sorry. You don't have to. At all. *Please* know there's zero pressure whatsoever."

Still he stared at his tea as if it were the most interesting liquid in the world. After a moment, "Do you not want me to come into your work?"

I stared at him, not sure what he was trying to say. "Um, do you *want* to come to my work?"

He looked at me then. His face was an enigma. And suddenly I was even more worried I'd offended him.

I started running my mouth. "You don't have to if you don't want to. I'll just tell her you're busy. Cause you are. Or to talk to your agent. Cause she should have. I'm so sorry."

He nodded. "Okay. I don't want to crowd you."

"Wait." I studied him, trying to figure out what we were talking about here. "Do you want to come in? Cause you can, you know. But you don't have to!" I was quick to add.

He looked like he was carefully choosing his words.

I threw my hands out. "What? What is it? Just say it. I can't keep guessing what you want, because I have no idea what that could possibly be."

He nodded slowly. "I had my agent turn down that job."

Mouth open, eyes wide, I stared at him, dumbfounded. "But—why? You said that new line was kind of a big deal. That you were hoping to get it."

At least, I thought that's the one he was talking about. Those kinds of details liked to get muddled or run away from my brain.

He nodded again. "Yeah, but that's before I realized the photo shoot was at *Voilà Magazine*."

My heart crashed through the floor and the two hundred–plus floors below it.

Tears filled my eyes. "You don't want to be seen with me?"

He startled. "What? Candace, no!"

But I was already backing toward the door. "I don't think you should give up a job just because of me. I mean, it would be on a completely different floor. You wouldn't even have to acknowledge my presence if you didn't want to."

Forgetting my jacket entirely, I was blindly grabbing for the doorknob behind me as he rushed my way and grabbed my shoulders.

"Candace, stop! That's not it at all."

I was still trying to get out.

"Look, can we please just talk a moment?" he asked. "I think there's been a huge miscommunication here."

I nodded. Though I dearly wanted to flee, I was too numb to run out on him. He turned it down because of me?

How could I possibly explain *that* to Vera?

Goodbye, job. It was nice living in New York City and raking in that kind of paycheck.

Even if half of it went toward rent.

He pulled me over to the barstools in the middle of his kitchen and sat facing me, my knees captured between his.

"I didn't accept the job because I didn't want to crowd you at work. You're always insisting you make it on your own, without my help. I wanted to respect that."

My eyes went huge. "But—you didn't help me get the job, did you?"

He shook his head emphatically. "Absolutely not."

A little of my insecurity about how I'd won the coveted position rushed out of me. "Then why on earth would a photo shoot bother me?"

His mouth parted a little. "So you wouldn't be upset if I took the job?"

"Upset?" I popped up and started pacing. "Gavin, I would be thrilled! I might even find an excuse to come down there and watch the whole thing."

I spun on him.

"If you don't mind, of course. Only if you don't mind."

"Mind?" He followed me, stilling my frantic motions with gentle hands. "Candace, I would love to come see you at work. I just haven't because I knew the kind of stir that would cause. Maybe jealousies and buttering up, too."

"But if we're both working…"

He grinned. "If we're both working, it might not be that inconvenient for you, do you think?"

"Inconvenient?" I threw my arms around him. "Oh, Gavin, I'm so sorry I made you think that. I would love if you accepted the job so I could unashamedly stare at you all day!"

He laughed and kissed me. "Let me call my agent."

He hurried into his bedroom and came back with his phone already to his ear.

"James, have you declined that Amour Ami ad yet? No? Great. I want to accept. Yeah, add it to my schedule with the studio. You're the best, thanks."

He got off the phone, grinning from ear to ear. "I guess I'll be seeing you at work."

I couldn't help my overly sappy grin back. "I guess you will."

His oven clock caught my eye, and I squinted at it, currently hiding behind the electric kettle he'd used to warm water for tea. "Hey, what time is it?"

He glanced at his phone as he grabbed his mug and settled next to me. "Almost midnight. You have been working late, haven't you?"

I groaned. "You have no idea. But seriously, your agent is fine if you call him in the middle of the night?"

He shrugged, his eyes smiling as he watched me, heating the room by a thousand degrees. "Never know when you gotta jump on opportunities. We're both used to it."

"Oh." And once again, it was glaringly obvious how little I knew about the acting industry.

And it was obvious what he was thinking by the way he was staring at me. Hello, heated makeout session.

I scooted back my untouched tea. "So, uh, I should go…"

Had I mentioned how delicious the man's smile was? It could melt solid rock.

"That's probably best," he agreed. "But I'll see you at work?"

I melted. "I'll see you at work."

He stalked me to the door, gave me the best kiss of the century, then handed me my coat and saw me out before neither of us wanted to leave.

I happy sighed on my way to the elevator. I was actually going to see Gavin again. In the daytime. At work. And bonus points: my boss would be thrilled with me.

Best. Boyfriend. Ever.

CHAPTER TEN

The next morning, I found out how grateful Vera was.

A stainless steel brand-spanking-new espresso machine sat on the narrow table that lined the only non-clear wall, a simple note attached to it.

To Candace. We can move mountains together.

Lola's eyes burned with jealousy all day, but I was too high on cloud nine to give it much thought.

Gavin was coming here—here!—and I might get to sneak away to see him. Score!

Stan came in to see the machine, shaking his head and making mournful sounds. "You've done it. You've really done it now, Miss Marshall."

I couldn't imagine what would upset him about his wife's gift.

So, of course, I officially freaked out. "What? Is this a bad thing? Should I refuse it? Do I take it home? Or does it stay in the office?" *For the love of doughnuts, man, tell me what I did wrong!* I didn't shout.

He just continued to shake his head. "You've done the worst thing you possibly could. You've proven yourself invaluable, Miss Marshall. Now it's going to be a disaster.

'Miss Marshall, can you do this?' and 'Miss Marshall, can you do that?' and 'Miss Marshall, only *you* can do this impossible thing.' You should get out while you still can."

I stood there frozen, staring at him, no clue how to react. Was he suggesting I quit? *Should* I quit? When everything was going so well?

Lola stomped around the office, slamming cabinets and banging drawers. I'd never really noticed how quietly she did everything till now.

Stan finally left, taking his mournful attitude with him, and I couldn't handle Lola's obvious jealousy.

"Lola?"

She didn't look at me, though she didn't slam things for a hot minute.

"I'm sure this was intended for both of us."

Her jaw tightened, and it looked like she was about to send the cupboard through the wall.

Oops! Wrong thing to say.

"Um, would you like to take it home with you?"

The cupboard door didn't hurl itself closed. I held my breath.

She turned to me with a bright smile. "Why, I think that's exactly what she meant!"

And she picked up the machine right then and there and made her way out of the clear glass office.

I had no idea where she was going to stash the thing until she could take it home, or how she was going to get it home, for that matter, but I watched her go with a sinking heart. What had come over me? Why had I offered it to her? Was I really that much of a coward?

Stan was in my office within seconds, his back to me, watching Lola. He looked at me. "Where is Lola taking your machine?"

I didn't know what to say. "I think I accidentally gave it to her while offering to share it?"

It was all kind of hazy. I hated when people were upset with me.

Oh my gosh, Stan was Vera's husband! Was he going to be offended for both of them? Oh my goodness gracious heavens, was he going to *tell* her?

I turned to him in agony, not knowing how I could possibly apologize enough.

He just shook his head. "Candace, you are too nice."

But his tone said, "Candace, what were you thinking?"

I groaned. "I know! She was just so upset and I was trying to make her feel better and then all these words came pouring out of my mouth and—"

He came over and kissed my forehead.

Only Stan could get away with that.

"The world needs more nice people like you."

I may have been sporting my deer-in-headlights look again.

He just grabbed what he came for and went back to his office, shaking his head the whole way.

✗

On Monday, my day off—but not Gavin's, this time—I made myself a cup of joe and settled in front of my brand-new computer. I ran my hands lovingly over its sleek silver surface.

Even if Stan had ordered me a brand-new computer and had it delivered right before I'd gotten there—which was what I highly suspected happened—I couldn't have been more grateful.

It was the most beautiful piece of tech I'd ever owned in my life.

I opened it and got to work. Only one goal for today—find out anything I possibly could about Mr. John Withers. How many could there be?

A whole heck of a lot, according to the internet.

I dialed the first number, holding my breath, and my phone had the graciousness to work.

Hours later, I'd made so many phone calls—and had spoken to so many living Mr. John Withers, I kind of wanted to cry.

And no matter how many times I called the morgue, Dr. Greenley was never in.

At least one young intern was happy to answer as many questions as I threw at her, even if she didn't know much. I scribbled "Tessa" in my notebook, just in case I needed to talk to her again, then went back to researching the millions of Mr. John Withers who had apparently moved to New York City and the surrounding area just to make my life difficult.

Oh my gosh, what if he wasn't even from NYC? He could be from somewhere else in the state. New Jersey, even. He could *commute*. Or be visiting from somewhere else entirely.

Why did I think I could do this again?

It was getting close to closing time for most white-collar businesses when I dialed the next number from the white pages. "Hello, may I speak to Mr. John Withers, please?"

After a pause in which I almost hung up, an elderly-sounding woman said, "This is his office. Whom may I ask is calling?"

And that meant he was alive and working there. I sighed and sagged in defeat. "No, that's okay, I was just looking for him, thanks."

"Young lady, wait."

But I heard it as I was hanging up. I stared at the phone in horror, then jumped and dialed—got a busy signal—and dialed a few thousand times more before I was finally able to get through.

It was *not* easy with my cracked screen, let me tell you.

I was breathless by the time she picked up again. "Ma'am, is that you? I'm so sorry, I heard what you said as I was hanging up and—"

"Young lady, take a deep breath and slow down."

I held my breath instead, just dying to hear what she had to say, and almost passed out. I tried to gulp air silently. Would she just tell me already?

She sounded like she was choosing every word carefully. "You are looking for Mr. John Withers, you say?"

I bobbed my head all over the place like a freaking bobblehead, even though she couldn't see it. "Yes, that's right. I am. You wouldn't happen to know where he is, would you?"

I was being vague on purpose. I didn't want to shock any unsuspecting coworkers or friends with news of his death, if they hadn't heard already.

She hesitated, then said, "Actually, I was hoping you might be able to tell me."

Clamping my phone between my shoulder and my face, I threw both hands into the air, and this time, I was thankful she couldn't see me. I tried super hard *not* to sound sarcastic. "Yeah, well, that's why I was calling, sooo…may I speak to him?"

I clamped my mouth closed before it could take off and cause more trouble than this sweet old woman deserved.

"My deepest apologies, but you can't. You see, he hasn't come into the office this past week, and quite frankly, I'm worried about him. It's not like him to miss work or even be late."

I was scribbling notes madly in my vampire notebook. "When was the last time you saw him, ma'am?"

She hesitated again. "I'm sorry. Who did you say you were again?"

Now it was my turn to freeze. I wildly looked about the

room, scrambling for what to say. "I'm a nosy do-gooder trying to right some wrongs" just wouldn't cut it.

"I'm...Candace Marshall, and I'm with—"

My eyes darted around the apartment while I frantically scrambled for what to say.

"I'm a reporter."

I smacked my forehead. Like that would make her talk to me more. I couldn't give her my credentials at my old job, since that was fake and splashed all over TV screens across America. What was I missing...?

"With *Missing News*?"

Oh my word. Did I really just say that?

A pause. "Never heard of it," she said slowly.

I laughed like a ditzy airhead. "Oh, that's because we're new. I mean online. I mean..."

"Young lady, stop."

I did.

"And why would a reporter be seeking an interview with Mr. Withers?"

I was quiet for a few heartbeats. "You mean...you don't know?"

"Know what?" Her voice was steel, demanding an answer.

I sighed. "I think that's something for Detective Sawyer to explain."

I eyed the clock. Which also meant I needed to get down there before he banned me from speaking to anyone at Mr. Withers's office.

Or maybe if I went during my lunch break tomorrow, I would miss him completely. Yeah, that sounded like a good plan.

Would it be more suspicious or less to ask her not to mention me?

"I'll have him call you," I settled on, trying to be helpful.

Now she was quiet a long moment.

"After, may I come down and interview you for an article I'm writing?"

A slight hesitation, then, "I suppose that would be all right…"

"Great!" I didn't give her a chance to change her mind. "I'm free tomorrow around one. See you then?"

She agreed, and I hung up, blowing out a massive breath of relief.

Oh my gosh, I was so close to finding out *something*, I just knew it.

I stared at my cracked phone, unable to see much through the rainbow of colors, and grumbled at it.

Guess if I were going to be from *Missing News*, I'd better create something online.

But first, Detective Sawyer.

A great deal of snooping later, I left a voicemail with a random tip about Mr. Withers's office on the number associated with his name, assuming it was a tip line, wondering how on earth the detective hadn't been down there yet.

"Really."

I froze. Detective Sawyer's dry, disbelieving voice interrupted my long, drawn-out tirade on how the people at Mr. Withers's office didn't know anything more than he hadn't shown up for work.

"Miss Marshall, don't you have anything better to do than pester me?"

My mouth popped open, and I blurted, "I'm so sorry—I thought I was leaving a voicemail!"

"I gathered that," he said with absolutely no inflection at all. "May I ask how you found something, several somethings, actually, on our John Doe when we've hit nothing but dead ends?"

I didn't know what to say to that. How to put this delicately so he didn't think I was putting my nose where it didn't belong? Which, well, I was. But still.

"I called a bunch of numbers. You know, in the phone book?" My neighbor had lent me hers after much cajoling and a promise to feed her cats whenever she took that trip to visit her sister. I was not holding my breath. They'd been feuding for years. Anyway.

He was quiet through my inner tangent.

I sighed. "Look, I just want justice for that poor old guy. Is that too hard to believe?"

I didn't add that the thought of vampires creeping around New York City and lapping up people's blood had me on the freaked out side of things.

Something creaked in the background, probably his chair, and it sounded like he leaned closer to the phone, as his voice got simultaneously quieter yet more distinct. "Let me make something clear, Miss Marshall. I want you far away from this case. I don't want you to talk about this case. I don't want you to think about this case. I don't even want you to dream about this case. Am I clear?"

"Yes, sir. So clear. I mean, like, crystal. Absolutely."

He grunted, sounding more annoyed, not less. "Then what are you still doing on the phone?"

I squeaked and hung up, not even saying goodbye.

Sooooo...did that mean I should or shouldn't keep my appointment tomorrow?

CHAPTER ELEVEN

The next day, I hurried down to Mr. Withers's workplace, just barely making it there by one o'clock. I scurried into the little hole-in-the-wall office, beside myself with excitement that I just might find out something worthwhile.

Also, I was hoping the police weren't still around.

Specifically the one who hated me so much.

I fought off a yawn. I'd gotten a few solid hours last night, but all this not sleeping was really catching up with me.

No one greeted me, and no one came to see who'd entered their workplace, so I started "looking" for someone to help me.

And by that I meant I was totally snooping.

I was leaning over, peeking into an empty cubicle when someone came up behind me.

"May I help you?"

I popped up and gave the woman a bright smile. "Hi! I'm Candace Marshall. With *Missing News*?"

In other words, the blog I'd thrown up last night and backdated a million hastily written articles from college so

I'd have something somewhat legit online in case the woman decided to look up the fake news name I'd given her.

Maybe I should've put more effort into the name. And the website.

"Uh-huh." She eyed me most suspiciously. "Interesting website."

I blew out a breath and sagged. I *knew* that had been a brilliant idea. "Thank you! We report on odd stories, things that slip through the cracks at other more, well…"

I searched for the right word.

"Reputable?"

"Yes! Reputable. I mean, no!"

"More established?"

I gave her a wobbly smile. I'd worked on that stupid website most of the night, trying to give myself some legit credentials, nodding off for a few hours only for my pre-set alarm on my phone to jolt me awake in time for work.

Thank God I had all that college and first job stuff to fluff things out with.

"Everyone has to start somewhere," I said quietly.

Her suspicion eased ever so slightly. "True. And what is the nature of your article, Miss Marshall?"

I knew this question would be coming. Everything I'd rehearsed on the way here flew right out of my head, and I said the first thing that came to me. Ho, boy.

"Because it isn't right. It isn't right what happened to Mr. Withers, and if I can help him, if I can encourage one person who saw something to call it in, if I can honor his life with a well-written article, as small and unimportant as my online paper may be…well. I will have done my part."

Actually, that wasn't half bad.

She got a little misty-eyed, then turned away quickly. "Very well." She waved me to follow her and started making her way past a dozen cubicles. "Mr. Withers kept mostly to himself. Showed up early, stayed late, didn't like to socialize."

She stopped in front of a tidy, mostly empty cubicle.

"The police already went through everything. We would have had the rest cleaned out already, but lucky for you, some rather large accounts asked for expedited work, and we've been rather busy."

I gave her a wide smile. "That's wonderful!" At her look, I thought that might be the wrong thing to say. "Uh, I mean, what do you do here?"

That woman and her looks! Was I really that disheveled, smarmy, or unbelievable? Probably.

I looked around. "At…this…company…?"

My pen hovered over my vampire notebook that I'd been clutching this entire time but had not yet used to take one note. I was too tired. Also, I sincerely hoped she wouldn't get a peek of the cover.

Both her eyebrows climbed her forehead as she tapped the sign directly behind her. "Johnson & Sons Title Company? What do we do at a title company?"

Oh. There it was. Right in front of my face.

I should really get more sleep.

I tried for another smile. "Humor me. For the article. Describe it as if my reader has never heard of a title company and doesn't know what you do." Like me.

Another deep sigh. "We search titles on homes before they are sold to make sure no legal issues arise to complicate matters."

I nodded and made a scribble on my paper. Not a word. A scribble.

"You mentioned on the phone that this job entails a lot of travel?"

"Yes, most of our employees travel to various county capitals within the state of New York to research property titles. We also have an office in New Jersey, and those employees research New Jersey property titles."

Yawn. So boring.

To be clear, I didn't actually yawn, but I wanted to.

I nodded, hoping I remembered this later. *Please, dear God, may I remember this later,* I silently prayed. Never hurt to have backup.

I entered the little cubicle and began poking around. "Yet Mr. Withers's job didn't entail travel?"

"No, he entered data at this office, verified what our traveling employees found, and prepared documents in case of legal issues or litigation."

Desk, chair, slate-gray walls—no pictures, no decorations, no personal touch of any kind. His filing cabinet was empty, and his drawers held only office supplies. A light dust ring said a computer monitor had rested there at some point. Sigh.

"And was he social with his coworkers?" I asked, finishing my search.

I swear I'd already asked that or something like it, but oh well.

She eyed me. "He kept to himself mostly."

"Right." Another scribble. Then another, for emphasis. "And did he have any quirks, any hobbies he spoke of, or did he ever have any outside-of-work correspondence others might have known about?"

I glanced around at the nearby cubicles. Surely someone knew something.

"Well, I suppose I would know more than anyone else since we took our lunch breaks together."

My eyes brightened. Which was rather hard to do when all they wanted to do was close and go to sleep. A few hours here or there just weren't cutting it.

I needed to sleep tonight, all night, and sleep hard.

I scribbled the word "sleep" across my notepad.

A slight smile touched her lips. "Don't get too excited. I liked to talk while he politely listened, or we both sat in silence."

I nodded and waved my pen a little to show I was ready and waiting and for the love of doughnuts, talk, woman!

"Let's see…he did the crossword, ate homemade meals only."

I opened my mouth.

"He lived alone, had no living family."

I closed my mouth, made a scribble. Yeah, the police had told me that too.

"This may not be the most glamorous job, but if you work hard, save, and invest well, you can make a fortune, which Mr. Withers did. And he was a bit obsessed with all things steampunk and vampires, which was rather odd for a lonely old man."

That got my attention. I glanced around his cubicle. Nothing would've told me that from the sparseness. "And how do you know that?"

"Oh, he subscribed to several steampunk and vampiric magazines, and for our Halloween parties, he would come dressed as either or both."

I smiled. Now here was a detail I could work with. "Yet he didn't interact with his coworkers?"

"No, he only dressed up, grabbed some snacks, and worked quietly."

I eyed her, suspicion growing. "And you know all of this because…"

She threw her shoulders back and straightened. "I know all of this because I was his boss. I am paid to know about my employees and look after their well-being."

I made a show of being deferential. I didn't want the poor woman thinking I was attacking her.

She softened. "Besides, I felt sorry for him. People avoided him. He was odd, after all, and I got the feeling he was that awkward kid in school who never quite grew out of it."

Tears burned the backs of my eyes, and I got a little choked up. Poor guy. To be all alone and awkward like that.

And for heaven's sake, Candace Marshall, get more sleep! Then you won't go crying over some guy you've never met.

She looked me over. "You know…come with me, please."

Great. Not only did she think my website was unreputable, now she thought I was unprofessional as well. Way to go, Candace.

I trailed her to her office, fully prepared to be asked to leave or shackled to the desk until the police arrived. Instead, she sat and dug around in her desk's bottom drawer before coming up with a large key.

"I forgot to tell the police about this, but I didn't think it was important at the time. Here."

I took it from her. It was old-fashioned, ornate, and beautiful. I didn't see keys like this every day. "What's it for?"

"He asked me to go with him to his club."

My eyebrows climbed my forehead. "Like a date?"

Oh my gosh, can you not say every thought that pops into your head?

Her cheeks turned a subtle pink. "I was afraid of that, which is why I declined."

"Why not?"

"I was kind to him, not attracted to him. He was far too odd."

Right, okay, but I was odd. Why was Gavin dating *me*? Oh my gosh, was I going to end up old and alone and odd, in love with all things steampunk and vampire?

Not that I was into those things. But still.

"And then when I was promoted, it no longer seemed

appropriate." She busied herself with something on her desk. "Besides, my reasons are my own."

Gotcha. Don't ask personal questions. But a fair amount of panic had already set in.

"Right, but do you know what kind of club? Did he say? And how long ago was this? Didn't he want his key back?" I cut off the stream of questions and waited.

Turn the faucet on, and questions poured out. I was amazed I was able to stop myself.

"He gave it to me a few months ago with an address"— she dug around in her purse—"and said not to lose it. 'Anyone with a key and a code will be granted entrance.' His words, not mine."

She handed me a slip of paper.

"He said the location changes monthly, so I'm not sure how helpful this will be. I apologize."

I did a double take, not at the address, but at the string of gibberish below it. What on earth? I'd never seen anything so unintelligible.

Well, except for random computer-generated passwords.

But this thing was way more complicated.

Sitting across from her, uninvited, I carefully copied it into my notebook in case I lost the slip of paper, because it was me.

"Thank you. This is more helpful than you can possibly know. Oh! Do you happen to have his home address or phone number? The only number I could find linked to his name was here. His workspace." Not that I'd made it through all the Mr. John Withers in this city.

She shook her head. "His worldly possessions were to be donated to charity in the event of his untimely demise. I gave the police his address, but I doubt anything will be left by now."

"Please?" I asked. "I don't want to leave any loose ends."

Besides, expecting the police to empty it in one day? I might actually beat them there.

She reluctantly gave it to me, then leaned back in her chair and studied me. "I hope you will treat Mr. Withers' life—and death—with all the respect he deserves, Miss Marshall. He was an odd man, a quiet man, true, but that made his life no less valuable."

I met her gaze. "I think more people need to look at the world like you do, ma'am. It would be a better place."

Again that light-pink hue came to her cheeks. "Good day, Miss Marshall."

"Ma'am." Because it was respectful, okay? Not just because I'd forgotten her name.

Though that was true, too.

I left the office, a huge smile on my face. Finally, I was getting somewhere!

This key would get me in. To where I didn't know. All I had to do was find the current meeting location—and I knew exactly who could help me with that.

And as long as they weren't real bloodsuckers, I might even leave with some answers. If they let me leave at all.

I swallowed. Yikes. But still, answers were right there. Within my grasp. Finally.

One of the things I'd learned at the school newspaper and again at my job at the Acción newspaper—before I'd found out the whole thing was a hoax—was that a story usually wasn't dumped in my lap.

No, I had to dig it out piece by piece, little bits of information at a time, from many different sources, until a full story presented itself.

And I had one more piece of that puzzle.

Now I had to figure out how to word it on my new blog without interfering with the police investigation. Or my fashion pieces at the magazine.

That would be fun to get all those switched around.

Oh no.

I froze, right there on the sidewalk, right in front of power-walking New Yorkers. They do *not* like it when people stop in front of them. Then again, who does?

But that didn't matter. Not their not-so-subtle shoves and protests, not the story that I wasn't really writing, not the police investigation.

I'd signed a non-disclosure agreement with *Voilà Magazine* when they'd hired me, and that included a non-compete clause, which they were overly emphatic about explaining to me on days one, two, *and* three.

And they were serious about suing. Seriously, their legal department was insane. So many cease-and-desist letters. Which they also made a point to show me.

If detective what's-his-name didn't find a way to throw me in the slammer, my own workplace just might do what he'd been dreaming of since he'd met me.

Things were already precarious at work as far as all things vamp-related were concerned. The last thing I wanted was getting fired, sued, thrown in jail, then sued again because of a stupid little blog I'd only put up because the stupid police wouldn't talk to me about a stupid investigation that Gavin insisted I drop.

Maybe I was the stupid one here.

With a groan, I took off running.

CHAPTER TWELVE

Out of breath, I stood in front of the legal department's secretary, holding the stitch in my side and trying to pretend I wasn't gasping for air like a dying fish.

"Hi. Hello. Hi. May I speak with Gertrude, pretty please?"

The receptionist eyed me up and down, her perfect eyeliner, pencil skirt, and ruffled blouse at odds with my windblown look.

At least I wasn't sweating. No, wait…yes, I was. Gross.

At least I was wearing black? But wait, was it true black? Would it still show? She interrupted my subtle attempt to look at myself.

"I'm sorry, but Gertrude has been terminated due to a breach of contract."

I was wrong. *Now* I was sweating.

I burst into laughter and slapped her desk. "Good one!" I sobered. "No, really, I need to see her. She handled my contract when I was hired?"

Little Miss Perfect twirled in her seat and started typing away at her computer. "Name?"

"Candace Marshall."

"Date of hire?"

"Uh…" Did I mention I hadn't slept much last night? "Not sure…don't remember…"

It was right there, but I couldn't grasp the information to save my life.

"Address? Date of birth? SSN?"

As she took down more info than the government on tax day, just like when I was hired, I wondered why she wasn't just reading it all from my file.

Like I said, insane legal department.

"ID?"

I handed it to her.

She compared it to whatever was on her computer.

I leaned over to look, but she just moved the monitor away. I was too tired to care. Not that I could see anything anyway with the privacy screen.

She scrolled through a few pages. "Let's see. It says here Marion has taken over your case files."

I blanched. I had a case? And files? Were they already preparing to sue me over that stupid website?

Maybe I should've taken it down before I'd run all the way here.

She squinted at the screen. "This is odd. She has time right now if you'd like to see her." She swiveled back to me, suspicion on her face. "That never happens. Most employees have to make an appointment several weeks out. Sometimes months."

Like that was my fault.

I laughed and waved my hand like an airhead. "Oh, that's me. Just lucky, I guess."

If only my luck would hold out for this meeting.

"Would you like to see her?"

I nodded too many times. "Of course. Right away. Thank you."

The only noise in the office for an excruciating amount of time was her typing.

I jumped when she spoke. To no one. "Miss Li, your one o'clock is here to see you. Yes. Please check the schedule. Very well. Thank you."

I looked all around, but nope. Still just me.

She turned an imperious look my way. "Have a seat. She'll be right with you."

I eyed her as I passed and was relieved to find an earbud in one ear. I let out a relieved breath. Whew!

For a moment there, I'd started to panic all over again about vampires speaking in people's heads.

A door opened and I stood.

"Miss Gruyere? May I please see you a moment?"

The receptionist stood and entered the woman's office, shutting the door behind her.

I sat. Twiddled my thumbs. Tried to stop sweating. But I was a bundle of nerves and still cooling down from my run. It might be a hot moment or three.

The door opened, and I jumped to my feet.

The receptionist came out, raised a portion of her desk so she could work standing, and went back to clacking on her ergonomically-designed keyboard. I'd ask if they had a quieter one if I was her.

Come to think of it, I should get one of those.

I groaned and rubbed my forehead. What was I doing here? My brother always said, "Ask forgiveness, not permission." But I was a rule follower, a firstborn, and I hated to get in trouble. I asked people for permission when they flat-out told me they didn't care.

Besides, this was way more important, I argued with myself. I could actually get *fired* if I didn't ask permission here.

After the longest five minutes of my life, the same door opened once more, and an older Asian woman, straight black hair in a bob, stepped out and looked at me. "Miss Marshall?"

I stumbled to my feet, berating myself for not standing in the first place, and looked at her with hopeful eyes. "Yes?"

"Right this way." She stepped back and let me enter her office first. "Please, have a seat." She shut the door and moved around her desk. After sitting and folding her hands on its surface, she asked, "And how may I help you today?"

It all tumbled out. The blog. The article I was writing. My experience at the college newspaper and the few short weeks I'd worked at Acción's little local paper.

"And it occurred to me I should make sure I'm not in breach of contract before I pursue future articles."

She turned smartly to her computer. "Name?"

I tilted my head. "Candace Marshall."

"That's your website name?"

"Oh! Oh. No. It's missing news dot com." I swallowed. It sounded even worse when I said it aloud the second time. Or was this the third? Either way, it was just getting worse.

"And the point of your publication?" She began scrolling through all the articles I'd written and-or copy-pasted from previous things I'd written that hadn't been published or that I had the rights back to. Had I mentioned how late it was when I'd thrown all that up?

Holy Moses, I hoped I hadn't misspelled anything. I was an editor for most of my pre-fashion career, for heaven's sake!

She started squinting at a few things, and I started talking to distract her from any stupid my brain had thought was brilliant the other night.

"Um, missing news, like things the news doesn't report on or doesn't think are important, or even little factoids that my readers might find interesting or unusual." I swallowed hard.

"Uh-huh." She didn't sound, look, or most likely feel impressed. "Anything about fashion?"

"Oh no!" I shook my head furiously. "Not a thing. That's my first love, and I dedicate anything fashion to this job. Other stuff is just a hobby."

Big, fat, stinking lie. My first love was photography, and I'd only put up the website as a cover for snooping.

I let out the worst, fake-sounding laugh in the history of mankind, then snapped my mouth closed. Pretty sure that laugh right there would make her fire me on the spot.

Apparently I could justify anything if I thought I was doing it for the right reasons.

That thought sobered me right up. So did that make what I was doing right? Or just set up my hastily thrown-up lies to come crashing down even harder when I inevitably ran out of them? I needed to think about that. Later.

When I wasn't awaiting my fate in the company's legal department.

She scrolled through a few more pages, then clicked out of the website. "Well, I don't see anything here in breach of contract, but I'll make a note in your file in case it comes up again in the future."

She stood, I stood, she held out a hand. I clasped it, hoping my palms weren't sweaty too. They probably were.

"Anything in particular I should avoid?"

She released my hand and clicked my file on her desktop closed. "Just don't talk about fashion, celebrities or models in the fashion world, or anything about working here, and the company shouldn't have a problem with your extracurricular activities."

Which meant nothing about Gavin or any other part of my life, since all I did was fashion right now. Not that I would publicize any part of Gavin's life. Not cool. For him or for me.

I nodded, smile crumbling. I needed so much more sleep

than I'd been getting lately. "Thank you for your time, Miss Marion. I mean, Miss Li. Miss Marion Li."

She gave me an odd look—who didn't these days?—and waved me toward the door.

As I sprinted to the elevator, I had only one thought on my mind: Take down that stupid website the moment I got home tonight before Miss Li sent the entire legal department after me. I was paranoid like that.

I'd figure out some other way to snoop.

CHAPTER THIRTEEN

I couldn't focus. I couldn't focus!

Gavin was in this very building, or at least if he wasn't yet, he would be soon, and every part of me thrummed in awareness.

Gavin was in my building! As a *model*. A very hot model.

One I got to unabashedly look at with no shame.

I flitted from task to task to task, Lola silently going behind me and fixing everything.

Stan popped his head into the room. "Well, aren't you coming?"

I looked between him and Lola. Pointed to myself. To Lola. Back at myself.

"Yes, you. That good-looking man of yours is here and all you want to do is stare at photos of other models?"

"He's here?" I squealed and threw my stack of photographs straight up into the air. "Oh my gosh, I can't believe he's here!"

I scrambled to pick everything up.

Lola sighed and dropped her head into her hands. "Please, just go. I am begging you."

She didn't have to ask me twice. Neither did Stan, for that matter. I sprinted for the door.

"Aren't you forgetting something?" Stan asked.

I froze. "Oh!" I retrieved my purse and almost ran into Stan on the way out.

"Hold it." He grabbed my arm. "Really, Miss Marshall? Really?"

I just stared at him. What on earth was he talking about?

"Your camera?"

My jaw dropped. "You...mean...I...but...how?"

"Please just take tweedle-dumb downstairs before I lose my mind," Lola groused behind me.

Stan ignored her. I was too frazzled to pay her any attention.

"How will you be a famous photographer someday if you don't submit some of your photos to Vera too?"

I squealed, threw my arms around him, danced around my office like a crazy person, and snatched up my camera—the one Stan had emailed me to bring this morning—locking my purse in its place.

It too may have been from my college days, but I kept this baby in pristine condition.

Lola grumbled to herself in the corner. "I'd hate to see her actually excited about something."

"What are you waiting for? Let's go!" I hauled Stan behind me to the elevator, and he laughed the entire way.

※

Jack's eyes brightened. "Candace?"

"Oh, hey, Jackson. I mean, Jack. I'll never get used to that, you know?" I strained to see past him, prattling the whole time. "So has, you know—is he here yet?"

The light in his eyes died, and now he just looked disgusted. "Go on back. He's in makeup."

I squealed and darted past him.

Stan had shaken me loose from his arm outside, heading back up to his office, yet I'd still somehow found my way in here. Gavin had me, hook, line, and sinker.

Another saying I wasn't sure was allowed in this building.

I darted all over the room, looking for him. Quite a lot of models were in hair and makeup at the moment.

"Candace!"

I spun around. "Gavin!" And launched myself into his open arms.

I'd tried the whole demure and reserved thing. Hadn't lasted five minutes, unfortunately.

He gave me a warm kiss. I melted into him.

"Mr. Bailey, please! Your makeup?"

I jerked away. Smoothed his shirt. Touched his face. And the little napkin thingies tucked into his collar. "Oh, Gavin, I'm so sorry! I didn't mean to mess anything up."

His smile could melt the entire North Pole. Or Antarctica. Both. All of it.

"You didn't." He laced his fingers with mine and pulled me over to his hairdresser.

She was gorgeous too. Everyone in this business was gorgeous. Ugh! What was I doing in this industry again?

"Rosie, meet my girlfriend, Candace. Candace, Rosie."

"Hi!" I said brightly with a wave.

She just gave me a disgruntled look and went back to fixing whatever makeup I'd messed up. Couldn't really tell. It looked the same after she'd finished.

"You watching or shooting today?" Gavin asked.

My eyes met his steel-gray ones. I held up my camera with a huge grin. "Stan said I should submit some of my photos too!"

This apparently was too much for makeup girl. She rolled her eyes and walked away. Some people just couldn't be happy for happy people.

Or I was just as annoying as I thought I might be, and Gavin was blissfully unaware. For now.

"Mr. Bailey? We're ready for you, sir," said an extremely young-looking intern, hiding behind his clipboard.

He smiled at the young man. "Thank you, Lucas." Then he turned the full ray of that smile back on me. He touched my face. "Go get 'em, you. You're going to set this world on fire."

And that was why I loved this man. He saw the good in me when no one else could. The good even I couldn't see. And how on earth could he remember everyone's names like that?

He left me, a messy pile of mushy goo, and walked over to the backdrop to get to work.

I stood there and sighed like an idiot. There was no one on this planet better, nicer, taller, or more gorgeous than Gavin Bailey.

Okay, there were probably taller people, but still.

"So you're shooting today too?" Jackson asked from right beside me.

I sighed. "Uh-huh." Ugh. Could I sound any less like a moony teenager?

I straightened and did my best to deepen my voice and act all mature.

"I mean, yes. Of course. Lead the way."

He didn't move. Just looked at me like I'd lost my mind.

I swallowed. "Um, what do you want me to do?"

He pointed to a spot where I could see everything. A spot close to Gavin. Not good. For my sanity.

"Stand there and observe. When we've got all the shots we're looking for, I'll work with you to get a few more."

I nodded, my eyes constantly drifting back to Gavin. To think he was interested in *me*...

Jackson rolled his eyes and tugged me forward, leaving me in the spot he'd indicated, then walked away to begin the shoot.

He called everyone to their places, and flash after flash and pose after pose began.

I sighed and melted a little. Gavin was just so darn handsome! I could watch him all day.

And he could apparently tell. Because he was not flirting with the camera. Oh no. He was flirting with *me*, and the camera just happened to capture it all.

Heat filled my face, my body, my brain—but I couldn't look away.

And it was working, because they got the shots they were looking for right away, something I would've thought would make Jackson—Jack—happy.

But it didn't. He grunted as perfect shot after perfect shot was checked off his list. He tried a few spontaneous shots, probably trying to get him to crack, but those came out perfect too.

And me? Well, I was a hot mess over there, standing where I was told to stand, not able to do much more than gape and sigh and fan my face while the room warmed to broiling temperatures.

What? Those light stands were *hot*.

"Okay, Marshall, get over here."

I tripped happily to Jackson's side, somehow making it all the way there without actually tripping. Not sure how. I didn't have any memory of walking over there.

"Okay, I want you to do some free shooting first, get a feel for the different angles, the weight of the camera, then you'll use the tripod for some steadier shots."

Gavin glanced up as makeup girl touched up his face, saw me watching him, and winked.

I may have sighed and giggled. At the same time.

I was not proud of what that man did to my brain, but I'd given up fighting it.

"Ugh. Are you even paying attention?"

I snapped my attention to Jackson, repeating what he'd said word for word. And *then* what he'd said made it to my brain. I smiled at him innocently.

He still looked like he didn't believe me. He lowered his voice. "I don't think you recognize the opportunity you've been given here, Candace. You can make it. Big. And when certain things don't work out…"

His gaze drifted to Gavin, and my face heated for an entirely different reason.

"Such as maybe getting a new job, or moving states, you'll have this to fall back on. A real portfolio. Experience."

I nodded soberly, feeling betrayed. I knew what he'd meant.

Gavin. When things with *Gavin* didn't work out.

And oh my gosh, had he heard something about my job? Was I getting a new job sometime in the near future? Was mine not working out?

Pulling me from my spiraling thoughts, he touched my arm, lightly. "Don't throw this opportunity away. Give it all you've got."

I nodded, serious for the first time all day, and the stage manager called everyone back into position. Jackson handed off directing the shots to someone else—something I knew he liked to do himself—and came over to assist me.

"Ready?"

I nodded, unable to keep the grin off my face. "Ready."

Jackson rolled his eyes. "Of course you are. Let's do this."

I turned to Gavin—he winked, I giggled—and the best photo shoot of my life began.

CHAPTER FOURTEEN

"Incredible. These are perfection. Better than mine, even."

I sat on Jack's desk, one leg swinging, surrounded by sheer bliss: Gavin's face on every monitor. Was I ridiculous or what?

Best. Day. Ever.

Jack's scowl couldn't even ruin it for me.

"Wow, I mean, really, Candace. Look at these."

I did. Grinned. "Yep."

The whole shoot had been magic.

Jack eyed me suspiciously. "I knew you were good, but dang. These are *good*."

"I know." My grin was mega-watt huge. My foot, swinging even bigger.

Had I mentioned this was the best day of my life? And we won't even mention the mini-make out session in a random closet after.

Jack made a sound of disgust and gave me a gentle shove. Even if he wasn't happy about me and Gavin, he still was too kind to outright shove me on the floor, thank goodness.

"Go. Please. You're driving me nuts. I'll get these edited and back to you."

I hopped off the desk. "I don't think so."

His eyebrows shot high in surprise.

I plopped into the chair next to his, pulling the monitor there closer. "I'll edit mine, you edit yours. Capeesh?"

He still looked disgruntled, but a grin fought to break through. "Capeesh."

"That's better."

I started clicking through my pictures, choosing the best and discarding the rest (in a hidden file in case I had to access them again one day, also secretly air-dropping myself the entire file so I could stare at it as much as I liked), as he clicked through his. Then I started chatting about everything and nothing at all, and he started to relax by degrees.

After a while, it started to feel normal again between us, kind of like when we were in college together. And for a moment, I was overcome with gratitude.

I just might have my friend back.

Even if we were more like acquaintances back then.

But for the first time since we'd both moved to New York, things felt better between us.

We edited, chatted, and laughed, deep into the night.

✝

Stan came to see me after most of my work was done for the day. He sat in his usual spot. "Well? How did it go?"

I grunted and tossed a stack of photographs in front of Stan.

Jack and I had edited until his alarm went off to get ready for work. Hey, look! I was calling him Jack in my own thoughts now. Score!

We'd laughed and gone to the cafeteria for breakfast.

Definitely better than old times. In college, I could

barely string two words together in his presence, and I'd most certainly never had breakfast with him. Peter would've thrown a fit. But I wasn't thinking about my controlling ex.

And Stan was still staring at me, waiting for an answer.

"Uh, what?"

He shook his head. "How much sleep did you get last night?"

"Uh…" I scratched my head. "None?"

"Oh, Candace. You're impossible."

He thumbed through my pictures. And let out a string of curses. I flinched.

"I'm sorry, dear, I know how you feel about poor language, but I meant every word. These are incredible." He looked at me expectantly. "And your write-up?"

I jerked awake. "Write-up?"

"You know, how you envision ad placement, color scheme, ad copy, etc.?"

I stared at him blankly.

He stood. "Go home. I'll run interference with Vera. You sleep, and as soon as you've woken up and had two pots of coffee—no less, you hear?—you email me. Understand?"

I nodded. Off. Not in agreement.

He groaned. "Lola. Take her home. Now."

Lola made all kinds of screeching objection noises. I winced. How could her voice reach such decibels? I rubbed my ear…then started nodding off again.

"Never mind," he groused. "You, young lady, come with me."

He took me to a dim interior office, shooed out whoever was working there, and settled me on a couch, throwing a light blanket already there over me.

"As soon as you wake up, go home, freshen up, and send me that write-up, yes?"

I was asleep before he closed the door, because when I woke up, I found a note with the exact same instructions. I staggered out of the office when I could finally stand and looked out the closest window.

It was dark outside. Of course it was.

Well, as dark as it got in NYC, anyway. More orangish-yellowish as the streetlights lit everything with their unique New York City glow.

And it seemed no one else was in my building.

I stumbled to my office, rubbing sleep from my eyes, and pulled out the pictures that had been approved by Vera and returned by Stan.

I did my write-up, emailed it to Stan, and left the moment I got his approval. Which wasn't saying much. His response was pretty much immediate.

I yawned as I made my way to the elevator, not even wanting to know if I had dragon breath or how bad it was. I was going home, and I was going to sleep for a week.

Well, at least for most of the day tomorrow, since Stan's email also told me to come in as late as needed. He even gave me the option to take the day off, reminding me to let HR know I was taking a personal day if I did.

I smiled happily to myself. I was gonna catch up on so much sleep.

※

I got back to my apartment as the sky was lightening and took a deep breath.

After checking every corner for lurkers and turning on every light to erase shadows, of course.

I was home. By myself. My plan? To get some decent sleep, *not* on a random couch that had left a crick in my neck. I had so many missed nights to catch up on, and even sleeping most of yesterday evening away, I was ready for round two.

I did all the things normal people do as a routine:

brushed my teeth, changed into real pajamas—couldn't remember the last time I'd slept in those—and brushed my hair till it was shining. Stuff I usually did on the subway or in the bathroom at work or so quickly I was left wondering if I'd actually done it or not.

I was on my way to my bedroom when my phone pinged. The email ping.

Yes, I could turn those off, and yes, I always thought about doing so, but my job generally frowned upon ignoring texts, calls, or emails.

I tried to walk past it, but it pinged again.

"Gah!" I went over to my laptop and booted it up. "Guess that's what I get for trying to sneak past it for bed anyway," I muttered to myself—

And froze.

It was an email. Not from work. From the morgue.

Asking me to pick up Mr. Withers's belongings as his next of kin.

"What on earth?"

Oh. Apparently when I'd asked all those questions of the younger, nicer of the two (Tessa, was it?), she'd assumed I was related to Mr. Withers.

Oh dear. I hadn't meant to mislead her, but…I eyed my jacket. How could I pass up this opportunity?

I threw on jeans, a long-sleeved tee, a sweater, and my jacket and was out my door.

Then went back for gloves and a hat. I didn't do cold so well.

I'd just have to tell her there'd been a mistake.

After I looked through old man Withers's belongings and asked questions to my heart's content, of course.

And if things went my way, just once, grumpy cop wouldn't even have to know about it.

I practically skipped to the elevator in my building.

Look, I tried to be honest, okay?

I showed up at the morgue, hoping the chief medical examiner, Dr. Greenley, wasn't in, but fully prepared to explain that there had been a misunderstanding.

Someone young and pleasant asked if she could help me. The girl I'd spoken to? Or someone else?

"Oh, um, yes. Hi."

She waited for me to get my words in order.

"I got an email about a Mr. Withers? Mr. John Withers?"

The girl's face brightened. "Oh, yes! Family signs in here, and if you'll give me a second, I'll go get his things."

She turned and walked out, leaving a grungy clipboard in my hands. I tried to sign, but I just couldn't. Feeling guilty and like I was going to get caught, even though I wasn't doing anything wrong—yet—I just stood there with my mind screaming at me to do the right thing.

She came back in with a manila envelope. "There wasn't much on him." She held it out.

Have I ever mentioned how curious I am? How I can't let things go? How if something's right there, in front of my face, I have to touch it, investigate, discover what the heck is going on?

Okay, so maybe I'd tell her there'd been a misunderstanding *after* I'd looked at his things.

Without giving myself time to talk myself out of it, I scribbled an illegible slash across the next blank line and snatched the envelope out of her hands.

She bowed her head respectfully. "I'll give you a moment."

Guilt showed up and told me how this was such a bad idea and how I was such a terrible person, but she walked out before I could work up the courage to be honest.

I dumped it all out in a little tray she'd set there for that reason, then took a pen out of a mug sprouting with them to rifle through it all without leaving fingerprints.

Hey, I'd seen a few detective shows, okay? Well, back when I had time for such things.

Keys, wallet, a few peppermints, and—jackpot!—an ornate, old-fashioned key. Just like the one at his job. I was sure it meant something.

The interior door whooshed open, so I plucked the key out of the tray and shoved it in my pocket—oh my gosh, was I a thief now? My grandma woud kill me when I got to heaven. If they even let me in now. I started to sweat.

I dumped the tray back into the envelope and held it close to my chest, trying not to look as guilty as I felt.

"Can I help you with anything else?" she asked.

I nodded. Licked my lips. "May I see him?"

The girl looked unsure for the first time. "Wouldn't you rather wait for, um, you know, the funeral?"

I shook my head. "I'd like to make sure it's him, please."

Her eyebrows raised.

"Oh! I mean…I'd like to make sure…to pay my last respects."

Still she hesitated.

"Please. It would mean so much to me."

She looked like she wasn't sure she was supposed to be doing this, but she nodded and took me to the back.

I followed her down the long corridor and into a room resplendent in stainless steel on every surface.

She read a chart, located a tag, then opened a square door on the wall and pulled out a tray that could have held a person. That *should* have held a person.

That was now empty.

She looked at me. I looked at her. Her chin trembled.

Not a good sign.

I cleared my throat. "Did you, uh, move him?"

She let out a strangled little laugh and slid the tray away. "No worries, Miss Marshall. I'm sure he's around here somewhere." She bit her lip. "Though I saw him on *this* slab. When he was brought in."

Which meant over a week ago. Two weeks now? I knew we were getting close to the two-week cutoff where the body would be taken to Hart Island for burial.

What? I'd most definitely done more research in my nonexistent spare time.

I loved my new laptop a little too much.

She started checking charts and opening the square doors one at a time, reading tags on toes and identifying bodies, then sliding them away to check the next.

I turned away quickly at my first peek of gray skin. I didn't handle things like that well. Not after all the zombies. Or before that, even. I kept expecting these guys to jump up and run at me, slathering and moaning and snapping their teeth.

On second thought, I made sure those gray toes stayed in my periphery in case they started twitching.

This was, like, the perfect zombie setup. Why hadn't they included *that* in my movie? Not that I wasn't grateful. I don't think I could've taken it.

I started to sweat, big time. I needed to get out of here.

The girl spoke again, voice thick and close to tears. "Maybe they moved him to the funeral home. Not that I've received a funeral home order. There wouldn't happen to be a rushed funeral early tomorrow, would there?"

I shook my head. Not that I'd know that info, anyway.

Her eyes flew wide. "The body's just…gone!"

She covered her mouth with her hand, and I freaked out. She'd just been touching dead people's toes!

I staggered out of there, doing my best not to hurl, and made it to the reception area before she caught up with me.

Composing myself, I turned to her, asking the question I

couldn't get out earlier without accompaniment. "How could the body just disappear like that?"

"Shh! Lower your voice, please!" The nervous girl peeled off her gloves, tossed them in the nearest trash can, and wiped her hands down her uniform's slacks.

Score one for cleanliness, but I hoped she kept her mouth far away from me. And disinfected it soon. And maybe her hands too, because who knew what had touched her uniform.

Ugh. I would not make it as a nurse. Or a mortician. I couldn't handle blood, wounds, germs, gross things, or dead people. Nurses were pretty much superhuman superheroes and had every ounce of my respect.

I nodded in abrupt agreement and whispered in a hoarse voice, "How could the body just disappear like that?"

Tears pooled in the girl's eyes. "I don't know. I don't know how this could've happened. I cleaned the body, tagged it, and put it on ice when it first came in. There was a no-autopsy order, so we didn't mess with it after that. We're super busy, you know. And now it isn't there!"

"What about embalming?" I asked. I knew they had about twenty-four hours to do some kind of embalming before there was decomposition, but I didn't know how a no-autopsy order would affect that.

Also, that was normally something a funeral home did, but as he had no family and there'd been no funeral…

She frowned. "Oh, I'm sure there was some kind of embalming. Had to be. It's been too long. Most of his organs would have liquified by now."

I couldn't help it. I gagged.

"But he still shouldn't be missing…"

The girl burst into tears. I sighed and patted her shoulder awkwardly, and she flung her arms around me. Me. A complete stranger.

With that gross uniform and germy hands and dead people–touched face.

Right. Next. To. Me.

I barely touched her back with two fingers and said all kinds of soothing nonsense while my mind raced with what could've happened to Mr. Wither's body and *when* it could've happened and how soon I could step away without being rude. And how to burn my clothes safely.

"I'm gonna get fired! I need this job! I've always wanted to be a mortician, and if I can't keep this job, then I won't be able to go to school. And if I can't go to school, I'll never get to do autopsies."

Dream job, right there.

The door leading into the back opened.

She might have said more, but I shushed her, grasped her arms, and pulled back to look her in the eye. "It's going to be okay, you got that? Nobody's getting fired."

I glanced up. Uh-oh. I'd seen that dude's picture plastered all over the government website, and by the way his head came up at my voice, he knew me too.

Probably from the thousands of times I'd called. And left voicemails.

I grumbled under my breath, "Unless, of course, *he* sees you talking to me."

She gave me a quizzical look as I moved away.

"Just tell them exactly what happened, and I'm sure you'll be fine. I, um, I've got to go."

I spun to leave, but his nasally voice filled the green-hued passageway.

"The tenacious Candace Marshall, I presume."

I turned slowly and nodded at him. "The elusive Dr. Greenley, I presume," I parroted right back.

The morgue attendant looked flustered and covered her flushed cheeks with shaking hands.

Could she *not* touch her face right now? Or ever?

"You just couldn't stay away, could you?" Dr. Greenley's voice spun my attention back on him.

I lifted my chin. "It's a free country. Besides, I just want some answers. I'm here to get them."

"Not when you poke your nose in my business and upset my workers, you're not." He nodded at the girl who'd grown quiet and was studying our exchange. "What do I have to do to get you to stay away from here? Will a restraining order do?"

"That won't be necessary. You should talk to your worker-person here, though." I nodded at the girl.

"Tessa," she said quickly. She looked like she couldn't decide whether to be hostile or indifferent to me. I was about to make that decision easy for her.

"The body's missing. Maybe you should've spoken with me earlier."

I turned and walked toward the exit.

"Another one?" he hissed at Tessa, then called to me, "Wait!"

I looked over my shoulder in time to see her shrink back. Another one? What?

"You say the body's missing? Mr. Withers?"

I nodded, trying not to look as scared and guilty as I felt. I had no idea why I felt guilty about the disappearance—it just always seemed to happen when people stared at me with accusation in their eyes, whether I deserved it or not. Like the morgue guy was doing.

He jerked his head. "Follow me."

My legs felt weighted as I stumbled after him. Was he going to call the cops? Put me in jail until they found out what had happened to the body?

I gagged when the door opened and they slid the empty tray out. Cold or not, faint or not, empty tray or not, formaldehyde and real dead people smell permeated the room. I would never get used to the smell. Not ever.

And I'd just seen far too many of those dead people for comfort.

Both looked at me strangely then back at the tray.

"Huh. It is gone," said Dr. Greenley.

Obvious statement of the year right there.

He turned to me. "Miss Marshall, I'll need you to stay here until the police arrive for questioning."

I groaned. *Please, oh please, oh please, Lord, keep Detective Sawyer far away!*

I nodded and held my shirt collar over my nose. "May I please wait somewhere else?"

Dr. Greenley nodded to his assistant, and Tessa took me to the front reception area. Apparently not trusting me, she seated me on this side of the locked and coded door. No escape happening through that tiny reception window.

Snatching the manila envelope from my hand at the last minute, she left to join the doctor, and I glanced around. Spotting the roster I'd just signed, I tugged it into my lap. My full intention was to snap a few pics, but my shattered screen disabused that notion real quick. Still, I fumbled to what I hoped was the camera app and clicked a few times on where the button should be.

I barely had it in place again before she checked on me.

I smiled at her, but she crossed her arms and glared.

Guess she'd decided not to like me. I sighed. It couldn't be helped. But now I had a list of names to start looking up—maybe—right after work. I wouldn't know till I pulled up the photo app on my computer.

The smile disappeared off my face. I hoped they let me go before I was late to work.

Maybe I'd have to use that personal day after all.

CHAPTER FIFTEEN

"Why am I not surprised?"

My head came up at Detective Sawyer's dry tone. I gave him a halfhearted smile. I should've bet money somehow.

I started to open my mouth, but he just pointed at me. "Stay there. I'll talk to you next."

I crossed my arms and slouched in my seat as he made his way to Dr. Greenley and the intern—attendant, assistant—whatever she was. I could never keep morgue terms straight.

Let's see...the attendant was like an intern, checking bodies in and doing paperwork, needing two years' experience to become an assistant. The assistant helped the coroner prep the body for examination or autopsy, and the chief medical examiner—Dr. Greenley—was in charge of all the sticky cases.

Like this one.

At least some of my research had stuck around. I stared at my phone dejectedly, where the rest of my notes were buried behind a cracked screen.

Those hadn't uploaded to my new computer.

I really needed to get that fixed. ASAP.

"Miss Marshall!"

My head snapped up.

"Get in here, please."

Shoving my phone away, I scurried down the hall and poked my head into the room where they kept the bodies. Again.

Nope. Still wasn't used to it. My shirt came up and over my nose.

Detective Sawyer, Dr. Greenley, and Tessa were glaring at each other in turn.

"A dead body doesn't just disappear!" the detective practically shouted.

I super unhelpfully pointed at the empty slab seconds before I realized he wasn't even talking to me.

He shot me a dirty look anyway.

Go figure.

Then he turned to me fully. "Did you or did you not see Mr. John Withers's body?

I began emphatically shaking my head no. "But not for lack of trying," I blurted. "I knew something was wrong, and I just…I wanted to make sure it was the same guy as was in that alleyway."

I couldn't tell him *why* I thought something was wrong—that dude grabbing me and threatening me—but it had made me more determined than ever to solve this.

He grunted and turned away, his laser-like focus zoning in on the intern. "When did you last see the body?"

The morgue attendant trembled from head to foot. "John Doe, I mean, Mr. Withers was here that first day, I swear, and then she"—now I was the one being pointed at—"said she was family and wanted to see him. That's the only reason I found out he was missing."

I immediately went into deer-in-headlights mode as the cop glared at me.

"Is that true?" he demanded.

"T-t-technically, I didn't say anything about being f-f-family…"

He looked like he didn't believe me. For good reason.

Tessa crossed her arms. Now she, too, was glaring at me. "When I said family had to sign in, you signed in."

I started to sweat. Like, big time. That cop was just itching for a reason to put me in jail, and I'd just handed him one. On a silver platter.

Or maybe a dead-body slab thingy?

My mouth took over, and I started backpedaling like crazy. "T-t-technically, you assumed I was family, though I didn't correct you," I hastily added, when I saw they were about to gang up on me, "and you ushered me in the back before I could set the record straight."

Dr. Greenley groaned. "Tessa, is this true?"

She turned flinty eyes on the bad cop. Er, my cop. I mean, the cop who wasn't nice. "I was told someone would be along soon to collect his things. Then she walked in."

She failed to mention *she'd* emailed *me*.

Detective Sawyer looked like he'd just swallowed a roach. "Did you at least check her ID?"

Tessa sniffed, clearly offended. "Of course I did. I'm not completely new."

Though she looked young enough. And she'd only glanced at it long enough for me to know she hadn't really been looking.

"You"—the detective pointed at me—"wait outside. You"—at least he was pointing at someone else, right?—"I need you to tell me everything."

I took as long as I possibly could leaving the room, hoping to overhear a snippet of their conversation. No such luck. They glared at me like I was the cause of all their problems, and they didn't make one sound until the heavy door clicked shut—and locked—behind me.

I slumped into a puke-green chair in the puke-green waiting room and waited for my puke-green sentence.

My head popped up as the detective slammed through the door. He eyed me, disgruntled. Much like I'd imagine someone would eye a fruitcake.

Or how I'd look at one, anyway. Nasty stuff.

"Well, it's pretty clear you had nothing to do with the body's disappearance," he said, as though that particular fact pained him.

I popped upright. "That's right! I mean, of course I didn't." I slumped a little. "Thank goodness."

He eyed me with his beady little eyes. "Is there anything you'd like to tell me, Miss Marshall?"

I jabbed a finger at my chest. "Me?" I squeaked. I cleared my throat. "Detective, the only thing I want to tell you is I know what I saw. I'm not crazy. It wasn't my imagination. And the only thing I want more than anything in the entire world is to get to the bottom of this." I tagged on as an afterthought, "Like you do."

"Huh." That's it. Nothing more. But I didn't sense as much hatred rolling off him as before.

Well, I told myself that, anyway.

"Come on. I'll take you home."

I picked my jaw off the nasty puke-green floor and gaped at him. "What? Are you serious?" Was he being nice?

Wait a sec…

I eyed him with suspicion. "Is this your coy way of 'accidentally' taking me to jail?"

Yep. I did air quotes and everything.

He took a deep breath, closed his eyes, and counted to ten. Out loud.

When he opened his eyes, his stare was obsidian. "Miss

Marshall, I have never been coy a day in my life, and if I were taking you to a holding cell, I would be happily reading you your Miranda rights."

I gulped. Oh. Well, then. Couldn't argue with that.

I stood, grasping my bag in two fingers—it was definitely getting tossed for even crossing a morgue's threshold—and let him herd me outside and into his waiting car.

It wasn't until we were almost to my apartment—should I have been more worried that he hadn't asked where I lived?—when he spoke. "Do you have anyone waiting for you at home, Miss Marshall?"

I sighed, deep and long. *Oh, you mean like Gavin? Oh wait, who's he?* "No." I eyed him, my suspicious nature coming out to play. "Why do you want to know?"

He turned onto another street, not looking at me. "Just wondering if anyone will be worried that you're out, once again, at all hours of the day and night, sticking your nose into things that might be dangerous for you."

"Dangerous?" I sat straight up. "What do you mean, dangerous? Is that a threat?"

He sighed. "It's just a question, Miss Marshall."

Oh. Thank goodness.

I plunked my head on the window next to me before jerking upright when he gave me the stink-eye. "Oops. Sorry."

Apology not accepted, if I read his face right.

"Parents, siblings?" A pause. "Movie-star boyfriend?"

Was that a note of bitterness I detected in his voice?

"Hey, what do you have against Gavin?"

His face went blank, and any attempt at conversation came to a screeching halt.

Not from my end, of course. Nope. I officially freaked out.

"Wait. Do you know something about him I don't?"

Nothing.

"Did you hear something? Gossip? Rumor? True story? Should I be concerned?"

Not a thing.

"He isn't hurt, or you wouldn't be asking about him," I mused. I snapped my fingers. "Did he say something to you? Something about me?"

Nada.

"Did that other detective say something? Your partner…Lawson, right? Dan Lawson?" Now how on earth had that name popped into my head? I'd only heard it the once. I gasped. "Is Gavin going to break up with me? Date someone prettier and much more famous?"

Complete silence. From him.

"Oh my gosh, is he cheating on me?"

Because every time I talked to my mother, that's exactly what she said all famous people did, just because they could, and I was lucky to even be noticed by one of them. And to enjoy it while it lasted. Ugh.

Gavin was not just some famous person. He had a heart. And a soul.

He was kindness itself.

Still, her words couldn't help but pop up at the most inopportune times.

Detective Sawyer jerked the cruiser to the curb and reached for me. I gasped when I thought he was going to strangle me, but instead, he just pushed my door open.

At his death glare, I tried to scramble out. Then remembered to untangle myself from the seatbelt I hadn't unfastened.

He watched me with absolutely no sympathy in his steel gaze.

As soon as I was free of the vehicle, he peeled out. I watched him go for a sec before I realized he'd dropped me off roughly three blocks from my apartment building.

Not that I didn't mind the walk—I loved the exercise

and would often go out of my way to choose walking over riding—but he couldn't at least have endured me for three more stinking blocks?

I raised shaking hands to my burning cheeks, humiliated that every doubt I'd had for the past month, every insecurity I'd shoved down deep, had come pouring out in front of the one person who hated me most in the world.

Would he tell Gavin? Would it be on the news? Would mean cop look at me with even more disgust than usual?

Peeling myself away from my personal pity party, I headed for my apartment. I was going to be calm, wash morgue grime off my body, dump my clothes and handbag down the trash chute, go to bed for two hours—or however many I had left after that morgue visit—then go to work and pretend absolutely nothing out of the ordinary had happened.

But no matter how much I tried to quiet my mind, niggling thoughts ate at me.

Why on earth had he been asking about my family and Gavin? For that matter, why did that detective hate me so much?

And more importantly, *should* I be more worried about Gavin and the ever-yawning distance between us?

✗

I was halfway to my apartment when I remembered I had Mr. Withers's address.

So…go to work smelling like a morgue? Shower and take a quick nap before work? Or use this info before Detective Sawyer banned me from it too?

Hopefully he wasn't headed there right now.

Then again, it had been a few days since I'd gotten the address, so he'd probably already been.

Could I pass up this opportunity to snoop? Who knew

the next time I'd be able to get away from work during daylight hours.

Decision made, I headed for the closest subway station.

And I had to buy an old-fashioned touristy map since I couldn't use my phone.

Several subway lines later, I stood in a quiet neighborhood across from a quieter park. Everything was neat, tidy, and made me want to move here, even if it was ridiculously far from work.

I made my way into the brownstone—someone held the door open for me with a smile—pretty sure that meant I was on an alien planet right now—and was soon standing before his door. I timidly knocked.

I had to knock a few more times before a middle-aged woman with platinum-blonde hair in a ponytail and wearing yoga pants came to the door. She had a light sheen of sweat and was jogging in place. A workout video was paused in the background.

"Yes? May I help you?"

I started at her, dumbfounded. First of all, if I were working out, which I kept meaning to do, I would *not* answer the door. Second, I'd most likely look like a drowned rat. Pretty sure an angel chorus sang for this chick as the door opened.

The lighting in her apartment was *fantastic*.

I shook myself back to the present. "Oh, um, yes. I'm looking for a Mr. Withers?"

She flicked bangs out of her eyes. "Is that who lived here before? I'm sorry, I just moved in."

Then I noticed the boxes.

I mean, sheesh. Mr. Withers's boss wasn't kidding. That was fast.

I wilted a little.

"Perhaps you can ask for forwarding info at the office? They're really nice, and in today till five."

I was definitely on a different planet. My office was "open when we're open!" and if things went wrong, you were the one fixing them.

And it was still an amazing place to live by New York standards. Well, until I'd seen this place.

I mumbled some kind of thank you and scurried away. The office told me the same thing, that once the movers came for Mr. Withers's possessions, the apartment had sold immediately.

It smelled nice, the people smiled, and the main office worker shoved candy in my hands as I left.

I kinda wished I'd had a chance at that apartment myself.

I shook myself out of the self-pity spiral with a "the grass is always greener" pep talk and slowly made my way back to the closest subway station.

Well that was disappointing. Another dead end.

As I rounded the corner, two blocks to go, someone grabbed me from behind and wrapped a sickly sweet smelling cloth around my nose and mouth. Before I could tense, fight back, or scream, I sagged against whoever it was and promptly went to sleep.

✗

I slowly came to after the best sleep of my life.

I smiled and moaned a little. I mean, I felt so good. I'd slept so hard, I hadn't even dreamed. I just woke up with this happy, light feeling and a sense of being completely rested. That was rare, let me tell you.

But my neck hurt a little. And I didn't usually sleep sitting up, did I?

I started to move my arms to stretch, but they wouldn't budge. My eyes flew open.

I was somewhere dank, dark, and dismal, water dripping

and echoing from not that far away. Ropes tied my hands to a wooden chair, and I was far more comfortable and far less cold than I probably should've been. A single beam of light glared into my face.

"Ah, Miss Marshall, you're awake. Good."

That woke me up real fast.

I craned my neck all over the place, but I couldn't see who was talking to me. "Who's there? Who are you? Why am I here?" I shook my wrists, trying to rattle them against the chair for emphasis, but the silent ropes wouldn't cooperate. "And tied up?"

"All in good time, Miss Marshall. All in good time."

I blinked back tears. "Where am I?"

"You don't listen well, do you?" The man stayed in the darkness rimming the room. "You have meddled in things that do not pertain to you, and I must insist that you leave them be."

I nodded furiously. "I'll do that. Whatever you ask. Just get me outta here and let me go home."

"Don't you want to know what I'm talking about first?" I could hear the smile in his voice.

"Um, maybe?" I mean, no, not really, but I didn't want to tell him that.

Now he did step into the single beam of light, and as he did, the room began to lighten. Recessed lights came on, highlighting garish art and weapons on the walls, as well as a spotlight right in my eyes. I recoiled, blinking to adjust my vision.

"If you promise to be a good girl, I'll have my men untie you."

I nodded all over the place. "Yes. Of course. I promise."

A knife made a distinct whooshing noise, and someone behind me cut the ropes and helped me stand.

I blinked owlishly against the lights still in my eyes. "Are you going to let me go?"

My voice wobbled and my chin trembled and I just wanted to be anywhere else but here.

He stepped close, then smiled, fangs on full display. "That depends entirely upon you, my sweet."

As I focused on him, I couldn't believe what I was seeing. Besides fangs that looked like believable implants or like they actually belonged to him, everything else was just so…fake. Black cape, red highlights underneath, and high collar. White shirt with ruffles at his wrists and neck. Velvet suit that would've been right at home under a disco ball. Can you say cheesy horror flick?

I expected him to say at any moment, "I vant to suck your blood. Ah-ah-ah-ah-ah!"

But he didn't. He just leered at me like some creepy old guy in a velvet suit that should *not* have been a thing. I was probably the most unfashionable person at *Voilà Magazine*, and even I knew that suit was the worst.

I gave him a wobbly smile. "So, um, are you going to let me go now?"

"After we have a little conversation, yes."

Not a smidgeon of sunlight made its way into this underground lair.

And I was definitely freaking out right about now.

"So, um, what are you going to do with me?" My voice quavered like a leaf in the wind.

And that made me think of Wash from *Firefly* dying right before a mob of reavers attacked, which made me think of my zombie movie and the mobs of zombies that had attacked, which made me think of a mob of vampires attacking right now…I may have whimpered a little.

"Why, not a thing, Miss Marshall. We're going to let you go."

I eyed him suspiciously.

His laughter filled the room and grated on my very last nerve. "I can see you don't believe me, but I'm telling the truth. You have nothing to worry about." He leaned close. "Yet."

I backed up to get away from him, but I ran directly into the dude standing behind me. He steadied me, then removed his hand. Talk about freaky.

But I couldn't take my eyes off creepy vampire old guy all up in my face.

Cheesy vampire backed away, making a circuit of the room. His finger trailed along the edge of his desk as my eyes became accustomed to the subdued lighting elsewhere and the glaring light right in my face.

"You see, if you leave well enough alone, if you stay out of our business, we'll stay out of yours."

I laughed. "Yeah, right. Like I believe that after you just *kidnapped* me."

"No, that's exactly right."

I snapped my mouth closed. Did I always say everything that popped into my head? Sheesh.

"But keep poking your nose into our business? Keep meddling? Keep stopping by the morgue and Mr. Withers's office and apartment and asking uncomfortable questions of the police? Then I guarantee you won't like what happens. To you *or* your friends."

Instantly my fear vanished.

I glared at vampire dude. Or dude who thought he was a vampire, anyway. I didn't take being intimidated well, and I especially didn't like it when someone threatened someone I loved. Besides, this was the second time I'd been threatened.

And this one included kidnapping. Not cool.

They wanted me to stay out of it? Then they should've let it fizzle out on its own.

Let me keep running into all the dead ends I had been.

"I see," I said, my voice tight.

He glanced my way, slowly taking me in after the

change in my voice. Then he dismissed it with a flick of his fingers and kept pacing.

"Mr. John Withers is our responsibility. He came to us, wanted to be a part of our coven, then someone took his life before that could happen. You see, Miss Marshall, we are his family, and we shall take care of any justice to be done."

I gasped. "Wait. He came to you? Wanted to be a part of"—I glanced around—"this?" Whatever this was. I still hadn't seen anything but this room and that horrible costume. "And now he's dead? So why is his body missing from the morgue?"

I snapped my mouth closed. Whoops. Maybe I shouldn't have said that.

The pale dude paled even further, which I had not thought possible. "Missing? His body is missing? Ahem. Anyway."

"No, not *anyway*," I insisted. "What's going on? Why am I here?"

He smiled. "Because, Miss Marshall, I want to emphasize how very serious we are. The vampire you saw is a dangerous murderer, and we shall see to his demise. You need to stay out of our way, or we shall see to your demise as well."

CHAPTER SIXTEEN

It took exactly five seconds for me to burst out laughing.

Vampire dude looked startled, but I was wiping my eyes and laughing too hard to care. "Good one!"

Not the reaction he was looking for, apparently, by the stunned expression on his face.

"All right, who put you up to this?" I started listing people's names at work, certain this was some kind of prank. "It wasn't Lola, was it? I mean, she's so straightlaced, she's gotta have fun at my expense at some point, right?"

It was official. I was starting to crack.

But no way this wasn't a joke. Or a movie set.

"What studio put you up to this?" I waved at the darkest corner. "Hello, there, movie people! Just gotta say, I'm not playing along this time. But I give you an A for effort!"

I gave a huge grin and two thumbs-up, not about to give them even a second of usable footage. Hopefully I was facing wherever the camera was.

My head snapped around at a noise behind one of the curtains. Something tin-sounding dropped. Muffled voices shushed each other.

Victory surged in my chest. A relieved grin stretched

across my face, and I shot toward it. Dude behind me grabbed for me but missed. "Ha! Did you think you could hide it from me?"

"Wait. Don't!"

I ripped the curtain aside.

Two pale beauties, their figures accentuated by ornate, low-cut red velvet gowns—was everything here velvet?—with blood-red lips—I mean, bright-red lips—stared at me with wide eyes. One licked her lips and stared at my neck. Creepy.

"Ah, daughters."

I scrunched my neck, ready to defend it at a moment's notice, and peeked around them, begging the good Lord to see lights, cameras, directors, something. Anything.

I swallowed hard when I realized I hadn't prayed about this. At all.

I'd been too busy stressing. Too busy trying to figure it all out on my own. Well, I was going to remedy that right now.

Dear God, please get me out of this. Somehow. And, uh, help me figure out what's going on? In Jesus's name, amen. Also, I'm so sorry. And really scared right now. And—

One of the velvet-clad women spoke. "Forgive us, Father. We heard you brought an outsider and wanted to see for ourselves what one looked like."

"Aha!" I spun around, jabbing my finger in what's-his-name's direction. "Vampires can't have kids!" I'd heard that somewhere. I think. "You can't be real."

The women glanced at each other, confusion on their faces.

He smiled. A slow, cunning, totally creepy and also chilling smile. "Whoever said they were borne to me?"

Something in me snapped—something that had been happening all too frequently lately. "Oh, for heaven's sake! They've got to be somewhere around here."

I started yanking pictures from the walls, climbing on chairs to inspect corners, jerking curtains aside, trying door handles. Locked, all of them but one.

"Father brought back a crazy one."

"She's not contagious, is she?"

"Maybe we should let this one go, Father. She isn't right in the mind."

"I'd hate to catch whatever she has."

Both women stopped speaking as I stared at them, unlocked door pulled partially open. They stared back.

I bolted.

Pounding down the corridors, I flung open every door and checked every nook I could find. There were cameras here, and I was going to find them. Or a way out. Either would work.

Clusters of freakishly pale people of multiple nationalities watched me as I raced past. The only word I could think of to describe the looks on their faces was delight, but I wasn't going to think about that right now.

Lost and turned around, I grabbed the wall and doubled over, gasping for breath. How many rooms were down here? The tunnels wound endlessly, and rooms were sprinkled everywhere—all lavishly decorated, dark, and peppered with gothic, vampiric-looking people.

I caught my breath and made another circuit, somehow ending up near the same room I'd started in. What on earth?

"Giving up?"

I spun, slamming my back against the tunnel wall, instantly regretting the damp feel and moldy smell it let off.

He glanced at the two women still hovering nearby, holding each other tightly, as if they were scared of me.

Hey, I was the only one allowed to be scared around here, thank you very much.

"My daughters were right about one thing. You are too

unstable to be taken into confidence. Goodness knows what you'll tell people tomorrow as it is." He smiled as if picturing how that blessed event would be received. "Come."

Before I knew what was happening, he'd grabbed my arm and was dragging me after him. His fingers clenched painfully around my arm.

"Listen and listen well. You will retract your claim of what you saw. You will remove your help, as questionable as it may be, from the police investigation. You will not call them, will not go anywhere near them. You will stay out of this, and you will go back to work and eating out and shopping and whatever else you humans do. In other words, your idea of normal." He spoke low and harsh, using threatening to his best advantage.

Vampires started to trickle out of rooms I'd investigated.

I kinda wanted to curl up in a ball and sob for a few hours. My brain was screaming so loud, I wasn't sure what words started tumbling out. Just that I was attempting a lot of them.

He pulled me back into the first room I'd been in and yanked me around to face him. I was still blubbering, so he slapped me, hard. I gasped.

"You do this, or I will kill you, and they will *never* find your body."

I nodded a bunch of times. Sure thing, scary dude. You want me to stay away? I got it this time. Staying away.

"Now, is that any way to speak to a lady?"

All eyes whipped to the speaker, who dropped to the ground from a dark corner of the ceiling.

The hope in my eyes died when I saw who it was. The murderer. The one who'd killed that poor old man and had taken time to *drink his blood.*

Fire started to boil in my stomach. I welcomed it.

I was *not* going to end up the same way.

"Guards! Security!" the main vampire shrieked.

In one bound, the man leaped onto the vampire's desk and knocked him out cold with one blow.

The man who'd cut me loose earlier ran in just then, fumbling for a weapon. The murderer jumped at him—over my head as I tumbled to the ground—and soon had the guard sleeping peacefully as well, blood trickling from the corner of his mouth. He pulled the door closed and jammed the chair I'd been tied to under it.

"Sorry you had to see that, love." He tugged me to my feet.

They obeyed him, even while I told them to stay put.

His eyes roved my face, then he gently touched my cheek with three fingertips. "No man should treat a woman like that."

I'll admit it. My heart thawed the teeniest-tiniest bit toward the murderer.

Murderer. Right.

I jerked away. "Don't you mean a vampire should never treat a blood bank this way? Or however you people— things—see humans? And more importantly, what are you *doing* here?"

At a crash near the door, I jumped and spun around. Still closed, chair still under the handle.

"Sorry about this, love."

"Oof!"

I was suddenly dangling from his freakishly strong arm as he carried me out another door. The guy was way too scrawny to be this strong. In a slim yet muscular way. The all-dark costume made me think of a dueling prince, come to rescue his fair maiden.

Ugh. Seriously? Thinking about something else now. And never watching another romantic movie in my life.

Dangling from his arm was uncomfortable. Kinda. Yes, I'd think about that.

He grabbed one of the towering candlesticks and

whacked anyone who got in his way, finally dropping me on my feet in a circular part of the hallway.

I stumbled and grabbed for anything. He steadied me.

"What do you think you're doing?" I slurred, completely disoriented. His grin caught me off guard. Incredibly handsome and non-murderer-like.

"Rescuing you, my fair lady."

Footsteps echoed from not so far away.

He grabbed my waist, pulled an old-fashioned crossbow from his back, one I hadn't noticed earlier, and pointed it at the ceiling. "Wish me luck."

His lips careened my way, and I turned my head just in time. He planted a sloppy kiss on my jaw and fired above our heads.

We barreled through the opening in the ceiling as those below us converged at our feet. An opening I hadn't seen and was so freaking thankful was there. It swallowed us whole.

I stared at those shouting at us far below. "Why aren't they coming after us? You know, climbing the walls like on all those vampire movies?"

Which I most definitely hadn't seen.

"There are all kinds of vampires, love." His roguish grin was not lost on me. "And because they can't. But I can."

I stared at him in awe for a moment, then glanced over our heads.

We reached the top of the shaft, and hands pulled us over the rim, onto a rooftop. I barely spared a glance for those helping us before my eyes were on the dark hole we'd just come out of.

"Then why are you using a rope?"

"Sorry about this, love."

"About wha—?" I saw his fist too late.

Exploding pain—a grunt—my grunt—and then darkness.

My eyes opened. I was in my apartment. In my pajamas. In my bed. It was still daylight.

I bolted upright, biting back the scream building in my chest. They'd undressed me? I covered my chest as if that could protect me from what had already happened.

I peeked down my shirt, then noticed they'd just stripped off my outer winter layer and had added a long-sleeved tee over my cami. And pulled off my boots. Whew!

Probably because my clothes were such a mess after rolling all over the ground.

I pulled back the covers and stared down at my sleep shorts. The ones I most definitely had *not* been wearing earlier. I ground my teeth, ready to give those vampires a piece of my mind.

But my head hurt and my jaw was throbbing…

I worked my sore jaw. Vampire dude had *bit* me? What the actual heck? After he'd been upset over the other guy slapping me, too.

Some knight in shining armor.

I stared at my hands. Which were shaking.

Someone had stalked me, followed me, waited for the moment I wasn't paying attention to *kidnap* me.

I couldn't even express on how many levels that wasn't good. Terrifying, in fact.

And the funny thing was?

They'd been trying to scare me off. And the thing was, I was going to drop it. The morgue had been a dead end. Mr. Withers's office and apartment had been a bust.

But now, *now*, I couldn't let it go. I was getting close to something.

And Mr. Withers was still dead, if missing, his murderer roaming free. Coming *inside* my apartment.

One thing was certain: I needed to protect myself.

I ground my teeth, growled a little, and jumped out of bed. After thoroughly checking the apartment for intruders, I dug around in the top of my closet, where I'd hidden my gun, purchased after my zombie movie had made sleeping nearly impossible. It used to be within easy grabbing range, but my tendency to shove everything in the first available spot had buried it deep on my high shelves.

My mind wandered back to the weeks I'd spent in the desert during what I thought was the end of the world. I'd learned how to shoot, how to protect myself, how to survive. Even a little of how to fight.

Apparently that had flown right out the window while I was in creepy dude's vampire lair.

That needed to change ASAP.

I pulled it out of its case and stared at the gun and fully loaded clip, stored separately.

I couldn't take this with me. My movie-issued weapon had shot blanks—nope, hadn't known that either with squibs exploding and spraying blood when they wanted me to think I'd hit something—and what if this was some kind of joke? Or setup?

I didn't want to legit murder someone.

Besides, my weapon was perfectly legal inside my apartment, but take one step outside my door, and it shot to illegal status real fast. Although I'd never needed a gun permit before in my life, apparently I'd chosen the most difficult state in the U.S. to apply for my first.

Thank you, New York City.

I weighed the weapon in my hand. Would it even be effective against vampires? Didn't I need silver bullets or something? Or was that for werewolves? Maybe I needed to look into the lore a bit more.

Ha! Listen to me. Like vampires…or werewolves…were *real*.

I was only hunting them down because vampires couldn't possibly be real and I was going to *prove* it.

But no way was I shooting anyone. Or staking them. That'd go over real well should these jokers be pretending to be vamps just to scare the crap out of me.

I'd have to figure out another way.

I carefully put the gun away and hid it where it couldn't be seen but where I could easily reach it. Just in case those guys came back into my apartment for any reason.

And then sent a belated email to HR that I was taking a personal day, since it was well past five.

As I did, one thought wouldn't leave me alone.

What on earth was I going to tell Gavin?

I supposed he'd find out anyway when *Vampire Feud* joined *Zombie Takeover* in a double feature matinee. No need to spoil the surprise.

CHAPTER SEVENTEEN

A few days later, I glanced up to see Jackson leaving Vera's office. He spared me a quick glance and lifted a few fingers in greeting. I gave him a huge smile and almost broke my arm waving back, to which he laughed and got onto the elevator without stopping in. Even though he usually did.

The elevator doors closed, and I sighed. It was because I was with Gavin, wasn't it?

Jackson—Jack—still hadn't quite forgiven me for getting back together with Gavin after our zombie movie. I hated losing any friendship, no matter how loosely that term could be applied to ours.

"Earth to Candace."

I jerked myself back to the present and grabbed the ad inserts from my assistant. I grumbled at them. My least favorite. Some were stunning, but others, like drug ads, left pages of unsightly disclaimers I couldn't make pretty no matter what. They paid well, but seriously, so ugly.

Thank goodness Vera rarely approved those.

At least Gavin's ad was in next month's issue. I may have sighed again, but for a completely different reason.

"Careful, or you'll make Gavin jealous."

My eyes flew to hers. Jealous? Over his own ad?

Lola tilted her head meaningfully to where Jackson had disappeared moments before.

Wait. Jackson? What? Wait. Was that a threat?

Her face remained impassive, her smile plastic as she bent her head over her own ad layouts. We both tried to get these over with quickly.

I crossed my arms. "Gavin has nothing to worry about, and I'll tell that to anyone who needs to hear it. Including Gavin. Jackson and I are *friends*, like we were in college."

I frowned out the glass wall. Well, we had been.

Lola shrugged delicate shoulders in the reflection. "If you say so."

"I do." Ignoring her, I started marking ad placement between my carefully laid-out pages, matching them with content and color schemes. At least I didn't have to design full-page ads, just insert them. Still, I wanted them to complement our content as much as possible.

And certain ads had to be placed in order of importance, of course.

Next week was crunch time, when we went to production and ran around for a full week like our heads would explode if we stopped for even half a second.

I was determined to get as much done as possible this week so next week wouldn't be quite as horrible.

What was I saying? It was our spring/summer Fashion Week feature. On New York, London, Milan, *and* Paris. As well as exclusive new designs only we were allowed to showcase, which meant it was our second highest selling edition. The fall/winter Fashion Week feature was our highest seller.

If the frantic pace, another week of zero sleep (one I at least planned for), and the amount of coffee I was about to consume didn't kill me, the inevitable last-minute changes would.

Which was why I *had* to put what had happened to me out of my head. I didn't have the capacity to deal with it and production week. So I was ignoring it. For now.

I took a deep breath and focused on controlling the one thing I actually could—these ads. Ugh. Hated them.

Except for Gavin's, of course. That one would be featured multiple times, with multiple poses from both me and Jack, and I was all for it.

Rumor had it that Vera had invested heavily in the new fragrance for men, one she'd created for Stan. Whether true or not, it was a romantic story, and I loved it.

I loved even more that Gavin was the face of it.

And thinking of Gavin brought Lola's and my argument back to mind.

We worked in miffed silence—okay, that was just me… pretty sure Lola was over there gloating—until a voice interrupted our workflow.

"Miss Marshall, may I speak with you a moment, please?"

My head came up, and Lola went perfectly still. I couldn't blame her. I could barely make my brain work.

Vera was at my door. Again. Making this the second time she'd dropped by, coming to me instead of calling me to her. I wiped my now-clammy hands on my business slacks and realized I still hadn't spoken.

"Oh, um, yes. Of course. Please, come in."

Before I could move, her eyes drifted to Lola, and Lola jumped. "Oh! I'll just, um"—she shot me a look, as if she'd never said such a horrible filler word before meeting me—"check on how our ads are coming along for next month."

Vera gave her a brilliant smile. "I think that's a lovely idea."

Lola grabbed her purse and skittered out, giving me one more bewildered glance before the door closed between her and Vera, shutting her out and me in.

I swallowed. What had I done now?

Vera took a few steps in and leaned against my table, folding her hands. "I just had a very interesting visit from Jack Holmes in photography."

I swallowed hard and tried to get my voice to work, to make it sound less like I was being strangled. "Oh?"

I mean, I'd seen him leave, but I hardly thought that had anything to do with *me*.

"He recommended you for Paris Fashion Week."

My elbow slipped, and I almost faceplanted on the layout table. "*Me?*"

I pointed to myself, just to make sure we were talking about the same person.

A hint of an amused smile graced her perfectly lovely face. "Yes, you. It isn't fall Fashion Week, which as you know is our biggest event of the year, but spring is perfect for getting your feet wet."

I was super close to hyperventilating. Paris? Me? I'd only wanted to go for my entire life!

Then I started to panic for a completely different reason.

My French was dismal. I'd taken it in high school and again in college, but I could barely ask where the bathroom was. I could read it, but the moment I tried to speak it, my accent fled and my mind screamed, "But what if I make a *mistake?*" causing everything I knew to simply disappear.

I needed to add French lessons to my schedule. ASAP. I could shove it in there somewhere, right?

She interrupted the thousands of plans that had exploded in my mind simultaneously.

"I assume Jack already spoke to you about the main feature session?"

I gulped and nodded, scared to open my mouth for all the blathering that might spill out. How did one person possibly deserve so many wonderful things happening all at once? I certainly didn't.

Wait. Main feature session?

"Do you think you can manage it and your current workload?"

My voice was breathless and a little gaspy. "Oh, yes, ma'am. I'm sure I can."

"Vera," she said with a slight smile.

"Vera," I practically breathed out.

She straightened away from the table. "Good." She offered me a quiet smile. "I look forward to seeing what you can do."

She left, but I felt like I'd been bulldozed into a pile of rainbows and sunshine and happiness, and it wasn't long until Lola was shaking my arm and rattling me back down to earth.

"Well? What did she say. Oh for heaven's sake, snap out of it!" She snapped her fingers in my face a bunch of times. I jerked toward her, and a curious, frustrated, wide-eyed Lola stared back.

I gripped both of her arms in a stranglehold and got right in her face. "I'm going to Paris Fashion Week. Can you believe it? Me. Paris!"

I started to squeal and jump up and down, and Lola peeled me off her and stepped away. "Good for you."

I started stuffing work into my bag, remembered I couldn't take it home with me, put it all back, and then collected my personal stuff instead.

"Oh my gosh, I have to go tell Gavin right now."

She glanced at the clock. "But what about…?"

I waved her off and headed for the door. "When I get back. I'm taking an extended lunch break!"

She called after me, "But it's after dinnertime!"

I laughed. "Then I'm taking a dinner break. Don't worry! I'll be back in an hour, tops."

And then I was hurrying toward the elevator, floating on clouds miles above the skyscraper I worked in.

I bounced on my tiptoes outside the final security checkpoint to get on set, everything I needed out and ready for the guard to verify.

Most filming took place stupid late or stupid early while it was dark to get as many city shots as possible, or so Gavin had told me. They did have a few bar and pool and other indoor sets, which was where I was headed.

Don't ask me how, but I somehow remembered he'd be shooting on set this week, and in the city, or on location, next. (Good luck finding him then.)

Also, props to me for remembering such random information. I couldn't figure out how my brain decided which thoughts would stick while others fled like cockroaches from sunlight when I tried to find them.

The security guard confirmed everything, laughed at me for being so bouncing excited, and then escorted me to Gavin's assistant.

As soon as I saw her, my mind completely blanked on her name. "Oh, um, hi, yooou…"

She quickly masked her surprise and went expressionless, her all-business look. "May I help you, Miss Marshall?"

The security guard left me in her care, and I tried to tamp down my excitement. For her sake, because I didn't want her to think I was a moron. "Hi, um, yes. May I see Gavin?" I tried to do something with my hands, and just ended up wringing them as I gave her a dopey grin. "I've got some exciting news I just couldn't wait to tell him."

She pulled out a tablet and swiped through to what I assumed was Gavin's schedule. "He has a break in thirty minutes if you can wait that long."

I really couldn't—that was pushing it, and I'd just run off before getting more details from Stan or Jackson or somebody about whatever main feature Vera was talking about—but I had to tell Gavin the rest. "Um, okay…"

She didn't miss a thing as my thoughts flitted across my face. "If you'd like to watch him work, you might be able to catch him between scenes, if you're pressed for time."

My mouth almost fell open. She'd let me do that? I nodded quickly. "That would be perfect. Thank you."

She turned and led me toward a giant warehouse-type building. I trotted to keep up with her endless, sculpted, model-worthy legs. And wished she didn't hate me so much.

Don't get me wrong, everything she said and did was completely professional, efficient, and as expressionless as an android. (Yes, I love *Star Trek*. I'm a total nerd and proud of it.) She didn't give me any reason to think she didn't like me, but I just knew she didn't.

She probably hated that a nobody like me was dating her cousin, and she had no idea what he saw in me. I saw it every time she looked at me, and it just made me want to apologize.

It also didn't help that the first time we'd seen each other, Gavin had accidentally spilled coffee all down her front in his haste to talk to me.

He hadn't known, and I doubted she'd told him, because he would've felt horrible.

One more thing for her to hold against me.

She led me through a series of doors, then held her finger to her lips as we went into a darkly lit area. Then she pointed to the lit-up red letters on the wall that said, "Quiet. Recording."

The atmosphere instantly changed. Charged is the best way I can think to describe it.

At a quick glance, I saw an indoor scene, someone's lavish office, dark muted colors of purple, blue, and green splashed on the walls.

Gavin was talking in a New York gangsta accent, and let

me tell you, all the gold bling around his neck, slicked-back hair, and buttoned-up shirt with sleeves rolled to his elbows made him look like a completely different person.

But that's not what stopped me cold. Oh no. It was all the foul language pouring out of his mouth. My eyes got wider with every syllable.

I didn't think he knew those words! *I* didn't know most of those words.

Then he whipped out a gun and held it to another guy's temple. The guy begged for mercy, but Gavin just laughed at him, wrapped his arm around the other guy's neck, and then proceeded to curse some more right before he "broke" the guy's neck and dropped him to the floor.

I jumped and covered my mouth with my hand.

Then he swaggered off the set, which had just become way too real, and someone called, "Cut!"

A flurry of activity followed, and I jumped again, my eyes glued to Gavin.

He instantly changed, back to his normal self—though if given a choice, I'd ask him to burn those clothes. He and someone else—the director, maybe?—watched the footage they'd just gotten.

"I think we got it," the other guy said before slapping Gavin's shoulder. "Set up for the next scene!"

Everyone scurried to comply.

Gavin rolled his neck, and his assistant made a beeline for him. He reached for the tablet she held, but she spoke quickly and quietly to him, and his head whipped up.

His eyes found me an instant later and brightened, and he hurried my way.

I offered him a wobbly smile. It didn't matter that it was fake—I'd just seen him kill a man, in anger, seething with hatred, completely unprovoked.

It's fake, it's fake, it's just fake, I chanted to myself.

He walked right up to me and kissed me. I clung to him and returned the kiss, letting him ground me in reality.

Which, according to Jackson, wasn't.

And oh my goodness, had they doused him with an entire bottle of cologne?

He pulled back, and his face was a little flushed. "Candace! What are you doing here?"

I tried to give him my brightest smile. It wobbled a little, and I wished, not for the first time, that I had a smidgeon of his acting skill.

Why was I here? Oh! "I have some exciting news, and I just couldn't wait to tell you."

My eyes went to the previously dead dude, who'd stood and was getting his makeup touched up. I breathed a sigh of relief.

I mean, I knew he wasn't really dead, but ugh. What a brutal scene.

Gavin pulled me farther to the back of the room and out of the bustle. "I'm sorry you had to see that. It's, um, a pretty hard-R film."

As I took in his face, I realized it was flushed from embarrassment, not from it being warmer in here. Oh my gosh, what else about this film did I not want to know?

I blurted, "Vera asked me to go to Paris with her. For fashion week. In spring. Early March, I think."

His eyes widened, and a smile stretched across his face. "Why, Candace, that's wonderful." He gave me a hug. "I'm so proud of you."

And just like that, I had my Gavin back, and I was able to shake what I'd seen.

I returned the hug, and my bubbly excitement flowed back in spades. "I'm sorry I just popped in like this, but I had to tell you right away."

"Places, everyone!" someone called.

Gavin pulled back, kissed me hard, leaving me breathless, and leaned his forehead against mine. "This Monday, you, me, and some veggie sushi. Tell me all about it?"

I melted. "You can count on it."

He kissed me again and was off, taking his place under the darkened lights. I blinked. The backdrop of an office had been removed.

The whole wall, moved, just like that.

Now the set was an indoor pool, an actual pool, and an actress in the skimpiest bikini ever lounged in the background as two mobster thugs approached Gavin with machine guns.

But was I focused on the guns? Oh no.

I couldn't stop staring at Miss String Bikini over there.

My mouth fell open. I couldn't help it. How could she be practically naked like that in front of all these people? I'd be hiding behind a towel and shouting, "Don't look!"

Once again, one of the many reasons I would not make it in this industry.

As Gavin took his place, his cousin handed him her tablet. "Your lines."

He scanned them as the flurry settled, and then the same person called, "Ready? And"—Gavin handed the tablet back—"mark!"

They slapped that white and black marker thingy, or whatever it was called, and Gavin's assistant headed back my way. "May I see you out?"

I nodded, and we quietly made our way from the scene. She saw me safely to a cab, then I returned to work in a daze.

Just what did Gavin mean by a hard-R film? And why did it bother me so much? And *who* in their right mind would ever *wear* that? In front of people?

CHAPTER EIGHTEEN

A date with Gavin Bailey.

Monday was here, the Monday *after* production week, and that meant it was sushi time.

I practically flew to the restaurant, floating on so much air, I was pretty sure I needed to be tethered to the ground, or maybe the table, for the evening.

Gavin had gotten us reservations at Chopped Stix, only the most gourmet Asian-food restaurant in NYC. Reservations were a year out, at least, and only celebrities or those wealthy enough could merit one.

Believe me, I was not the kind of girl who needed fancy dinner reservations, but I was a little impressed and a lot giddy all the same.

I set my clutch on the hostess stand and beamed at the beautiful girl working there. Normally exquisite people intimidated me, but I was too happy to shrivel into a ball of self-doubt. She eyed me back warily.

It didn't faze me. I got that look from most people.

"Candace Marshall. Table for two. Reservation under Mr. Bailey?" I beamed some more.

She typed in the info and then looked surprised. "Your

table isn't ready yet, but we don't seat until both parties have arrived."

She settled a cool, level look on me.

I mean, I couldn't blame her. I didn't belong in a place like this. They should probably pad the wine glasses and hide the fine china. I was used to being a disaster.

I nodded and tried to keep the same wattage to my smile, but now it was a lot of work. "Of course. I'll just…"

She pointed. I turned around. Saw the waiting area. Nodded.

"I'll just sit over there."

I gave her another smile that wasn't returned, then settled in to be watched and gossiped over by the wait staff.

Time for dinner came and went, and still no Gavin.

I called a few times, still unable to text or email, and obsessively checked the reservation confirmation he'd sent me. (I'd printed it at work, simply because I knew I couldn't see it on my phone.) I *still* needed to get that fixed.

Plus, the pitying and exasperated and amused looks I was getting were starting to sting. Okay, they were past stinging. I blinked back tears.

Where was he? Why wasn't he here? Was he standing me up?

I called again. He picked up on the fifth ring.

"Candace? What is it? Is it an emergency?" He sounded harried—rushed.

I rolled my eyes and threw my hands in the air. "No, I'm fine. Just fine. Are you okay, though? Not dying or anything?"

He sounded like he was in a closet. Why was he in a closet? His voice sounded muffled. Tinny. Was he hiding?

"Look, Candace, I've got to go—if everything's okay…?" His words hung in the air.

Heat flooded me, and not from the overhead vent's warm breeze. Was he kidding me right now?

His sigh was heavy. "Candace, do you need something?"

I tried to sound as nonchalant as possible, but I was seething inside. "Oh, you know, nothing important. Just our dinner date? I was hoping you weren't dead somewhere. Though now I'm rethinking that."

He groaned. "Oh, Candace, I'm so sorry—I completely forgot. I'll make it up to you, lass, I promise I will."

It was kinda hard to stay mad, hearing all the regret in his voice. But if I stopped being mad, tears might start, and I was already being scrutinized and thoroughly judged by the wait staff.

She thinks she's got a date with Gavin Bailey? What a loser! Someone duped her big time.

Gavin interrupted the internal beating I was giving myself. "Look, I've got to go. No cell phones on set. My assistant thought there might be something wrong with how many times you called."

Now I was the one who felt terrible. Though I shouldn't. Not really.

"I'm so sorry—" I started to apologize, even though this totally wasn't my fault.

"I'm in my trailer—I really need to go."

Wait a sec… "I thought you weren't working today?"

"Got called in—I'll explain. Soon. I love you. Bye."

I pulled my silent phone away from my ear. Mouth open. Yep, he'd hung up on me. The hostess hovered over me, willing me to leave with every ounce of her being.

"Will your party be joining you now?"

I could tell she didn't think I'd ever had a party in the first place.

Tears filled my eyes, but before they could streak down my face and turn me into a blubbering mess, I stuck my nose in the air, pulled my bag over my shoulder, and left without saying a word.

My stomach reminded me I hadn't eaten in ages. I

should've ordered something, but the prices were outrageous, and I never would've chosen to eat there on my own.

Because I was furious and didn't know what else to do, I marched to the nearest bistro and choked down half a sandwich and half a bowl of soup. I sat with my back to the other diners, facing the widow, and cried my eyes out to my reflection.

Even tears were not going to keep me from a perfect sandwich, okay?

Once I'd finished my meal and composed myself enough to walk past everyone I didn't know to find the restroom, thankfully this place actually had a restroom for customers, I locked myself in a stall and cried some more.

Then I blew my nose, washed my hands, and splashed water on my face.

The last time I'd cried my eyes out in a bathroom, Gavin had rescued me from being dumped by my then-boyfriend Peter.

And here I was again.

I sincerely hoped this wasn't the omen I felt it was, no matter what Jackson said.

My phone buzzed, and I pulled it out of my clutch.

Someone had texted me, and I rolled my eyes and then turned my phone every which way to try to interpret it through the cracks in the screen and the messed-up background. I found if I pressed on the screen in different places, I could make out a few words…

Apparently, possibly, Gavin had texted me right after hanging up on me?

Stay…sending…driver…

I yelped, used makeup wipes on the trails of mascara that had somehow escaped the brand's waterproof memo, and practically ran out of the bistro.

"Stumbled" would've been more accurate, because heels.

That should've been my first clue Gavin had forgotten.

Unlike Peter, he always picked me up for our dates, but this time, I'd been so excited, I hadn't even thought twice of making my way to the restaurant without him.

Then again, it had been a while.

Slipping off my heels before I killed myself—I was a comfy-and-cute flats kind of girl—I ran down the sidewalk for Chopped Stix, and sure enough, a huge black SUV waited at the curb.

I slid in, thanked Gavin's driver, and tried not to gulp air like I'd been running. Which I totally had. Gavin's driver, whatever his name was, eyed me in the rearview mirror and looked like he wanted to say something.

Instead, he pulled out into traffic, and I was on my way to my empty apartment.

I leaned back and took a deep breath. The car smelled faintly of Gavin, and it made me miss him that much more. What a great evening this had turned out to be. A whole day off, wasted.

As I tried to maintain a non-sobbing face for Gavin's stoic driver, I told myself one thing over and over.

No matter what, I was not going to cry myself to sleep.

✗

I was totally going to cry myself to sleep.

As we neared my apartment, I held in another shuddering sob, hoping Gavin's driver hadn't heard the last one.

I'd had lots of practice crying silently as a kid—people were made fun of in my family for splaying real emotions for the world to see, which as anyone could imagine had been killer for me—but I was making every effort to unleash elsewhere, not where Gavin could hear about this later.

Oh my gosh, what was he going to tell Gavin?

I had to escape this dude and his eagle eyes.

Taking deep breaths, I blinked back tears and tried to

think of anything other than being stood up. Honestly, this night would be so much worse if I fell to pieces in front of him. I needed out.

"Right here is fine."

Gavin's driver didn't say anything—he was the size of a linebacker—just grunted and pulled over in a no-parking zone.

If anyone could get away with it, it was this guy.

Not wanting to get in trouble—or be there when he did—I fell all over myself to get out of the SUV as quickly as possible.

"Thank you!" I called as I tried to close the door and missed.

Then I got it closed but dropped my purse.

I retrieved my clutch, but upside down, so everything in it fell out all over the sidewalk—including the notes I'd brought with me in case I got a chance to go over them. The pages unrolled and fanned out all over the ground.

"Are you kidding me!"

Driver dude just sat there, watching me.

Several people walked by as I frantically retrieved pages I wasn't even supposed to take out of the office. But crazy deadline, and new designer trying to get featured in our magazine, so…I was researching him and his skill and his professionalism.

Besides, Stan had handed it to me as I left work yesterday. What else was I to assume but that it was homework? He knew I had a working laptop.

No one helped. One person might have glanced my way, but even that was questionable.

I took my flurry of pages, upset purse, and humiliated self to my apartment's keyless entry. I waved my purse all over the pad, but nothing happened.

Stupid purse. Stupid keyless entry. Stupid fashion proposal!

I found my not-key I kept in the small zipper area for when my phone didn't work, only dropping three more pages, and held the door with my foot as I snatched them up.

I waved at driver dude, still waiting, still watching, face completely emotionless behind a dark film of glass, and let the door slam behind me.

I dumped everything on the entryway table, took a moment to rearrange everything, and flipped through the proposal.

Oh my gosh, a page was missing.

I frantically searched for it, then a piece of white caught my eye. Outside.

Oh no.

I ran out and snatched it up. The door shut behind me with an ominous click.

Slowly turning, I saw my purse, the rest of the proposal, everything, just sitting there on the entry table, waiting for someone to take it.

And this was NYC. Someone was gonna take it.

And with my luck, they'd do it while maintaining eye contact the whole time.

I squeaked and sprinted for the door—tugged and begged and tried to pry it off its hinges—but nothing. The door remained firmly locked. My *purse* was inside. My proposal. The one I wasn't even supposed to have outside of work's safe walls.

I glanced behind me, but Gavin's driver was gone.

✗

What felt like a million years later, I stood huddled against the door, refusing to budge in case someone came.

Of course, if they were inside, they'd probably just take

everything and walk away, smiling at me, knowing I could do nothing about it.

Please God, please God, please. Send someone. Anyone. Just not a thief.

"Can I get that for you?"

"Oh, thank God!" I spun toward the voice.

And froze. Him. The murderer. With fangs. *Vampire* fangs.

Though they looked a lot bigger when he was carrying me all up close and personal.

"What are you doing here?" I demanded.

Suave, almost-handsome vampire dude smiled, pointy teeth sharp in the cloudy moonlight. Or rather, NYC-light. Because NYC had its own look at night. Anyway.

"I came to see you, actually."

Well if that wasn't just creepy. My eyes narrowed. "You punched me."

He bowed his head and spread his hands a little, in acceptance of what I said. "Sometimes we must do distasteful things to keep those we love safe."

I wasn't even going there. I scowled. "You undressed me."

He barely stifled a grin. "Couldn't leave any DNA with you. Besides, sometimes sacrifices are necessary. And some of those sacrifices are rather enjoyable."

I blinked. I hadn't even realized those clothes were missing. So of course I glowered harder. "I woke up in my bed."

"Only to keep you safe, my lady. Would you rather I had left you unconscious in front of your building?" He raised an eyebrow.

I sputtered and couldn't come up with a response.

Oh wait! Yes I could.

I frowned at him. "Don't you need to be invited in or something? How did you even get inside my apartment?"

His grin was positively devilish. "Oh, you invited me in, all right. Told me to make myself at home."

I grumbled to myself. Well, okay, fine then. That sounded like me. Especially if I was delirious and had slept through being *undressed*.

"May I?" He gestured at the door.

I stepped back, my eyes still on my purse. My *life* was in there.

He waved his hand over the door pad, and it popped open.

My mouth fell open. "How did you—what on earth—how did you do that?"

He smiled, bent and retrieved the paper I'd dropped, again, and handed it to me. "Another delicious secret, I'm afraid, my darling."

I didn't care. Well, I did, but it was too cold to care. And I wasn't his darling.

But I was laser focused on my belongings.

I darted inside, and he followed me. I quickly stuffed the page where it belonged, checked to make sure everything was in my purse—though no one had been near it—then reluctantly faced him, loose pages clutched to my chest.

In hindsight, totally should've bound those after Stan handed them to me.

He watched me with an amused expression. "All better, lovely?"

I eyed him. "You're like an odd mix of *Once Upon a Time's* Captain Hook, *Pirate of the Caribbean's* Captain Jack, and a *Lost Boys'* vampire. Not that I ever saw *Lost Boys*. Just a poster. Because I don't do scary."

"Don't do scary." He prowled around the little entryway, four elevators facing each other in the small space, as if he couldn't stand still for long. "Yet you somehow find yourself in a vampiric lair and simply must uncover what's going on?"

My face felt like it was a million degrees. "Yeah, well, you know what they say about curiosity and all."

He paused and raised an eyebrow. "That it killed the cat? Or Bluebeard's many wives?"

I felt lightheaded all of a sudden, and I was pretty sure my face had gone sheet white. "Uh, yeah, no. Not that one."

He resumed his prowling. "Then which saying did you mean?"

Dude could be an actor. His presence filled the room and made everyone pay attention. Unfortunately, I was his only audience. Talk about uncomfortable.

I shrugged. "Just, you know, about needing to be solved. Or found out. Or something."

"Or something. Oh that one."

He smiled at me, and I relaxed a smidge and returned it.

No, Candace, bad! Vampire, remember? *Murdering* vampire. Who *threatened* you.

"Right, okay, I need to go...um...thank you again for your help."

"Ah, but you see, I haven't gotten what I came for yet."

I froze, a thousand warning bells clanging in my head. "And that would be...?"

He smiled, most likely thinking he was devilishly handsome and charming.

Well, he was. But I would not be swayed.

"You."

CHAPTER NINETEEN

Oh heck no. Not happening.

I convinced him to walk half a block to the all-night pizza joint on the corner just to get him out of my building. And to be surrounded by witnesses. I eyed the single guy behind the counter who'd gone right back to his phone after handing us our slices.

Not sure he counted, but still.

We stood at a little table right outside their doors in full light.

I didn't understand how they could stay open all night with the crime in this city.

But I was grateful. This was sometimes the only food I got all day, usually between two or three a.m.

My pizza was gone, he hadn't touched his—duh, vampire—and he was getting more animated the longer we sparred. Er, talked.

I jabbed an angry finger in his direction. "Yeah, but I saw you. I *saw* you sucking blood from that old dude's neck!"

He was too scrawny to be handsome. Too greasy to be suave. Too pale to be attractive. Yet he leaned against the brick wall, just shy of the light spilling from within, and was all those things anyway.

"What you saw, my dear, was me tasting the blood splashed all over that man's neck to make it look like he'd been attacked. I didn't kill him. And he wasn't supposed to be dead."

"Wait, what? You were tasting the blood? That's disgusting. Why? If that's even true…" I eyed him suspiciously.

He shrugged, his grin far too confident for someone who'd just admitted to drinking blood. Sooo gross.

"When blood is the main part of your diet—or rather, the only part of your diet—then you know what different blood tastes like. And that wasn't human blood."

I started gagging, just a little, and my pizza threatened to come back up for a visit.

Nope. I refused to let him know how gross I found this conversation. Or to waste what was actually incredibly amazing pizza.

"But…why?"

He ducked his head a moment before returning his magnetic gaze to me. "I'd seen it several times around the city, couldn't figure it out. It wasn't our coven. We're not that messy."

I didn't want to ask. But there it was, coming out of my mouth anyway. "But…you do drink human blood?"

Huh. Maybe I should've asked about the other dead bodies instead. I'd meant to.

He moved right past my question with an ease I found enviable. "Something's going on that shouldn't be. You see, Mr. John Withers chose a life as one of us. He chose to join my coven. He is quite a wealthy old man, and he wanted to leave his life as a mortal behind, no strings attached to anything from before."

I leaned in, fascinated, perfectly willing to let vampire dude tell me this outrageous bedtime story.

He shrugged. "We have ways of doing that. Of faking a death, donating their worldly goods to the coven of their choice, disguised as a charity—but something has been going wrong lately."

"Like dead guys showing up in alleys instead of dying peacefully in their beds?" I guessed.

"Exactly. We've been finding more bodies dumped instead of brought to us, their wills rewritten or funds going elsewhere, places we cannot trace. Mr. Withers was to die peacefully in his bed, then we'd arranged to have his body transferred to the funeral home and removed before he could be embalmed, a closed yet empty casket on display with strict instructions not to open. He would then be awakened in a resurgence ceremony. He never made it to the funeral home. I was looking for him when I found his body in that alley."

"But you said Mr. Withers wasn't supposed to be dead."

"No, he wasn't. Only made to look that way to you humans."

I tilted my head. "Is that why his body went missing from the morgue?"

All of a sudden, I had his full, undivided attention. It felt like a weight between my shoulders. "What did you just say?" he asked in a low voice.

I shrugged and looked away, uncomfortable. "They said they'd cleaned his body that first day, put him away, and hadn't touched him since. He had a no-autopsy order or something. So no one had any idea when he disappeared. Are you saying he might still be alive?"

He pulled back with a grin. "Oh, that's good news. He might indeed."

"What do you think happened to the body?" I asked.

"I don't know. It's bothering me, too. The other bodies

haven't disappeared that I know of. It's so similar to what we do—but whoever is doing this is actually killing people and involving the police and accusing members of my coven of murder. They've gone too far."

"No, Dr. Greenley said this isn't the first body that has disappeared," I said absently.

His sudden, direct stare was unnerving. "What did you just say?"

"I said it wasn't the first body to disappear. Why? Is that important?"

He just grunted and looked away, pondering something, so my mind wandered.

I craned my neck to look at the pizza slices on display. Should I get another? Because I could definitely eat more. "Any other coven have a grudge against yours?"

He was quiet so long, I suddenly remembered we were having a conversation.

I hyper-focused on him. He had a funny look on his face.

"Yes," he said simply.

I shrugged. "Sounds like they found a way to stop you from doing whatever you guys do to get new members, stealing them for their own coven or whatever."

"That makes your involvement more vital than ever."

I still wasn't convinced. I huffed and crossed my arms. "And you need me involved because…"

"Because you're the only one who can find them again. Find their location."

I threw my hands in the air. "I was knocked out! Drugged! And if you recall, *you* then knocked me out when we left. I couldn't take you back there if my life depended upon it! Besides, you were there. Can't you just go back?"

He ran his fingers through his hair a few times. Gavin did it better. "You were the only reason we found that hideaway. If we hadn't been watching Mr. Withers's apartment…"

I gasped. "You mean you used me as *bait*?"

"And now they've surely moved. Or enhanced their security so it's impossible to get back in. Besides, they're not the ones I'm looking for. They don't know where the old man is, either. Or so they say."

I sighed. "Look, I don't even belong in your world. I stick out like a, well, like a person just asking to be drained like a juice box. I don't understand why you can't find these people on your own. You fit in and everything."

I waved a hand over his all-black garb, more suitable in Victorian times or pirate times or some other time period around there.

History was not my strong suit. Facts liked to flee, remember?

He did *not* look happy with me. "Where is the key, Miss Marshall?"

I gasped, and, instinctively, my hand went to my chest. He searched my neck as if looking for a necklace chain—or a snack—and I dropped my hand. "What key?"

"The one you stole from Mr. Withers, of course. The one I didn't have time to retrieve from his body, thanks to you."

I floundered like a fish. "I didn't—I don't—how dare you…"

He gritted his teeth. "The Midnight Coven are my sworn enemies. I've been trying to find them for years to mete out justice. That key ensures I find them. And I swear by the great Dracul, I will have my revenge. *Especially* if they are the ones doing this to us."

My eyes progressively widened with every syllable of his tirade.

Coven? Enemies? Dracul?

This was one crazy train I wanted no part of. My life was exciting enough as it was, thank you very much.

"Oh, okay. If I find some old ornate key, I'll let you know…" I eased my clutch off the table, papers stuffed back inside for this little jaunt, and edged toward my apartment building, my eyes on him the entire time.

"I never said the key was old nor ornate," he said in a deeply satisfied voice.

I froze like a deer in headlights. Yes, that happened quite often in the little town I used to live in, so I definitely knew what it looked like.

Another heavy sigh from wannabe vampire over there. "I can't stress to you the importance of that key. If you 'find' it, you will tell me? Many lives depend upon it."

I could hear the air quotes around "find" and everything.

I let out an unbelieving laugh. "What, like undead lives?"

He speared me with a look, and I froze. "It is not a laughing matter, Candace Marshall. You've already seen what they can do. How they can kill anyone they want and blame it on anyone they like. How far their reach is."

So he still maintained his innocence. Didn't everyone? The guilty and the innocent alike? Now I just had to figure out which one he actually was.

Ugh! Why was I involving myself in this again?

I nodded, ready to agree to just about anything so I could leave. "Yeah, framed you for murder, made it look like a vampire attack—"

He shot me a look filled with scorn.

I lifted a hand, hoping to calm him. "Whether it was or not, you have to admit the police don't believe a word of it, and the vampire forums are all too happy about the evidence that 'real' vampires live among us."

His posture relaxed a little.

"Then they made the body disappear." I thought about it. "So like a vampire mob. I mean, this is New York City."

He shot me another look of scorn. "Please. Your human mafia have nothing on the evil that fills this city's underground."

I swallowed. Hard. "Oh."

On that note, I was going to my apartment and never coming out again. Except for work and to see Gavin. In other words, in the daylight or with people. Lots of people.

Real people. Not vampire people.

I faked a yawn, but it turned real. "I've got to go. Early day tomorrow, not much rest to be had, thanks to this mess."

His look softened. "Sleep well, Candace Marshall. I shall place a guard on your dwelling so no evil befalls you."

"I really wish you wouldn't."

"Remember, invite no one in. They cannot come in if you do not give your express permission. You are safe within your walls."

My eyes widened, and all hope for sleep evaporated.

I nodded, far too many times. "Y-y-you can c-c-count on it."

He smiled. "Good."

With that, he suddenly unfolded himself from his casual resting place against the wall and took off.

Not that I minded. I was beyond ready for this conversation to be over.

I looked behind me every three seconds as I sprinted to my apartment. Why did he have to make everything so freaking creepy? Vampires weren't real. They *weren't*.

I paused right before I entered my building, door held open, and glanced once more behind me.

He was bending over a homeless dude.

No. Oh no oh no oh no.

Pretty sure I was making the worst mistake of my life, I let the door drop and sprinted back his way.

"God bless you, sir," said a low, wobbly voice.

I stopped as the low words washed over me, then ducked into a darkened doorway.

Vampire dude turned and walked the other way.

Some homeless vet, according to his sign, sat there happily munching on a slice of New York City's finest pizza.

My heart softened toward the supposedly innocent vampire dude. I really should learn his name. Maybe he wasn't such a bad guy after all.

I stiffened. Unless he was trying to enthrall the guy for his next meal.

I eyed the guy, but nothing seemed out of the ordinary. Unless I called living on the streets ordinary. Which it shouldn't be.

At least he had something warm to fill his belly. I made a mental note to look for him when hunger drove me to the pizza joint in the middle of the night.

I tiptoed back to my apartment building, certain at any moment, the next vampire on "scare Candace" rotation would grab me for a non-friendly little chat.

And I'd fall over dead from a heart attack.

✝

After a restless night of jerking awake at every noise my building made, I was nodding off, again, when I heard dishes clank together in my kitchen.

I shot out of bed.

Not even taking a moment to think things through, I grabbed the closest thing and tore out of my bedroom.

And froze.

There murdery vampire goth dude stood, calm as you please, cooking eggs. In my kitchen. With a pan I didn't even know I had.

He gave me a lazy grin. "Morning, beautiful. Sleep well?" His eyes slid to what I held in my hand, and his grin widened. "Going to pelt me to death with your stuffed animal?"

I eyed the red teddy bear I was pretty sure came from

Gavin at some point, threw it down, and pointed at my unwelcome guest.

"What are you doing in my apartment?" I demanded.

"Why, making you breakfast, of course."

He offered me a cheeky grin I wanted to scratch right off his face.

I scowled harder. "Wait a sec. If you're a real vampire, like you *claim*, how are you inside my apartment? That shouldn't be possible."

"First of all, I am a real vampire. Second, your previous invitation still stands. When I brought you home the other night."

My mouth fell open. "After you *punched* me?"

I still wasn't over that.

He rubbed his chin and looked slightly disconcerted. "I had no choice—"

I interrupted. "And after you *undressed* me?"

His beyond-pale face flushed just slightly. "As I said, couldn't leave any DNA behind." He talked right over my spluttering. "Besides, I'm sure you noticed you were still wearing what you had on under your outer clothing."

I glanced down at my sleep shorts, then pointed at them for emphasis. They were the same ones I'd been wearing when I'd woken up that day.

"Well, except for those." He grinned.

I slammed my eyes shut, then thought better of it with a freaking vampire in my kitchen. "Please tell me you at least closed your eyes."

His grin widened. "If that makes you feel better. Sure."

I started to die of humiliation, then glanced around frantically. "But those were my favorite jeans! Where are they?" I gasped. "You didn't throw them away, did you?"

Not that I'd noticed they were missing until he mentioned it.

He saluted me. "Now don't let that worry even pass that

pretty little head of yours. I'll have them dry cleaned and delivered."

I blinked. Wait, was I supposed to dry clean those? Oops.

Then I squinted. "Isn't it morning? How can you be out in daylight?"

Another grin. "Ah, the sun isn't quite up yet, my lovely. Besides, we never finished our conversation."

"We most certainly did too," I insisted in a petulant voice. This dude was in my apartment. I couldn't even begin to express how many ways that was *not cool*.

He raised an eyebrow, still an amused cant to his lips, darn him. "Oh? You know all about the dark web and our secret codes and how to find this month's meeting place?"

My jaw may have dropped open and stayed that way.

I shot a quick glance to my paper calendar on the wall. Still on June.

Not because I'd forgotten to change it, but because I liked that picture. Okay, both things were true. I'd honestly forgotten I even had a calendar till just now. Anyway.

Pretty sure it was November.

"I thought not," he continued. "Shall we begin while you eat?"

He picked up a full plate of lightly scrambled eggs, crispy bacon, and diced fresh salsa, then poured a glass of freshly squeezed orange juice—not that cooked, pasteurized crap—and set it before me.

As a rule, I did not eat food offered by strangers. Unless, of course, you counted every takeout meal or cafeteria sandwich or late-night pizza slice I ordered. Which I wasn't.

Okay, fine. All my food was made by strangers. I never cooked.

But this was different.

I stood there, unsure, until my stomach gave an angry growl, reminding me I hadn't been taking care of it.

At my hesitation, he smirked. "Poison and enthrall free, I promise."

Like I could trust him.

But he'd already had plenty of time to do something nefarious and hadn't…

I caught a waft of the deliciousness he'd set under my nose, and before I knew it, I was plopping down on one of my two bar seats at my kitchen counter and stuffing my face with eggs.

I pointed my fork at him. "This doesn't mean we won't have words about you breaking into my apartment. Again."

He didn't look overly threatened by me. He just leaned on his elbows on the counter across from me and watched me eat with an intensity that made me uncomfortable. Until I realized he was staring at my food with longing, not me.

Oh, come on. How far was he going to take this joke?

At my glower, he straightened, leaned against my counter, and crossed his arms. The move was so Gavin-like, I blinked.

But the moment passed, and he no longer even held a candle to Gavin Bailey.

The food grew into a tasteless lump in my mouth. I missed that man.

Even if he'd stood me up for the first time ever.

I narrowed my eyes and resumed chewing. "Tell me everything."

"I can't tell you everything—you'd have to join us for that." He grinned as if he found that idea overly pleasing.

I rolled my eyes. "Not happening. What about this dark web thingy, then?"

I shoved another bite in my mouth. One thing was for sure, this vamp could *cook*.

If he ever decided to go into the chef business and stop pretending to be a vampire, I'd hire him on the spot.

Good food was one of my love languages, and this breakfast was perfection.

He yammered on as I downed one of the best breakfasts I'd had since, well, possibly moving here. The salsa added just the right spice to the eggs, and that fresh tomato was a heavenly contrast to the bacon and eggs.

I mean, coffee and the occasional pastry weren't the healthiest on those days I remembered to eat.

I forced myself to focus on his words, which were becoming slightly worrying.

Dark web? Secret codes? A meeting place I was to go to, *alone*?

"Wait, what exactly is this dark web?" I interrupted.

He spoke after a slight hesitation. "It's the online black market. You can get just about anything there. Illegal guns, drugs, fake IDs…and other things. It's untraceable, can't be indexed, and isn't viewable on a standard web browser." He held out a funny-looking piece of tech. "You'll have to use this software to access it."

I eyed it warily. It would definitely hook up to my new computer, where they'd changed the access ports yet again with the latest model, but I did *not* like putting unknown software on my computer. I didn't want anything bad to happen to it.

Or to go to jail. Which, hello, black market?

I would object just as soon as I finished my plate.

Unless there was more…

I craned my neck to see past him, but nope. He'd given me all of it.

He waited, as if he just knew I'd gotten distracted. I gave him a sheepish smile and waved for him to continue.

I wondered if he'd notice if I licked the plate. Probably.

Oh well. It was delightful while it lasted.

"Let me see if I get this straight," I finally said, pushing my completely clean plate away. I hoped I didn't accidentally put that thing back in the cupboard. "You want me to go online, access a very illegal and untraceable site that could land me in *jail*, then take this cipher"—I held up the piece of paper he'd slid my way while he was talking—"decipher your rival coven's meeting place for the month, then go there all by myself?"

It sounded like something I absolutely was not going to do.

He gave me a confident grin. "Yes, just so."

I raised an eyebrow and gave him a *look*. One I was quite proud of, in fact.

His grin stretched wider, and I sighed. What would it take to learn to be intimidating? Confident? For my *no* to mean *no*?

"You'd best copy that down, love. I've got to go soon, and I can't leave it with you, I'm afraid."

I grumbled all the way to my vampire notebook and back.

He laughed aloud when he saw the cover, but I tucked my burning face over the pages and carefully copied each line, each slash, each little mark, checking it over several times before I was confident I'd gotten it all.

It took up several pages. And was freaking complicated.

He snatched the paper back and shoved it into his overcoat's pocket. "And that, as they say, is that. I'll be seeing you."

He headed toward my door, and I tripped over my feet to chase after him.

"Wait! How will I get in touch with you?"

He flicked a hand in dismissal. "You have my number."

Yeah, but I couldn't text anymore. Did I have time to get that fixed before work today?

"If you think for one moment that I'm going to this place *alone*…"

His fingers on the handle, he offered me another fang-filled grin. "Oh, I think that's exactly what you'll be doing. Want to know why?"

I shook my head, but he answered anyway.

"That blessed curiosity."

Then he was gone, and the lock clicked shut after him. I hurried over, and yep, sure enough, he'd somehow locked my door.

All I could picture was him waving his hand to unlock my building door, and I shook my head and backed up.

Nope. I was jumping off this crazy train right now.

I had no way of finding Mr. Withers, dead or alive, now that his body was missing.

And I wasn't going by myself to some vampire meeting just to prove these jokers weren't real.

CHAPTER TWENTY

I scribbled madly in my vampire notebook, copying the code from the super-sketch website before it kicked me out again.

It took a while to get the hang of this dark web thing. Thank goodness for vampire dude's instructions.

Granted, there were sooo many things I didn't want to see on here. Body parts, anyone? I couldn't tell if they were real or fake, but you know what? I didn't want to know.

But now I had one more motivation in finding Mr. Withers. I didn't want him to end up as one of those body parts.

The deeper I got, the less I wanted to be here. Torture devices I couldn't quite figure out what they'd be used for? Pretty young girls and boys with dollar signs next to their smiling faces? For *sale*.

How were these people not rotting away in jail?

Because I'd happily help put them there, if I could.

According to pirate vampire dude, which was his official name until I asked what it actually was, everything on the dark web was untraceable, but it wasn't right.

But it made me feel gross and it made me feel filthy and sad and disheartened to see the absolute filth humans were willing to wade through when they thought there'd be no consequences.

I didn't talk about my Christian faith often or well, but if these people didn't repent and change their ways, stop selling other human beings, for heaven's sake, breaking their souls in pieces if not their bodies, there would be a reckoning.

And I didn't know how I felt this way, but I didn't want that for them either. I wanted them all to be free, victim and captor alike.

I wretched my concentration back on my pen and paper as the website did that little blip thing before it crashed and I'd have to go looking for it again.

Code complete, I checked it over line by line to make sure I had it right.

The website blinked out, and my screen went blank.

I sagged against my desk chair and sighed. That was close!

And now I was done wandering the dark web for the rest of my life, thank you very much.

Putting all depressing thoughts firmly from my mind, I popped upright, grabbed my cipher, and began to—you guessed it—decipher the uber-secret code: where the vampires were meeting this month.

Vampires. Yeah right. These movie people were going above and beyond this time. Hey, at least I wasn't living in a bus in the middle of the desert, right?

Code complete, I stared at the Queens address.

And the meeting that was *tonight*.

"Ha! Take that, Sherlock Holmes!"

Only my favorite detective ever. I didn't care what Mark Twain said.

I held up the address and keys together. "I have you now, my pretty."

I cackled just like the green witch, then started throwing things together for my night on the town. Pretty sure delirium from such little sleep wasn't good for me.

It was the next day after pirate vampire dude had given me the code, after work, and the first opportunity I'd had to work on it. I didn't want to mess with this anywhere near production week, so it was now or never. Thank goodness I'd actually looked it up tonight, or I'd have to wait another month. And November was freaking cold as it was.

I was in Manhattan, thanks to Gavin and my job, and I'd been too busy to explore the other four main suburbs of New York City. Was this area of Queens a good area? Bad? How long would it take me to get there?

And would I be safe if I did?

I eyed the gun I kept in my apartment for self-defense purposes only. I'd just been reading some pretty scary stuff, after all.

New York City had such extreme concealed carry laws, I'd been jumping through hoops for months to try to get a permit. And they'd been leading me on for just as many months, no end in sight.

I mean, I got that they only wanted cops or active military to carry weapons, but after all I'd been through, I wanted to protect myself.

Gavin, on the other hand? They loved him. What am I saying? Everyone loved that man. When he'd first moved here, far before I did, it hadn't taken him long for NYC to trust him with an armed escort on their streets.

Me, though? I'm pretty sure I had a file somewhere that read, "Potential Unabomber." Or at the very least, "Potential to accidentally aid a Unabomber."

If I carried that thing outside, seeing the inside of a jail might become more of a reality than I cared to experience.

If I were caught.

But if I didn't take it with me, I might get murdered by the people who thought it was normal to drink someone's blood. Or sell body parts. Ack. I mean, really!

Then again, if they were real vampires, then nothing but a silver bullet would work. Or was that werewolves? I'd forgotten to look that up.

I groaned and dropped my head into my hands. I didn't know the lore. I didn't *want* to know the lore. But I didn't want to go exploring vampire lairs without some protection, either.

Impulsively, I grabbed it and had it shoved halfway into my waistband when another thought struck me. If it was some kind of *club* club instead of a gathering of murderers, as I'd been picturing, there would be guards. Bouncers.

I'd be sent home, or the thing would be confiscated.

Ugh! I threw my hands up. What was the right thing to do here?

I sprang for my closet and dug out my duffel bag, the one I'd put together to help me sleep at night after my disastrous zombie movie.

I was prepared for every zombie, vampire, or ghost (hey, it could happen) apocalypse with this thing. But mostly it was camping gear and water filters and bullets for my gun.

Surely I had something that wasn't illegal to carry in NYC.

✗

My rideshare took me as close as I dared, then I struck out on foot.

Thank goodness I'd bundled up. It was freaking cold.

If this was where the vampires were meeting this month, then I was going to settle this thing once and for all. Somebody was going to tell me something, dang it.

I mean, it was kinda ridiculous that the different covens used the exact same code, but hey, easier for me. And if they were truly meeting here to initiate new members, then I was going to be in on this.

I entered the abandoned waterfront warehouse through a side entrance, gun out and held low before me.

Yes. I'd also brought pepper spray, but I'd practiced most with the gun, okay? It just made me feel safer.

I just hoped I didn't have to use it.

The warehouse was divided by still and silent giant machinery and conveyor belts running through the open space, creating lots of creepy hideaways and shadows I swear were moving.

I explored the entire area but found no one. Whoever had set up this meeting had already left, and I'd missed it.

I turned to go, then tripped over something bulky and… soft. It took me a few extra steps to keep from face-planting into heavy machinery, but like a vampire walking past a slumber party, I immediately changed course and went back.

A faded blue sheet covered something far too body-shaped for my comfort. I eased the corner back, and glassy eyes stared at nothing.

I groaned. I was too late.

Not only had I missed whatever meeting this was, but now whatever hopeful initiate this had been was dead.

I pulled back the sheet just a little farther and checked both sides of his neck. Yep, two jagged, puckered, torn fang holes, spilling blood onto the ground.

Just like Mr. Withers.

So, so gross.

Gun aimed low with one hand, eyes darting everywhere, I dug out my phone and called Detective Sawyer.

I didn't care how much the guy hated me. This was beyond my expertise, and he needed to know.

Gun tucked safely away—I only checked eight million times to make sure, one, it was within easy reach in case other vamps showed up, and two, it was well hidden from the cop who hated me—I stayed within the shadows of the warehouse until Detective Sawyer's nondescript police car showed up.

Vehicles with flashing lights weren't far behind.

I stepped out as he did.

He eyed me. "This better not be a waste of my time."

"It isn't," I said solemnly. Maybe I'd been *too* vague.

He followed me inside and over to the body, which was, thankfully, still there. He grunted and crouched down to inspect it with his penlight.

I glanced away as more details became apparent. Younger than Mr. Withers, heavyset, ash-colored hair, and pale eyes. Vampire puncture wounds too real to ignore.

I didn't want to see more.

"Do I want to know what you're doing on private property in the middle of the night, Miss Marshall?"

I shrugged, even though he was totally facing away from me. "I was invited."

He sent me a sharp look.

"It's true. But when I showed up, no one was here, and I practically tripped over this guy."

He grunted again. "You do realize this is the second dead body I've found you hovering over in my town?"

I went paler than a ghost. Pretty sure I swayed a little too.

He went on, almost nonchalantly. "No gunshot wounds, no signs of being strangled or even a struggle."

"Don't forget the vampire fang wounds!" I pointed out helpfully.

He shot me a look. "Some kind of injection site in his neck. I will be asking for your alibi for the past 48 hours."

I stuttered, "Of c-course."

Did I even *have* an alibi? Did obsessively checking the dark web and talking with supposed vampires count?

Pretty sure it didn't.

He stood. "And this is where you found him?"

"It is."

"Please start from the beginning."

So I did. I mean, I was a little vague on the dark web and secret code stuff, leaving murdery vampire dude out of it entirely, but I started really getting into the telling.

I bent over to demonstrate how I'd checked dead guy after I'd tripped over him, and my gun fell right out of my concealed-carry holster—that I swear I'd been saving for when I had a real permit and everything—and slid toward him. The cop who hated me.

And this was New York City, even if I was on the outskirts of Queens.

They technically had "may issue" concealed-carry laws, but they practiced "no issue." Which meant I'd been fighting to get one since I moved here.

Because I still had nightmares about zombie attacks and felt safer with a gun, okay?

All excuses that flew through my head but didn't make it out of my mouth. Not that they would've helped me in any way whatsoever.

My eyes raised reluctantly to his. They were sparkling.

"Why, Miss Marshall. Is that what I think it is?"

Sweat popped up in all kinds of unattractive places. Most noticeably, my upper lip and hairline. No way a cop trained to read people wouldn't notice that.

"I, uh, well—what would you have done if someone asked you to come to an abandoned warehouse in the middle of the night?"

"Not gone," he said promptly, then grinned—the first smile of any kind I'd seen on the man's face—and he looked like I'd just handed him a Christmas present. One he'd wanted his entire lifetime but never thought he'd get.

"I believe I need to see your NYC-approved Pistol License."

I started to backpedal. Big time. I pointed to the incriminating weapon. "Oh, that? That's not mine." It so was.

Great, not only was I going to jail, now I was going to hell for lying. *Just shut up, Candace!*

"I just was, uh, carrying—I mean! *Not* carrying it. Because it stays in my home. Like the law allows. Because I'm a law-abiding citizen. And I like it here in New York. But you didn't expect me to show up at a place like this without some kind of protection, did you?"

I didn't listen to me very well.

He just smiled and let me talk.

I snapped my mouth closed. Oh my gosh, is this what they meant when they said "Anything you say can and will be used against you in a court of law" on the cop shows?

I was so dead. Un-dead. Not dead!

I sighed. I hated zombie references.

"Is that all?" His smile hadn't dimmed.

I covered my mouth to keep from saying anything else and shook my head.

"In that case"—he pulled out a pair of handcuffs, his smile growing—"Candace Marshall, you have the right to remain silent."

"What? I mean, wait. What are you doing?"

He grinned. "I'm taking you to jail. For impeding this investigation, and for concealing a weapon without a permit. Anything you say can and will be used against you in a court of law."

I knew that part was coming!

"But, but—you can't! I'm *helping* this investigation. You

wouldn't have found this guy without me! And I can't go to jail. What are my parents going to say?"

"You have the right to an attorney."

"What if my job finds out? I'll get fired!"

"If you can't afford an attorney, one will be provided for you."

"And Gavin…" I snapped my mouth closed. He couldn't find out about this. He just couldn't.

With a firm grasp on my shoulder, bad cop turned me around and snapped a pair of handcuffs around my wrists. I winced as the strobing red and blue lights bounced off my face. He herded me toward his car.

Okay, I was officially freaking out.

My worst fear had come true. I was going to *jail*.

I was a blubbering mess before he was anywhere close to finished.

You know in those movies, where everything turns to slow motion? Yeah, it felt like that, everything drawn out so I could experience it in intricate detail.

He finished reciting and stuffed me in the back of his car.

I was in a daze, snot and tears streaming down my face as I made every excuse he'd probably heard a thousand times over.

I didn't belong in a jail cell!

My mom would disown me. My grandma would come back from the grave to strangle me. And Gavin—oh my gosh, Gavin.

I dropped my chin on my chest and sobbed my eyes out.

I was only trying to help. To get to the bottom of this. To prove I wasn't going crazy by seeing a freaking vampire. This was the *first day* I'd ever carried a gun outside my apartment in this city!

His partner's gentle objection—"Hey, man, is that really

necessary?"—didn't do a thing to soothe my complete and utter despair.

I hadn't even noticed Lawson was here too, of course he was, but I tucked my chin further, not wanting to meet his eyes.

He'd most likely call Gavin first thing, and my life would be over.

I was going to jail. To *jail*.

CHAPTER TWENTY-ONE

"Miss Marshall?"

My head came up seconds before I shot to my feet. "Yes? Yes! That's me!"

I clung to the bars, their griminess making me think this holding cell housed every deadly disease ever.

I couldn't wait to wash my hands.

The woman cop gave me an expressionless stare. "You have one phone call."

"Oh, thank you!" I rushed to the door.

She took a wide stance, like she was ready to take me down. "Stand back, ma'am!"

I scrambled back. I wanted to let this hard woman who looked like she was ready to tase me—and like she'd thoroughly enjoy it—know I was no threat.

I was happy to do anything she said.

"I don't belong in a place like this. Really. It was all a misunderstanding. A mistake."

And I was babbling.

Her expression told me she wasn't buying it. Everyone in here ever had tried that one. It didn't matter that it was actually true for me.

The door squealed open, and she had me proceed her to a room with phones. "You have two minutes."

"Yes, ma'am. Thank you, ma'am. I'll hurry, ma'am."

I bobbed my head and tried to look as compliant as possible.

"Time's almost up."

That couldn't possibly be true, but I rushed to a phone anyway. My finger hovered over the phone, the first two digits of Gavin's number pressed.

I couldn't call him. He would kill me.

He would also kill me when he found out I hadn't called him first. But my fingers wouldn't work. I physically couldn't do it. Who else could I call?

My brother would laugh and leave me in here for weeks. He'd probably only come to record me so he could post vids all over the internet. My dad would only pass the phone to my mom when he heard it was me. My mom would only cry and do nothing else. I didn't know any lawyers. And Gavin…

My fingers dialed a number I hadn't called in ages. Years. Two years, to be exact. I was amazed I even remembered it. Would she even talk to me?

"Yo, this is Jemma. Leave me a message, and I might call you back. Maybe. I'm living life large with my hottie husband and my awesome fam!"

She hadn't changed one bit.

Beep.

"Uh…hi. Hi, Jemma. It's me. Candace." I blew out a breath. "I know I haven't talked to you in a while…"

My guard lady cleared her throat.

Words tumbled out in a jumble. "But I can't call Gavin and I don't know what to do and I'm in *jail*—can you believe it? Me? In jail? And I don't know any lawyers. I don't know what to do. They said they'll assign someone, but I don't want someone who doesn't care!"

Oh my gosh, was I crying? Would she even be able to make out my words through all the hiccups?

"And I don't know what to do and Gavin is going to kill me and I thought—well, I thought…" I sighed. "I'm sorry. I'm sorry I suck at keeping in touch and I haven't talked to you since your wedding and I'm a big, fat, lousy liar friend, who said she'd keep in touch but didn't, but I don't know what else to do…"

"Time's up."

I let out one final, pathetic sob, rattled off the jail's contact info listed next to the phone, and the call cut off, cop lady's finger on the hang-up button thingy.

She took me back to the holding cell, a sobbing, blubbery mess.

I was suave like that.

The other zoned-out girl in the cell kept staring at the wall, and the two hard-looking older women gave me disgusted looks and scooted away.

That cell door closing was the worst sound in the universe, and I drew my knees to my face and sobbed my eyes out.

No one was coming to help me, and I was going to die here, spending my final days as a jailbird. (My grandma's words, not mine. It was probably the worst thing a person could be, in her opinion.) Why did this have to happen to me?

More importantly, why had I done this to myself?

⚔

"Marshall. Up."

I jumped to my feet, my face crusty and tight and my eyelids gritty like I'd rubbed sand in them.

And Gavin Bailey walked around the corner.

My heart stopped. I couldn't breathe.

Not only was he the most delicious sight in the world, what was he *doing* here? He couldn't see me like this!

He took one look at me, and his jaw went tight. "Was this really necessary?"

Cop lady didn't answer him.

The clanging door slid open, and she jerked her head.

I didn't move. I couldn't.

She stepped toward me, grasped my arm, and pulled me out of the cell.

Gavin shrugged out of his overcoat and draped it over my shoulders, holding me tight. "You can believe I will be pressing charges."

Cop lady had apparently heard that before too—though probably not from such a good-looking movie star—and it didn't faze her. Much.

I caught the flicker in her eyes, but that was it.

He ushered me out to a slick-looking dude who started talking fast. "You don't need to say a word, Miss Marshall. Everything is being taken care of. You didn't say anything, did you? Mr. Bailey, bail is set, and I will be demanding they drop all charges at once."

I could only listen, my world slipping off a precipice.

My life was officially over.

Gavin hustled me past all those watching in the precinct, lawyer dude prattling nonsense the whole time. Thankfully I didn't see Detective Sawyer anywhere.

A giant SUV waited outside—a freaking top-of-the-line, cannot-be-missed SUV—and a line of bodyguards in sunglasses and with earpieces held the crowd back, one holding the door open for us. Gavin shielded me as camera flashes went off everywhere.

As if this night could get any worse.

Nothing like a huge SUV parked outside of a police

station and bodyguards in earpieces to scream *Come look at me!*

Zombie Takeover had nothing on the awfulness of this night.

Gavin didn't say a word the whole way to his apartment.

One of his bodyguards saw us upstairs, swept the room, then stepped outside, settling in front of the door as Gavin shut and locked it.

He turned on the bathroom light and wordlessly held out a stack of clothes, tags still dangling from them.

I couldn't meet his eyes as I took the clothes and slinked away.

As my favorite redhead liked to say, "I was in the depths of despair," and I wasn't coming out anytime soon.

※

I didn't want to leave the bathroom.

I'd taken the longest shower in the history of showers. I still didn't think that jail grime would ever wash off. Plus there was the musky base of warehouse slash dead-guy slash back-of-cop-car fustiness, which made it that much worse.

Maybe I should hop back in?

I stood on the other side of the door from Gavin, fully clothed, steam swirling around me, shower fan buzzing in the background, and I couldn't move.

It was over. We were over. If I went out there, everything would change. I couldn't do it.

"Candace?"

My throat seized up, tears burning my eyes.

"Candace, we need to talk. Can you come out, please?"

I stared at the doorknob. Stupid thing. I couldn't turn it if I wanted to.

"Candace, please unlock the door."

I did. The doorknob turned halfway. From the other side.

"May I come in?"

I nodded. Which of course he couldn't see.

I cleared my throat and squeaked, "Yes?"

He gently pushed open the door.

My eyes flicked from his eyes to the wall to his chest to his eyes to his chest to the floor.

"Candace. Why didn't you call me?"

And stupid me started to cry.

He pulled me out of the bathroom and into his kitchen, wrapped me in strong arms against a firm chest, and held me while I sobbed my eyes out.

When the torrent slowed—slightly—he spoke over my sniffling and hiccuping. "Detective Sawyer agreed to drop all charges if you stay away from this."

I nodded furiously. I never wanted to see the inside of a jail cell again. Holding cell. Whatever.

"Why didn't you call me?" His voice cracked.

I pulled back at that. The heartbreak in his eyes did it. I started blubbering out words all over the place. "I'm so sorry…it's all my fault…I should've…"

And then I was soaking his shirt again.

"I was in jail, Gavin. In *jail*. It doesn't even matter that Paul and Silas went to prison, my super-strict religious grandmother is spinning in her grave, probably pounding on the casket to get out so she can strangle me. I went to *jail*!"

Gavin raised an eyebrow. "I can't believe with all you've been through that you were comfortable making that reference."

Images of undead zombies immediately swarmed my mind. I threw my hands in the air. "It just shows you how upset I am!"

"Yet I get a call from a best friend I didn't know you

had, have never met, and that's okay? I thought it was a joke!"

My eyes widened. Everything had happened so quickly, it hadn't even occurred to me that Jemma might've gotten my call and done something about it. I owed her big time.

"Thankfully, Lawson called me next," he continued.

I knew it.

Easing away, I leaned against the counter, steeling myself. "Gavin, I couldn't tell you. You're so busy and I'm such a mess and after you missed our dinner, I didn't know if you would come…"

My voice trailed off at the stricken look on his face.

He gave me his crooked grin, but this one looked kinda sad and made my heart squeeze. "Better I hear it from you than the front page of the newspaper, aye? Or national TV?"

My eyes widened. Reporters had gotten the story, definitely—oh my gosh, I could lose my job!

I plunked my forehead on the cool countertop. "Oh, Gavin, I'm so sorry. I made a stupid decision. I seem to be doing that a lot lately."

I heard his footsteps. They seemed to be walking away. I sagged. Guess I didn't blame him.

I jumped when he squeezed my shoulders. Stupid carpet. He must've walked around the kitchen island, not away from me.

"Hey. It's okay. If anyone can relate to being on national TV or the front page when they don't want to be, it's me."

I peeked at him. "What am I going to do?"

His jaw tightened. "Get some rest. Eat something. Leave the rest to me."

Too weary to protest that I was a strong, independent woman—because at this moment, I absolutely was not—I nodded and followed him to his guest room, where he tucked me in, kissed my forehead, and left to make some phone calls.

Lulled by the cadence of his voice through the wall, even if I couldn't tell what he was saying, I started to drift off.

That Scottish brogue that came out when he was playful —or upset—yum.

I snuggled deeper into the covers, so very thankful for this man in my life.

CHAPTER TWENTY-TWO

I picked up the phone on the second ring, a bit breathless from scrambling to answer. "Candace Marshall speaking."

"Candace Marshall. Now that's a voice I've been wanting to hear for a while now."

I squealed and threw whatever was in my other hand. "Gavin! Oh my gosh, it's so good to hear from you! How have you been?"

Lola went completely still. I hardly noticed.

"Missing my girlfriend and wondering if she has time to see me." I could hear the smile in his voice.

"Time to see you? Of course I do."

Lola gave me a look, so I turned a little to make the conversation more private, even though it totally wasn't. But I couldn't leave until this spread was done. I shouldn't have taken this call, really.

We were in production, and Lola and I were working late. November was almost gone, and I hadn't seen or heard from Gavin since the night I'd stayed in his guest room.

His driver had taken me home the next day, and then nothing. For two weeks.

Was it bad I was getting used to not seeing him for weeks on end?

In the glass's reflection, Lola bent and retrieved the two photographs I'd thrown. The rest of the office outside our cube was bathed in darkness. Most everyone else had gone home.

"What did you have in mind?" I asked, a dopey grin on my face.

A slight hesitation, then, "Only the most romantic date of all time."

That pause said something was up.

I raised an eyebrow, handing Lola an ad that had come in last minute. I moved the phone away from my mouth and said in a low voice, "Ask them to shift the colors to a cooler shade to complement our theme this month." Then to Gavin, "Oh?"

"Want to run down to the station with me to pick up my car? They're done with it." I could picture the sheepish grin on his face. "It's also kinda an apology for, well, you know."

I most certainly did. Not only had he missed our date, I hadn't seen him since he'd flown to my rescue. Not that I could complain since he'd bailed me out, quite literally, but I decided not to be hurt or offended about the missed date, which still stung.

It had been *so long* since we'd spent any real time together.

I laughed and eyed the clock. "Well, I don't know…that might be too much excitement for me. What time were you thinking?"

Lola tried to flag me down, but I waved her off. I could choose between the two photos she wielded in just a moment.

"I have some time first thing tomorrow morning," he said.

I shook my head, even though he couldn't see it, I realized belatedly. "I can after work, maybe?"

"Not sure they'd be open then…."

Lola huffed and propped one fist on her hip.

"Maybe after the weekend?" I suggested.

He laughed. "You sound just as busy as I've been."

"Don't I know it," I mumbled.

Gavin was quiet, and Lola shoved the photos at me again.

"Okay, fine, that one," I finally told Lola, just to get her off my back. I raised an eyebrow. "That ad?"

She huffed and pulled up her company email account on the layout table, typed out a quick email, and sent it off with a flick of her fingers.

"Okay," Gavin said, "I can tell you're busy…"

"Want me to call you the moment I'm done?"

"Please do," he said in a deep, sultry voice that immediately made me want to throw all my work at Lola, go track him down, and kiss the living daylights out of him.

I sighed. "I miss you."

His voice got even lower, but this time he wasn't acting. "I do too."

Lola made some obvious gagging sounds, and I laughed.

"Okay, we're officially grossing out my assistant, so I'm going to go so I can see you that much faster."

"I love you," he said and hung up.

"I—love you, too," I said in a daze to no one.

He still loved me? I honestly wasn't sure I'd ever hear those words again after how we'd left things. With the whole bailing-me-out-of-jail thing and not calling him first and the silence for two weeks. I was officially freaking out.

I needed to kiss him so badly I could hardly stand it.

"Earth to Candace." Lola waved her hand in front of my face. "You going to get this done so you can go see…him…

or are you going to stand there and daydream the rest of the night?"

I caught some of what she said, jerked myself out of my daze, and looked down at the magazine section we were working on.

I frowned. "Lola, where's that other picture? This one doesn't look quite right."

She rolled her eyes and handed me the photo I'd dismissed a few moments ago.

※

I went back to my apartment around two in the morning, fell in my bed fully clothed, and got up in time to throw myself together and make it to work with three minutes to spare.

Was I living the life or what?

It wasn't until Gavin called me on Monday—after production, so I actually had the day off—that I even remembered about picking up his car.

Let's just say I was beside myself—a wriggly puppy came to mind—when he stopped by my apartment to pick me up.

My face was glued to my spyhole from the moment Gavin texted that he was on his way.

Okay, in between peeking, I was running all over like a crazy person, trying to straighten up the place—pretty sure I was just making it worse.

So when he walked up to my door and raised his hand to knock, I flung open the door and tackled him in a hug.

I didn't even know what he was trying to say when I kissed him so long and so hard, he went from laughing to serious and returning the kiss like I was oxygen and he was desperate for air.

Which hopefully wasn't the case.

I heard a disgusted grunt and somewhat greeted my neighbor with my face still attached to Gavin's as I pulled him inside.

He pulled back after I'd let him know just how much I'd missed him and wrapped me in his warm, muscular, delicious arms.

I sighed and laid my head on his chest, just listening to his heartbeat and breathing in the wonderful scent that was Gavin. I couldn't name it if I'd wanted to, but whatever cologne he used was subtle and heady and mixed so well with whatever scent that was his alone. I could breathe him in all day.

Pretty sure I sighed aloud again, because his chest rumbled with a deep chuckle.

"Miss me that much, huh?"

I hugged him a little tighter. "You have no idea."

"You eat yet?"

I shrugged, not letting him go just yet. "Maybe. I think so. Yeah, I grabbed something at the cafeteria before I left. Pretty sure."

He settled his arm around my shoulders and guided me to the couch. "I have to admit, I was impressed when I had my shoot there. When you said cafeteria, I immediately thought of barely edible food."

We settled next to each other, and I went in for another hug, my head on his chest again. He leaned back and just held me as we talked.

At some point I'd sit up and talk to him like a normal person, but right now, I just needed his arms around me. It'd been too long.

"Do you really think Vera would let barely edible food anywhere near her?"

He chuckled. "Probably not."

"Most definitely not." I settled deeper into the hug. "Besides, with my employee discount, food is cheaper there than most other places. At least, places with such healthy options."

I tried to be healthy, but that didn't mean it always happened. When things like ice cream and root beer and cheese crackers got involved, my health kick went on vacation real fast.

But I was trying! That counted, right?

Again, that delicious chuckle rumbled against my ear. Happy sigh. I could listen to that all day.

"Are we ever going to go get my car?"

I finally pulled back. "Hey, you could've totally gotten it the other day. Why didn't you?"

He stretched and gave me that grin that made me go all melty, then settled deeper into the couch and looked at home and…relaxed.

I'd forgotten how he could just be himself around me. How although he was gracious and somehow remembered other people's names and was rated one of the most down-to-earth actors by all the gossip magazines—I should totally lie and say I didn't read them, but my grandma frowned upon such things, both the lying and the magazines—he was just, well, different around others. When we were out in public. A little on guard, a little cautious, smiling all the time and being what people expected him to be.

He had on his actor's face.

Here, all that fell away. He laughed and smiled when he felt like it, didn't feel like he had to perform for me—let's face it, I was performing for him nonstop, whether I meant to or not—and just relaxed, like the weight of the world rolled off his shoulders when it was just the two of us.

All this washed over me in a few seconds, and although I'd kind of noticed it before, I hadn't really had a spare moment to just sit and think about it. Not like this.

I couldn't help the beaming smile that spread across my face.

Even if no one else in the world knew how to take me, even if everyone thought I was too much crazy to handle, if I had one person who liked me for who I was, who could be themselves around me and wanted me to be myself too, I had the world. I didn't need anything else.

I had no idea what Gavin was saying, but I leaned forward and kissed him in the middle of it.

He looked surprised, but he accepted the kiss. I mean, duh. Who wouldn't?

"You like that ended up too busy to get the car?" he asked when I broke away.

I beamed at him. A little of what he'd said trickled in. "I like that you waited for me so we could spend time together, even for something as small as getting your car. I like that you can be yourself around me, and I like that I can be myself around you too. Thank you for that."

He went so serious so fast, and the way he was looking at me—I started to sweat. Not the ideal reaction around Gavin Bailey ever, let me tell you.

He also looked like he wanted to ask me something, and I started to panic. This was as serious as I got.

Opening up to someone, sharing my feelings, saying what I thought without being ridiculed—it was all new to me. I couldn't do too much at once. And I apparently needed to take things as slowly as he thought I did.

I was pretty sure he was about to tell me something I wasn't ready to hear. "Candace…"

I popped up before he could do something crazy like propose. Not that I was expecting that *at all*. "So are we ready to go?"

For a moment, he looked like he couldn't keep up, then he laughed and climbed to his feet. He took me in, his look appreciative. "After you, my leading lady."

I melted into goo and giggled at him—the poor man put up with *way* too much of that from me—as we collected our jackets, hats, gloves, and everything else that would protect us from a New York winter.

I paused just as I grabbed my scarf from the coat rack. "Hey!" I whipped around, nearly knocking him in the face. "Do you think nice cop will talk to me?"

He backed up a step. "Who?"

My hands started flailing. "Nice cop—good cop—you know, the super-cooperative, pleasant gem of law enforcement you got to talk to at the crime scene while I got the detective bent on destroying any smidgeon of self-respect I've gained over the past few years?"

Gavin rubbed the scruff starting to emerge on his chin. Man, I missed the stuff. This shoot had him clean shaven all the time. "Lawson?"

I almost got distracted, but I was on a mission here. There would be time to admire the scruff later.

I snapped my fingers. "Lawson! That's right. Will you take me to see him? You know, while we're there?"

"Candace…"

I put on my best puppy-pleading face as I looped my scarf around my neck. I didn't even want to know how pathetic it looked. "Please? If I could just talk to someone who would listen, even pretend to listen, I can get all this off my chest and stop running after questionable characters to get answers."

He didn't look convinced. "I don't know…"

"He's always too busy when I try to talk to him, but I just know he'll see me if you're there too. Please, Gavin. Please." I wasn't too proud to beg, apparently.

He held up his hands, laughing. "All right, all right. I'll ask him." A stern, pointing finger cut off my squeal. "On one condition."

I tried to look innocent, but I couldn't help it. I squirmed a little. Was he going to ask me to drop the whole vampire thing? Even after promising that very thing, now that I knew Mr. Withers might actually be alive, I wasn't sure I could stay out of it.

Lives could be at stake. Especially one very missing and supposedly dead old man who'd signed over all his wealth to a vampire coven in exchange for them to fake his death.

So many things just didn't add up. And I still wasn't convinced I wasn't on another movie set. I bit my lip.

He gently lifted my chin with one finger. "That you call me *first* the next time you go to jail."

I threw my arms around him so he wouldn't see the relief on my face and ask for a second condition. First of all, he was just too good for me. Second, I sincerely hoped I never saw the inside of a holding cell or jail cell—pretty sure those were close enough to the same thing—again.

"I promise, baby." My words were muffled against his delicious-smelling shirt. "I'm so sorry."

He pulled back. "It's forgiven. Maybe not forgotten yet, but forgiven. Let's go see Lawson."

I tilted my head, taking on that innocent pose classy girls got when they were about to do something dreadful. "Gavin?"

A wary, suspicious look came over his face, one he hadn't used on me yet, just on fans who didn't understand boundaries. My heart stuttered, and I almost didn't go through with it.

"Yeah?"

"I could really use an 'I'm glad you're out of jail' kiss."

His relief was as immediate as my own. A sly grin spread across his face. "I think I can manage that."

He jerked me close and kissed me hard. As I began to lose myself in the passion of the moment, I made a promise to myself.

Do not ever try to play Gavin Bailey, even in fun.

Neither of our hearts—or our pasts—could take it.

CHAPTER TWENTY-THREE

My fingers drummed a staccato beat on the ugly brown vinyl armrests of the torture device masquerading as a chair in the police station. Dingy yellow stuffing spewed out of the armrest, throwing off what should've been a satisfying rhythm.

Drum, drum, *poof*. Drum, drum, *poof*.

Warily studying the bulbous cameras sprinkled around the police station, I wondered for the umpteenth time how long it could possibly take for Gavin to sign some papers and get his car keys.

Gavin's car had been kept by the police to search for fingerprints, as well as to get all of the blood cleaned off. Not something they normally did, but Gavin knew someone who was doing it as a favor. Of course he did.

I tried to sit still, but I just couldn't.

I hated to admit it, but I was nervous about meeting with Detective Dan Lawson, Gavin's good cop.

Yes, I only remembered his name because Gavin had been coaching me on the way here.

A subtle click signaled the end of his time cloistered in the tiny records room, and the door swung open. I bolted to my feet and charged him the moment his foot crossed the threshold.

Gavin eased out of the room, Detective Dan Lawson not far behind. I faltered, whatever I was about to say forgotten. Gavin offered me a kind smile as he and Lawson chatted like best buds who hadn't seen each other in years.

As Gavin and Lawson exchanged pleasantries, I hopped from foot to foot as I was largely ignored.

This was it! Someone might actually believe me, might actually look into what I saw—might actually not despise the air I breathed as I told my story.

I sneaked a glance at Gavin. Then again, I hadn't told him anything about pirate vampire dude or getting kidnapped. Should I have? Before telling the detective?

Gah! I should've thought of that earlier!

"What brings you down here, Mr. Bailey?" Lawson was saying. "You know I can always come to you so you don't have to make a trip to the precinct."

Gavin waved away his offer. "I'm here to get my car, actually, but…" He dropped his arm around my shoulders and pulled me close. "My girlfriend has some questions about the case. I was hoping you wouldn't mind?"

I grinned foolishly at the detective. Gavin calling me his girlfriend would never get old.

Lawson's cautious gaze sought mine. I couldn't help but notice the tight smile he gave me was loads different than the brilliant smile he turned back to Gavin.

The bottom dropped right out of my stomach. My eyes sought the rest of the office for my own miserable detective's desk. Had he warned him about me? That nothing I said could be trusted?

My stomach dropped further. Well of course he had. They were partners, on the same case, Lawson had seen me go to jail, and I just bet everyone on this floor laughed at me, the crazy vampire-believing lady, when they were on break or discussing the case. Or whatever it was cops did.

Lawson's voice came through my panic. "Anything I can do to help. The captain's office, perhaps?"

"Perfect."

The aisle was narrow, so I stepped behind Gavin. They chatted while we made our way to the office. We were just rounding a corner, and thankfully I was still behind Gavin and partially hidden by a tall filing cabinet, a vigorous plant sprouting fronds in my face, when a voice barked "Lawson!"

I froze, gripping Gavin's leather jacket in my fists. No, no, no. I would recognize the growly voice anywhere. Detective surly-cop Sawyer.

"You get anywhere with those prints I asked you to check on?"

Gavin stood a little taller, arms at his sides, making sure I was completely blocked. At least, I hoped he wasn't about to step aside with an introduction and a "remember us?"

I clutched just a tad tighter, willing him not to move.

Lawson sighed. "Sorry, man. They said it'd be another week."

The other detective cursed and slapped a file against a nearby desk. "Goodnight! It's like they think we've got all the time in the world down here to solve cases before the trail gets cold. You!"

For one panic-stricken moment, I thought he was talking to me.

"You bail your girl out yet?"

Gavin nodded, his voice and stance tight. "I did."

Lawson spoke, "As a matter of fact, she's—"

Gavin cut him off. "Come up with any new leads on who could've made the body disappear or why?"

Sawyer's voice was tight. "I can't discuss an active case with you, Mr. Bailey, movie star or not."

The tension was thick all up in here ta-night.

Lawson tried again. "Where did she—?"

This time, Sawyer cut him off. "She gonna keep her nose outta this?"

I sagged against Gavin in relief. He didn't flinch. Whatever he was doing to block me was working fabulously. I just wondered how long it would last.

Gavin took his time crossing his arms. "I think a holding cell was the wrong way to go about it. If anything, it might have made her more determined than ever to figure this out. But to answer your question, yes, she's going to stay out of it."

The officer grunted. "Good. I wouldn't want her to get hurt."

I thawed a little. Maybe he wasn't so bad after all.

He slapped the desk with his file once more. "Nosey girl can't stay out of trouble! She's the most meddling, irritating, irresponsible chit of a girl I've ever met, and I can't wait to see the last of her." A pause. "No offense."

Gavin knew me so well. I bristled and started to march around him to chew the officer out, my pointer finger up and ready to shake in his face, but Gavin blocked me, gently knocking me in the face with his elbow as he casually leaned against the filing cabinet.

The irate officer kept going. "I can't wait to put this case to rest. Probably isn't going to get solved anyway."

"Oh? How's that?" Gavin asked.

"It's that darned girl of yours!"

"Sawyer…" Lawson warned, but the other officer must've been too worked up.

Let me tell you, it's *awesome* to hear yourself torn apart while eavesdropping.

Not.

"Before I can get one question answered, she unearths

twenty more. Now with that body disappearing, there's not a solid piece of evidence remaining. No fingerprints—none, not from the entire case—no usable DNA that matches our database, nothing. Did you hear the blood was from an animal?"

My mouth fell open. That's what vampire dude had told me too!

Sawyer continued. "This is going in the unsolved pile if you ask me."

Gavin crossed his arms again. "Then what's the harm in letting her help you? Giving her a few things to do to bring closure to what she saw?"

"Because she's playing detective, Bailey, without the authority to back it up, and it's going to get her killed."

If that wasn't a sucker punch to the gut, I didn't know what was.

"That's enough." Lawson's voice was firm. "Mr. Bailey, this way, please."

Apparently a showdown was going on, because Gavin didn't move. It wasn't until I heard Sawyer huff and stomp away that Gavin turned to Lawson and said pleasantly, "After you."

I peeked around Gavin to check if the coast was clear. Lawson's raised eyebrows mirrored my own. I just knew he'd never heard Sawyer talk so much in his life. Or maybe that was just me.

A chair squealed, and Sawyer heaved himself into it, typing away on a desktop that was older than my great-great-grandmother. Coast not clear.

A few steps away, Lawson opened a door, standing next to Gavin. Creating a barrier for me, I realized.

Lawson nodded at Sawyer's desk on the precinct floor. "What was the name on those prints you needed again?"

I peeked through the triangle Gavin's arms made. Sawyer sighed and turned away to dig through a file. I darted into Lawson's office and crouched beside a chair. It wasn't much cover, but it was something.

"Smith. Of course."

"That's right. We'll get one of your cases solved yet. Thanks, Sawyer."

I smirked as I imagined the look on Sawyer's face.

Lawson and Gavin entered, and Lawson pulled the door closed, shut the blinds, and looked at me. I straightened awkwardly.

He blew out a breath. "Well." He stared at me. "Care to explain what's got his shorts in a twist?" His face colored just slightly. "Pardon the expression."

I plopped into the closest chair.

"You guys aren't going to believe this."

⚔

Maybe I shouldn't have led with that.

I was right. They didn't. If only I'd caught on sooner.

I sat back with a relieved sigh. I'd given my statement in full, and deep satisfaction streamed through me for the first time in weeks. Months, even. Maybe ever.

Apparently I was a darn good storyteller. Gavin and Lawson were enraptured the whole time I was talking. Or maybe they just couldn't believe the words coming out of my mouth.

That one was more likely.

"Sooo..." Lawson drew out the word, alternately chewing on his pen and scratching out notes. "These people think they're real vampires."

I nodded far too enthusiastically. "They do. They have these underground Victorian or steampunk or something covens, and apparently their rivals absolutely hate each other and are feuding."

Gavin did *not* look thrilled that I'd been to one of them. Definitely should've mentioned that to him first. Oops?

Besides, I was repeating some things by now, but I barely believed it myself. I figured it would take several doses before they believed me either.

Lawson's look wasn't hard, but it wasn't entirely convinced either. "As a detective with the NYPD for over twenty years, why have I never heard of this, Miss Marshall?"

I opened my mouth…and just sat there. Huh.

I shrugged. "No clue. They said joining members were sworn to secrecy, leaving everything in their pasts behind." I snapped my fingers as a thought struck me, certain I'd hit pure gold. "Must not be paying their taxes then, huh?"

He looked interested for the first time ever. He mumbled something and looked down at his notes. Then back up at me. "I've lived here a lot of years and have seen many strange things, but never a real vampire cult. Sure, some cosplay for a few nights here or there, and a few fringe groups hang out on the web, and there are definitely a few vampire-themed clubs, but why the extreme? Why leave an entire life behind instead of meeting on, say, weekends or even occasionally? Hmm?"

I had no answers for him. None.

But when did that ever stop me?

I jabbed my finger in his face. Thank goodness a desk was between us. "See? Exactly what I mean! Why the extremes? Why tell me all this if it's fake? Why kill a guy, then steal his body, then kill other people who actually want to join them? This is all so crazy, I just can't understand it."

After a few moments of silence, he snapped his little notebook closed.

I was most satisfied to see perfectly scribbled notes there, not a Spongebob or Patrick in sight. This dude was a straight-up real detective.

He stood and shook my hand, like I was important or something. My jaw practically fell open, and I did my best to rein it in.

"Thank you, Miss Marshall. This certainly gives me something to think about and look into."

My grin was a thousand watts strong, and I may have squealed. "Really? Oh my goodness, thank you so much!"

And just like that, I undermined everything I'd just said. Doubt crept into his expression, so of course I started talking right away to combat it.

"I'm sorry, I'm just so happy to be believed for once. Well, not necessarily believed, but at least listened to. Well, you know. Like maybe justice will happen. Maybe old man Withers will be found. Maybe it *is* an elaborate hoax, but at least no one else will get hurt, right? Or, at least, if you really do look into it…"

And I was still shaking his hand and babbling like an idiot.

Gavin stood and offered me his arm. "Shall we?"

I latched on to it, laughing like the biggest airhead on earth. "Oh, um, yeah. Okay. Thanks."

I wiggled my fingers at the officer like we were best buds as Gavin shook Lawson's hand himself.

The detective offered Gavin a smile I couldn't read. "I'll go run interference."

"Thank you, Dan." Gavin nodded once more at the detective as he left, waited a few moments, and ushered me hastily out of the bustling police station.

I peeked, but Sawyer's desk was empty, thankfully. Whew.

Tension built the entire walk through the precinct, but it wasn't until we were in the parking garage that I groaned and dropped my head on Gavin's shoulder.

"Ugh, seriously? You let me keep talking?"

Gavin laughed, and I couldn't help but notice he looked

slightly embarrassed. Great, just great. He'd gotten me an interview, and I'd bombed it in the last three seconds with all the word vomit. Fan-freaking-tastic.

He kissed my temple anyway. "Oh, it wasn't that bad."

I just looked at him.

He laughed. "Okay, maybe it was, but don't worry."

I threw my arms wide. "Don't worry? How could I not worry? That was the world's biggest explosion of stupid in the history of mankind!"

He winked at me, and for a moment there, I forgot what I was saying.

"It's okay. I warned him about you."

I stopped dead in my tracks. I mean, *alive* in my tracks. Not dead.

New sayings, ASAP.

I sent a glower his way. "What do you mean you *warned* him about me."

He tried to tug me forward, but I just glared at him and crossed my arms. No way was I going anywhere until he explained that.

He sighed and glanced around the deserted parking garage we were in. It should've been enough to get me going—the place was uber-creepy—but I didn't budge.

"Warned him about what?" I demanded.

He gave me a sheepish grin. "I told him when you get nervous, you tend to, uh, talk. A lot. And sometimes it doesn't make sense."

If that wasn't insulting... "Then why on earth did you introduce us? And why did he act surprised I was there? He acted like he didn't even know me!"

He rubbed the back of his neck, looking extremely guilty. "I asked him not to. I didn't want you to be nervous. I thought if you were at ease, it would go better." He shrugged. "And for the most part, it did."

I stomped away from him and back a few times, flinging my arms around but too upset to make words happen.

He caught me on one of my passes. "Look, don't be mad. I was just trying to help, and I'd much rather talk about this over a waffle cone and mint chocolate chip ice cream instead of a mostly deserted parking garage."

The man knew how much I loved towering mint chocolate chip scoops in waffle cones, but I was not going to let that distract me.

I spun away from him again, and when I did, someone familiar caught my eye. I gasped. The figure was bending over Gavin's car, like he was trying to break in, then he saw me and ducked away. I took off running.

I'd taken to wearing comfortable flats I could run fast in, and thank goodness for that.

Gavin's footsteps rushed to catch up. "What? What is it?"

He didn't even sound out of breath, and I was running fast. Me? I was already gulping for air.

I pointed, not breaking my stride. "It's him! It's that vampire dude!"

How was I not more in shape with all the walking I did around New York City? Sheesh.

A flash of black cape with red undertones swirled down and around the steps leading deeper into the underground parking garage. Goodnight, he wasn't still wearing that ridiculous outfit, was he? And how could a guy that old run that fast?

And what was he even *doing* here? Didn't he have people for…whatever this was?

I ran pell-mell down the steps, apparently not even caring if I broke my neck. I was being so reckless, in fact, that I started losing Gavin on the stairs.

Never thought in all my life *that* would happen.

I rounded the last curve of the staircase and ended up in a mostly dark level, no cars in sight.

I took one step forward.

"That's far enough."

Gavin came up behind just in time for us both to hear the click of a gun being cocked. He shoved me behind him and covered me with his body.

"Don't do anything rash," Gavin called out.

Old vampire dude just laughed. "Rash? After you keep drawing attention to my coven by telling the police everything you think you know?" He glowered at me, his eyes reflecting reddish in the darkness. "Even though there isn't a lick of evidence left? Really, Miss Marshall. I told you to leave this alone, and you haven't. I said there would be consequences if you didn't."

Sheesh, this old guy liked to talk.

I peeked out just far enough to yell, "It's you, isn't it? You're the one who keeps making evidence disappear."

He laughed. "You can't prove that."

My jaw tightened. "I can and I will."

Although he was shrouded in darkness, he stepped forward just enough for the silver and mother-of-pearl gun he held to glint in the light. His eyes still glowed. So freaking weird. "You've gone far enough, Miss Marshall. It's time to end this."

I rolled my eyes. "In a police station parking garage? Really? Enough of this fake vampire act already!"

Ignoring my words, he waved the gun a little. "Step out from behind your shield, please."

The flare of light off its barrel caught my attention. "Hey, is that real silver? I thought vampires couldn't touch it."

Gavin and pretend vamp groaned at the same time.

"Candace, not now," Gavin said in a low voice. "And whatever you do, do *not* get out from behind me."

"Oh, right." I raised my voice. "Listen, you aren't going to get away with this here. There are cameras. And police. This is a terrible idea, really. You should just let us go."

He barked a laugh. "If you recall, the last time I let you go, you promised to stay away from this. Yet here you are, not doing so."

I cringed, and Gavin and I exchanged a quick glance. He took over. "I can assure you, we are more than ready to step away from this. In fact, we're only here to pick up my car. Nothing else."

"Oh? And your girl here didn't just give her statement to a detective, one who's actually willing to listen to her?"

The bottom dropped right out of my stomach, and my shoulders slumped. If he knew that, there was no use denying it.

"As you said, there's no evidence, so they can't do anything anyway," Gavin reminded him. "Now, we're just going to back up slowly…"

"I don't think so."

Before he could make good on his threat, a door slammed above, and loud voices laughed and chatted.

The vamp stepped back, letting the darkness swallow him whole. "I'll be watching you, Miss Marshall. You step out of line again, even once, and you'll be seeing me or one of mine very soon. And I promise you, it will be the *last* thing you ever see."

Gavin stepped forward, but vampire dude waved the gun our way.

"Now, turn around. Walk up those stairs, all the way to the top, and don't come back down to your car for fifteen minutes." His voice was pure steel. "Or call anyone in that time. I'll know if you do."

CHAPTER TWENTY-FOUR

Gavin and I sat in his car. Neither of us moved. He didn't even attempt to start it or leave. He took a deep breath and rested his hands on the steering wheel.

They were shaking.

"That was the guy who kidnapped you, wasn't it?" he said quietly.

My whole face brightened, and I jumped a little. Finally! "Yes! And then that other wannabe vampire rescued me and dropped me off in my apartment, which I didn't know till I woke up."

He spun on me so fast I blinked. "He *what*?"

"Oh, um…" I bit my lip. "I texted you about it?"

"Candace. You did not."

Apparently I hadn't included that in my police statement. But I wasn't sure I should mention the dark web, secret code, or monthly meetings, either.

I flicked my fingers. "Oh sure I did. Remember? When I asked, um, if vampires can speak in a person's head? It was the same guy. That we saw in that alley, only he claims he didn't kill anyone. That Mr. Withers might still be alive."

He did not look pleased. "That was a question about lore."

"Well, yeah." I gave him a sheepish grin. "Cause he kinda did that. I think. Not sure how that even happened. Super creepy."

"Candace, I want you to leave this alone. And you are moving."

My eyes shot to his. "What?"

He didn't even flinch at my raised voice. The guy was a rock.

"I mean it. These guys are dangerous. You should have told me the moment someone broke into your apartment. Or called the police. Both things, actually."

"But—but—" I spluttered, no comeback at the ready. I mean, he was right, but still. "But the police haven't believed a word I said, and you were too busy!"

He turned to me, his features diamond hard. "Stalking you at work? Going *inside* your apartment? They killed a guy right in front of us, Candace. And they just threatened to kill you. You leave this to the NYPD, and you get as far away from it as you possibly can. No more digging."

"But—but—"

"Promise me."

I stared at him, mouth hanging open. He didn't budge; I couldn't move.

Why couldn't I promise him? My life had just been threatened, and Gavin had been there to witness it. What was it about this crazy situation I couldn't let go of?

I wilted a little when the tension got to be too much. He was absolutely right. So why was I holding that against him?

"Fine." I huffed and crossed my arms.

He relaxed just a smidge and opened his car door. "Thank you." He jerked his head. "Come on. We should report this."

I craned my neck to look all around the garage. "Think it's safe to do that? He literally just said I would die if I did that very thing."

Gavin rarely looked unsure of himself, and this was one of those times. "I think he would've taken this time to get away."

His "I hope" vibrated in the air between us, unspoken but all the more potent for being unsaid.

We marched back into the police station in silence, my still-crossed arms far too petty for my liking.

Was I twelve? He wasn't bossing me around, but I was pouting like he was. It was my choice. He was completely right. I agreed with him, for heaven's sake.

So why was I so frustrated?

An eternity and two statements later, Gavin ushered me out of the police station, quietly explaining they were going to keep his car and check for prints, just in case.

I highly doubted that would do any good, but what did I know? I only knew how to spin wild stories and make more work for the police department, apparently.

Something bigger was going on, I just knew it.

But was it bigger in a "we're a giant movie company throwing millions of dollars at this little deception" kind of way or a "we're vampire mobsters and will kill anyone who gets in our way" thing?

Though the second was way scarier. Definitely.

I blinked back tears of frustration as we made our way outside to hail a cab, ice cream completely forgotten.

By him. Not me. But I was too miffed to remind him.

✗

The next day at work, I warily eyed everyone who walked by my office.

I wanted to call Gavin and say, "Don't think I didn't notice that bodyguard you had follow me to work today."

But my message would just go to voicemail, and who knew when Gavin would actually hear it or respond.

He'd either gone in to work early, slept in his trailer, or took public transport so he could sic his driver on me. Though, I had to admit, if it had been anyone else, I would've freaked out and called the police. As it was, I was just annoyed.

Part of me knew he'd done it for my safety. Part of me knew he'd done it because he loved me and didn't want anything bad to happen to me.

But an annoyed little part of me whispered in my head that he'd just done it to make sure I didn't go back on my word.

I knew that little voice was false and completely lying to me, but dang it, it still felt the most real of all the rationalization I was doing.

And besides, didn't Gavin need his burly mountain beast bodyguard to protect *him* from mobbing fans?

I grumbled some more, and Lola sighed. "If you're going to mutter to yourself for the rest of the day, can you please just tell me now so I can go home?"

I looked at her a bit blankly. I mean, I hadn't exactly forgotten she was in here…okay, yes, I had. "Are you not feeling well?"

She rubbed her rock-hard and completely flat tummy. "Breakfast isn't sitting well."

I adjusted this article's fonts for the eight hundredth time and mumbled under my breath, "Maybe if you actually ate breakfast, I'd believe that."

"Seriously, what is *with* you?"

Stan walked in and snapped his fingers. "Lola. Coffee. Now."

She shot him a disgruntled look but scurried off. She'd probably use the time to take a long break.

I faced Stan and spoke before he could. "It was a misunderstanding. All charges were dropped."

He crossed his arms and eyed me.

I sighed and leaned against the table. "I found another dead body, and due to a…misunderstanding…they took me in for questioning."

"It seemed like a bit more than questioning," he said quietly.

I sighed again. "Yeah. But they let me go and…apologized."

I mean, kinda.

"Miss Marshall, I spent the morning of the incident calling in favors and getting the story scrubbed from most media outlets before it could go live. You do realize had your little…mishap…been leaked, it would not only reflect poorly on you, but on the company as well?"

My throat burning, I tucked my head and nodded. "Yes, sir."

"You are a valuable asset, Miss Marshall, and Vera is quite taken with you."

I think that was a clever way of saying they both were. *Why*, I had no idea.

"But make no mistake. If you don't leave this whole mess alone, things could get worse. Much worse."

I nodded without saying a word.

"Let your assistant know she can come back, and let's focus on work, shall we? Our holiday edition is one of our bestsellers, and we need everyone on board and your full attention on the job, yes?"

"Yes, sir," I whispered.

"Chin up, Miss Marshall. We aren't through with you yet."

He chucked me under the chin and was gone.

That "yet" seemed to echo loudest in the room.

I gave myself a moment or three to compose myself before sending Lola an email. From the layout table. Because I *still* needed to get my phone fixed.

Ugh. How was it December already?

It was like she was waiting around the corner. She set down a coffee from my favorite local shop—I moved it off my layout table—and leaned forward. "What happened?"

In an extreme lapse of judgment, I told her of the old dude who thought he was a vampire pulling a gun on us at the police station parking garage last night, though I left out everything about jail. Even I couldn't go through that again.

"And now that Gavin thinks I'm on someone's hit list, he sicced his bodyguard on me on my way to work." I snorted. "Like I'm going to get kidnapped or something."

I barked out a laugh that fizzled into a choking sound, because that's exactly what had already happened. I sighed. My life, right?

"Now he's insisting I need to move and…I just don't know. I can't use a gun to protect myself because it's illegal, but I just don't think pepper spray will cut it." Thinking about it all was making my head hurt.

And now my job was at stake, if Stan's not-so-subtle warning meant what I thought it did. Then again, I didn't do so well with subtext. I wished he'd come right out and said it.

Though that would've made my freakout later this evening when I got home tonight about a thousand times worse.

Lola was biting her lip, her expression not giving me a single clue to what she was thinking. She finally said, "Have you met Martha?"

I blinked and tried to keep up with the sudden turn in conversation. "Martha?"

She nodded. "She works a few floors down"—in other

words, she was lower-level scum Lola refused to talk to unless forced—"and sometimes eats in the cafeteria the same time we do."

I blinked again. I wasn't even aware Lola went to the cafeteria. I never saw anyone I knew, so I always squeezed into the smallest space available, ate as fast as I could, and got back to work as quickly as possible.

Lola was usually in our glass office as I left and when I got back, so I just assumed she stepped into the coffee room to eat, even though food technically wasn't allowed on our floor.

Technically, because there were rare exceptions, mostly when Stan cooked something delicate and exquisite and brought it in for us to try. Though those bite-size appetizers always left me ravenous for more.

No one knew how to eat around here.

Lola sighed. "You checked out on me again, didn't you."

I snapped back to attention. "Yes. I mean, no. I mean, what?"

She rolled her eyes. "Come to lunch with me. I'll introduce you."

My mouth fell open. Lola was willing to be seen with me?

I could hardly concentrate as the minutes ticked slowly onward toward lunchtime. This had to be good.

CHAPTER TWENTY-FIVE

Gavin kissed my hair and whispered, "Be confident." Then he said to the sheriff headed our way, "Thank you for seeing us."

Gavin and I shook New York City's sheriff's hand in turn.

This was a big deal. Like, huge. No one got an appointment with the sheriff. He was one busy dude. But Gavin equaled connections, so here we were.

"Please, sit."

Gavin and I sat in the chairs across from his desk as he scanned my concealed-carry application.

"It says here that you were detained for carrying without a permit."

I blanched, but before dumb words could spill out of my mouth, Gavin answered.

"Those charges were dropped, Sheriff. Someone threatened to kill Candace, and she's been trying to get a permit for six months now. She needs to be able to protect herself."

Smooth, calm, confident. So nothing like me.

The sheriff leaned back in his swivel chair and stroked his beard. There wasn't much to stroke. "Well, now, being caught with a weapon without a permit is a serious offense, Miss Marshall. Although a misdemeanor is allowed in rare circumstances, this should have been a felony charge."

"The charges were dropped, sir. A misunderstanding."

Gavin again, not me. No, I was sitting over there, quaking in my boots, in awe at even being allowed in this office after seeing the inside of a holding cell.

The sheriff didn't look like he wanted to argue with Gavin, but he raised an eyebrow anyway. "A misunderstanding?"

Like he didn't hear that every day of his life.

"Yes, sir. It was my gun, purchased legally and registered with both the state of New York and the city, of which I have a valid carry permit."

Yikes. I'd forgotten all about that.

"But she does not."

"No, sir. But someone threatened to kill her, a wanted murderer, in the police station's own garage, and I want her to be safe."

The sheriff nodded. "I remember seeing that in the report. I am truly sorry that happened on our property. All cameras on the bottommost level had their wires cut and have since been repaired."

Gavin crossed his ankle over his knee. "I'm glad to hear that, sir. But I'd feel a lot better if my girlfriend could defend herself if the criminal in question were to come after her again."

The sheriff looked to be wavering, but then his eyes fell on me.

I shrank back a little.

That seemed to make up his mind. "She has not been trained."

Ugh. Seriously, Candace? Seriously?

"She *has* been trained. And I'm sure she would be

willing to take any additional training or classes you require."

I jumped after a few heartbeats of silence, then nodded far too many times.

He was still looking at me, reading me, and I was sweating big time.

Could I please not look so guilty over just existing? Please?

The sheriff spoke directly to me. "I am sorry, but I have to deny your application."

Gavin got that look in his eye that said he was going to make it happen anyway, but I licked my lips and asked in a timid voice, "May I please ask why?"

Gavin held off on whatever he was going to say, watching the sheriff to see how he would respond to me.

"Miss Marshall, you have every right to defend yourself. And you may do so within your apartment with your weapon of choice. But once you take your weapon outside on my streets, I not only have to worry about you, but everyone else who comes in contact with you."

It was like he knew me or something. "What do you mean?"

He folded long, slender hands over my application. Guy could be a pianist.

"You don't strike me as an overly confident individual. If I place a gun in your hands and let you loose on my streets, I want to know you've had training—"

"I have," I squeaked.

"That you won't startle and fire your gun prematurely—"

"Yeah, well, that's legit."

Gavin cut me a glance. I shrugged.

"And that it won't fall into the wrong hands. I am very selective of whom I hand guns in my city, and if it were up to me, only police and active military would carry. So until our gun laws change, I am going to do everything in my power to make sure only the right people carry weapons in the city."

Yikes. He'd be voted right out of office in my little country-yet-Californian town where everyone had a gun and a truck.

I didn't fit in there either. Or here. Or anywhere.

"I can respect that," I said.

Gavin took a deep breath and let it out slowly.

The sheriff gave me a nod, grabbed a stamp, and slathered a big, fat, red *denied* over my paperwork.

I stood. "I hope to one day change your mind."

A hint of a smile touched his eyes. "I would very much like to see that." The smile faded. "But unless you join the military or my police force, I honestly don't see that happening."

In other words, don't waste his time. "That's fair," I said.

I preferred to know exactly where I stood with people, and this sheriff was pulling no punches. I appreciated that.

I offered my hand, Gavin offered his—with another "thank you for seeing us"—and we left his office.

As we walked, Gavin rubbed my neck under my scarf. "I'm sorry."

My skin tingled at his touch.

I shrugged. "I didn't expect it to go any differently. Not after jail and illegal carry and impeding an investigation and back-of-cop-car rides and *jail*."

Didn't think I'd be getting over that anytime soon.

Gavin's voice held a smile. "A holding cell is quite a bit different than jail time, Candace."

"Okay fine, Mr. 'I spent a week in real jail to research a role though they got rid of the really bad guys so I'd be safe' Bailey. It felt just as bad, okay? At least you knew you were being protected and could get out any time you wanted."

"That's right. Because I knew the right people to call."

I winced. "Ouch. Not getting past that anytime soon, are we?" I glanced at him.

His look said no, he wasn't exactly over that. "Would you?"

I shook my head and said in a small voice, "No. You're right. I'm sorry."

We stepped outside into the freezing weather. Why did people live in places this cold? Oh, right. Magical New York City.

At least it was magical when people weren't trying to kill me. Or throw me in jail.

Though even I had to admit the Christmas lights and decorations were incredible.

Gavin wrapped one arm around my waist as I shivered. "No, I'm sorry. I said I forgave you, and that means I shouldn't bring it up again."

Gavin's driver opened the door for both of us, and we slipped inside.

I gave him a grin. "I kinda walked right into it, though."

He grinned back. "Yeah. It was too tempting. But I do. Forgive you. And I won't. Bring it up again."

I wrapped my arms around his firm waist and breathed in his tantalizing scent. This man. "You're too good to me."

He held me for a few blocks before his phone rang. I sat up. After a hushed conversation with his assistant—I still didn't know why she disliked me so much, I tried everything I could think of to get her to like me—he dropped his phone in his pocket.

"Dave? Change of plans. I need to get to the studio."

The driver made two right turns to go back the way we'd come.

"Sorry, Candace. I took some time off to come down here with you, but the director wants to reshoot a scene we've been having trouble with. Do you mind if Dave takes you home after he drops me off?"

"Oh, I don't know. Would it matter if I did?"

His eyes widened. "Well…I could always take a taxi…"

I touched his arm. "I'm kidding! Of course that's fine. Thank you for meeting me."

His grin spoke of relief. "Oh good."

We chatted about light things the rest of the way to the studio currently throwing millions, maybe billions, of dollars at New York City to film here.

Hey, I was grateful. If Gavin were filming in LA, I'd either be looking for opportunities out there, or we'd be trying the whole long-distance thing.

We pulled up in front of the studio. He grabbed my knee. "Hey, see you for Christmas, if not before?"

"What, the two whole days off they've given us?"

Christmas Eve and Christmas Day, to be exact.

Concern filled his eyes. "Are you okay?"

I rubbed my face. No, I was not. Being threatened, then denied a way to protect myself had rattled me more than I'd thought.

I met his eyes and attempted a smile. "It went how I expected, but I guess I was really hoping it would go differently."

Sympathy filled his eyes, and he kissed me. "Just wait till Christmas. I've got an amazing two days planned for you."

Leave it to Gavin to try to make me feel better. He knew how I felt about presents.

My smile was more genuine this time. "I can't wait."

Gavin kissed me again and slid out of the SUV, not making me or his driver go through security to get on set.

He shut the door, and the smile dropped off my face. I took a deep breath and let it out slowly.

This shoot would be over in a few months, and then we would have to have the long-distance relationship talk.

If I hadn't destroyed everything good in my life by then.

The next two weeks were chewed up by the holiday edition's early release so employees could have a few days off. Gavin and I had a lovely Christmas Eve and Christmas together, no drama, no arguing, no more mention of my moving once I put my foot down.

I really couldn't find another place in Manhattan at my current rent, and I just didn't have *time* to uproot my life.

Plus I couldn't do it all on my next day off, half of New Year's Eve and all of New Year's Day, which Gavin understood completely. He was incredible at gift giving and experience planning, and New Year's passed much like Christmas: a small gift that said he knew me so well, then a whirlwind of NYC-only experiences that left me smiling till my cheeks hurt, then evenings cuddling in front of a movie that we in all honesty didn't pay much attention to. The holidays were over way too fast.

No dead bodies or wannabe vampires, thankfully.

Then I was back to work like normal.

Our January edition was always extra thick (to match the previous holiday edition, I imagine), filled with articles on how to set attainable goals for the new year, fashion predictions (that were mostly accurate, thanks to Fashion Week), losing weight, or how to dress your size and feel fabulous doing so.

I was taping that one up in my office, as I did last year. It didn't stop certain girls from harassing me, but I could hope.

I safely went from my apartment to work, nobody grabbing me, threatening me, or otherwise bothering me and making me fear for my life.

Still, I couldn't get my run-ins with NYC's vamps out of my head. I wanted to protect myself the next time some bozo thought it was a good idea to put his grimy hands on me, vamp or not. I just hadn't figured out how to do that yet.

I also wasn't sleeping the best with worrying so much, so I was a little bit loopy and a lot slaphappy.

That meant my love for musicals was on full display for my coworkers, and I didn't even have enough working brain cells to care.

I hummed to myself, something I only did when I was alone in my glass-encased office…with the door closed.

At least, I hoped that was the only time I did it.

I broke into song, from one of the Broadway plays Gavin and I had been to before holidays were over and work started and he'd basically disappeared from my life. Again.

So now I listened to soundtracks nonstop to make up for it.

And to keep from spiraling about the next time some vamp would try to pop up in my life. The only thing in my arsenal right now was pepper spray. Would that even work on vampires? Right. Not thinking about that right now.

I trilled off something nonsensical in my off-key voice, then stilled, hands hovering over the partially completed layouts on my backlit table.

Someone was watching me. I could just tell. My eyes lifted to find out who it was. He was tall, skinny as a beanpole, had thick glasses, and sported a sweater vest. And he was giving me a weird look. I straightened and returned it.

Hey, what I did in my office was none of his business! And I loved that song.

Oh my gosh, was I dancing? I flushed. I sincerely hoped not.

Someone walked by, and scrawny dude ducked his head and pretended to walk away. He just made a little circle then was back to watching me.

I threw up my hands in a "What the heck are you looking at?" gesture.

He glanced around, then furtively waved me his way.

I shook my head. Yeah right. Like I was falling for that.

He waved harder. I rolled my eyes. Fine. I wasn't getting any work done now that he'd distracted me. Might as well get this over with.

I haphazardly tossed textures and articles all over, knowing I would perfect them when I returned, and made my way out the door and over to where he was slinking around in the hallway.

"Yes? What do you want?"

So I was testy when I averaged two to four hours of sleep per night, only to crash hard on my day off. For weeks. So what?

He looked furtively around. "Not here," he hissed, then made his way over to the staircase and disappeared inside.

Okay, I was sooo not following him into a dark staircase no one used. These were executive offices. On the top floor. Of a mega-huge office building in the middle of Manhattan.

He cracked open the door and waved me in.

But then again, I was so curious I could hardly stand it.

I walked over to the door and stopped there. "Who are you? What do you want?"

"Keep your voice down! Come inside and I'll tell you."

I just looked at him. Not happening.

"Um, please?"

I shrugged. "Or I can just call security."

His tan face went uber-pale in an instant. "Please don't do that. Martha said you wanted something from me?"

I tried to remember someone named that. "Martha?"

"Look, I don't even want to be here, but she said it was important. And I owe her a favor. So do you want the stuff or not?"

Favor? Stuff? Martha? What the actual heck was going on? I didn't budge.

He started to sweat. "I didn't want to come up here anyway." He scribbled on a piece of paper and handed it to me. "This is the floor I work on. If you want your silver bullets, you can come to me next time."

He let the door close between us.

I stared at the paper as it slowly dawned on me who Martha was.

The loud, older, laughing woman I'd had lunch with a few weeks ago. Before the holidays. The one, well one of many, overly curious about my brush with vampires.

The one Lola had introduced me to.

Mind swirling, I made my way back to my office. She'd been serious about knowing someone who could help me protect myself from vampires? I thought she'd been joking around, like everyone else. Making fun like I was. Like I was trying to.

I went back to my quirky layouts, physical before I made them digital—I needed to get my hands on textures before they became visual only—but I couldn't concentrate.

I glanced up in time to see what's-his-name slip out of the staircase and head toward the bank of elevators.

I kept rearranging items, looking for a theme to complement Vera's and run throughout the January edition, but I kept zoning out. My brain was downstairs with some guy who sold vampiric weapons.

What on earth did people in this city sell to protect against vampires besides silver bullets?

And how hard would they all be laughing when my curiosity won and I went down there to find out?

I groaned and grabbed my jacket, giving up on this month's current magazine. Fashion could wait. My brain wouldn't focus on a blasted thing while obsessed with something else. Yay, me.

CHAPTER TWENTY-SIX

Nerdy dude saw me coming. He jumped up and darted down the hallway made of cubicles and around the corner. I should probably turn around and leave, right? But I'd come all this way...

I followed and peeked around the corner. He was waiting for me.

As I watched, he yanked open a door and darted into what looked like...a supply closet?

After a moment of my standing there, staring, the door cracked open, and a hand came out, waving me in.

I cautiously made my way forward, wondering what side of crazy I'd gotten myself into now. I stopped right outside.

The door popped open, crazy dude latched on to my arm, and he yanked me inside.

Fortunately, the place was lit and roomy. Because I was starting to panic.

Guess I could get murdered just as easily in a supply closet as thrown down the stairs at the top of my building, right?

"I knew you'd come!" His grinning face looked far creepier in the dim light of the storage closet than it had in the well-lit stairwell. "Is it true? You've seen a real vampire?"

I didn't know how to answer that. "Oh, um, maybe?"

He punched the air. "Yes! I knew it!"

He got way too close and spoke quickly. "I've got everything you need. Everything. But we can't be seen talking here."

I pointed to the door, thinking of the note he'd given me. "But you just told me to meet you here…"

He waved away my words. "I know, I know. But I can't do business here."

Yeah, cause we were in a *supply closet*.

"Look, meet me here, and you can go over the merchandise."

He handed me a business card. In code. The same code that had disguised the vampire's club thingy.

I tried to look innocent. "But how will I ever decipher what this means?"

He grinned and rubbed his hands together like a mad scientist.

Didn't make me feel any better about him.

"Just like you deciphered where the vampires were meeting before. Man! I would've given anything to be there, watch you walk into their lair without a care. You must be some badass chick!"

I preened a little and didn't bother to mention it was nothing more than an abandoned warehouse by the time I'd gotten there. Apparently I wasn't above succumbing to a little flattery.

I straightened and tried to look how he described. I gave what was supposed to be a carefree laugh but mostly just choked. "Yeah, that's me. Badass."

He moved close and dropped his voice. I edged away the slightest bit.

"Those vampires have taken over our city long enough.

Fighting, feuding, using up valuable resources. Killing the homeless and depleting our blood banks." He pounded his fist on a shelf covered in office supplies. "It's an outrage."

My back hit the door. I couldn't go any farther. "Uh, yes, exactly that. An outrage."

His eyes gleamed. "I knew you were one of us!"

I kept his business card between us as some form of protection. Super helpful, that.

He nodded at it. "Meet me there, after work, and I'll set you up with anything and everything you could possibly need for the hunt."

My eyes widened. "The *hunt*?"

He shoved past me, mashing me up against shelves, and furtively looked out of the supply closet. "It's clear. Go!"

He shoved me out, and I almost sprawled face-first in the middle of the office hallway.

When I regained my balance, I turned to find him wagging a finger at me. "And remember, tell no one! Your very life could depend on it. Those vamps are everywhere…"

He glanced furtively from side to side and slid back into the closet, shutting the door as he went.

I stared at the door until someone walked by, then turned and made my way to the elevators.

I snorted as I pushed the button for the top floor. Yeah right was I meeting that guy. At a place of his choosing, no less.

Nothing this side of millions of dollars could make me.

✗

The next day, I hurried out of work a tad early, on my way to meet that guy.

The rest of yesterday had been a wash. I couldn't concentrate on a dang thing. Today hadn't been much better. I just needed to meet that guy, kill my curiosity, and take a long nap.

The elevator doors opened, and I broke from the crowd and sprinted toward the front doors, my speed walk in full swing.

"Hey, Candace!"

I yelped and flung my folder across the lobby floor. It slid and landed against the handsome security guard's feet. He was always so nice to me, but I could still never remember his name. Sigh.

Whoever had called out to me burst into laughter, the sound all wheezy and hacking and smoker-cough worthy.

The security guard gathered it all up—things had fallen out, of course—and headed my way with a smile. "Here you go, Candace."

I took it from him with a mumbled "thank you," and he touched his cap and moved back toward the desk with a smile. My face burned. I kind of wanted to die.

Coughing smoker lady latched on to my arm and pulled me to face her as end-of-the-day employees streamed around us. Martha. Oh goodie.

"That was priceless, Marshall. Priceless! What're ya gonna do for your next act?"

She elbowed me then bent over her knees, laughing so hard I was concerned a paramedic call was in her near future.

Security guard watched us from his post, laughter in his eyes.

I attempted a smile, then pulled Martha out of the stream of workers. "Did you need something?"

She calmed herself enough to look at me with sparkling eyes. "So I hear you met Brandan. A riot, am I right?"

She elbowed me again, and I hunched over a little with an "oof!" and rubbed my side. Was I bleeding internally? Cause that hurt. "Sure, a riot."

"Did he offer to set you up with any 'special gear'?" She did huge air quotes and everything.

I squirmed a little. "Well, um, yes…"

"Can you believe it? He actually thinks New York is overrun with vampires! What did he offer you?"

"I'm not exactly sure…"

"Wait a minute." She pushed on my shoulder with wide, sparkling eyes, almost knocking me over. "Wait just a minute! You're going to meet him, aren't you?"

I rubbed my shoulder where her bony fingers had dug in. A sheepish grin grew on my face. "You can't tell me you aren't the slightest bit curious?"

She hiked her purse higher on her shoulder. "Slightly curious? Girl, we've been making fun of him for years. Years! I'm dying to know what he sells."

I laughed, shaking my head. I couldn't believe I was actually considering this. "You wouldn't want to track me with GPS or anything, would you?"

She squared her shoulders. "I'll do ya one better." She leaned forward and dropped her voice. "I'm going with you!"

"With me?" I took a step back. She didn't just sound like a smoker. She most definitely was one. How to offer a breath mint politely? "Wait, you think I should still go? You think it's safe? I was just curious. Like, insanely curious, but still. I don't have to go."

"Don't have to go?" She latched on to my arm and dragged me outside. "I'm not giving this up for the world! Besides, I'm serious that you need some kind of protection. I don't care if they think they're real vampires or not. Someone pulls a gun on me or one of my friends? Oh, they're gonna die."

We were already three blocks away by the time I could get a word in. I pulled up, but she just yanked harder.

I pointed at the building. "Sorry, kinda need to go in here."

She squinted up at the sign. "American Bank? Let me guess, cash only?"

I nodded, feeling more foolish by the second.

She laughed and dug a cigarette and lighter out of her purse. "Go on, then. I'll be right out here."

I couldn't escape fast enough.

A few minutes later, I was tucking cash deep into my secret pocket in my purse and zipping it closed as I pushed back out into the frigid air.

I'd emptied most of my emergency cash reserve buying that computer from Stan, and I kept meaning to get over here before closing to stock it back up. Couldn't do that now, however, just in case this Brandan guy lived in a bad area.

A part of me couldn't wait to get over there to see what goods he peddled. The other part was screaming at me that this was such a bad idea. On so many levels.

Martha squashed out her cigarette, her eyes still dancing, and breathed right in my face. "Ready?"

I nodded, pulled a little metal case out of my handbag, and opened it, smiling brightly. "Breath mint?"

※

"Brandan, darling!" Martha wedged her way through the jail-style barred door, giving him a hug and ensuring he wouldn't leave her out of the fun.

He looked rather nervous and jittery, which did nothing to settle my stomach. This guy could be on drugs for all I knew.

"Oh, Martha, hi. I wasn't expecting you…" He darted me a quick look.

I shrugged in a helpless manner. What could I say? The woman was a leech.

"Oh, darling, I wouldn't miss this for the world." She prowled the room. "So where's the stuff?"

Brandan locked the door behind me. "I can't stress the importance of this remaining a secret…"

She waved off his words like she was waving away smoke, the lie second nature to her. "You know how long I've kept your secret, my dear. Now, onward! My friend Charis here—"

"Candace," I corrected.

"Cadence here needs what you've got." She checked her watch. "And we don't have much time, sooo…"

I blinked. The woman was a force of nature. And I was suddenly thrilled she was here with me. No matter how much she'd make fun of us both tomorrow.

Maybe with her here, I wouldn't spend all the cash I'd brought with me after all.

I was a pushover like that.

Which is why I'd brought his asking price and no more.

I followed them both to a stairwell leading down, past where his mother sat at the kitchen table in curlers and a bathrobe, intent on her word search, not looking up once as we trailed past.

I sincerely hoped we weren't about to be murdered in their basement.

✗

I took it back. I highly regretted ever meeting Martha.

She piled one more "ooh, you simply must have this too" item in my arms, and I sagged under the weight.

Brandan's eyes danced with greed.

Did I mention how expensive everything was? Stupid

expensive. Like, ridiculous. I could've made half of this stuff with five bucks and free rein in a dollar store.

"Don't forget the holy water!" Brandan held up a super-soaker water gun, half blinding orange and half glaring blue. "Vampires hate it, of course."

Martha seized it with joy and added it to the pile in my arms, which was on a slow slide to the floor.

Enough! I was *not* going to hunt down vampires with a water gun. I wasn't hunting vampires, period.

"Look," I said, parroting Brandan's favorite phrase in the world. "This is too much."

Fold-up tables lined the room, covered with all kinds of things Brandan swore was all I needed to fight darkness and eee-viiil.

I let my armload spill onto the closest table.

Brandan looked crestfallen. Martha simply watched with dancing eyes, perfectly happy with being entertained. She wouldn't be disappointed with me around. Or Brandan, apparently. Dude was cray-cray.

All she was missing was the popcorn.

"Look, I just want a few things." And I needed to stop saying *look*. ASAP. "Some guy, whether he's a real vampire or not, is trying to kill me. And whether he's a real vampire or not, he likes to make his killings look like a vampire did it."

Brandan was enthralled by my every word. Martha looked like she'd never been happier.

I rubbed my forehead. "Look—I mean—do you have any real weapons? Tasers, knives, pepper spray, anything? My gun permit has been denied, so maybe not something illegal?"

Brandan's eyes widened. "You applied for a gun permit in New York City? Brave lady. I could've told you it would be denied." He seemed to shake himself out of that vein of thought. "But illegal doesn't matter. Not when you're fighting for your life against vamps."

"Yeah, no," I insisted. "I've already been caught with a gun once by the police. Next time is a felony. No, thank you. Not happening."

All of a sudden, Brandan looked like he regretted even meeting me.

Not the first time I'd seen that look.

Martha looked even more delighted. Oops? Maybe I shouldn't have said that last bit.

I perused all the cheap, fake stuff he'd just tried to peddle on me. "Something, you know, good quality?"

He huffed and stomped over to one of the tables with a black table skirt and dug around underneath. He pulled out what looked like an old-fashioned wooden treasure box, rubies inlaid in a swirling pattern on the lid. From it, he retrieved a padded gun case.

I started to sweat. I was serious. I didn't want to go to jail over a gun, again, or be charged with a felony. NYC cops were serious about illegal carry. And I had a cop with a personal grudge against me for some reason.

He popped it open and pulled out a Walther PPK.

What? My brother watched a lot of James Bond. The gun was surrounded by—can you guess? Silver bullets.

"Wow!" I reached for one.

He slapped my hand. "You touch, you buy."

I snatched my hand back. What, was this gun, like, two million dollars? I wouldn't put it past him.

He put on cloth gloves and reverently lifted a bullet. "One hundred percent silver alloy, blessed by a priest. You won't find these just anywhere in New York City."

He had that right. I couldn't believe I'd found them *here*.

Plus, hadn't I heard somewhere that those were impossible to shoot with any kind of accuracy?

He put it back. Snapped the case closed. Then he laid

out wooden stakes, fancy containers that held something jagged and powdery—rock salt, maybe—and a row of dark-blue glass vials of liquid.

He'd most likely tell me they were filled with holy water too.

And a slingshot. I blinked at it.

Then two belts that looked like they'd strap on Rambo style, little pockets interspersed all over to contain the stakes and the vials and the salt potions. Oh, and some kind of knives. And two bundles of…something…in some kind of holster.

And a giant cross that tucked into the belt portion of the Rambo straps.

From the bottom he pulled out one last black case. He opened it, pulled out a metal object, and unfolded it into a mini crossbow with a wrist strap.

My eyebrows could not possibly get any higher.

Good grief. I didn't want to *kill* anybody. Just, I don't know, scare them off? Make sure they didn't kill me? Keep myself from getting grabbed again?

And how were these thousands of weapons to be tucked about my person any kind of subtle?

He pointed to each item and explained. "Wooden stakes. Mallet to get 'em past the ribcage and into the heart. Silver powder. Use with the slingshot. Aim for the face. Holy water. Throw on any exposed skin. Like this."

He demonstrated, splashing me right in the face. I jumped and blinked at him. Had he really just—?

"Not a vampire. Good. Anyway, easy storage and transport for all your gear. Cross to keep 'em from getting too close. Silver-edged knives. Silver-tipped bolts. Wrist crossbow. Use at closer range than the gun."

"I'm not using a *gun*—" I tried to insist, still dripping holy water.

"Five hundred for the lot. This is the last one I have. No returns. No takebacks."

Because we were twelve.

I was interested in the wrist crossbow, dang it, and maybe the slingshot, but not anything else. I mean, stakes? Really?

Cause I could just see me staking some poor delusion guy dressed in velvet in an abandoned subway station. And then going right back to jail. For life.

"Yeah, no. I don't want the stakes."

His jaw got all tight, and he looked like he was having trouble even processing what I'd just said. "You take the whole thing, or not at all."

I wavered. I couldn't remember all the other weapon laws of NYC, just that there were eight million of them, but this seemed like a bad idea. Plus, Martha…

My eyes drifted to her.

She hadn't lost her enthusiasm, and she gave me a thumbs-up with a huge smile. "That's a bargain, if you ask me," she said.

Well in a way, I was.

I turned back to Brandan. Sighed. "You got a receipt for any of this? Proof of purchase?"

Man, I needed to look up all those weapons to make sure nothing else in this pile was illegal. Brass knuckles were, if I remembered correctly. And ferrets? Or was that just California? Anyway.

He went rather pale. "Oh no, you're not tracing this back to me. You want a receipt, you make one up."

Oh my gosh, this was horrible on so many levels. I needed to walk away right now.

But I was here. Being stared at. About to lose a good chunk of my savings, by the looks of things. Not that I spent much anyway.

Why the heck hadn't I just gone home after work? I was

going to regret this so, so much tomorrow. Probably in five minutes. But silver bullets…

"Wait." I fingered the gun case hesitantly. "I thought silver bullets were for werewolves?"

I cringed inwardly, just knowing how often my brain liked to scramble up facts without my permission.

Instantly a mask of superiority dropped over his face, and I had a feeling I was gonna be here for a while.

"Actually, it's a little-known fact that silver bullets kill both vampires *and* werewolves. It was first introduced in vampire lore, then the vampires worked hard to turn it around for use solely on their enemies, all while knowing they had the same weakness."

He might have droned on a bit longer, but my eyes had started to glaze. I interrupted him mid-something. "I'll take it."

His mouth hung open for a beat, then his superior air was slowly replaced with a gleam in his eye. Pretty sure it was greed. "As in, the whole lot?"

I pointed at the box. "That box and everything in it. Only."

I didn't want to try to make it home juggling fifty super-soakers and all the other crap he'd tried to sell me.

Brandan looked like he'd won a million bucks. Because, well, to some dude living in his mom's basement, it probably felt like he had.

What could I say? I was a sucker.

Brandan packaged it all up into the ornate wooden box, counted my money twice, and sent us on our way.

We waded through snowy slush on the way to the bus stop.

Martha got on the first bus while I waited for the next.

I shook my head as her bus pulled up. "That guy, huh? Kinda felt sorry for him."

She smiled. "That why you bought all that junk?"

I gave her a sheepish smile. "Why else?"

She gave me a calculating look, then smiled and waved as her bus pulled up. The severity of my situation didn't hit me until her bus pulled away.

I shivered, and not just from still being damp with holy water.

Now I just had to get all the way to my apartment without getting mugged or caught or thrown in jail with all these weapons…carrying them in an ornate treasure box.

Was I dumb or was I dumb?

CHAPTER TWENTY-SEVEN

On my way home, the bus swayed, and I nodded off. At one of the stops, I jerked awake and made sure I was still holding my box of contraband.

The last thing I wanted to explain to any cops was why I held a box of stakes, a mallet, holy water, and an ornate cross. Not to mention the illegal gun with silver bullets wedged in the bottom, along with knives, bolts, a wrist crossbow, and vials that could be full of anything, really.

I clutched the box just a little tighter.

A tall, intimidating guy stepped on the bus and spoke to someone outside. "Look, I'll just check it out and be on my way back to LA."

I heard something like a disgusted, "Bah!" from someone else, then the guy turned and made his way down the bus toward me.

I tried not to stare, but I couldn't help it. The guy was so tall! And in a dark overcoat with a hat pulled low over his eyes, I expected him to call someone out for a gunslingin' duel at any second.

He tipped his hat at me—I made sure to stare back with my signature wide-eyed look—then he started to pass me.

He caught sight of my box, hesitated, then sat a few seats down and across from me.

I clutched the box a little tighter.

I was so dead. Not only was I flashing how nervous I was to every person on the bus, of which there were few at this hour, now I looked like I carried pure gold and was terrified of anyone stealing it.

There were times it sucked to be me.

We were in the row of open seats near the front, facing opposite sides of the bus, and he spoke to me after a few streets. "That's quite some box you've got there."

My fingers were going to puncture the wood with how hard I was clutching it. I let off a mortifying, high-pitched laugh. "Ha! You know." That wasn't right. I tried again. "Uh, thanks."

I ducked my head and hoped he'd get off at the next stop and that next stop would be in two seconds or less.

After an awkward silence, I peeked at him and noticed a flash of red around his neck. "That's quite an interesting—necklace?—you've got there."

He didn't really smile, but his lips made an upward motion. He tucked the silver cross inlaid with a red jewel in its center into his shirt. "Thanks."

I stared out the window and wished for my stop with every fiber of my being. I could feel his stare broiling into me from across the bus.

Unable to help myself, I peeked at him to find the guy squinting in my direction. He said, "You look familiar. Have we met before…?"

"Oh, I get that a lot." I gave off an airy laugh and pretended to fluff my hair. No clue why *that* was my reaction, but I was nothing if not awkward. "But sure. I'll sign an autograph. If you want."

I shrugged, the picture of cool nonchalance.

Now he just looked confused. "Why would I want your autograph?"

My face flamed. People still asked for my autograph from my zombie movie, so *of course* I'd immediately assumed that.

This guy probably didn't even *watch* movies.

"No reason," I muttered to the floor, hoping I could somehow just slip through it, roll across the pavement, and walk home.

After an eternity of awkward, he nodded at my box. "Do you know what that symbol means?"

I craned my neck to look. I'd forgotten anything was on the box, besides the fake rubies. They were fake, weren't they? Surely Brandan wouldn't have parted with it for so little if they weren't.

As soon as I saw the swirling pattern, I gave off another airy laugh. No wonder strangers assumed I didn't have enough brain cells to hold a legit conversation. Of course, anxiety made that a real thing half the time.

"Oh, this thing?" I traced the symbol I'd seen on the dark web. I rolled my eyes and spoke out the side of my mouth. "It's supposed to be for the feuding vampire covens of New York City, before they were at war, but like that's even a real thing, am I right?"

Again, a hint of a smile. "I don't know. You tell me. You're holding a sacred burial chest for a vampire's heart. They're said to hold enormous power."

I simultaneously threw the chest and lunged to catch it before it crashed to the floor. I caught it just in time. I then plopped it next to me, between us, and tried not to touch it.

"You're kidding me."

He shrugged, his steady gaze tracking my movements. "It's one of the reasons I'm in this city, actually. Can you tell me where you got it?"

"Dude," I said, "you can have it." I chewed on my lip.

"Well, um, actually, I paid quite a bit for it, and I need a few things from inside…"

I eyed the box, knowing there was no way I could open that thing and start pulling out half that stuff to stash about my person.

But I was serious he could have the rest. The bullets would fit my legal gun—legal as long as it stayed inside my apartment—which the police department had finally given back, and I wasn't using a stake on a vampire. Ever.

I mean, seriously. What if it was another underpaid actor? That I staked? Because no one would tell me what was freaking going on? No, thank you.

He leaned forward casually, his eyes intense. "Do you know what's inside?"

I nodded, and my mouth just started telling him without my approval. "Oh, yes. Stakes, holy water, silver powder, silver bull—"

My face heated to inferno levels and I choked. I quickly guzzled from my water bottle before I could speak again. Even then, I could barely look at him. Who admitted things like that out loud?

"You know how to hunt vampires, do you, miss?"

I shook my head, trying to take it all back. "Oh no. Not even close. I mean, they're not even real, right?"

I didn't say it, but I wanted to beg him to tell me they weren't real. Apparently that was all over my face, because he offered me a kind look.

"Then why are you decked out and prepared to fight them?"

I sighed, and the whole story spilled out. How we found the dead guy, whose body had up and disappeared, how no one believed me, and how I'd been kidnapped and taken underground. How I'd found another dead body, been arrested, and was now desperate to defend myself. Somehow. Legally.

And I hadn't forgotten that Mr. Withers might still be alive. Though for how much longer? It had been months since his body had disappeared.

I didn't even know this guy, and he now knew more about me than most people.

"He asked for my help. Asked for it. I was kidnapped. Kidnapped!" I noticed I was spiraling and took a deep breath. "Sorry. I just feel like, well, if I don't do something, who will?"

The bus stopped, and he stood. He scribbled something on a piece of paper and handed it to me. "This is where I'm staying for the next few days. When you get done with the box, send it here?"

I took the paper, noted the address, and nodded.

He checked his pockets. "I'm a little low on cash…"

I waved him off. "If it's as important as you say, I certainly don't need it."

He studied me a moment. "You're a good woman, ma'am."

A warm glow filled me, and I kind of wilted into the seat with relief. He didn't know it, but I needed to hear that. And he'd been such a good listener. Not a hint of doubt or disbelief in his expression at all.

And he'd been kind. That meant the most of all to me.

He made his way to the exit and paused right before he got off. "Sometimes it takes just one person willing to do the right thing to change the world."

He stepped off before I could come up with a response, and I watched until the bus left him far behind.

My goodness, if I didn't believe in angels before, that would've done it.

Though he didn't *seem* like an angel with the scary demeanor and mystical necklace and knowledge of vampires and all…

Thank God for sending someone to tell me what I needed to hear, right when I needed to hear it.

I sat back, more determined than ever.

Did I think vampires were real?

Heck no.

Was I going to keep looking and find out what had happened to old man Withers?

Why, yes, Mr. Stranger Man, I most certainly was, thank you very much.

※

The next day at lunch, I made my way to where Martha was sitting, a rapt audience spread around her as she smoked and waved her hands in the midst of storytelling.

I shook my head. No one was supposed to smoke in the cafeteria. Yet she somehow got away with it. Near our food. Ugh.

Still, curiosity wouldn't let me find a nice, quiet corner to disappear in as I usually did. I wanted to hear her take on last night.

First thing this morning, I'd sent a courier with the box emptied of everything to that dude—because let's be honest. A stash of vampire-themed weapons seemed like a great idea.

And on the way to work, I may or may not have stopped by a jeweler and bought a pure silver cross and had it blessed by a priest, parting with even more of my savings.

Not that I was superstitious or anything. But if it worked, it worked.

I would not be unprepared this time.

Lola threw back her head and laughed, something I'd never seen her do before. The moment her eyes met mine, her lip curled slightly. Not a good look on her. Even if she was drop-dead gorgeous.

I faltered, then swallowed and kept going.

My assistant couldn't rattle me. I wouldn't let her. I wanted, no, *needed* to know what was being said about me.

Uh, about Brandan. Not me.

She bent her head and said something, and everyone hushed, turning to look at me at the same time.

Oh my gosh, it was like high school all over again. My hands turned clammy, and I prayed I wouldn't drop my tray. High school had been a nightmare.

Which is why I was more than thrilled to leave that time in my life behind and never look back.

I slid into an open space. "Hi, Martha."

Her eyes danced, her lips smiled, but none of the friendliness from last night was present. "Marshall."

I laughed and prepared to take a bite. "That was something last night. Brandan, am I right?"

Okay, that came out way worse than it sounded in my head. I wasn't *trying* to be cruel. Just…trying to lead the conversation back to him.

Still, if I could take back my words, I would in a heartbeat.

Her gaze turned cool, and several of the others turned away. "Brandan? My dear, he's on my floor. In my office pool. It's not *Brandan* I'm worried about."

A few of the cultured, adult-not-high-school ladies around me tittered, still obviously listening but pretending to ignore me.

I choked on the bite I'd taken, chewing hastily and swallowing before I should've. It didn't go down well.

I stared at her with wide eyes. "But you said, I just, you only…"

Martha looked at all those around her as she spoke to me. "My, cat's got your tongue? What could you possibly be hiding?"

A cough. "Vampire slayer," someone I didn't know said under her breath.

More titters.

My face flamed. "Oh, come on. We both know I went just because you wanted to see what he was selling."

"Me?" Martha leaned forward, eyes cruel. "I went because you were scared of being killed by vampires and were on your way to buy weapons, possibly illegal weapons, I might add, to protect yourself from said creatures of the night." She tilted her head. "Who's the crazy one? Brandan? I don't think so."

My mouth was hanging open at this point. My eyes darted around the table of poised, suave, and gorgeous women, even a few of the models Jackson knew, and those who weren't outright ignoring me were watching with open disdain, no kindness in sight.

Lola watched the whole thing, blood-red lips curved into a smile, eyes hooded and unreadable. Well, except for the enjoying this part. That was obvious.

I took a deep breath to stop the tears. "I see."

Standing, I grabbed my tray and walked away to laughter and whispers. No one tried to stop me.

I dumped my full tray in the trash, mourning the loss of my lunch, but wanting to get out of there too badly to keep any of it.

This building had a strict "no food anywhere but the cafeteria" policy. And I was a rule follower, dang it.

I hurried to the elevator, not returning the security guard's smile, and I never did that. It just wasn't polite, but my lips weren't working.

Pounding on the elevator button, I kept my head lowered as I got on.

I had plenty of work to do. I could always eat later. After everyone else left.

My throat still burned, but at least my tears were mostly gone by the time Lola came back from lunch.

Yep, I'd gone in the bathroom and cried like a baby. Twice.

I hated remembering high school. And I hated crying. But that hadn't stopped me from doing both.

Stupid mean girls.

I kept my head down as she came in, knowing my voice wouldn't cooperate for a little while yet.

She had a slight smile on her face the entire time we worked silently together.

Falling into a familiar rhythm did much to keep me from blubbering all over the place again. But I was still curious—Lola hadn't defended me, but what did she think about what had happened?

Stan poked his head in just as I thought I would scream from the tension in the air.

"Lola? Be a dear at take care of the 2 p.m. pickup."

That wiped the smile off her face. "Me? But—"

I tried not to smile. Because it was an intern's job? Or perhaps a delivery service's job? Teach her to make fun of me.

I sobered. Not that I wanted to be unkind too. Also, not that I hadn't done that a time or two myself, but they were usually crazy-important pickups.

Stan just raised an eyebrow, and Lola went.

He sat. Looked at me. "Care to explain why I have some lower-level employee in my office right now? Talking about vampires?"

I blanched. "What?"

He studied me a moment. "I thought so." He leaned forward. "Am I firing her?"

I sat down, horrified. And tempted. So very tempted.

"You can do that?"

"Please, girlfriend."

Right. Second-in-command. I waved my hand. "I mean, right. Of course you can. But should you? Really? Over that? A misunderstanding?"

He leaned forward. Clasped his hands. "Unless you give me a reason not to, yes."

A heartbeat passed before the entire story spilled out. The whole thing.

Stan had that way with people.

And I cried like a baby for the third time when I described the cafeteria scene. He handed me his handkerchief, and I wiped my eyes, uncomfortably aware that I was sitting in a glass cube where the entire office could walk by and watch me cry.

Ugh. How was this even a little professional?

"I only went because I was curious. Honest. I don't want anyone to get in trouble. Not Brandan. Not Martha. I mean, really. What on earth would a guy sell who thinks there are such things as real vampires?" I fiddled with Stan's handkerchief. "I don't want anyone to get in trouble. I don't want anyone to get fired. I was just curious. And I felt bad for him. I mean, seriously. He lives in his mom's basement and was trying to sell me wooden stakes."

I rolled my eyes, but I didn't mention the illegal part of the sale. Ugh.

I wrung the white, embroidered cloth—who embroidered handkerchiefs these days? Who carried them, for that matter?—and had trouble meeting his eyes.

Was he laughing at me? Feeling sorry for me? Going to set me up to be made fun of too? If he told his wife…

Oh my gosh, was he considering firing me too? He'd already warned me about dropping this whole vampire thing. More than once.

He slapped his knees, and I jumped, my eyes flying to his. "A warning, then. She needs to know not to mess with top-tier employees. *My* employees."

My heart warmed as I realized he wasn't talking about giving *me* a warning. I may have smiled a little. And I didn't object.

He swiped away a few stray tears with his knuckles, then tapped my shoulder twice and walked away.

How could anyone not love this man?

I buried my face in my work, now choked up for an entirely different reason. Everyone needed to experience someone else having their back, just once. It was bliss.

"Oh, and Candace?"

My head came up.

He stood at my clear door, ready to open it. "Let's drop the vampire thing altogether, but especially at work, shall we?"

I nodded a million times. "Oh, yes, please. I can't tell you how many times I've tried to do just that. I want *nothing* to do with it."

He gave me a nod and a smile and left, whistling.

Only Stan could get away with that on Vera's floor.

Lola still wasn't back when I moved a page, and Stan's handkerchief fell to the floor.

Oh! I'd forgotten to give it back.

I scooped it up and stood. Martha was on her way back from Stan's office, and our eyes locked. Hatred filled her expression, promising retribution for whatever had just happened. And as angry as she looked, under it all, she looked like she might cry.

My heart plummeted, and I plopped back down on my stool.

Maybe I'd return it later.

CHAPTER TWENTY-EIGHT

A dirty note jammed in my apartment's doorframe caught my attention.

Come alone or don't bother showing up at all.

A barely legible address sprawled underneath it.

Oh my gosh, would this night never end? I already felt guilty enough about whatever warning Martha got. Lola had been subdued after she'd come back from the pickup, too.

And I'd worked my butt off to make up for it all.

I snatched up the note as I went inside. I found another note stuffed under my door. I sighed and picked it up. This note was in pirate vampire dude's handwriting.

At least he hadn't broken in this time, right?

To the Lovely Candace Marshall:

The leader of my coven, the Blood Coven, has agreed to meet with you and answer any questions you might have. I suggest taking this opportunity, Miss Marshall. I cannot hazard a guess when such an opportunity might present itself again.

Might want to bring that notebook of yours.

One more thing? Burn both notes once you memorize the address.

—Anders

I blinked. Anders? Was that his name? I'd have to remember that.

And memorize the address? He had much greater faith in my memorization skills than I did.

I used my trusty vampire notebook to scribble down the address, then found a candle in my kitchen and had *way* too much fun burning the notes.

Fear and excitement coursed through me. My heart raced and my palms grew sweaty. This was it. A lead. A real one. I'd finally find out what was going on.

"Yeah, or they plan on stuffing you in a body bag," I mumbled to myself as I made my way to my room.

Slipping off my work clothes, I quickly changed into something I could move well in, my mind made up.

At the risk of death or complete humiliation—not sure which would be worse—I was going to solve this mystery if it killed me. Which it wouldn't. Because it was clearly another movie set. Or a sick joke. I was sure of it.

Humiliation it was.

I fingered the gun filled with silver bullets. Should I take it? Because I would go to jail if I were caught. And Gavin wouldn't be able to get me out this time. He probably wouldn't even want to.

But I also wasn't going to wind up dead in some back alley. Jail was better than dead. I hoped. Maybe?

No, I couldn't do that to either of us again. It would have to stay in my apartment.

I strapped the mini crossbow on my wrist, added silver-tipped bolts that apparently auto-loaded (how freaking cool was that?), and made sure it was well hidden under my coat sleeve.

Then I shoved two sheathed silver-edged knives into my waistband, where I usually kept my concealed-carry holster.

Grabbing my phone, ID, and some cash, I locked my apartment door behind me and jogged to the elevator, certain this was quite possibly the dumbest thing I'd done in my entire life.

⚔

I hesitated on the corner of like, the worst neighborhood ever. Sketchy during the day at best, with night falling it was downright terrifying. Even dressed in nondescript dark clothing, my every movement was tracked by the scariest people ever.

Raising my chin, I walked faster.

I arrived at the address and couldn't move a step farther. I just needed to knock on the door and go inside the brownstone that looked like it was crumbling where it stood.

The trick was getting back out again.

I was looking forward to that part already.

Still I hesitated. Even the people who lived in this area had the good sense to stay in their homes, and anyone brave enough to be outside walked quickly to their destination, head down, and disappeared inside. That should've told me something right there.

Was I really dumb enough to do this? What was wrong with me? Why was I here?

"You that chick that found the body?"

I jumped a mile, maybe more, and spun on the guy standing. Right. Next. To. Me. "Ah!"

He tucked his cigarette in his mouth and held up both hands. "Whoa, calm down, lady. I was just told you wanted to see my boss. That true?"

My teeth were chattering so much, I could barely get the words out. "Your boss? The body? Who, me?"

His forehead creased, and he took several puffs, staring at me like I was crazy.

Which, let's face it, I was. What was I doing here again?

"Look, lady, I ain't got all day. You wanna see him or not?"

"Uh, yes, maybe. I think so."

He rolled his eyes, dropped his cigarette, and ground it out on the cracked sidewalk. "Follow me, then."

This was such a bad idea. Had I mentioned that?

But stupid me followed him anyway.

He punched in a code, and the door opened. He dropped the door on me—definitely not gentleman material—and I caught it right before the heavy door smacked me in the face.

"Thanks a lot," I muttered.

He waved a hand and dropped the inner door on me too. That one got me in the thigh.

"Think nothing of it. I just do what I'm told. If the boss wants to see you, then the boss wants to see you. Who am I to argue?" He glanced back and looked me up and down. "Even if you do look like some uptight uptown girl who don't belong here."

I had never been called such a thing in my life. "Um, thank you?"

"Like I said. It ain't a problem."

He took the stairs down, not up. I hesitated. A basement room? Really? What was the limit of my stupidity here?

"Ya coming?"

I hurried after him. I hated making people wait, even if I was certain I was about to be kidnapped, robbed blind, and ransomed back to Gavin for far more than I was worth. Especially since I'd chosen to come here *on my own*.

He went down another flight of stairs.

I clutched the sagging, creaking handrail. How far down did this thing go? We were almost out of natural light. And I was beginning to shake.

Could I change my mind now, please?

Something I should've done earlier. When I first got the note.

He kept going, and like a bug helplessly entranced by a light about to burn it to a crisp, I went after him. It was dark, the flickering lights not doing much more than letting me know that, yes, there were still walls and a floor.

And it got darker the farther down I went.

Goodbye, dear friends, I said in my head to everyone I'd ever known. Because I didn't want scary dude over there to remember I was still behind him.

At the third underground floor, he took off down a sagging hallway—yes, the floor, walls, *and* ceiling sagged—the light so sparse, huge gaps of darkness made me think I'd step into a hole and never be found.

He stopped at a doorway just past a flickering light and lit another cigarette. Then he unlocked the door and pushed it open. He stood back, puffing away and watching me.

"Uh…" I said.

I was about to get hit on the head. Kidnapped. Sold to a trafficking ring.

This was bad on so many levels.

He shrugged. "You was the one who set up the meeting. I don't care if yous go in or not."

Cause that made me feel better.

"Uh, do you mind taking a few steps back?" I asked timidly.

He eyed me like I was out of my mind—I was—but took a few shuffling steps back.

I edged forward. Pretty sure he could still jump me and sell me to the highest bidder, but I somehow made it to the door and peeked in, trying to keep creepy dude in my sight, too.

Off-white walls, very little furniture, no windows, all lit modestly.

The guy in the hallway moved.

I jumped back, my hand going to my waist, where my gun was hidden.

My hand closed around a knife handle. Right! Hadn't brought the gun.

Both of his hands came up. "Whoa, whoa, calm down, lady."

There was a new appreciation, a cautiousness in his eyes now. Oh. Good. Hopefully I wouldn't have to pull it.

"You've got some brass if you brought a weapon down here."

"It's just for protection," I stammered. "I won't use it, I won't even use it, but I'm a girl, by myself, here." I realized how that sounded. "Oh! I mean, my friends know I'm here and will call the cops if I'm not back in two hours, but I came alone. Like you asked."

He just shrugged, not taking his eyes off my hand.

"Anyway," I continued. "I won't touch it if you don't touch me."

His laugh sounded like he'd keel over any moment from all the smoke he'd inhaled over the years. "You can take that up with the boss. I don't really care." He pointed to the room. "In there."

I moved into the sparse room against my better judgment, which was apparently on vacation, or taking a nap, or just completely absent. I was ready to dart back out any second.

The guy leaned into the room and touched his hat in farewell. "He'll be right with you. Best of luck."

And he shut the door and locked it.

I almost died on the spot.

I squeaked and ran back to it, pulling on it with all my might.

But as I tried to jerk it open, a voice behind me said, "Ah, Miss Marshall. I understand you have a few questions for me?"

I spun toward the voice, both hands still on the doorknob. I rattled it anyway, but nothing. Looked solid.

An older gentleman stood there, in an exquisite suit that fit his frame perfectly. I could tell how expensive it was by how simple, unassuming, and clean the lines were.

I took a moment to appreciate his well-made suit, then remembered I was locked in here with him. Fashionable or not, I had no idea what he was about to do. Or who he was.

That sobered me right up.

"Uh, um, yes? That's me. Who are you?"

And where was Anders? Once again, should've gotten more information first.

He smiled in a way that avoided showing any teeth. "You can call me Bob. It's not my real name, of course, but it will do."

I looked at him, deadpan. "Bob. Bob the vampire."

Some of my fear ebbed away. I mean, how could it not with a name like that?

His tight-lipped smile grew a little tighter. "As I said, it's not my real name. As far as being a vampire…" He laughed. "He said you believed us, but I did not countenance it."

My face heated. "That's why I'm here, isn't it? To learn about this vampire feud between the other covens in the city and yours?"

I knew how stupid that sounded. Yet I was here anyway, saying it aloud anyway, waiting to be kidnapped anyway.

Another smile. "Answers await you, my dear." He waved me forward. "Now, my office is just here. Won't you come in?"

I shook my head, both hands still planted on the doorknob. "Um, no. Let's just talk right here. I'm perfectly comfortable." I gave the handle a rattle for emphasis. "And then you can let me out."

"Oh, I have every intention of letting you go. You need

not fear on that account. I am not like…others…of my kind. But first, this way, please?"

I edged toward him, and he backed away, just a little, giving me space. I peeked into the room he was indicating, keeping him in my periphery.

The room was warmly lit, had an extremely nice desk—probably cost a fortune, so what was it doing in this dump?—and gorgeous leather chairs that also looked like they cost more than this entire building.

Then again, it was NYC real estate, even if it was in an unlivable area of New York and most likely needed to be torn down.

But mostly I just noticed the huge linebacker slash bodyguard slash wrestler in the highest weight class possible slash mob dude standing behind the desk, sunglasses on, meaty hands folded in front of him.

Bob the Vamp walked right past me and calmly sat behind the desk. "You wouldn't begrudge me a little protection, would you? Especially since you brought a little protection of your own?"

I swallowed. "Of course not."

"Good. Now, what do you want to know?" He waved his hand again. "Please, sit."

I sat, got out my notepad, and started nervous-asking questions. "You are the leader of the Blood Coven, is that correct?"

He smiled, lips still firmly clamped shut. "I am. Anders has told me much about you."

Oh, uh, good, I think? "How…nice. And you are feuding with the Midnight Coven?"

He nodded. "And the Dark Coven and the Moonlit Coven and the Stabbed Heart Coven."

My brain derailed, and it took a moment to calm down from all the screaming it was doing. I cleared my throat, but it had gone bone dry. "Oh?"

I pretty much choked on the word.

"Yes, you see, at one time, the five covens were united under our two: the Midnight Coven, ruled by Horatius, and the Blood Coven, ruled by me. Tensions rose over how we harvested our food and how we initiated new members, and the covens fractured."

I was listening too hard to remember to write anything down, so when he nodded at my vampire notebook—of which I hoped I'd hidden the cover quickly enough—I jumped and scratched out a few notes.

He continued, a satisfied timbre to his voice. "Eighty years ago, the first blood bank opened in New York City. The public was told that it was difficult to get wounded patients blood in time, but only I and my brother, Horatius, knew it was a compromise between our covens and the then-mayor of New York City to protect his people from ours."

He sighed impatiently and stared at my notebook.

I jumped a little and tapped my temple with my pen. "Don't worry. Steel trap."

Believe me, this wild tale would be circling in my head for hours.

I mean, really, how could reporters *not* be fascinated by such incredible and unbelievable stories such as this one?

Oh, right. I didn't see other reporters jumping on this story for a reason.

I made a few notes to appease the old vampire guy while he went back to treating me to some supernatural slash horror slash history lesson.

"Horatius and I agreed. Our covens were being hunted and members eliminated, and the death toll in New York and the surrounding area was getting out of hand, even for us. Not all of our acolytes, unfortunately, agreed with our decision."

Now I was madly scribbling notes. If nothing else, this would make an awesome novel, right?

"The Moonlit Coven split from Horatius's, continuing to hunt the night of the full moon. Those who knew of us had warning enough to stay indoors then. The Dark Coven consists of mostly fresh recruits who want to live as normals by day and in the darkness by night. The Stabbed Heart Coven reaps from the weak and the forgotten and is responsible for most homeless disappearances in this city. That one, unfortunately, split from my own coven."

I couldn't help my shiver. Note to self: If my job and dating Gavin somehow didn't work out, do *not* be homeless in this city.

"But this time my brother has gone too far. A murder his coven is responsible for has gone public and has been blamed on us."

"What are you going to do about it?" I asked.

He snarled. "I am going to teach my traitor of a brother that he cannot go behind my back and expose my coven without consequences."

I nodded, still scribbling madly. This nonsense was pure gold. "And what proof do you have?"

When he didn't say anything, I looked up to see him staring at his bodyguard. Oh my gosh, were they having one of those silent conversations in their heads?

Just as long as they didn't try to have one with *me*.

"I can show you, if you like, but I do not think you would enjoy how you got there. We cannot allow our visitors to see the pathway to our home. Privacy and protection for my family, of course."

I shook my head emphatically and scribbled a few more notes. "Oh, no, that's okay. This is plenty, thank you."

He leaned forward, hands steepled and elbows propped on the desk. "You are planning on publishing an article on your website, are you not?"

My pen froze over the paper. I lifted my eyes to meet his. "My website?"

He nodded, eyes agleam. "I read your articles. Very good. Very objective. You presented the zombies of Arizona and New Mexico in a way that will ease people into knowledge of them. A movie, ha!" He cleared his throat. "I think you will represent our coven to the people of New York City well."

My mouth went dry. *That's* what I was doing here? And he thought my movie was real? "B-b-but I thought you wanted secrecy. Privacy. Non-exposure and all that. I didn't think you wanted anything published about you…all."

My eyes flicked to scary dude behind him.

They were all scary, okay? Every guy I ran across in this whole stupid, scary, vampire thing should be nicknamed scary dude.

Though it was a good thing I'd forgotten to take that website down, right?

"Privacy? That's what Horatius wants." He sneered. "No, I want every detail out there. I want my brother exposed, once and for all. On this world wide web, or whatever you young people are calling it these days. Apt name, is it not?"

"But why?" It just didn't make sense.

Now he smiled for real. Pearly, bleached, blazing whites in full view for me to see.

Fangs and all.

They were absolutely humungous. Hadn't I read somewhere the older a vampire got, the longer his fangs grew? I could believe it.

"Because I want the other covens that try to encroach on my territory to know that I am not afraid of them. That they cannot mess with me. That I will come after them if they try to pin a murder on me or mine ever again."

He sat back in his chair and grinned, fangs long and real and just so very there. I couldn't stop staring at them.

The rest of him may have looked suave and put together as if he came from money, but his fangs took that image and made him about a thousand times creepier.

"Besides, the right people will get the message." He leaned forward again, intense look on his face. "And you're going to give it to them."

I just sat there, frozen, not sure what was even happening.

Did that mean the other covens would then come after *me* for revenge?

You know what? I didn't want to be right anymore. I didn't want to try to figure out what was going on. I just wanted to go home.

"I'd like to go home now. Please."

He sat back and nodded at his henchman. "Of course. My thrall will take you home."

I slid a glance at the looming linebacker who hadn't said a word or changed his expression this whole time.

"Oh, that's okay. I'll just go home the way I came. Alone." I stood and started to edge that way.

Bob the Vamp displayed his fangs once more. "I strongly recommend against it, Candace Marshall. The other covens will not be pleased that you've spoken with me, and believe me, they will have someone watching. Anders was very clear that no harm should come to you, and I keep my promises."

He nodded at his thrall, then turned away, dismissing us both.

"Um, thank you," I told him. To the thrall, as he escorted me from the office, I said, "Just to the nearest subway station. Please."

He nodded, unlocked the door, then proceeded me all the way down the hall, up the stairs, and to the closest subway station. No one dared approach us.

He waited next to me until I climbed on, then I glimpsed his retreating back as the train rumbled away from the station.

I sagged against the dangling handhold. Oh, thank goodness. I'd been certain he would follow me home.

Stumbling to the nearest seat, I sank down and started madly scribbling in my vampire notebook, writing the article I'd be posting on my website tonight.

And then I was having nothing to do with these wannabe vamps ever again.

I paused, pen raised. Huh. How many times would I pledge that before it actually became true?

CHAPTER TWENTY-NINE

True to my word, my article was up that night (with a quick revision the next morning, before work), after double checking to make sure my site couldn't be linked to me in any way.

I didn't care about my byline. I just wanted to be left alone.

Maybe I was just being paranoid, but for the next few days, it felt like someone was watching me.

I happened to know that Gavin's driver wasn't, so had he hired someone else? Or had my article reached its intended audience?

You know what? As long as whoever it was left me alone, I didn't care.

But I was extra cautious all the same. Went to work early with lots of other commuters, came home at a decent hour—while the sun was still up, which was crazy early in winter—and worked my butt off in between so no one could say I was working less or slacking off or absolutely anything else.

But my job being my job, it wasn't long until production week forced me to work late.

I told myself it was okay. I told myself I'd done this hundreds of times, that next month was the start of the Fashion Week circuit, that I would be in Paris soon, that I had nothing to worry about.

Trudging through slushy snow, I chewed my lip all the way to the subway station and my apartment and back, chapping them horribly, which Lola was disgusted by, and jumping at every shadow.

Though I stayed far away from alleys and other places that had "grab Candace" potential.

So I was not even a little bit surprised when a van came squealing up to the curb, spraying slush. Two giant scary dudes jumped out and tried to wrest me inside.

I fought like a wet cat trying to escape a bath.

I went for my pepper spray, but they knocked it out of my hand and into the gutter.

I managed to pop open a vial of holy water one-handed and tossed it in the first scary dude's face. He blinked at me, but his face didn't melt off.

Right. Human henchmen.

Or, more logically, no such things as vamps.

Big dude number two pounced, wrapping his meaty arms around me and pinning my arms to my sides.

I was able to liberate one of the silver-edged knives and stabbed it straight back, into his thigh.

He howled, but he kept his hold on me, dang it.

But I was still somehow outside the van, which was my only goal in life right now, thank you very much. The next was running away.

I jerked and tried to slip down and away, using the dead-body-weight maneuver from days of wrestling my brother, but dude was having none of that. He stopped me about halfway down.

My arm caught on something sharp on his belt and tore. My skin, not the belt.

The pain sent my panic through the roof. I opened my mouth.

Before I could scream, a handkerchief and a meaty hand covered my face, something sickly sweet on the cloth.

Oh my gosh, not again.

Trying not to breathe, I bucked and writhed and fought, but then he yanked me up and my head connected with his chin—his freaking chin that was bigger than some people's faces—and I was out like a light.

※

I came to in another place altogether, my head foggy and feeling like it had been stuffed with cotton. Or clouds. Or something fluffy and insubstantial.

It took a moment or two to remember everything, and then it took even longer to be upset by it. Whatever they'd covered my face with worked well. Chloroform, perhaps?

I knew I'd care in a bit, that it would come crashing over me and I'd freak out, but for now, I was going to sit here and relax.

In this dim room with old stone walls. Velvet wall hangings everywhere. A familiar desk. Just as nice as the other desk in the crappy building.

As far as I could tell, I was alone.

A huge, plush, leather-coated chair with stiff arms propped me up, and I was quite happy to see I was untied. I probably would've been just as happy if I were tied up, though.

This sedative thing was great.

I glanced down at my arm, neatly wrapped in clean bandages.

At least, I hoped they were clean. Germs were invisible.

My body woke up by degrees, and soon I was thinking about standing. And about getting scared again. But I still wasn't sure about that. This whole not-caring thing was rather nice.

"I'm sorry, Miss Marshall, I did not want this for you, but you left me no choice."

I jumped and whipped my head around, causing the room to spin.

The vampire in velvet, his henchmen—the one I'd stabbed glaring at me—and a scrawny, skinny dude holding a goblet entered the room. The vamp came toward me, but the other three just stood there. He made a wide arc around me and sat behind his desk.

"I must say, you are lucky indeed. This is the second time you've been inside my home. Not many of the living have seen my humble abode."

My eyes swept the room, velvety curtains and goth decor that made an ornate—but scary—sitting room. One I'd been to before.

I swallowed, hard. "Were they still living? After that particular meeting, that is?"

He smiled but didn't answer.

Great. Just great.

You really are the dumbest person alive, Candace, you know that?

Now that I'd met Vampire Bob, I could see the resemblance. What did he say his brother's name was? Horatio? Horticus? Horatius? Whatever it was, Vampire Bob still needed to come up with a cooler nickname. I mean, really, would that scare anyone?

"Horatius, I presume?"

He spread his hands and made a bowing motion with his head, not taking his eyes off me the whole time. Total guess, but looked like I was right. For once.

I licked my lips. "Where exactly is here, by the way?"

He smiled at me, revealing long, pointy incisors. Freaking fangs.

Please someone jump out, shout boo, and whip out a camera?

He spread his arms all the way out now, and his cape went with them, jagged edge and pointy collar on full display. Can you say ridiculous?

"Welcome to the Midnight Coven, the father of all other covens in New York City."

My mouth hung open. Creepy velvet suit dude did *not* just say that. Which meant this was the coven feuding with Anders's coven, the Blood Coven, the one led by Vampire…Bob.

Still wasn't getting over that name anytime soon.

I shook myself out of my stupor. "Are you trying to tell me you think this whole vampire thing is…real?"

"Oh, I'm afraid it's very real, Candace Eileen Marshall."

I winced a little. I hated my middle name. My mother, Eileen, was rather proud of it and liked to call me "Eileen Junior" whenever she could. Ha-ha.

I did not answer to Eileen.

"Candace or Miss Marshall is good," I ground out.

He raised an eyebrow. "It was difficult to discover your middle name, I'll admit, but I'll agree not to use it if you agree to leave us alone."

Now my eyebrows tried to climb off my face. "Come again?"

"You see, you have it all wrong. Mr. John Withers was not murdered as you mistakenly believe…"

Did he mean the body in the alley that was wearing all its blood on the outside?

"You see, he is right here."

He spread his hand to the side, and a nervous-looking little old man came in, wringing his hands and shuffling his feet.

He too was dressed in velvet and a white linen shirt with excessive ruffles and a cape.

This had to be a joke, right?

I mean, Cheesiest. Costumes. Ever.

"John, will you tell the poor girl you're alive and well?"

He bowed a few times, something that looked more like a nervous tick than a bow, and wrung his hands while he did so. "Yes, Miss Marshall. Of course, Miss Marshall. I'm doing fine, Miss Marshall."

He had the thickest New York accent ever. If I lived long enough, I would eventually be able to tell the different accents apart, but all I knew was his voice was nasally and he could've been from a mob family.

And he did not look fine. Emaciated, huge bags under his eyes, skin thin and papery, which, honestly, could have been due to his age. Four months underground had not been kind to him.

"You see?" Fang dude bared his teeth in what he probably thought was a smile. "All is fine. He is fine. You are fine. No harm done, yes?"

My mouth was hanging open again. "You kidnapped me! Again! No, everything is not *fine*."

His beaming teeth baring got a little tight. "A necessary precaution, I assure you. You had to see Mr. Withers for yourself, and I could not bring him to you. Not without risking his capture. You will be returned unharmed."

I pointed at Mr. Withers. "You told me he was dead!"

He looked like he was putting in a lot of effort to keep showing me his teeth. "But he obviously is not."

I started waving my hands around. "You do realize this raises a million more questions, right?"

His fists were now clenched, as were his teeth, and he spoke through them. "Which is why I'm telling you to leave it alone. You do not have all the facts." As I spluttered, he turned and dismissed Mr. Withers with a careless wave. "You may go."

Dude liked to talk with his hands just about as much as I did.

Mr. Withers shuffled toward the door. He swung in a random, wide arc on the way, and when he got near me, he hissed, "Lady, get me outta here!"

I whipped my head around to see if anyone else had heard that—no one reacted as if they had—but when I turned back to Mr. Withers, the door was closing behind his stodgy little form.

Oh my gosh, had they kidnapped him too? After killing him?

I rubbed my forehead. And now my head hurt. What was going on here? And whose body had been at the morgue? Or had there ever been a body at the morgue?

And what did this mean for the second dead body I'd found at that warehouse?

The other paler-than-a-ghost man with long dark hair who showed fangs—yes, fangs—came up next to me and smiled, baring those awful teeth. I couldn't look away.

He set a goblet before me and backed away slowly, taking a deep whiff of my neck, followed by a heavy sigh, as if my scent sent him into ecstasy.

Ooh...passing out right now was *not* a good idea, no matter how lightheaded I suddenly was.

"Refreshment?" Horatius asked.

With shaking hands, I reached for the heavy golden cup set with rubies—more to clobber sniffing boy if necessary than to sate any thirst—and took an unintentional whiff.

Heavy, metallic, cloying, musty. I peered at the dark, thick liquid. Blood. Had to be.

"I'll pass," I whispered, sliding the goblet as far away from me on the desk as I could manage. Too late I realized I'd bereaved myself of my only weapon.

I mentally smacked myself. *Way to go, Candace!*

And *today* I was going to stop thinking in terms of death.

Horatius continued. "We don't want any more trouble. So now that you know Mr. Withers is alive—"

I snorted. "As if. You could've gotten any old man to play Mr. Withers."

I hated to admit this, but with all the blood and flashing police lights and darkness of the alley, I apparently couldn't identify him if my life depended on it. Nothing about him looked familiar while he was upright and speaking to me. Some help I was.

Annoyance flashed on his face. "And now that you know that he wishes to be here, with us—"

That wasn't at all the vibe I'd gotten from him. Jumpy, scared, nervous—dude was seriously freaked.

"We ask that you take down your…laughable…article, and put up a new one. One that reveals the other was a joke, no one was killed, and we all just want to live in peace."

My eyebrows shot up my forehead. "You want me to lie?"

His smile was brittle. "On the contrary, I am trying to respect Mr. Withers's wishes. He wants to leave his past behind and join us in unending solitude and everlasting life. Removing any unwanted attention will only help him live in peace."

I squinted at him. Guy really thought he was a vampire. Creepy.

I started nodding. "You got yourself a deal."

At his broad smile, I amended my words, holding up a hand.

"I'm not saying I'll lie for you, but I can definitely put up an article with the opposing point of view. But the other article stays."

His eye twitched. "Why you would want to keep up such blatant *lies*…"

"An opposing article can only help you," I insisted. I didn't know why I was insisting, but I was proud of that article. It read like a glorious piece of fiction, and I enjoyed every moment writing it. "And others will want to see the original article yours is combating. And then I will have nothing to do with any of this, ever again."

I mean, geez, Gavin, my boss, the cops, and now uber-scary vampires wanted me to stay away? I was going to stay away.

Getting kidnapped wasn't as glamorous as they make it seem on movies. Especially when there was no rescue in sight.

"No more articles?" he asked, a suspicious look on his face.

"No more articles," I agreed.

His smile revealed long, pointy canine teeth. I shuddered.

"Very good, Miss Marshall. I am thrilled you've come to see our side of it."

I gave him a half smile. I'd see anybody's side of anything if it meant getting out of here.

He folded his hands behind his back. "I will be watching for your article. Keep that in mind."

Yep, definitely glad I'd left the embarrassing thing up. Even if it was by accident.

"I did want to answer one of your questions, however. Yes, we are real. Very real. Brother Coptin will take you home now." He nodded to someone I couldn't see behind me.

Footsteps. Before I could spring away, another cloth covered my face.

I woke up sprawled outside my apartment door.

At least the other vampires had the decency to put me in my own bed, for crying out loud. Not that I wanted *more* vampires inside my apartment.

I came to with the words ringing in my head, *Remember to write your article, Miss Marshall. We will be watching.*

At first, I nodded in agreement with the disembodied voice, mumbling, "Write the article. Watching. Got it."

Then, panic smacked me in the face like a crazy ton of bricks. Once again, *how* were they talking inside my head? I grumbled as I tried to climb to my feet.

I felt someone watching me and slowly lifted my head.

My neighbor, in curlers, a fuzzy bathrobe, and bunny slippers, stood there with arms crossed. A cigarette dangling from her lips, she clutched a newspaper and watched me with judgmental eyes.

Huh. Wonder how long she'd been standing there, letting me drool all over myself?

Not that I'd expect any less from her.

Oh my gosh, what time was it?

I nodded her way, then pushed myself up the wall, checking my pockets for keys. Once I found them, I stumbled inside, locked the door, and leaned against it, breathing heavily.

I checked myself all over, but I still had everything non-vampire related—my wallet, ID, debit card, cash for emergencies—but the few things I carried for protection were all gone. I didn't want to go to work jangling with vampire-hunting paraphernalia, but I also hid a few things about my person each day, just in case.

A thought hit me, and I yanked back my sleeve.

Bright and too real to be ignored, a gash ran up the length of my arm, wrapping gone. The gash I'd gotten when they'd grabbed me.

It had been real. I'd been in a vampire's lair. Again.

I stumbled into my kitchen and worked around the mess to make myself some instant coffee. I cooled it down with oat milk and creamer, guzzled, and made another. I repeated this until my brain was officially awake and ready to start making decisions.

Unfortunately, that meant it proceeded to beat me up for

going to see Vampire Bob in the first place and writing the first article, scream at me for putting myself in danger when no one knew where I was, and finally, berate me for going against my word to Gavin. And my boss. And Detective Sawyer.

Oh my gosh, Gavin! Had he called me?

I scrambled for my phone, but once again, I couldn't read a blasted thing on my broken screen. I dropped it in disgust.

I rubbed my hands down my face and groaned.

Okay, so new plan. Put a second article on that site ASAP, get my phone fixed, especially since that Paris trip was coming up, and drop in on Gavin.

Hopefully he actually had today off.

CHAPTER THIRTY

I totally didn't go see Gavin. Nope, I chickened out like a big, fat, lazy chicken.

Instead, I wrote an article—all vague, no way could this thing be traced to me—and laid out all the facts. Those I'd seen with my own two eyes, and those the other vamp had told me.

My article ended with a plea that if anyone knew anything about the situation, the alleged vampire covens in the city, or the missing Mr. Withers, to please contact *Missing News*.

I snorted. Yeah, like this thing would get any views.

I spent way too much time trying to upload the article—they were doing some kind of update or the site was running stupid slow, because it took for-eh-ver to do the simplest tasks. But soon the second vamp would have no cause to kidnap me again. I hoped.

Then I made my way to the nearest phone store. I was getting a new phone right now this very second, and I wasn't going to step on it this time.

As I was opening the door, my phone in my coat pocket

vibrated against my hip. I let it fall closed and stood right there in front of the door to dig my phone free.

Apparently I stopped in someone's way because they shoved me aside. I mumbled an apology and attempted to answer my broken phone.

It finally swiped open after trying to embed glass shards in my thumb.

"Yes? Hello?"

"Candace, where are you?" Stan demanded.

I craned my whole body around the corner to read the shop signs hung in the wraparound window, even though I realized belatedly it was probably on the door in front of my face. I told him the store name and started looking for the closest street sign, because I had to give my exact location like that.

Stan cut me off mid-street designation with a huff. "Yes, yes, fine. Why are you *there* instead of *here*?"

I frowned. "Well, I dropped my phone, then kicked it under my couch—no, wait, was that the last time I broke it? Anyway, then I stepped on it. There's this crazy-long crack running right down the middle and spider-webbing out everywhere and I can't see a blasted thing on the screen and it's been like this for *months* and I thought, with the Paris trip coming up, that I probably should—"

"Candace, stop! Couldn't this have waited until after work?"

He started yammering on about layouts and Vera being mad and keeping up a good reputation by being on time, but my pulse was pounding so loudly in my ears, everything else turned into buzzing background noise, and I could just imagine a camera zooming in to my panicked face.

If this were a movie, of course.

I was supposed to be…at work? Right now?

Swallowing didn't do a thing for my bone-dry throat. "Um, Stan? Isn't today my day off? Isn't it Monday?"

I mean, I couldn't check my phone, but I was pretty sure it was.

I swear that's what my computer said. Had I even looked, though?

I'd been pretty out of it from my second dose of chloroform, or whatever that had been.

A long pause followed my question, where he'd either hung up on me or I'd passed out. I checked my screen, but no help there.

"Oh, girlfriend," he said, his voice pitying. "You are in so much trouble."

I shrieked and took off running for the nearest subway stop.

Dodging more people than I ran into, I made it to the subway station just before my train left. I elbowed people aside and barreled on board—who said I couldn't assert myself if necessary?—and collapsed on the nearest sticky, gross seat.

I usually stood on these things, but my flight had left me shaky and sweating.

I was so dead.

How on earth had I gotten my days off mixed up like that?

I was so good at being on time. Planning ahead. Putting reminders literally everywhere so I knew where I needed to be and was there well before people would start looking for me.

This was bad on so many levels.

I looked down at myself. Oh, great. My messy, non-designery, non-fashionable self was going into work. Like this?

Old jeans, frizzy hair in a messy bun, an oversized sweatshirt that almost didn't fit under my old brown leather jacket I'd gotten at a thrift store in college—*not* the one I wore to work, ever. Definitely no makeup. Had I even looked in a mirror?

This day could not get any worse.

⁂

I blazed into work, hands shaking, sunglasses askew with a smudge I could *not* see through on one side, clothes sticking to my sweaty, gross skin from running the whole way from the subway, completely beside myself that I'd gotten my day off wrong.

With sleeping in and taking hours fiddling with that stupid website—which *oh my gosh* was totally dated today and time stamped for when I was supposed to be working—if anyone down in HR was looking into reasons to fire me, that would about do it—I wasn't just a little late for work.

Oh no. I was hours late.

For a normal job, people would be going home in an hour or so. Here, I might get in a few hours of work before the office started to clear.

I rounded the corner to find Stan, Lola, and some intern I didn't recognize bent over my layout table, hard at work piecing things together and trying out colors and textures and patterns and themes.

They were apparently working the old-fashioned way—which I often preferred—with actual photos and cloth swatches instead of using the virtual features of my table.

That meant it was serious. A piece of the magazine that had to be even better than perfect, because it went closer to the front pages, was a main feature, or was a project near and dear to Vera's heart.

Or Vera was having us redo something.

Oh my gosh, they'd be going over the lead-up into Fashion Week, the one that prepared everyone for next month's New York, London, Milan, and Paris circuit, and I wasn't even there to help.

Tears filled my eyes, and my chin trembled.

Stan looked up right then.

Way to betray me, chin.

Lola also glanced up, and I wasn't able to read her expression in the brief glance she gave me, but when she looked back down quickly, I could've sworn she was hiding a slight smile. Maybe Stan had said something funny?

Stan very obviously sighed and waved me in, and I rushed toward my doom.

I swung open the silent glass door. "Stan, I am so sor—"

He shook his head. "No time for that. You"—he pointed at the intern—"get her coffee."

Guilt made an instant appearance, and I just wanted to apologize to the intern. I mean really, I didn't deserve coffee, even if I totally could use one.

She nodded and ran out of the room.

"You"—Stan pointed at Lola—"keep doing what you're doing."

She didn't even acknowledge him as she kept steadily working.

"And you." Stan pointed at me, and my stupid chin went visual again. Ugh. His stern look softened a little, and Lola gave me a look like I'd done that on purpose—I totally hadn't! "Come here."

I made my way over and accepted a Stan hug. He kissed my forehead.

"There you are."

Tears made their presence known by clogging up my voice and making it sound like I had a stuffy nose. "I really am so sorry, Stan. I messed up."

He kissed my forehead again and released me. "Just don't let it happen again, young lady," he said sternly and handed me another clean handkerchief.

Lola rolled her eyes in the background.

"Now, let me see your phone." Stan held out his hand.

I handed it over and turned to the layouts, getting right to work while I was sweltering in all the winter layers I hadn't taken off yet.

I might have also been prolonging revealing the sweatshirt for as long as possible.

He tisked and pulled my attention back. "Oh, dear, you're right. This is horrible." He eyed me over his glasses. "How can you possibly use this thing?"

Already laser focused, I shrugged and started rearranging a few things to my liking. More accurately, to Vera's liking. This probably had more to do with my hiring than anything else. I got her. I got her vision.

And I delivered what she liked.

I answered Stan offhandedly. "I pretty much can only answer and hang up when someone calls. Can't see texts or emails or anything else. I use my computer for that."

Lola added a swatch of bumpy muslin in eggplant purple.

"Oh no, not that one," I corrected. I switched it out for smooth satin in the same shade. "Here, this one. Vera doesn't like that texture with that color."

Lola flushed a little. I'd only seen it once or twice, and she only turned the lightest shade of pink I'd ever seen—I'd kill to barely blush like that instead of going straight for volcano red—which meant she was embarrassed not to have remembered.

I smiled at her. "It's okay. It took me a while to figure out which textures and patterns she likes with which shades, but you'll get it."

"Thanks," she said in a tight voice, with a vicious glare.

Oh no. I'd said something wrong again. But what?

My mind scrambled, but all I could figure out was that I'd been trying to be helpful, encouraging, helping her not feel bad, but had somehow messed up on one or all of those things. But which one?

Of course, she'd been here about the same amount of time I had...maybe she was just embarrassed she'd forgotten?

Although we'd interned together, since I'd gotten the head layout position, I'd gone through an intense training period, since most people worked their way up.

Apparently Vera had seen something in me she liked, something she wanted for her company, and I couldn't let her down. I couldn't. Even if it was hard to admit to myself, I did have an eye for design, layout, and photography, and those were the classes I'd excelled in at college.

If only I'd known at the time to major in them instead of flitting from major to major and taking extra time to work my way through college and pay for it all myself.

In a twist I hadn't seen coming, I'd actually landed a job that made saving and not going into debt super easy. Thank God.

And there my mind went, wandering again.

I turned back to Stan in time to see an appreciative look on his face. "You've blossomed in the time you've been here, Miss Marshall. I'm proud of you."

And there went my face, just trying to prove it could blush brighter than Lola's ever could. Ugh.

With a grimace, I started to take off my jacket. Sweat was worse than revealing this outfit, though I really wish I didn't have to in front of Stan.

He took me in from head to toe, then deliberately went back to the layouts.

Oh, thank goodness.

My face continued to burn, though. He didn't have to say anything for me to know what he was thinking.

The intern popped back in with a lidded cup, steaming out its single opening. "Let me get that for you."

She wrangled off my coat the rest of the way with one hand, nearly sending me to the floor in a tangled mess of twisted leather, then handed the recyclable cup to me carefully.

Her bright eyes met mine. "Just how you like it, Miss Marshall."

I gave her my deer-in-headlights look, startled at being called Miss Marshall by someone younger than I was. It made me feel old, not like a cherished daughter when Stan said it or a respected coworker when someone else said it.

Since when did I feel old around other adults?

I mean, I was in my mid-twenties, but this girl had to be what? Twelve? Fourteen? Um, eighteen? I was terrible with ages. How old did you have to be to intern here?

Whatever it was, she didn't seem old enough.

After she tucked away my coat, she beamed at me and moved closer, an eager look in her eyes. "Is there anything else I can do for you?"

Oh my gosh, had I been like that as an intern?

I backed up into my table and wondered if there was a kind way to ask her to step away from me and look at someone else like that.

I was *not* someone to look up to.

Stan handed her my phone and shooed her away. "Take this to the nearest store and get it repaired. Use the company card."

She was only too eager to run off and obey our every whim—after giving me a beaming smile, of course.

I turned my wide-eyed stare on Stan.

He shrugged. "We need to be able to reach you."

I flushed, my faux pas in the forefront of my mind again, but Stan still mercifully kept his attention off me—well, possibly my clothes—and onto the layouts, and we all got to work.

The intern, whatever her name was, arrived some time later, breathless. She handed me a bag stuffed full of papers and boxes.

She'd apparently gotten anything and everything the salesman had told her I needed. Wireless earbuds, wall charger, touchless charger, car charger—I didn't even own a car—wireless docking station, speakers for the docking station...

Oh my gosh, this must've cost a fortune!

Stan looked as though he couldn't have cared less, and Little Miss Intern started gushing.

"The guy said there was nothing they could do—apparently it was internally damaged, and he had no idea how you were still using it—so he backed everything up and said as soon as you sign into this one, you'll get all your apps and contacts back. Oh! And he factory reset the other one so that your personal information is safe." Her excitement ratcheted up a notch. "So you have a new phone! Isn't that exciting?"

She clapped her hands with a little bounce.

"Oh, thank you!" I gushed. I snatched everything from her hands, dug out my new phone, and stepped to the side to sign in as fast as I could.

I immediately texted Gavin. *Hey, guess what? I got a new phone! I can text again!*

I most definitely overused the dancing emoji, but that didn't stop me from wielding it once more.

And then I pulled up my notes app. Then my messages. Then my contacts.

My heart dropped. Oh no.

Half my stuff hadn't transferred. Mysterious texts from Anders, contact info for Mr. Withers's workplace, unsupported notes app that I used before I had my vamp notebook, all gone.

And then Gavin's text was returned undeliverable.

I felt like I'd been sucker punched. I looked at the intern a bit desperately. "I need my old phone."

Her face fell like I'd crushed all her hopes and dreams for life, but Stan waved off my words as he stayed bent over his task. "Oh, that old dinosaur needed replacing ages ago. Believe me, you'll be thankful once you see all the new upgrades."

"My phone wasn't *that* old…" I muttered.

Well, actually it was. I tended to run my phones into the ground, waiting till they no longer were supported to replace them.

Or in this phone's case, until I stomped it into the ground and could no longer even access it.

I loved new tech, I really did, but I also loved saving money, and replacing my phone every year seemed excessive, even for me.

I shook my head and turned back to the intern. "I'm sorry, but can you please get my old phone for me? I have important information on there…"

My voice trailed off. Not if they'd factory reset it, I didn't. I groaned and dropped my head into my hands. All that work, gone.

The intern sounded unsure. "He said there was nothing else he could do…"

I gave her my brightest, fakest smile. "It's okay. Thank you for everything you did for me. I appreciate it. Really."

Her smile was back, though a little unsure, and I turned away, trying not to cry.

They didn't understand.

Not only was a huge chunk of my vampire research gone, I'd forgotten Gavin's phone didn't accept calls and texts and emails like a regular phone. No, only approved numbers could get through to him. Important people, like his agent, his assistant, and…me.

Although my new phone had the same number, the device itself wouldn't be recognized and would now bounce back any of my calls or texts. As I'd been so rudely reminded of. It was a miracle Jemma had gotten through to his assistant.

And I didn't know when I'd see him again.

My badge to get on set, my digital key to his apartment building—not his suite of rooms, just the building itself—were both on that phone and wouldn't upload to the new phone, even with the transfer of info.

The number for Mr. Withers's boss, for the morgue, for Detective Sawyer—I was going to have to find it all again. They were in my recents, not my contacts.

Throat burning, I threw myself into my task until I could get home and try to repair all the damage the poor, clueless intern had unwittingly done.

Hopefully I'd written as much as possible in that stupid vampire notebook.

And hopefully Gavin would call or text me soon.

CHAPTER THIRTY-ONE

Before Stan left, he had two instructions for me. One, take a quick break and grab something fashionable from the closet downstairs. And two, check my emails.

I was insanely curious, so I checked my emails first.

There was one from Jackson, with instructions for the main feature next month.

My mouth fell open. Main feature? What main feature?

From the hazy past came a conversation I'd had with Vera, when she'd asked me to go to Paris Fashion Week. (Which was almost here! Squeal!)

She'd mentioned a main feature, but I'd been too focused on Paris. Was this what she'd meant?

Jackson's email detailed how to set up for the shoot, which kind of shots to include in my list, how to corral the models—which would be about a thousand times harder for me since they all swooned when he walked by and followed blindly wherever he led—and insisted I have it all done well beforehand. He'd only have enough time to come by and support the shoot before he was on a plane to Paris.

At the end, he asked me to stop by after work so we could go over it all in person.

I gasped aloud several times, my mouth well and truly wide open while reading.

"Main feature? What main feature?" Lola said from right over my shoulder.

I screamed and smacked her, still jumpy from being grabbed yesterday.

She beat a hasty retreat from my flailing arms and crossed hers. "Get a grip, Marshall. What. Main. Feature?"

She was scowling, but she looked more…worried?…than upset.

My heart still pounded like it was trying to run away, but I tried to laugh. "Oh, something Jackson recommended me for. I think? I don't know. I'm supposed to go see him about it…"

My eyes were back on the email, reading it again. I just couldn't believe it!

"Good for you." Lola grabbed her coat and left, which I realized when the elevator dinged.

I glanced up. "Oh, but Lola, you need to put away the…"

But she'd already gone, and I was the only one left on our floor.

I sighed. "I guess I'll just do it, then?"

It wasn't like her to leave tasks undone, but she'd helped me so much lately, I quickly straightened up, skipped the closet (Stan had gone home anyway), and rushed down to see if Jackson was working as late as I was.

Giddy with nerves—could I run a main feature? Me?—I let off a nervous laugh as I realized how very alone I was up here. I was usually too busy working to notice. A quote from one of my favorite shows ever, *The Dick Van Dyke Show*, popped into my head.

Dick Van Dyke had once said, in his best Dracula voice, "It's like being the last living cell in a dead building" when the writers were working late, and yes. It felt exactly like that.

Now to see if this email was some kind of hoax.

I bounced on my toes all the way to Jackson's floor.

Totally not a hoax.

The moment I saw Jackson, I pulled up his email and pointed at it. "Is this for real?"

Jackson, who was indeed working late, gave me a hesitant smile. "Oh, hi, Candace. Good to see you too."

I rolled my eyes and wiggled my phone. "Seriously. Did you send this to me?"

He gave me a laid-back, tired grin. "I did."

I bounced and barely refrained from squealing. "Really?"

I may have clasped my hands under my chin, but I would admit that to no one.

His grin widened. "Really. You have time to go over procedures now?"

"Oh, absolutely."

I claimed my chair, the one I'd edited Gavin's face in last time, and it was all I could do not to spin it around constantly. Hey, when I was excited, it just seemed to pour out of me physically, okay?

"So as I said, it's a shoot for Distance, a big deal, a main feature, and you're taking the lead."

I did *not* squeal. But I wanted to.

"I would be there to oversee, of course, but I already got permission from Vera to steal you for the time. You'd be in charge of background, setup, directing the team, putting the whole shoot together."

I pulled up the notes app—okay, I admit, my new phone was absolutely gorgeous—and started taking copious notes, even though he'd already emailed me. I didn't want to forget a thing.

"Stan assured me layouts would be taken care of—in fact, you can do the whole thing, if you want. Shoot, edit, layout, and submit to Vera. I hear there's a possibility of promotion too."

He rubbed the back of his neck and shrugged as if to downplay the hugeness of the opportunity he was just handing me here. For no reason.

"To be honest, I could use the assist. And who knows? If it works out, if layout can spare you, I don't know. Maybe we could work together. In the future."

"I would *love* that."

He smirked. "Let me show you my process."

We went over his checklist, of which he gave me a copy—my eyes got huge and he smiled and assured me that yes, he was giving it to me on purpose, and yes, I could use it anytime I liked and make it my own however I saw fit—and he showed me how to stage set design, who to hire if flowers or balloons or other props were needed, and what to do if snow was still on the ground, since it was an outside shoot.

It was a lot of information, but thankfully my brain hyper-focused on it, and I took copious notes. I was going to nail this thing.

Then he pulled up some photos and showed me how to edit them with his own program, something all his own that Vera was especially fond of and that gave our magazine an even more unique edge on other fashion magazines.

No wonder Vera had snatched him up. This man was a genius.

We were deep into editing when he started fiddling with everything in sight.

"So, um, I was wondering…"

My head came up, and I smiled at him. "Yes?"

His eyes took in my face a bit too intimately, but I shook

it off. It was just because we were sitting so close and were such good friends and had been working together for so long down here tonight. It was nothing.

He swallowed. "I hear you're going to Paris too?"

I nodded enthusiastically. "I mean, not London or Milan. They need me here to get the next issue out. But Paris, yes, definitely. Why?"

"I was wondering…"

And he just stopped, right there. I waited, a tad impatiently. I didn't handle suspense well. Give it a few more seconds, and I'd be bouncing in my chair.

"If I could take some pics with you while I'm there?" I guessed hopefully.

"Yeah." He blew out a long breath. "And if I could show you some of my favorite places."

My mouth fell open and just hung there.

He started nervous-talking, something I was all too familiar with. "You know, if you want to. Only if you want to! We could grab dinner a few nights—when we're not working, of course—maybe take a few extra days to see some touristy sights: Notre Dame, Opéra Garnier, la Tour Eiffel, maybe Versailles, if we have time for the hour-long train ride. Then there's Disneyland Paris, if you're into that kind of thing, but that's a full day trip, so I really don't see that happening…"

I still wasn't capable of words.

He shrugged. "You can say no, of course. I know it's a business trip, not pleasure, but you can't go to Paris for the first time and *not* see at least a few famous landmarks. And, well, I'd love to be the one to show you."

He fiddled with his standing mouse, not making eye contact.

"Jack, are you sure?" I couldn't help asking, but I had to admit, I was ecstatic. No way was I turning this down. It was Huge with a capital H.

Someone who had been there before? Yes, please.

"Of course I'm sure." He gave me that laid-back grin that had girls at my college sighing in despair and running into their lockers.

I'd only done it the one time, okay? My roommate was the one who'd made a habit of it. She'd been completely head over heels for him, and he hadn't known she existed. Anyway.

He hadn't changed much since then. Well, except for his awful nickname. Jackson was just so much better on so many levels.

But, I got it. I really did. New city, new persona. Making a new life.

So I'd respect that and correct myself when I called him Jackson instead of Jack eight thousand times a day.

When I finally realized he was serious and wasn't going to yell "psych!" or laugh at me, I squealed and bounced to my feet, beside myself with joy. I'd been waiting for an opportunity like this for most of my life.

The photography, yes, but also Paris.

He stood too, that lazy grin on his face, and I threw my arms around him and, without thinking, smacked his cheek with a giant kiss.

"Thank you, Jackson, er, Jack. You won't regret this! And I can't wait to see Paris with you."

I felt him tense, and his hands immediately went to my waist. I pulled away, but he stopped me.

Then before I even knew what was happening, he was kissing me.

It was soft, gentle, embodying all the longing I was just now realizing he'd held for a long time. Since college, possibly.

When he'd first tried to get me to work with him.

I just stood there like an idiot, no idea what to do, as my

friend, confidante, and coworker kissed me. And man, was he a good kisser.

My brain yelled at me—*Danger, danger, danger!*—like a klaxon siren, but it apparently bypassed my fight or flight instinct and went straight for freeze.

He pulled back, a dazed look in his eyes, probably matching my own. Then he started to head in for round two.

I placed a hand on his firm chest and pushed myself away from him. *What was that?* my brain was screaming. All I managed out loud was "Wha—?"

He looked sheepish and...triumphant. He let out a nervous laugh. "I've been wanting to do that for a long time."

"But, but—I'm with Gavin?" My voice rose as I pointed off to the side, even though Gavin was nowhere near me.

His jaw tensed, and his eyes flashed. "Candace, when are you going to stop dating guys who put everyone else before you? Who keep putting you second?"

"I'm not...I haven't...I don't..."

"Because believe me, he's putting everyone and everything else before you, including his career, and just expecting you to be there when he crooks his little finger. He only makes time for you, what? Once a month? If that."

My mouth was hanging open again, and I attempted to sputter indignantly.

And how on earth did he know that? Were the gossip rags following our relationship *that* closely?

He swallowed, his voice turning husky. "Can't you choose what *you* want for once? Can't you choose someone who will treat you well and will show you that you're his world? Someone who won't keep putting his career before yours? Someone who isn't too busy to make time for you?"

Tears filled my eyes. Gavin wasn't doing that. He wasn't. Sure, he'd been busy—we both were—but Jackson didn't have all the facts.

He looked at my mouth again, leaned forward, and I jumped back.

"I, uh, I…ve gotta go."

"Candace…" He reached for me.

I jerked away, immediately regretting the hurt that flared in his eyes.

"And, I'll, uh, thanks for the opportunity, but maybe I shouldn't…"

His mouth fell open. "You think *this* was because of *that*?"

Well, um, yeah. Duh. I gave him a look. Probably shouldn't see Paris with him either.

His jaw went hard. "I recommended you for that opportunity because you're one of the best photographers I've ever seen, not because I wanted to use you. It's yours, no matter what does or doesn't happen between us. I believe in you and want you to succeed, no matter what."

I didn't know what to say to that.

Hurt filled his face and bled from his eyes. "Why can't you see yourself like I do? Why can't you see how wonderful you are. How…perfect…you are. Candace…"

He advanced a step, and I backed up a step, the standing desk halting me from further retreat.

"Why can't you surround yourself with people who will support you, encourage you, build you up, not tear you down and make you think you're worthless? Because you're not. You have no idea how much light you bring to everyone around you. Why can't you be with someone who appreciates you for who you really are?"

I shook my head, tears clogging my throat.

"Someone like me," he whispered.

Tears made their way onto my face. "Oh, Jackson…"

And with that, I grabbed my bag and bolted like an entire coven of vampires were chasing me.

CHAPTER THIRTY-TWO

I blindly made my way to my apartment, aching for Jackson. Hating the way I'd hurt him. Regretting that I couldn't return his feelings.

But he was so wrong about Gavin. He had to be. We were still getting to know each other, still in the honeymoon stage of dating, sure, but we both respected each other and the life we'd carved out for ourselves. Didn't we?

I wrapped my arms around myself, shivering, wishing I'd grabbed my jacket, but I'd just left it like a dummy.

I needed to tell someone—no, talk to someone, more accurately. Ask for advice. About everything. But I'd been so busy, my few friendships from high school or college had slipped away.

Gavin was busy. Besides, I couldn't contact him anyway. I glanced down at my phone, then scrolled through my contacts. Peter? No way. How did I still have his number? My brother? Nope. Not even. Jack? That would just make things worse.

Just friends. Yeah right.

Jemma? My finger hovered over the screen. She may have been my best friend from college—pretty much my only close friend—but I hadn't spoken to her since she'd gotten married and I'd moved to Acción and been chased by zombies.

And the last time I'd called her, I'd begged her to bail me out of jail.

She'd probably kill me if I called her again, just because I was in trouble.

My shoulders slumped. I didn't have anyone to talk to.

I was terrible at keeping in touch. I hated talking on the phone, and I was pretty certain if I ever met the guy who'd invented texting, I'd kiss him on the spot. Best invention ever.

But Jemma didn't text. And I didn't call. Well, anyone but Gavin, that is. Or for work things. She had to be mad at me. But I was so desperate to talk to someone about this. Maybe she'd forgive me if I just—

My phone rang, blaring music, *not* on silent as it should've been. Then again, I hadn't had a chance to make it completely mine yet. I shrieked and threw it straight up.

No! Bad! New phone! I couldn't break this one *the day* I'd gotten it.

Gavin's name flashed by my face. Gavin? Hope swelled, and I sucked in a quick breath. *He* was calling *me*? Finally! I couldn't help my smile.

I snatched at it five or six times before I actually caught it, providing great entertainment for those who'd stopped to stare at the freak juggling her blaring phone.

Thanks, random strangers.

Several people laughed, one clapped, and I couldn't resist a bow before I spun away and fumbled to answer. "Yes! Hi? Hello?"

"Candace?"

I melted a little. His voice just did that to me. "Yes, yes, it's me. Is it you?"

I smacked my forehead, face awash in burning flames. Did I seriously just say that?

"Is everything okay? You sound a little breathless."

And he sounded like he was smiling, probably holding back a laugh. As usual. Normal. Normal was good.

I immediately held my breath and let it out slowly, trying to regulate the air I was sucking down. Didn't want to do anything weird in front of Gavin Bailey. On the phone.

All holding my breath did was make me gasp for air, desperate to get more.

"What? No, I'm fine. How are you?"

I hadn't meant to ask it. But it was polite, and my grandma had taught me above all things to be polite. I was bursting to talk to him. To just curl up at his side, tell him everything, and just let it all out and soak up his advice.

His heavy sigh told me that might not happen.

"Not good."

A thousand alarm bells went off, and I wanted to ask a million questions and crawl through the phone to make sure he was okay.

As my brother the Trekkie would say, why on earth hadn't they invented transporters yet? Okay, maybe that was me, because he always gave me a scientific explanation why they weren't possible yet while I was all huffy from crazy traffic.

Gavin kept talking, oblivious to the many tangents that often went off in my head. It was when they came out that it was a problem. Or when I zoned out. Like now.

"Hey, do you think we could get together today?" he asked.

"Of course! Is that even a real question? Do you want to meet somewhere? Go out?" *Catch up on the last million dates you've had to cancel?*

"I'd rather come over, if that's okay."

No "I love you," no sweet talk, no happiness that usually laced his voice when he talked to me.

Oh. My. Freaking. Goodness. He'd heard about Jackson, hadn't he? Somehow, he already knew, and I hadn't even had the chance to tell him first.

No, that couldn't be it. It had literally just happened.

And it couldn't be about the vampire craziness, could it? I hadn't told anyone about getting kidnapped a second time. Or, you know, seeking them out myself right before that.

Um, maybe he was just tired?

Now I was lying to myself. I had to face this. Whatever it was.

I tried to speak past my bone-dry throat. "That's always okay. You know that. What time?"

"I'll be over in thirty." His voice still hadn't lightened. "I'm on my way now."

I yanked the phone away from my ear and stared at the time. Oh crud. I'd be lucky to make it home by then.

"See you there?" he asked.

I forced a light smile, hoping it came through my voice. The light part, not the forcing it part. "Yes! See you! There."

"Thanks, Candace."

The line went dead. And I took off running.

✗

The elevator was down for maintenance. Again. Of course.

I dragged in another breath and tackled another flight of stairs. I could do this. I was in shape. Kind of.

And then I started to sweat. Great. Just great.

I sucked in another breath and vowed to myself to begin working out. Immediately.

When I made it to my floor—the 17th floor—I seriously hoped I'd have enough strength to make it to my door.

Without Gavin seeing me.

I stumbled down the hall, gasping for air, struggling to get my phone out, hoping if anyone saw me they wouldn't think I was dying or drunk and call the cops.

Twenty-seven minutes.

"Hah!" I gave a feeble fist pump, my victory shout practically soundless and using up far too much oxygen. I had three minutes.

It was uncanny how Gavin arrived exactly when he said he would, even in New York City.

I fumbled with my keys, praying for a traffic jam, praying for Gavin's watch to be off—in my favor—praying for a miracle.

The door next to mine opened. And my neighbor stepped out. Bathrobe, slippers, and hair curlers. Phone present and casually aimed in my direction. As always.

I'd never demanded to know if she was recording me, but I had a hunch. Once I worked up enough courage, I'd say something. I would.

Someday.

I nodded, hoping she didn't expect me to speak, and tried to find the right key harder. Since when did I have so many keys? I had one apartment and no car, for heaven's sake!

She eyed me up and down. "You should get rid of some of those keys, young lady."

I smiled halfheartedly, trying to be polite, but I just didn't know if I could stand to be criticized over One. More. Thing.

And Gavin would be here any second. I tried another key, my trembling fingers not obeying my totally freaked-out mind. *Just go in already!*

"That's...good idea, Mrs. Kennedy. Maybe they'll get... keyless entry...like they've been teasing...for so long, eh?"

My words came out all breathless, most of them not even there.

I may have jammed the next key in harder than I meant to. What did they all go to? And why did they all look the same? Though it could have been all the hair and sweat in my eyes…

She snorted. "Only make our rent go up. My sister told me—"

"Come on, come on, come on."

I didn't realize I'd said it aloud until I noticed she was looking at me rather strangely. I offered a somewhat feral grin and got back to it.

"You look terrible." My eyes shot to hers as she leaned forward and sniffed. "You smell terrible too."

Yep, that was my neighbor for you. Obnoxious.

"You don't smell like you've been drinking. Did you spend the night somewhere and forget deodorant?"

Just when I thought my panic had already peaked…

Success! I flung open my door and practically fell inside. "Gotta run, so sorry!"

Certain I'd be hearing about how rude young people were these days the next time I saw her, I slammed the door and ran to my bedroom, sniffing as I went. I didn't smell terrible, did I? These were my comfy clothes, but they weren't dirty. Then again, I'd run from metro stop to metro stop, then up all these stairs…I *knew* my deodorant was better than that. Still…

I flung clothes every which way—hoping I could distinguish dirty from clean later—and grabbed something that may have matched and hopefully was cute on my way to the shower.

After I took the world's fastest shower and dressed at lightning speed, I remembered Gavin had a key. For emergencies. Or for escaping my neighbor or snoopy reporters quickly.

Yikes! I swiped on deodorant, spritzed body spray—just in case—and rubbed my face clean for the second time. Then I attacked the mess in my apartment.

Oh my gosh, was I sweating again? I blew on my armpits and down my shirt as I threw pillows on the couch, more clothes into my room, stacked books in piles—everywhere—and eyed the kitchen longingly. No way would I have time for that.

My apartment looked exactly the same as it had the last time Gavin had been here, because I hadn't been. I'd been at work. And chasing down vampires. In New York City.

Sheesh. Would he even believe me?

You know, if we weren't having the breakup talk. My eyes welled, and I started to stress sweat in earnest. No, no, no! I wasn't going to think about that! It might not even happen, right?

A knock and I froze. A key jangled in the lock.

I squealed and rearranged the mess, throwing armloads in my bedroom and somehow not making it look any better.

Thank God I hadn't gotten the studio apartment I'd fallen in love with but was somehow more expensive. Only in New York, right?

The door opened slowly, and I heard voices. My heart skipped a beat. *Sic him, Mrs. Kennedy!* I threw in one last armload and kicked it with my foot to try to get my bedroom door closed. Ugh! When had I gotten so much stuff? I didn't even like to shop!

Probably because the design lady at work took pity on my fashion-less self and was constantly bringing me castoffs that "just might fit you" as she looked me up and down with a critical eye.

Once I heard his deep, slightly accented voice, I couldn't stop my foolish grin if I wanted to. Which I didn't. I'd missed him so much!

I sniffed myself one last time, totally freaked out now

about how I smelled—*Thank you, Mrs. Kennedy*—and ran toward the door, fears forgotten.

Pretty sure I smelled fine. Hopefully.

Besides, Gavin had just come from location. He was probably all sweaty and dirty and would need his own shower. This action flick set in the NYC underground of mobsters, money laundering, and strip clubs—wasn't thrilled about that last one—was kicking his butt, and the man was in shape. Unlike me.

Though I was pretty impressed with myself after seventeen flights. Geez, was that even humanly possible? Maybe I was a closet superhero and didn't know it.

I couldn't wait to see him a second longer. I flung open the door the rest of the way, grinning so wide my cheeks hurt, bursting to tell him my news. Well, the good parts anyway. I wasn't sure how to tell him the rest. But I would. Because he'd want me to.

Mournful eyes met mine. My smile froze.

"Are you okay?" I asked right away.

"May I come in?"

I jumped away from the door. "Of course."

He softly shut the door behind him.

Oh my gosh, oh my gosh, oh my gosh. For a second there, I'd forgotten why I suspected he was coming over. Jackson had just *kissed* me. I'd once again gone seeking vampire mobsters, who could murder me and make my body disappear just as easily as human people mobsters. And I hadn't called or texted him because I *couldn't*.

I was Doomed. Capital D.

He strolled in, more subdued than I'd ever seen him in my life, straight to my window and stared out over my glorious view.

"What happened?" I demanded.

He didn't even face me. "I could really use a drink."

"Right." And then I was going to die.

I ran to the kitchen, slipped on something wet, and knocked a mug into the sink when I caught myself. The thing shattered, but I just shrugged. It was dirty anyway. One fewer thing to clean.

And heaven knew my place was *not* in the kitchen. Or anywhere near one.

Oh my gosh, was that pan still out from when pirate vampire dude—I mean, Anders—had cooked me breakfast? Okay, I officially needed to clean in here. Someday.

"I'm fine!" I called, but I didn't hear footsteps headed my way. Hopefully it was because he was used to me by now, not because he didn't care anymore.

Don't panic. Just don't.

I yanked open the fridge. "I have water, milk—no wait, expired"—I tossed the half gallon into the sink on top of the shards and continued my perusal—did I really eat out that much?—"and, uh, water."

I slammed the fridge door and nearly leaped out of my skin to find him standing on the other side.

"Ack!" No matter how many times I screamed in his face, I still hadn't made him jump. The guy was a rock. I raised sheepish eyes to his. "Apparently I haven't been to the store in a while."

His eyes lightened for a sec, and he gave me that half smile I loved so very much. "Then I'll have your finest water, please."

And I almost turned into a blubbering mess right there. I didn't realize how stressed I was about our impending breakup. Er, talk. I meant *talk*.

I turned away so he couldn't see my eyes well up. *"Oui, Monsieur."*

Pretty sure I botched that accent. Oh well. At least I wasn't crying. Yet.

I only broke two glasses in my quest for clean, room-temperature water. I'd only made the mistake of bringing him cold water once. He'd been gracious, but I hated making mistakes. I still occasionally sat straight up in the middle of the night, freaking out about how cold water wasn't good for his vocal cords. Ugh. Issues much?

"Do you want me to—" he began.

"No! I've got this." Or I'd die trying, dang it. Slippery things were just slippery, that's all.

And my hands were shaky for no reason.

I triumphantly handed him his clean glass filled to the brim and tiptoed out of the kitchen, slipping off my shoes so I didn't track glass shards everywhere. A hospital trip was the last thing I needed. Or wanted. Or could even fathom at the moment.

Gavin chuckled. "Guess we'll need shatterproof dishes in our house."

I nearly fell over. Did that mean—he wasn't breaking up with me? And had he just implied…? Nope. Not going there. My default was to ignore significant things.

Like right now. I was definitely ignoring that.

In typical Candace fashion, I covered my flustered, close-to-tears, exploding self with the first thought that came to mind. "Wow, I can't believe you're not even sweaty!"

I'd like to strangle the neurons that fired off that one.

His small smile was back, but his eyes were still sad. I needed to fix that. Immediately.

He ran a hand through his hair. "I took a shower before leaving the studio. A long, cold shower."

My eyes widened. What on earth had happened? Was he okay? Had some bimbo come on to him? I still hadn't been able to purge the image of Miss String Bikini showing off her wares for the entire studio to see—and soon the rest of America.

I tried to ask what happened, I really did, but again, my

mouth took over. Ugh. Couldn't I have one serious conversation with the guy?

Even if I didn't want to know about some hot, sexy costar coming on to him?

I shivered. "I don't even get cold showers. They sound completely miserable. I'm not even okay with a shower unless they're nice and hot and warm and steaming."

Would I please just shut up already?

"But all those stairs!" Apparently not. "How did you make it all the way up here without getting completely drenched? I couldn't even breathe—"

He shrugged. "I took the elevator."

Guess he'd learned to jump right in if he wanted to say anything while I was nervous speaking. Good for him.

Wait, what? Elevator?

I spun around. Apparently I'd gone back to cleaning the apartment without noticing. My hands were full of takeout trash.

"Elevator? How'd you use the elevator?"

"Got on as a guy was removing an out-of-order sign. Said he'd forgotten to take it down earlier."

I threw the trash back on the coffee table and fell onto the couch, my legs throbbing.

"You've *got* to be kidding me!"

"Took the stairs, did you?"

At least my stupidity was making him smile. I nodded. "Excuse me if I can't get up the whole time you're here."

He dropped beside me with a chuckle. "All seventeen floors?"

I groaned. "All seventeen floors."

"Oh, Candace." He laughed. "I'm sorry."

"Me too."

He dropped a hand on my leg, and I winced. He started to move.

"Please don't," I muttered. "The pain is worth it."

He pulled my legs onto his lap and began massaging my calves, and I groaned in pain. It almost felt good, but there was so much pain.

"Can I get you anything?"

I gave him a tired smile. "A new set of legs?"

"Hurt that bad, huh?"

I gave him a completely serious look. "I've never been in such excruciating pain in all my life."

He laughed. "Oh, Candace. I love you."

He knew how to put a delirious smile on my face. "I love you too. So much. And I love to see your smile back."

Yes! Good one. I rocked this serious stuff.

His smile vanished. Worry replaced the lightheartedness I'd been able to pull from him, as unintended as it was.

Way to go, Candace. Erase that smile. Remind him of his terrible day. Get dumped.

I gasped. Why he was so upset? I glanced around my messy apartment.

Goodnight, I'd never purposefully invite *anyone* into a place that looked like this. Several months ago, I would've sworn I'd never *live* in a place like this. His personal designer would be horrified.

What on earth had happened?

Oh, right. Crazy work schedule. Crazy vamp schedule. Never home, except to sleep. But how'd I let it get this bad? Would a rat scurry by at any second?

Someone needed to clean this place ASAP.

"I shot someone at work."

I fell off the couch. Literally. Not joking. I'd started to get up to throw away more trash, he'd dropped that particular bombshell, and I just fell over. Like a dummy.

He lunged to help me, and I crawled up him to stand. We stared at each other.

"Shot someone? How?" I was trying so hard to make

sense of it. How was he here and not in jail? Oh my gosh, would I have to bail *him* out?

He sank back against the cushions, and I followed him, perched on the edge, holding his hand. He ran his other hand through his hair and blew out a breath, looking haggard for the first time ever. The premature gray at his temples that I adored didn't help.

"One of the scenes. There was a shootout in a bar, and when the take was over, one of the actors didn't get up."

I gasped. "But—how's that even possible? You're all shooting blanks! And how did they even know it was you?"

He went into teacher mode. As he often did with set-related stuff. "Blanks can still be dangerous, Candace. Scenes have to be blocked out perfectly, you have to be aware of your surroundings, and if a real bullet gets mixed in accidentally..."

I was going to be parched soon from all this gasping. "Oh my gosh, was that what happened? Is the guy okay?"

Now he looked even more miserable. "It was actually a woman. A really good actor, new talent, talk was she could go far."

I gulped. "Could?"

He closed his eyes. "She still hadn't woken up when they'd stabilized her enough to move her to the hospital."

I jumped to my feet. "Then why aren't we at the hospital right now? Gavin, let's go—if we hurry..."

I sprinted past him, but he caught my hand and pulled me back. "No, they sent everyone home. Said we could come in shifts tomorrow during visiting hours."

I dropped back beside him and rubbed his back. "Oh, Gavin, I am so sorry."

He dropped his head in his hands. "I feel like the world's biggest jerk."

"It was an accident," I said in my most stern voice.

"Don't beat yourself up." Like I had any room to talk. "Who did you shoot?"

And there went my mouth again, doing stupid things.

He winced. "My costar, Ava deMais."

Now I winced. Gavin didn't speak badly of anyone, but I'd gathered she was a helping of diva with a side of demanding. Gavin, the studio, and all kinds of people were in heaps of trouble.

"Ava? Aw, man, I'm sorry." Such an absurd thing to say over and over, but what else was there?

Gavin didn't move. "Me too."

"Want to talk about it? I mean, more? Or how it happened?"

He leaned back, dropped both hands behind his head, and blew out a deep breath.

And he proceeded to give me a play by play. I let him talk, asking questions when it seemed it was the right thing to do, wanting more than anything in the world to help him, to be there for him, as he so often was for me.

Hours later, he sat in the same spot, holding my hand, fast asleep.

I soaked in his beautiful face, his chiseled features, his expression that looked kind even in sleep.

I should be taking out a trash bag—or two thousand—and straightening up while he was out. He liked things tidy, and maybe that would subconsciously help him feel a little better whenever he woke up.

My legs screamed at me when I tried to move, so I snuggled closer to Gavin instead. I'd just wake up earlier than him and do it.

He gave a sound of contentment and tugged me closer in his sleep. We fit side by side perfectly.

It wasn't until I was drifting off that I realized I still hadn't talked to him about Jackson or the vampires kidnapping me or the articles I'd written. Oops?

I cracked my eyelids open. More like peeled them, actually, all crusty with sleep nasties. Yuck.

It took me a while to realize what I was seeing, but once it got through my early morning self—in other words, my dead-to-the-world self if I woke up before noon, even with coffee—my jaw dropped.

Spotless. Everything.

I staggered off the couch, legs protesting they weren't ready to get up yet either.

I could see my floor. Not a speck of trash or piles of whatever leftovers remained in my apartment. Somehow.

My bedroom door was even open, and folded clothes sat in great piles on the bench under my window. I rubbed my eyes, but yep, still there.

My dirty clothes were even missing. I gasped. Gavin didn't…touch them…did he? Ack! I wouldn't wish that on anyone. You know what? I wasn't going to think about that right now. I'd search for them later.

Though I half suspected he'd had a service pick them up. I was not that fancy.

I staggered toward the kitchen.

My kitchen was spotless, dishwasher humming happily, a towel piled high with more clean dishes. Broken glass, all of it, gone.

But one thing was missing. A super-important something.

Clean apartment. No Gavin. I sighed.

And I hadn't even told him about my new phone, so I couldn't call him.

Story of my life.

CHAPTER THIRTY-THREE

After work, I fiddled with my phone, staring down at the glorious uncracked shiny new screen, torn about what to do.

Not giving myself a moment to agonize further, I quickly dialed the number I'd had to hunt down once again and shoved the phone to my ear.

Then I jumped up to pace madly.

This time, I waited for Detective Sawyer's surly voice to demand I leave a message—as long as I didn't waste his time—and then for the beep.

"Detective Sawyer?" I said hesitantly. When he didn't respond, I rushed on. "Look, I know you said to stay out of this—so I am!—but I also heard this rumor, tip, gossip, thing...anyway, they said they give their new initiates something to make them appear dead, then remove their bodies from the morgue to bring them into the fold."

I was starting to sweat, but I was also doing all I could not to say the word "vampire."

"Anyway, I just thought you might want to check the morgue for the second body—"

A beep came again, cutting off my message, and I lowered the phone.

There. I'd taken my tip to the police instead of hightailing it down to the morgue myself. Like I wanted to.

I glanced at my phone again. I hadn't said anything about seeing the supposed Mr. Withers alive or about *Missing News*, because that would lead to a whole slew of uncomfortable questions.

Though I'd seriously debated telling him anyway.

Although I'd taken my byline off the website and erased any information that could lead to me, I still had a note in my file about the site at *Voilà Magazine*'s legal department, and I had no idea how long it would take Detective Sawyer to trace the site back to me.

But it would certainly make it easier to just shove both articles the vamp coven leaders had gotten me to write under his nose and let him investigate from there.

Then again, it had taken all my bravery to make the first phone call, and I wasn't certain I could handle another. Especially if he answered.

To distract myself, I pulled out my laptop and went to my website to read both articles again, just to make sure I hadn't forgotten to tell him anything vital, and my mouth dropped.

Both articles had gone viral.

Views were in the millions, they'd been shared thousands of times, and hundreds of comments crowded my site. I knew better than to read them, but I fell into the void of speculating, trolling, joking, encouraging the writer for great fiction, and arguing that vampires were real and when were people going to wake up and see what was right in front of them before they were killed, too?

I may have forgotten about Detective Sawyer entirely.

The next day, again after work, someone knocked on my door. I peeked through the spyhole, squealed, and threw open the door. "Gavin!"

I yanked him inside, then threw myself into his arms.

"I could get used to this whole having a boyfriend again thing," I said into his chest, flushing once I realized I said it aloud.

My eyes popped open, and I frowned. It wasn't that he wasn't returning my hug, he was just kinda stiff and wooden and seemed to be holding me with his fingertips only.

I groaned, pulled back, and smacked my forehead. "Of course! I'm so sorry, Gavin. I didn't mean to be insensitive. How are you doing? How is your costar. Is she better?"

I offered him a sympathetic smile.

Gavin just walked over to my kitchen counter—the one that had bar seats on the other side of the cutout—and he set pictures there, on top of a Manila envelope.

"Hey, what're these?" I smiled and looked down. The smile died on my face.

There I was, kissing Jackson.

Or more accurately, he was kissing me.

My gaze flew to Gavin's, and the heartbreak in his eyes about undid me.

"Can you explain it?" he asked softly, gently, like he wanted to give me a chance.

My mouth fell open. And words came pouring out like I was a bystander, quietly watching a train wreck and waving as it went by.

"First of all, Jackson kissed *me*. Second, who in their right mind was spying on me and taking pictures? Third"—I pounded on my picture's face with my pointer finger—"do you see my wide eyes? My frozen expression? My bewildered look? The fact I was taken by surprise? Who *does* this?"

I covered my face and let out an unflattering wail-groan,

feeling violated. Not only had I not had a chance to tell Gavin myself, now someone had taken that away from me. They'd imposed themselves in a fragile moment and ruined quite possibly the only good thing in my life.

I spoke through my fingers. "I told him I wasn't interested, that I was with you. If they would've stuck around for more pictures, they would've seen me falling all over myself to get away and then running out of there as fast as I possibly could. I even left my jacket! From college! And then you and I never see each other, so the one time we did, when you had enough going on, I didn't want to blurt, 'Hey, guess who kissed me?'"

I choked on a sob.

Gavin pulled my hands away from my face in time to see the epic start of an ugly cry. I mean, when I cry, there are no survivors. My face practically implodes.

His eyes held understanding…and deep hurt. "Hey, I believe you."

I stared at him, ugly cry forgotten, then blurted, "Why on earth would you do that?"

I didn't understand. I'd violated the most important thing to him—trust—and he was okay with that? How?

He looked down, rubbed the backs of my hands with his thumbs. "I, uh, had a little talk with Jack first." He met my eyes then. As well as my hugely open mouth. "That's what he told me too. Even said you tried to turn down the opportunity he'd offered you."

"Oh. Well. Oh." My brain was apparently broken.

"Besides"—he gave me a wry grin—"I get a lot of pictures of Stan hugging you and kissing your forehead. My assistant usually shreds those."

I gasped. "Seriously?"

Well great. She was going to hate me even more now.

He looked part amused and part regretful and part like

he wanted to tear off whoever's face was doing this to me. To us.

But then my eyes filled with tears again. "I'm so sorry."

"So am I," he admitted, then pulled me into his wonderful arms. "I'm sorry I haven't been here for you."

What? No, wait. What?

I pulled back and eyed him. "I never said you weren't." I licked my lips. "Who…?"

He grimaced. "Let's just say Jack had quite a lot to say to me. He wasn't right about everything, but he was right about enough. I haven't been here for you, and I'm sorry."

My eyebrows about lifted off my forehead. How were we not breaking up right now? Was this dude even human?

Jackson's words came back to me then, and I mentally shoved my finger in his face. Ha! See? Gavin didn't put me second.

No, Gavin held me while I soaked his shirt with snot and tears. Poor guy.

A text interrupted my cry fest, and I reached for my phone, wary about missing work after my brush with Stan.

I stopped crying. "Huh."

What can I say? I get distracted *really* easily.

Gavin pulled back and waited for me to speak.

"Detective Sawyer said my tip was good. Looks like body *numero dos* also disappeared from the morgue, which they discovered right before he was supposed to be buried. He wants to know if I had anything to do with it." I snorted. "As if I'd make *that* mistake again."

Oh wait. I absolutely had. So was this the right time to bring that up or not?

Another text popped up.

Once again, my mouth fell open. I could not believe what I was seeing.

"What is it?" Gavin asked.

"Now he's thanking me for the tip. And wants to know if

I've got anything else." I looked up at him. "He actually *thanked* me."

Wonder that the universe was tilting on its axis didn't fill Gavin's eyes, however. Oh no. He was eyeing me a bit warily. "I thought you were going to drop that?"

I flushed, all the way to the roots of my hair, my scalp growing tingly and hot. I squirmed under his gaze, knowing he needed complete honesty. "I was. I am! It's just…I heard something, about the bodies disappearing, and I left a message for Sawyer. Leaving it for the police to handle. Just like I'm supposed to."

I tried to say more, but I quailed under his gaze. I couldn't bear to see his disappointment after he'd just shown me pictures of Jackson kissing me. How could I bring this up without him hating me?

Another text pinged through.

I looked at it a fair bit eagerly to escape that penetrating gaze.

It wasn't that I was willfully keeping it from him. I just didn't know how to begin. You know, without blurting it all out horribly and making everything worse.

"Now he wants me to come down and give a statement." I glanced up.

Gavin grabbed his jacket and gave me a grin that lacked its usual exuberance. "Then what are we waiting for?"

I stopped him. "Wait. Gavin, are we good? Because I don't need to go down there right now. You're more important."

He took my face into both hands and kissed me tenderly, gently. The smile he gave me made my toes curl, although a touch of sadness remained.

Sadness I wanted to erase more than anything.

He wiped the tears still on my cheeks. "We're good."

I threw my arms around him and kissed him as hard as I

could, trying to express just how sorry I was. How grateful. How much he meant to me.

Dear God, I love this man. Please may I marry him.

Heat traveled all the way down to my toes, part embarrassment, part longing. I turned away to fumble around for my own jacket, my nice jacket, and tried to pretend I hadn't just thought that.

I hoped no one, especially those mind-reading vamps, could hear my thoughts right about now.

✗

Statement given, Gavin's car collected, and no hassle from any surly police detectives later, we fell into a routine that was divine.

I went to work, then Gavin either picked me up and took me back to my apartment or his for a gourmet dinner, conversation, and getting to know each other better.

I never wanted these days to end.

Today we were back in Gavin's apartment, ready to spend some time together. We settled on the couch, and Gavin pulled me into his arms.

I leaned back and sighed. "This is nice. I love when you're not working."

Gavin, currently trailing his fingers down my arm, stilled.

My eyes flew wide. "Oh! I mean, it isn't *nice* that you shot someone and had to stop working. I just meant it's nice that we get to spend time together, and I've missed you so much—"

His finger found my lips and gently pressed. "Shh…I knew what you meant."

I sagged. "Thank goodness." I leaned back so I could look him square in his face. "How are you doing?"

He took my hand and kissed it. "I too am happy I get to spend time with my bonnie lass."

My entire self melted as his Scottish brogue came through thick and oh so sexy.

His accent was like a gentle tide, almost unnoticeable now that I knew him so well. So when he brought it out full force…happy sigh.

He chuckled.

Apparently I'd happy sighed aloud.

We sat in front of his monstrous TV, nothing but a fireplace crackling on its screen.

It'd been so long since we'd spent any real time together, we'd immediately moved to our spot, but neither of us wanted to watch anything but each other.

Sappy, I knew, but our time together was precious.

Now how to bring this up…

"Um, Gavin…what Detective Sawyer said…about the missing bodies…what if I…"

"No."

"But if I just…"

"No."

"But I have to…"

He pushed me off him and sat up, turning me to face him.

"Candace, I bailed you out of jail. Jail!"

I squinted at him. Was he making fun of the way I repeated things when I got excited or flustered or nervous?

"They dropped all charges, but next time it could be a felony. A felony!"

Okay, he was definitely making fun of me. Rude. Though he looked completely serious. Oh my gosh, I hoped I wasn't rubbing off on him. One of me was far too many.

I gave him a look, and he grinned, not even a little abashed. Oh yeah, he'd done that on purpose.

"But don't you feel like you have to do something?

Bodies are disappearing, people think they're real vampires, and all of this just doesn't make *sense*."

"I don't think they'll drop the charges again if you meddle."

I spoke out of the side of my mouth in a gravelly, old-man voice. "You darn, meddling kids."

I freaking loved Scooby-Doo. It was about all the scary I could handle.

His half smile said he found that only slightly amusing. "I'm serious, my love. And worse than that, you might get killed." He visibly swallowed. "Don't make me go through that. I can't lose you to this."

I sobered instantly. "Never."

He eyed me. "So you'll stay out of it?"

I gave a single nod. "I'll stay out of it."

His smile lit up the entire world and set my belly on fire.

I pointed at him, mock stern. "But if I get any other tips, I'm calling Detective Sawyer."

"I can live with that." He leaned in to kiss me.

His stupid phone rang.

I groaned. He kissed me anyway.

I melted into him, not even caring about the phone, the world fading to nothing but him, me, and that's it.

He smiled against my mouth and pulled back. "Hello?"

I groaned, eyes still closed.

A voice on the other end said indecipherable words.

"Really?"

My eyes popped open as he undraped my legs from across his and set them gently on the couch. He stood and moved into his ultra-modern kitchen. He listened for a long time before he said anything.

"That's great news! All right, then. See you tomorrow."

He turned to me, eyes shining.

My smile was a little bit dead. "You go back to work tomorrow?"

"I go back to work tomorrow!"

"That's great." It really wasn't. That meant I was going back to being boyfriend-less. Not that I needed to see him every moment of every day. No, just once a week was enough.

Well, not enough. But I'd take it.

And now I wouldn't even get that.

He couldn't sit still as he bounced around the apartment, getting ready for the next day. Okay, well, Gavin didn't bounce—that was me—but he was restless, moving like an incoming tide always seeking, seeking, seeking but not finding what he was looking for.

"So…what happened to the girl? Your costar?" I asked.

He was stuffing workout clothes into a duffle bag. "She's doing great. Apparently there were other factors—exhaustion, an infection she was fighting off, and some diet-related issues—that made it seem so much worse than it was. The bullet hit a non-vital part of her body, which she's recovering from nicely, especially with antibiotics and rest and a balanced diet. Now the investigation is over, and the responsible party has been arrested."

I opened my mouth to ask a question, and he gave me an understanding smile. "That's all I know, and I don't even know how accurate the info is, but my agent said we'll have a court date later for when the person who planted a live round on purpose goes to trial. Everyone on set that day will have to give our testimony then."

I nodded. I definitely wanted more details when he had them. "And Ava?"

"She won't be back for a while—they're going to give her as much time as she needs to recover—but she'll be back in time to finish her shots." He grimaced. "I mean, her scenes."

I snorted. "Yeah, shop talk's not the best anymore, is it?"

He gave me a mild look.

I instantly regretted everything. "Sorry. I didn't mean it that way. I'm just all…" I waved my hands around my head like a crazy person to try to explain all the emotions hounding me at once. "Happy for you? Sad for me?"

His smile was gentle. "You don't have to apologize to me, Candace. How many times do I have to tell you that?"

I threw my hands out and waved them around some more. "It's just what I do, okay? I say sorry as often as I take a breath."

"I know, and I love you. Just know you don't have to around me, all right?"

"Okay, fine. I'll stop saying what I think around you."

"Don't you dare!" He laughed. "You are the most refreshing person I know. I take it back. Don't change a thing."

I smiled. "That's better."

As important as it was for me not to treat him like a movie star, even though he was, it was important for him to accept me just the way I was too.

I'd been trying to change me for years, and I was slowly accepting that it just wasn't going to happen. And I needed to be happy with it.

While still trying not to be so forgetful and apologetic and shy.

And since everyone I'd met in my entire life had tried to change me too, I wanted just one person, just one, to like who I was in spite of myself. And that person was Gavin.

Even though I had a feeling it should be me first.

"Care to celebrate?"

I glanced up, embarrassed I hadn't heard him. "Um, excuse me, what?"

He just grinned. "Care to celebrate? I'll have veggie sushi and sparkling grape juice sent up."

Him, because he didn't drink for serious reasons, and me, because I didn't drink for religious reasons.

He added, "Maybe a cupcake to split from the Cupcake Factory too?"

Because those things were monstrous. And like heaven in your mouth.

I moaned and rubbed my now-ravenous stomach. "Yes, please. That sounds divine."

He turned away to order, and I took a few moments to admire him. How did he make every day I spent with him better than the last?

No matter what life threw at me, I hoped he would be by my side through it all.

CHAPTER THIRTY-FOUR

"Whoa, you look dead."

"Thank you, Lola." I tried to look at her through my sunglasses, but it was just too darn bright.

Once Gavin went back to work, I started having trouble sleeping again. Also stressing nonstop. Because I hadn't heard anything from the supposed vamps in ages, so of course I worried when the next would pop up.

The wild theories and horror stories posted on my website's comment section didn't help.

Lola peered closely at me, trying to see through the dark lenses. "You either have the world's worst hangover, which is doubtful considering it's you, or you're trying out to be one of our models, in which case you'll want to give up right now."

Why was she being so darn loud?

"Don't drink, don't model," I mumbled, trying to make sense of the layouts spread all over the backlit table. Talk about way too bright...

I clicked off the light and rested my head on the corner without realizing I'd done so. Maybe just a quick nap...

She pinched my loose clothes between her bright-red fingernails. "Seriously, have you lost weight?"

I jerked upright. "Huh?"

"Weight. Have you lost it?"

I stared at her until the words made sense. "Oh. Uh, I don't think so?"

She just stared at me, her expression unreadable. "You're hopeless," she finally said.

She clicked the table's light back on just as my body was resting my head on it again without my permission.

I jerked away from the glare and hissed. Oh my gosh, I hadn't been bitten, had I? How had I even made it here in one piece?

"I was wondering the exact same thing," Lola said under her breath, getting to work on the layouts.

I stared at her. Was she a mind reader?

She took one look at me and rolled her eyes. "You said it out loud, stupid."

I was too tired to even notice she'd called me stupid.

Maybe I'd just do what I swore I never would and fall asleep in a bathroom stall for a bit. Or an empty office, if I could find one. I started to slink toward the door. "I think I'll just…"

Stan burst into the room, and I snapped upright, suddenly wide awake.

Or at least suddenly able to pretend I was, anyway.

"Oh, good, you're both here."

I nodded, grinning stupidly.

Stan did a double take. "Sunglasses again? And inside?" He tisked. "Dear, take them off."

I did so, and he stared harder.

"On second thought, you need those today."

I just nodded and slipped them back on. I guess the red eyes I saw in the mirror this morning were actually my bloodshot eyes and not some vampire's.

He slapped paper on our table, and I groaned when a cacophony took up residence in my head. He waved a vague hand in Lola's direction.

"Two aspirin, my office, now."

She was gone in a whirl of high heels, a tight skirt, and expensive perfume.

As soon as she got back, I downed the aspirin, and he got right to business.

"Our front cover shoot is a no-go. The designer apparently stole the designs, they're in litigation, it's a contract nightmare. Vera is throwing things, yelling, crying—you don't even want to know."

I'd never witnessed Vera throw one thing or even raise her voice in all the time I'd worked here, but I didn't question Stan when I was awake; I wasn't about to now. Especially when I had no idea what would come out of my mouth.

He looked at me. "You still have those practice shots?"

I stared back at him, comprehension not making it past my stupid brain.

He crossed his arms and sat back on a chair, shaking his head and peering over his half-rim glasses. "Oh dear. If you're going to get drunk, don't you know you're supposed to do it over the weekend? Well, a weekend we aren't working, anyway?"

I took off my glasses and rubbed my face, several times. I barely felt it. "Not drunk. No sleep."

"No sleep? No sleep! My dear, we're all running on no sleep." He snapped his fingers. Only Stan could do it inoffensively, and he knew it. "Lola, coffee. My office, now."

Her eyes widened. No one drank coffee out of Stan's office. He was a coffee snob, and no one touched his machine but him. And quite possibly Vera.

Though rumor had it even she wasn't allowed near it.

Lola came back all too soon, cradling a steaming cup of dark-brown goodness as though she held precious treasure.

Stan pointed at the cup while looking at me. "Drink. Now."

I didn't ask if it was a bad idea to drink it with aspirin; I just obeyed. Stan did that to people. Especially pushovers like me.

I drained it, feeling a feeble shot of energy, and nodded at him in gratitude.

He was still watching me like I was a dangerous machine about to implode. I probably was. "Now. Practice shots?"

I pulled them out of my locked cubby.

He flipped through them, pulling out a few and spreading them on the table. "This one for the cover, these for interior. Wait, give her this option, too. Think you can manage an article as well?"

I nodded. "Of course."

One thing I could do well was write in my sleep. At least, I sincerely hoped so since that was likely what I'd be doing.

Lola's eyes widened once again, and this time, they stayed wide. She kept looking between us, like she couldn't believe what was happening.

"Practice shots?" she ventured.

Stan nodded, still arranging and rearranging photos. "A new designer sent clothes for our guest model last month. They didn't work for Vera, so after the shoot, I had Candace take some shots while everyone else was packing up. Oh, yes, this one will do nicely."

I grunted, too numb to feel anything close to excitement.

He crossed his wrists, resting them on his knee, and looked at me in pity. "Are you ready for this?"

I nodded. What else could I be? I wasn't about to say no to this opportunity.

I would show my photos to Vera, coming to the rescue when she was in a pinch, and she would be grateful. Impressed.

And I'd most likely get that promotion Stan and Jackson had both hinted at.

Lola looked at me with something like awe, but something else too. A flare lit up her eyes, and she turned away before it could sink into my brain.

"Wow," she said. "I'm so happy for you."

I should've felt the same way, but I was only disgruntled I'd spent most of the last seventy-two hours wide awake and was about to walk into the biggest meeting of my life with a fuse as short and fast burning as Wylie Coyote's dynamite.

Stan, Lola, and I spent the next ten minutes setting up a layout proposal—something Stan rarely did with us—then Stan shoved me out the door with lots of "be brave," "don't let her intimidate you," and "remember, they never found the last employee who made her mad" following me down the corridor.

Stan followed as well, since he was a part of Vera's meetings.

As I padded down the carpeted hallway in my designer flats, I tried to find some excitement. To tell myself I was finally doing something I wanted. And I had a supportive team.

But my own pep talk fell flat. I just wanted to go home and sleep.

And for someone who'd wanted this more than anything else for so long, it surprised me how little I cared.

※

Apparently exhausted me was somehow the best me for the meeting. I was no-nonsense direct, immediately got down to business, and didn't accept any haggling from the department heads. I told them how it was going to be, finished my presentation, and looked to Vera, arms crossed.

Only because I was pretty sure I would fall over and sleep right there on Vera's floor if I didn't stand stiff as a board and hold myself together.

She took me in, eyes lingering on my sunglasses, and gave me an amused smile. "Approved."

I thanked her and left, not even waiting for the others in the room who wanted to discuss "one more thing" or had "just a teensy smidgeon of an idea" or "the smallest quick change ever."

I knew my job, and I was going to do it.

I spent the rest of the day like that, hovering near wakefulness by sheer willpower, a crackling powerhouse, directing everything and setting everything in motion that needed to happen for the shortened timeline of this month's magazine.

I even ate my lunch right there, in my glass cube, for all to see.

It wasn't a conscious decision, really—I was too tired to even attempt the cafeteria, and I needed to stay standing to stay awake. So I sent for a sandwich and ate it, rules be darned.

Lola watched me in something akin to awe, or perhaps respect—maybe a touch of shell shock—as I treated her like my assistant for the first time ever. And she jumped to her tasks and was more helpful than I'd known she could possibly be.

It was a glorious day—if only I would remember it all and somehow replicate this after I slept through my whole day off tomorrow.

As I was leaving, someone tugged on my arm.

I hadn't removed my glasses once today—surely my colleagues thought I was doing this whole new persona thing as they treated me with a newfound respect—so I peered through them hard.

It took a hot minute to recognize Jackson.

I allowed the smallest smile to peek through. My whole face hurt. "Jack."

He released me, suddenly looking sheepish. "Sorry, I just—" He put his hands in his pockets and rocked up on his toes. Something he did when nervous. "Just wanted to say good luck."

I stared at him blankly.

"About the photo shoot first thing Tuesday?" He grinned. "I heard your shots got front cover and main feature this month too. Nice, Candace. I'm proud of you."

I nodded, my face too dead to work properly. "Night."

I turned and walked away, only briefly glimpsing his confusion, then his face slightly crumpling.

Oh, right. The kiss. I was kinda surprised he was talking to me after that, especially if he and Gavin had words. Then again, he was still my professional coworker.

But I was too tired to work through that right now.

The moment I got home, I happily faceplanted on my couch and didn't move until late the next day.

CHAPTER THIRTY-FIVE

I'd barely begun to join the living, stumbling around my apartment like a zombie and grunting when I ran into things, when something scratched at my door.

Probably more zombies.

I looked at it blankly, wondering if I should investigate or go back to bed. I mean, most of my sleep lately had been short cat naps instead of the deep sleep I craved and my body needed, after all. I could use the extra sleep.

Dusk was just beginning to fall outside my window.

A double tap shook me out of my befuddled state, then light footsteps hurried away. I sighed.

Guess if I didn't want my neighbor to snatch up whatever that was, I'd better hurry.

I peeked through my spyhole, but no one stood or crouched on the other side. I eased the door open, and a note fell in. I quickly locked up before seizing it. It was a string of gibberish.

You've got to be kidding me.

I went to my kitchen, made myself some coffee, scarfed down the five strawberries in my fridge that hadn't molded

—after meticulously washing them, of course—and went back to the note.

Who had left this garbage on my front door? And how was I supposed to know what it meant?

It took, like, fifteen years to dawn on me that it was the same code the vampire covens used on the dark web to hide their meeting locations.

In moments, I had my vampire notebook out, had deciphered the string of text, and sat there staring at an address a good hour away, on the outskirts of the Bronx.

In all honesty, the life-altering shoot I was in charge of early tomorrow morning barely flitted across my mind.

I'd be back in plenty of time for that.

Besides, everything was packed and ready to go—all I had to do was grab my gear and show up. The models and assistants had already been briefed, and Jackson would be there for at least a few hours before he had to catch his flight to Paris.

Huh. I wondered who was in charge of the Milan photo shoot this week, since it was usually him. He'd been there for New York's Fashion Week two weeks ago, and had been off to London last week—he hadn't missed Milan and flown here just to be my backup, had he?

My mind hiccuped over my brief interaction with Jackson yesterday, and I barely had time to wonder if I'd been rude in my sleep-deprived state when my mind was back to that address.

Holy freaking Moses. I was *so close* to getting to the bottom of this.

It took me less than three seconds to make one of the worst decisions of my life.

I picked up my gorgeous new phone, cradled it lovingly in my hands, then texted someone I'd sworn I wanted nothing to do with.

I slipped on a knee-length black dress that I could run in and didn't show too much skin. I adjusted the high collar that came to a V at the base of my neck and hoped it covered enough so the vampires wouldn't be too tempted to drain me like a juice box.

I then wedged myself into lined black tights and some super-short running shorts in case I had to—you guessed it—run for my life, then strapped on my mini crossbow and its bolts under the full skirt on one side and the silver dagger in its sheath on the other.

I risked losing them both tonight, especially if they used metal detectors or patted me down, but at least I wouldn't die first thing, right?

My heart pounded wildly, and I barely had time to wonder if I was really going to do this when someone rapped at my door.

I held my breath. That wouldn't be Gavin, would it?

I quickly added pepper spray and a silver letter opener that looked like lip gloss to my black clutch with a wrist strap, slipped on dark flats I could run in, and rushed to the door.

Totally random, but I loved the way my skirt swished around my knees. I twirled it a few times on the way.

I peeked through the eyehole, gasped, and jerked open the door. "What are you doing here?"

Anders just grinned at me. "Why, I'm here to escort you to your ball, milady." He eyed me appreciatively, then took my hand and kissed it. "My, but don't you look lovely."

I snatched my hand back. "You were supposed to meet me there."

He looked affronted. "And let something happen to you along the way? I don't think so."

I rolled my eyes, though his point was legit. "Fine. Let me grab my jacket."

"May I come in?" he asked innocently.

"Um, no." I mean, just in case my previous invitation ever ran out, I was not knowingly issuing it again.

Anders grinned and opened his mouth.

The door next to mine started to creak open, and I gasped and shut my door to just a slit. "Go, hurry!" I hissed. "I'll meet you downstairs!"

He gave me a puzzled look but left, thank goodness, and I saw him give a pleasant nod to my neighbor just before I gently eased my door all the way closed and pretended it hadn't been open in the first place.

I could just picture her curler-laden head scowling at the guy leaving my door who wasn't Gavin. She was probably recording it, too.

I covered my mouth with my hand. How was I going to sneak out now?

And of course guilt showed up and let me know just how horrible a person I was to go behind Gavin's back like this. But I was getting answers, dang it.

Mr. Withers's "Get me outta here, lady," was on a near repeat in my mind lately, I was having nightmares about the next time his dead body showed up—for real, this time—and I couldn't let him live in that dank vampire lair for the rest of his life, however long that might be.

I slipped on my coat, gloves, and scarf, listening till her door shut to ease out.

Holding my breath, I silently shut my door, and the minute the stupid-loud bolt slipped into place, I tore down the corridor and around the corner.

Her door jerked open, and I didn't dare press the button for the elevator until it closed again.

Good thing, too, because I shrieked the moment the elevator doors popped open.

Anders laughed. "Jumpy much?"

Covering my heart with my gloved hand, I took deep breaths. "Why aren't you downstairs? You don't even know how difficult you're making this on me."

He beckoned me in, then pressed the lobby button. "It was easy enough to hold the elevator for you." He gave me a look I couldn't quite figure out. "If you're placing yourself in my world, you need some protection."

I crossed my arms and gave him a look. "And that's you?"

I didn't hear his response, because just before the elevator doors closed, my neighbor rounded the corner, curlers bouncing and pink robe flying. We locked eyes, and the doors slid shut between us.

And I felt like the elevator had just plummeted all seventeen floors.

Oh my gosh. Was she going to contact Gavin somehow and let him know I was going out with someone else? Was *she* the one following me around and sending Gavin incriminating photos? Or hiring it out? I wouldn't put it past her.

I buried my face in my hands and groaned.

Anders stopped talking. "Is everything okay?"

I shook my head and groaned some more. I felt him shift and glanced back in time to see him cross his arms and lean against the elevator wall. "You know, I don't mind if you back out. You don't even know who left you that note. Besides, this underworld isn't the place for one such as you."

He eyed me again, taking in my covered-from-head-to-toe appearance in a style I was just now starting to worry might be too young for me.

I glanced down at myself. Did it look that bad? I didn't go for the slinky, skintight, clubbing look.

"Listen, I'm going. I need to know what happened to Mr. Withers." I changed the subject. "By the way, can you tell me where we're going tonight?"

He just smirked. "Now where would be the fun in that?"

I rolled my eyes and muttered, "Because someone couldn't just give me a straight answer for once. Of course not! Pretty sure the universe would implode if that happened."

He changed the subject. "Now, where we're going, you need to be careful, Miss Marshall. Please don't leave my side, and please don't strike out on your own. Most of the people in the club itself are in no danger, but those who wander are fair game."

A chill swept my insides, and I shivered and huddled deeper in my coat.

The door opened, and he escorted me into the night.

✝

I did *not* like the area Anders took me to.

"Last chance to back out." He eyed me as if I was having the exact reaction he was looking for, a slight smirk on his face.

Okay, we needed to set a few things straight. I stabbed my finger his way, poking him in the chest a few times for good measure.

"I'm not going anywhere. I've had enough! You people have harassed me, made me think I was crazy, and have taken this vampire thing to epic proportions. Enough is enough! If anything I do here can help Mr. Withers, then I'm all in."

His smirk grew into a lazy grin. That just kinda riled me up more.

"I'm serious. It's time I know what's going on. All of it."

His grin hadn't dimmed in the slightest. "Are you sure about that, Miss Marshall? You might not like it."

I huffed and propped my fists on my hips. "I don't like what's happening now! I'm done playing this stupid game where everyone in New York City thinks I'm willing to be kidnapped on the slightest whim."

His smile just got bigger.

He really should consider adding more to his diet than blood. And maybe getting rid of the blood part. He could be rather handsome if he just learned some basic hygiene and bought a few thousand breath mints.

He leaned closer, his voice turning husky and subtle. "It might scare you."

I backed up a smidge. Blood was not good on the breath. "I'm already scared. But now I'm angry. And I'm tired of feeling scared all the time."

He got that look Gavin sometimes gets right before he kisses me. Gavin wore it better.

I blinked. Oh my gosh, was he going to kiss me?

Steel entered my spine. Let him try. I'd deck him.

My thoughts must've come across my face, because he backed up a little. Just not enough for my comfort level.

His voice didn't lose a smidgeon of the smarm, however. "You might not believe me."

I pushed him back to arm's length—I couldn't take one more whiff of his breath.

"I've been scared to death by ghosts"—that was another time I never, ever wanted to think about again for the rest of my life, thank you very much—"pranked by fake zombies who pretended they were going to eat me, and now a gaggle of NYC crime lords want me to believe they are honest-to-goodness, real-life vampires? For the love of doughnuts, give me something real here!"

"Very well." He raised an eyebrow. "Got that key?"

After a startled moment, because I'd forgotten he'd known about that, I dug around in my bag and came up with the ornate key I'd hidden there. I held it up. "This one?"

He grinned. "That's the one. Best keep it close."

I nodded and hid it deep in my skirt's pocket.

Then he held out his hand. "Come with me."

I looked between his hand and his face a few times. "This isn't some kind of trick where I pretend to come willingly but you kidnap me anyway, is it?"

He laughed. "Believe me, Candace Marshall, I don't think anyone could make you go where you didn't want to."

I grumbled a little. Tell that to the line of people I'd let make decisions for me my entire life. I'd done nothing *but* that for most of my life, which is why I was in New York City, trying to live my dream for once.

Then why was I in fashion instead of photography?

I squashed that uncomfortable thought like a pesky bug and took his hand. Then I shook my finger at him like every little granny at church had been known to do once or twice. "This had better not be a prank, young man."

He kissed my cheek, then pulled me after him, laughter in his eyes. "Yes, ma'am."

I flushed as he hauled me down the sidewalk and into a smelly dark alley.

Just my luck, that kiss would be all over the tabloids tomorrow morning, just waiting for Gavin to see it first thing.

He turned to a warped door, tapped out a rapid succession of secret-code knocks (what else could it be?), and pulled me after him when the door opened.

The darkness swallowed me whole, and one last comforting thought struck me as I followed him down, down, down into New York City's underbelly.

I was an idiot.

CHAPTER THIRTY-SIX

I was lost. Completely, irrevocably lost.

The path he'd taken me on twisted, turned, never went up, and left me feeling like I was buried alive under brownstone rubble.

Which I pretty much was.

I cleared my throat. "How, um, are we going to get back?"

I could hear the smile in his voice in the dimly lit tunnel. "Oh, we never enter or exit the same way twice. We need to make sure you're good and lost."

Well he'd nailed it, then. And it totally wasn't creepy how he'd switched to "we" all of a sudden.

I swallowed audibly. "So, um, by 'we' do you mean you and the other vampires? Or you and your bat persona?"

I let out a high-pitched laugh, then snapped my mouth closed and wished I had duct tape for it. Who said things like that?

His chuckle said he didn't know whether to be amused or concerned. "We. Of the Blood Coven. The only true vampires of New York City, dedicated to preserving our way of life, even though others of my kind seem bent on destroying that very thing."

I stopped right there, in the middle of a darkened hallway where I couldn't see more than a few feet ahead—nor the creatures of the night I was positive were tracking our every movement—as something dawned on me.

"You mean, *you* sent that note? You lured me down here? Why?"

He turned and raised both hands. "Be at peace, Candace Marshall. I didn't send that note, no, but you said you wanted answers. I nudged members of the right coven to issue you an invitation."

Okay, I had officially entered cray-cray town. And I'd let him bring me down here willingly.

See? Idiot.

My eyes darted to the walls on either side of me. Was the panic exit nearby? Because I wanted out. Right now.

"So, um, where does this coven of yours meet? Are you taking me to a club? A hideout? A torture chamber?" I laughed, but it stuck in my throat.

He held a finger to his lips and winked. "All in good time, my darling girl, all in good time."

Then he turned and kept going down the endless underground tunnels.

"You can't tell me anything?" I asked his back.

He shrugged. "It's neutral territory of sorts. For all the covens. Keep up. Unless you'd rather try to find it on your own?"

I scrambled after him, and we passed just enough light that I could see the smirk on his face.

I shut up for the rest of the trek, but by the time we came to a nondescript door, I was sweating. Big time.

Stress sweat is not attractive, let me tell you.

At least I was wearing all black.

He placed me in front of it and stepped back. I looked at him, the door, then him again.

He raised an eyebrow. "The key?"

I jumped. "Oh!" I dug it out of my pocket and held it up to the pathetic light.

Intricate scrollwork was carved into the metal, and I searched the door. Just barely could I make out matching scrollwork in the middle of the door, a keyhole in its center.

"Here goes nothing," I muttered and stuck it in.

Gears whirred, and slowly the key turned all by itself and was sucked out of sight. I scrambled away from the door, but Anders was there to push me toward the yawning darkness.

Because strobe lights, a rave, and partiers bathed in blood were not on the other side of that door like I was expecting.

Oh no. Complete, utter darkness stretched before me and threatened to swallow me whole.

"Um," I squeaked and tried harder to back up.

He pushed me right inside, and the door closed with a heavy thud, like a vault door. Sounds I hadn't even known were there—dripping, scurrying, soft whispering of air currents—immediately snuffed out, and I felt like I was in a pressure chamber.

Would anyone even hear me scream?

I immediately spun and put my hands out like a mummy, searching everywhere for him. Anders could not be found.

I whimpered, and a deep voice echoed in the chamber.

"Who goes there?"

I whimpered some more, but then the words from their dark web website came to mind. "Um, someone who seeks to be worthy?"

The same voice boomed out, "Then enter and enjoy your brush with the underworld and with *death*."

Chilling laughter spilled out, and I felt like I was drenched head to toe in spiders, I was so creeped out.

It *might* have been laughable had I not been so freaked out, but they'd done a thorough job of scaring the living daylights outta me.

A round door at the far end of what looked like a painted-black tunnel opened, spilling in red strobing light, deep throbbing music, and sounds of people having a good time.

I honestly didn't know whether to move forward or try to get out through the door at my back.

Considering it sounded like a vault door with all the pins and chambers closing, forward and through?

I sprinted toward the light, wanting to be anywhere but here, and passed some dude in a cloak that covered his face. He held out my key. I shied away, snatched it from him, and darted through the circular door.

I came out on a small platform that looked down on an open floorplan.

The people dancing to throbbing music below weren't actually drenched in blood, but the red lights sure made them look that way.

The music rattled my chest, I went dizzy from the strobe lights, and I tried to get out the way I'd come. The second vault-like door was locked tight at my back.

Guess that meant I had to be brave. Or stupid. Probably both.

I clung to the rail and made my way down the staircase, taking everything in.

We were deep underground.

The building looked like the inside of a giant concrete box that had been buried years ago and either painted or aged some dark color. Decorations were sparse, but they mostly consisted of flashing lights and dark wall hangings. Maybe to mute the sound?

They could use a few thousand more.

A DJ controlled the music on a raised station above the bar, but speakers were placed all over the room so people weren't mobbing the bar to get closer to the DJ.

Blacklights made everything glow weirdly, including the fangs on all the people below. They must've been rather proud of them with how much they were showing them off.

Or everyone had gotten the memo that it was scare-Candace day.

Dressed in shiny, skintight leather with lots of skin showing, they wore some kind of body glitter that looked like blood spatter and glowed under the blacklight, because it shimmered and winked out of sight as soon as they went over to the covered bar with normal, softly glowing lights.

Then they just looked like normal people in leather clothes with fangs.

Everything combined was crazy disorientating. I wished I'd known to bring earplugs. Or giant earmuffs. Or anything to protect my hearing, really.

Because I didn't know what else to do, I stumbled my way to the bar and claimed a stool there.

Like a wet blanket had settled over my ears, the music was more muffled here, and I couldn't have been more grateful. It was still ridiculously loud, but better.

Sure enough, everyone had what looked like gold dust all over their faces and arms, and as soon as they stepped away into the blacklight, it lit up like starlight in a blood spatter pattern.

Seriously? Anders had taken me to the glitter vampire club? We were having words as soon as I found him.

"What'll it be?" The bartender somehow spoke over the noise.

"Oh, um…" I looked around for a menu, but there wasn't one. Let's just say I didn't have much experience with bars and the drinks you could get there. But did I really want to order something from a vampire club? "Water?"

At his incensed look, I quickly backtracked.

"Oh, um, I mean, something non-alcoholic?"

He looked at me like he was trying to figure out what I was doing there—that made two of us, buddy—and got out a skinny dark-glass vial of some kind. "How about the night's special?"

Yeah, but was that non-alcoholic? Somehow I sincerely doubted it. Unless it was, you know, something else I never wanted to drink.

I wilted in my seat, too intimidated to ask questions or say no. "Sure. That'd be great, thanks."

He'd already started pouring before I agreed to it. Then he set it before me in a little stand and stood there, watching me.

I eyed him, then the glass, then him again.

Oh my gosh, was he going to watch me until I drank it?

A smirk lifted one side of his face. "Sans alcohol."

"Oh, um, thank you?"

He nodded. "That'll be twenty-four dollars."

My mouth fell open. "For a *drink*?"

I eyed the glass. That skinny little dark-glass vial didn't look like it held enough to possibly cost that much. Unless I was drinking liquid gold.

Sheesh. Considering I was too cheap to order a four-dollar soda at most restaurants, opting for free tap water instead, no way was I paying twenty-four dollars for this measly amount of liquid.

Well, except my coffee.

Coffee was life. Coffee kept me awake. Coffee made sure I could do things like work when I hadn't gotten more than a few hours of sleep three nights in a row.

But even then, I tried to make my own or use the office

single-cup maker as much as possible. And they were, what? Like eight bucks now?

Not twenty-*four*.

I think my cheapskate was showing.

"Sure I can't just get water?" Just my luck he'd charge me ten bucks for that.

That got another half smile out of him. "No offense, but how'd you get in here?"

Great. Was it that obvious I didn't know what I was doing? I hooked my thumb over my shoulder and wilted even further. "Some guy."

I didn't add: "Who shoved me in here and locked the door behind me and left me to die and is there a safe way out, please?"

But I wanted to.

Considering my face was an open book, he probably got some of that anyway.

He glanced behind me briefly, even though I'd been abandoned. "Ah. I see." He winked. "First one's on the house. Enjoy your drink."

I couldn't help it; I gave him my slow-burn signature Candace smile.

My smile hates me. It's slow in coming, and by the time it reaches my face, it transforms into something magnificent. But most people don't get to see it.

No, I didn't believe it either, but my best friend Jemma from college swears up and down it's true. And it's nice to think I have one thing going for me in the attractive department.

Most people are gone or turned away or moving on to the next customer before they see it, but I've seen enough weird reactions from those who stick around for it to think Jemma might not be completely crazy.

What can I say? I ugly cry and have a killer smile, and my face pretty much just does its normal thing between.

He gave me a startled look as I picked up my drink. See? Weird reaction.

I sniffed it warily and almost fainted from relief. Wasn't blood, thank the good Lord above. It smelled kinda sweet, was a little fizzy, and made me hopeful I wouldn't spit it out everywhere.

Someone grabbed my elbow, and I shrieked, jumped, and threw my drink right in his face.

A dripping-wet Anders stood right behind me, quite possibly looking the most annoyed since I'd met him. And that was saying something.

The bartender handed him a rag, and he wiped down his face, hair, chest, and shoulders until he was mostly free of blood-red liquid.

Guess that little vial held more than I thought. But at least I didn't have to drink it now, right? And thank God I hadn't actually paid for it.

Anders grinned at me with effort. "Having a good time?"

I just raised an eyebrow. I debated saying, "Does it look like I'm having a good time?" or "Why, yes, I just love being abandoned in a place where vampires want to eat me," or perhaps "Is being scared to death a good time?"

Before I could decide on which to go with, he spread his hands wide and grinned.

"Welcome to the Convergence, neutral territory for the five covens of New York City."

CHAPTER THIRTY-SEVEN

I just stared at Anders. He couldn't be serious.

He smiled at me, fangs on full display, and I realized he was. Completely, absolutely serious. He thought he was a real vampire.

As I looked around, one thing hit me stronger than anything else. These people didn't look right. Emaciated, skin palish and translucent, hair thin.

Maybe there *was* blood in that vial.

But something else about all the strobing lights and writhing bodies struck me as odd. "Mr. Withers wanted to bring that nice old lady *here*? To a vampire *club*?"

Anders tracked my gaze and said nonchalantly, "Some weeks it's a club, some weeks it's a tea party. Without, you know, tea. Sometimes it's something else entirely. The location isn't the only thing that changes." He gave me a lazy grin. "Who's to know which they were into?"

"Certainly not this," I muttered into my empty drink, not brave enough to say it to his face.

Anders tapped the bar, and like sleight of hand, the bartender had two more vials full and waiting for us.

"So…the Convergence?" I shouted over the bass-deep

music. It was rattling my chest so much, it felt like I had a second and third heartbeat.

Anders shook his head and spoke in my mind. *I can hear you just fine.* He tapped his temple. *In here.*

My mouth fell open. How on earth did he do that?

He leaned close and whispered in my ear and mind at the same time. *"Magic."*

I snorted, even as a chill swept my body. Yeah right.

He shrugged as if he didn't care whether I believed him or not, then took a sip of his drink.

I left my drink sitting where it was, thank you very much.

I squinted at him. "I thought you needed my help? To infiltrate this place or something."

His eyes flashed. As in, red. *Oh, I do. And you will. Believe me when I say I couldn't have gotten in without you.* He nodded toward the bartender. *Show him the old man's key.*

I swallowed, really hoping the whole red eyes thing was just a trick of the light. Before I could say anything, he slipped into the crowd and was gone.

Freaking disappearing vampires. After telling me to stick close, even.

So there I sat, all alone, at a rave club thingy surrounded by vampires, looking lost, scared, and like a tasty snack.

Not my favorite moment, let me tell you.

As I sat there trying not to vibrate right off the bar stool from nerves, I glanced at the guy behind the bar, wondering if I was brave enough to do what Anders asked. Well, told me, really.

The barkeep spoke over the music, barely raising his voice at all. "Can I top off your drink, miss?"

I shook my head and immediately cradled my drink. "No, thank you. But thank you. Really."

I got a half smile at that.

Some moments passed until he spoke again. He jerked

his head in the direction Anders had disappeared. "He coming back?"

My eyes went the widest they'd ever been, probably. "I certainly hope so."

Again that half smile.

He regarded me for so long, I started to feel uncomfortable. Sure, he was good looking, I think—I mean, most people looked good in dim light—and sure, I was alone at a bar, but I most certainly was *not* looking to be picked up.

Especially not by people who thought they were vampires.

And especially if they were real vampires, which they weren't.

"Who're you waiting for, then?"

I dug in my pocket and came up with the key. I waved it around. "I'm looking for—"

I never got to finish.

He grabbed my hand and shoved it down on top of the bar, covering the key with his warm hand. Warm? Shouldn't it be ice cold?

"Best keep such things close, lovely." He jerked his chin to a door behind him and off to the side of the bar. "Right through there."

I just wanted my hand back, please and thank you, but he kept it.

I licked my lips. "Um, me? Go back there?"

He followed the movement—which I absolutely regretted now—and gave me a smolder he most likely used on all his customers for bigger tips. "Now you've got the idea."

He released me, and I shoved the key away. I couldn't get to the back door fast enough.

As I went, I noticed movement around me had stilled, people nearby watched me closely, and several sniffed the air as I passed. Some of the people dressed as vamps were so convincing, I almost gave up my whole "this can't be real" mantra. Almost.

As I reached the door, lifted my hand to knock, but the bartender was there, opening it for me.

I gave him a wobbly smile, and he ushered me through with a hand at the small of my back.

I practically jumped through the doorway to get away from that hand, and with a wink, he shut the door behind me. The throbbing pulse of the club snuffed out to almost nothing.

I reeled, putting my hands to my head, thankful the horrible noise was gone. Still, that headache wasn't going away anytime soon. I'd probably hear that throbbing music in my sleep.

Then I noticed the others in the room, who had gone still, watching me.

Five people sat at a poker table, bright-red velvet lit up like Christmas in the single lightbulb above. The bulb had a flared stained-glass cover, shielding the light from the rest of the room and guiding it down to the table and those sitting below.

A woman sat directly across from me. She had dark hair, a pale face, and blood-red lips. Dark skintight clothing covered every inch except her hands and face. Her fingers clutched cards, and her red fingernails matched her lips.

To her left were two men, one in a bowler hat with vibrant red hair peeking out that made him look Irish, and the other of Arabic descent and looking dapper in a shiny high-collar suit, and to her right were two more men, one older and Asian in a crushed-silk suit, and the other with dark skin and wearing a deep-purple suit that threw off a sultry sheen.

I noticed expensive clothes now, okay?

And to make it worse, they were all watching me stand there and grab my head like an idiot.

I dropped my hands. "Oh, um, hi."

The woman with the jet-black hair and blood-red lips spoke first. "You have a key?"

I dug around in my pockets and came up with both of them. "Two, actually."

Everyone at the table looked surprised, and the woman nodded at a chair set off to the side. "Pull up and we'll deal you in."

I backed away, just a little. "Oh no, that's okay. I mean, thank you, but I don't play. I don't gamble. I mean, I don't know how."

Suddenly Anders was there, in his dark overcoat and stringy, straight dark hair, guiding me to sit with a firm hand.

How did he keep popping up all over the place like that?

He stepped back, along the wall, and folded his hands in front of him, standing as a bodyguard might. But his eyes gleamed as he stared at one of the gentlemen, the one in the crushed-silk suit.

Who studiously ignored Anders, as if he couldn't be bothered by someone so beneath him.

My eyes adjusted, and that's when I noticed those at the table had their own bodyguards, alert, hands folded, standing behind each chair. Anders was acting as mine, and I didn't know whether to be grateful or scared out of my mind.

Especially if he was about to murder some dude I'd led him to.

I blinked under the glaring light as they dealt me in, trying to keep up.

The guy in the purple suit spoke in a deep, raspy voice. "The game is simple. You'll do fine."

As creepy as the whole situation was, something about this guy put me at ease. He seemed like a grandfatherly type, and his deep voice was soothing. He could easily compete with Morgan Freeman over narrating everything in sight.

I startled a little. Unless that was their plan all along. Soothe me into relaxing, suck me almost dry, and turn me. Then I'd wake up as one of them.

I frantically searched for Anders, and he gave me a calming look, slightly moving his hands in a "it's all good" gesture.

"How did you get the keys?" the woman asked. "It's rare for a player to have two."

I started to answer, but Anders cut me off. "You know that's not how it works, Mirvas."

She gave him a sharp look as the gentleman in the dark-purple suit rumbled a deep laugh. "Just play the game, Mirvas," he said. "You'll find out what you want to know soon enough."

I started sweating, and my hands went all clammy. Not only did I have no idea what they were talking about, what I was doing here, or how to play this stupid game, I had no idea what the keys meant or anything.

Mirvas laid out a row of cards that had various vampire symbols on them that were familiar and many that weren't. "The key gets you into the game. With two keys"—she flicked a glance at Anders—"well, I suppose we'll come to that problem when we need to. Put your keys in the center of the table."

I did, then snatched my hand back. Didn't want to just offer something tasty they couldn't refuse.

She dealt us ten cards each, starting and ending with me, so I had eleven. Once they picked up theirs, I looked at mine.

Whoever had drawn and painted these cards was an amazing artist. Only five symbols repeated on my cards. One was a dagger through a heart, one was a landscape bathed in the light of a full moon, one was of blood overflowing a goblet and pooled around its base, one was the cycles of the moon, and the final was a person hiding behind a red-lined, pitch-black cape, eyes only peeking out.

I got a little distracted studying the cards, then jumped when someone cleared their throat. They all watched me.

I tentatively laid out a card. The stabbed-heart one, because it was the prettiest.

It may have sounded gross, but believe me, the cards were gorgeous.

The woman raised an eyebrow. "Interesting choice."

The other five players quickly played cards, and someone snatched up the trick.

Then they all stared at me again.

I had no idea what had just happened. It was too quick to follow. But they were waiting on me, so…

I laid out the full moon next. It was so vibrant, I wanted to visit the little hut on the grassy knoll with the massive full moon taking up most of the night sky. I squinted. It looked like a little person was slipping into the darkened doorway. Hadn't the hut's door just been closed?

Please tell me these cards were not moving. Come on! I hadn't even had anything to drink.

Someone threw a card on top of mine, and I jumped back.

They quickly played another hand, and a different player snatched up the trick.

There seemed to be no rhyme or reason to it. Not only was it too fast to follow, it didn't make sense who won or why.

Or was I winning by getting rid of them? I didn't know.

It went like this for the rest of my cards, until I had one left, and they had none.

The final card was the goblet full of blood.

I tentatively laid it out, wondering what would happen next.

The woman, Mirvas, smiled, then slid the card under one of the keys and set it aside.

Then she dealt all over again.

I looked up at Anders, and he gave me an encouraging smile and a wink.

Once again, cards were laid out, and once again, I had no idea how tricks were won, but won they were, and soon, I was down to one card again.

This time, I kept back the stabbed heart card. I wasn't sure if it would've been better to have two of the same, or if I should spread out my chances of whatever this was, but I tilted my head as I laid it out, as if to ask, "Is this okay?"

Mirvas's jaw went hard as soon as she saw my card, and the gentleman next to me chuckled again.

"Now it's up to you, Mirvas. Are you going to contest it?"

Her stormy eyes met mine, and she seemed to struggle. "No," she finally said. "I won't contest it. Anders," she snapped. "Take your little pet home."

My spine went straight. "Wait just a minute. I didn't come all this way—"

"I too have business here—" Anders spoke over me.

"Not here, not now," Mirvas snapped. "This is neutral ground. You will have another opportunity."

Anders seemed to physically struggle, his glare back on the Asian dude.

Who now smiled, as if gloating, still ignoring Anders.

"Go, thrall," the guy in the deep-purple suit rumbled. "Your master will have his revenge soon enough."

Whatever this was, I wanted no part of it. "I'm here about a Mr. Withers—"

I got a sharp look from the Asian guy, but Mirvas cut me off with a brisk hand gesture. "Enough. Your fate has been decided, your houses chosen. Your time here is done."

After a stare down between Anders and Mirvas that had

my skin prickling, Anders gently grasped my arm and pulled me to stand. "I thank you all for your time and consideration." He turned to the dude he'd been glaring at. "My master challenges yours at a place of your choosing." His fangs gleamed in a smile that was more of a glare. With bared teeth. "If your master is still vampire enough to engage in the rules of combat, that is."

The guy in the crushed-silk suit dropped the cards he'd been gathering, everyone else at the table went still, and the bodyguards put their hands to their sides like they were seconds from drawing weapons.

And with that, Anders hauled me past them all and out through a back way.

I desperately wanted to demand to know what was going on, but I had to run to keep up and was soon breathless as he led me through crumbling abandoned tunnels.

What on earth had just happened?

✝

After being dragged through another maze of tunnels until I was thoroughly turned around, I stood under New York City's yellow lights and hoped to never see its underside again.

I rubbed my temples. I didn't do clubs for a reason.

Anders crossed his arms and leaned against the side of a building, back to his nonchalant self. "So. What did you think?"

I spun on him, my patience completely gone. "What do I think? I'll tell you what I think. I think you're all completely insane. Pretending to be vampires in an underground club? Drinking your blood punch and drenched in blood light and crawling through darkness like it's a good place to be? And what was up with that challenge? I thought they were going to shoot you!"

I huffed and waved my arms.

"Meanwhile, some scary dudes are out there who are perfectly willing to kidnap people, drink their blood, and let's not forget—actually *kill* them—and I'm no closer to answers."

He shifted, his look uneasy, and I had to assume I was starting to damage his calm. "First of all, Jorge could tell you were new, so you didn't get the real stuff—"

"Save it." I spun and marched away, no longer scared of this dude. Or at least no longer wanting to be a part of his mess. "When you're ready to save someone's life, call me. Until then, just save it."

He didn't follow me as I searched for a cab, then took it home to shower, sleep for two hours, then go straight into work.

My head throbbed with ghost beats of club music, and I wondered how long until it left me alone too.

When I got home, I skipped the shower, set my alarm, and buried myself deep in my covers. I'd been missing sleep far too much for far too long, and I'd had enough.

I was getting back on some kind of normal schedule ASAP.

CHAPTER THIRTY-EIGHT

Obnoxious. Insufferable. Excruciating.

What was that noise?

I peeled one eyelid off my grimy eyeball and stared at my bedside table.

My phone danced across the table with each buzz. It gyrated itself right off the flat surface into my trashcan. I smiled. Finally.

Drifting back to sleep, my eyes shot open.

The photo shoot!

I bolted out of bed, covers still attached. They tangled around my legs, and I fell face-first into the designer rug by my bedside.

I rolled down the side of the bed, but the covers tightened around my legs, leaving me half dangling there. I fought with them until I finally wrested myself free.

Tugging back the heavy curtains, I cried out and grabbed my head. Why was it so bright?

I glanced at the clock and squinted, trying to read it. I stumbled over to it and pulled it close to my face. My eyes wouldn't work.

"Come on come on come on."

My eyes adjusted, and I tried to make my brain tell me what my eyes were seeing.

"Oh no. No. No, no, no, no, no!"

I headed for the bathroom, changed my mind, and dug around in the trashcan.

Pulling my phone way too close to my face, I waited for my brain to catch up. Again.

Sixteen missed calls.

Thirty-two texts.

The very last message caught my eye.

I DID NOT give u this big break 4 u 2 stand me up. If u aren't here in 2 seconds, consider R deal off.

I shrieked and threw the phone on my bed, bolting for the bathroom.

I threw water on my face and turned to leave. Thankfully, I glanced in the mirror before I did. The wrinkled black dress was still present from the vampire lair. Makeup ran down my face. Frizzy hair stuck in every direction. I sniffed under my arm.

Yep, smelled like something dead.

Which meant I'd have to torch those sheets whenever I got a chance.

I couldn't go within ten yards of a fashion designer smelling and looking like this. Turning on the water, I took the second-fastest shower of my life.

✗

The cab dropped me at one of the entrances to Central Park. I clutched my camera bag with one hand and my portfolio of shot setup sketches with the other.

I ran down paths and around joggers until I came to the spot where we were supposed to be shooting. I rushed around the corner and into the open square and stopped.

The square was deserted.

Water trickled musically out of the fountain, grating on my every nerve.

Not one photographer, model, designer, or piece of equipment was left.

I dropped my head and took a deep breath.

Man, was I going to get it.

※

I opened the glass door as noiselessly as possible and slipped into my office. Lola wouldn't even look at me. I slipped my camera case into the place where I normally kept my purse. I vaguely hoped I'd left my purse in my apartment before I turned to my layout table.

I looked over everything. "Do you need…?"

"Nope."

"Did you get…?"

"Already got it."

"Do you want me to…?"

"Absolutely not."

I sighed. I couldn't fault her for being angry with me. *I* was angry with me.

Hopefully Jackson had caught his flight in time?

Stan burst into the room. "First of all, what are you wearing?"

I looked down. The first thing I grabbed out of the closet. Definitely not fashion-magazine worthy.

He clutched his nose and waved his hand. I stared at him, horrified. It was a fast shower, but I was absolutely certain I'd gotten the vamp club smell off. Certain.

"Phew. Get those off-brand rags out of here before you jinx us all. Tell Evie down at the closet it's an emergency and Stan sent you. She'll know what to do."

I started to get up, mortified. I paused. "What was the second thing?"

He dropped his hands and gave me a look that had me wanting to find a hole to fall into and pull in after myself, like in a cartoon. "I think you know."

He left quietly, which did more to scare me than if he'd sniffed and strutted out of the room, nose exaggeratedly in the air. I was worse than dead.

I trudged toward the door, all my late nights making my legs feel like lead. The door opened, and I lifted my head, expecting Stan.

Harold, team leader and final say for all hiring and promotions, stood at the threshold, nostrils flaring. I felt Lola straighten behind me. He looked me up and down in disdain, disgust wiping any previous admiration from owning that meeting away.

He looked past me, ignoring me, at Lola.

"Darling, would you be a dear and bring me your portfolio? Thank you."

He paused to give me one last scalding look before disappearing. I stared at his retreating back until it disappeared around a corner.

My shoulders slumped, and Lola chuckled.

"I guess you can help me with these layouts after all. Be a dear and take them to Stan when you're done?"

She grabbed a wide canvas binder from her personal cupboard. She, too, paused at the threshold.

Her ice-cold gaze was back, no fire, no warmth. She tapped her naked wrist. "Four o'clock deadline. Don't forget."

She wriggled her fingers at me and blew a kiss, likely keeping up "professional coworkers" appearances. Only I could see the daggers of hate she shot me.

I sighed and looked at the clock.

Four o'clock. Just a few hours.

Everything was crashing down on me, and I didn't know how long until I buckled.

I rushed as fast as my beyond-tired body could take me out the door and down to the third floor.

Evie took one look at me. "Stan?"

I nodded.

She clucked and pulled out an outfit—just one—and shoved it my way. I changed right there, not caring who was bustling through on the way to the next wherever.

I heard her gasp and glanced up.

She was staring at my bra and panties. "Oh my. That's hardly…my dear, you really shouldn't, you know, wear such…"

Dingy? Old? Granny panties? Sports bras? What?

I'd kept meaning to replace them.

"Things…" She started to reach for the lingerie rack, but I shook my head.

"No time," I muttered, sounding half dead, even to me.

Evie didn't look convinced, but her voice was kind. "Best hurry, dearie."

I nodded and pulled my beautiful—yet highly uncomfortable—clothes over my head. She tossed my clothes in the trash as I hurried to the elevator.

I sure would miss it. All of it. Everything. Especially Stan's over-the-top demeanor.

I trudged off the elevator and back to my studio.

I skipped the desperately needed coffee and furiously slapped layouts together. The perfectionist in me wouldn't let them go into the completed pile sloppy, and my heart sank faster the further past the hour the clock hands ticked.

Finally. Finished. I looked up at the clock. Five thirty. Yikes. I grabbed the final draft and rushed to Stan's office.

His assistant shook her head at me from behind her headset. She pointed to the conference room.

I tapped lightly before opening the door and sticking my head in. I flushed when Vera, Stan, Harold, and the rest of the movers and shakers of *Voilà Magazine* stared back at me.

I shakily walked the length of the room—the longest walk of my life—to Stan, and placed the packet in front of him.

"Layouts. Sir."

I hadn't called him "sir" since my first day. I'm not sure why I added that now, considering he forbade me from calling him that ever again. The occasion might call for it.

He held my gaze for far too long before dropping his gaze to the layouts. "Mm-hmm. Yes. Impeccable as always."

Why did that not sound like a compliment at all?

"We had high hopes for you, Miss Marshall."

A loud buzzing filled my ears, and I felt lightheaded. Was he really going to do this here, in front of everyone?

"Yes, sir," I managed to rasp out.

He stared at me a moment more before shuffling through a few more pages. "Unfortunately, as perfect as these may be, they lack ingenuity."

"Excuse me?" I couldn't help it. It burst from my lips before I could stop it.

"You've done layouts like these before. They are too bland. Too basic. Already been done. Your creative spark is gone, along with your punctuality and reliability."

I opened my mouth to protest, but nothing came out. Where was my brain when I needed it?

Oh, yeah, that's right. Asleep, like the rest of my body.

"If you would just give me one more chance…"

I stopped. The words fell flat, and I knew it. They'd given me so many chances, what with vampire drama and missed work and being late.

"You've run out of chances, Miss Marshall. I want your things cleared and your workspace organized. Come see me in my office before you leave, please."

I nodded and backed toward the door, groping for the handle. I froze. Couldn't even turn around. "Um, Paris?"

Vera spoke up for the first time. "Lola will be going with

me, Miss Marshall. I need someone along whom I can trust."

I nodded again, my voice thick with tears. "Yes, ma'am."

Then I fled. Stuffing back a sob, I hurried toward my hard-won workspace. Why hadn't I fought harder to keep it? Stupid vampires, that's why.

I slipped inside and put my back to the clear door.

No, stupid me.

The blame rested squarely on my shoulders. I couldn't push that off on someone or something else.

And the worst part was, I'd seen it coming. Even warned myself of what could happen if I let too many things slide. But I thought I was invincible, that I could manage it all on my own, that I could focus on everything except my job and still keep it.

I'd let the important things slip away, obsessively chasing something the cops told me over and over again—they had it under control.

But I was so convinced some part of it was real…that I could save Mr. Withers…

And it drove me crazy that no one believed me, so I was beyond determined to solve the mystery, expose the movie, or find real vampires, dang it.

And worst of all, Gavin didn't even know. And I didn't know the next time he would be available to talk. Not to mention he'd told me this would happen if I kept chasing this insanity.

It was my own fault. My own crazy, stupid fault. I had no one to blame but me.

I made everything as neat as possible, ready for Lola in the morning. At least, for as long as she still worked layout. Until she got the promotion I didn't realize how desperately I wanted until right now.

I straightened everything one more time.

I had to face it: I could no longer delay my meeting with Stan. I crept to his office.

"Come in," his grave voice commanded when I barely peeked around the corner.

I sighed and stood before his desk, twisting my fingers until they hurt.

"Space cleaned out?"

I swallowed and nodded.

"Desk organized?"

I nodded again, forcing back tears. My eyes stung.

"Good."

He scribbled out my severance check and stretched it out to me. I took it, but the number blurred. He sighed, then ran his fingers through his thick gray hair.

"I didn't want it to end like this, you know."

"I know," I whispered. "Me neither. I'm so s—" I choked on a sob and couldn't get the rest of my apology out.

"Go! Before you make us all cry. Off with you now!"

I jumped at his loud voice and turned away.

"Oh." I looked down. "The clothes?"

"Keep them."

I nodded and left.

⚔

I stumbled toward the door, then remembered my camera. I wasn't one to leave things behind—even if I never wanted to show my face around here again—so I slunk toward my former office, praying no one would see my walk of shame.

Thank God it was after when most decent people went home. Not that people around here kept regular hours.

I paused as I rounded the corner. My completely clear-glass office held someone I most certainly didn't want to see.

Maybe I could just leave my camera?

Better not.

I crept forward and knew the instant she spotted me. Her cat-like, snake-like, demon-like expression turned positively smug, and I wondered if I could scratch her eyes out and get away with it.

Again, better not.

I offered Lola a halfhearted smile as I tried to unlock my cubby with shaking hands as I tried not to make eye contact as I tried to pretend I wasn't there…you get the idea.

"Heeey…yooou." I drew out the words and made myself sound like an idiot. Could I get any more pathetic?

I grabbed my pack, left the key, and took a moment to look around, to make sure I hadn't forgotten anything else. Most everything here belonged to the company. My designs, company. My office supplies, company. My espresso machine…

Well, Lola had stashed that thing somewhere, and now probably wasn't the best time to ask about it.

Digital pens, tablet, even the sticky notes: all provided by the company.

There wasn't anything else of mine here to take.

Lola crossed her arms. "Well that couldn't have gone any better."

I mumbled, "You mean worse."

She shrugged. "Nope. Better. For me."

My head came up at that. I'd never heard her voice so full of hatred, loathing. "What? What do you mean?"

She looked at me like I was an idiot. "You mean you don't know. Seriously."

I shook my head, dumbfounded, wondering what had happened to my emotionless assistant, the one I thought was my friend. Well, at the very least didn't hate me.

But now I was starting to remember little glances, little remarks, the whole Martha incident…

"You mean…you *wanted* me to get fired?"

She threw her hands up, a quick, jerky motion that was more expressive than anything I'd seen her do before.

"Yes! I should've had your job from the beginning, and now it's mine. Thank God! How does a little nobody like you—from a little town only God knows where—end up lead layout artist? And me, the shoo-in, your assistant? It's unfair on so many levels. Am I upset you lost your job? No. It was only a matter of time, especially with how all the ludicrous vampire stuff was making you crazy. Am I glad to see you go? Absolutely."

I stared openmouthed at my assistant—former assistant—as Lola's chest heaved, her eyes flashing and her fists clenched.

She barked a laugh. "And then you insisted on keeping me. Did you know another employee got fired over that? They didn't need both of us—our positions were redundant—so they let her go. That was all *you*."

Guilt swarmed me, and I remembered an older woman who had comforted me over Stan's teasing, how she'd told me he did that to absolutely everyone *not* in danger of losing their jobs, then hearing about someone getting let go not long after that. Was that her?

Lola sneered. "You make me sick."

I was too shocked to even cry, and that was my go-to for literally everything. "But I thought we were friends…" As soon as I said it, I knew I'd chosen the wrong word.

She rolled her eyes. "Girl, please. I don't even like you."

I couldn't help sputtering at that. She didn't even *like* me? Since when? She'd always acted like she did. Well, kind of. Well, at first…

"And Gavin Bailey…"

My head came up, a trickle of fire making its way to my spine. "What about Gavin?"

"Do you really think you would've gotten this job without your connection to him?"

"I wasn't…he didn't…he said…"

She parroted me, her voice high and mocking. "'He said, he said.' Surely you can't be that naïve, cupcake. Did you know they were going to hire me until, all of a sudden, you and Gavin Bailey show up in the tabloids as getting back together after falling hard for each other in your movie? You think I had a chance after that?"

I spluttered, trying to deny it, but I'd never heard Lola talk so much in my life. It was throwing me off big time.

She snorted. "Maybe if I'd gone out with him more than a few times, I'd be running this company by now."

My head jerked back, and I stumbled back a step. "You…dated…*Gavin*?"

She saw every nuance of my reaction and, from the smirk growing on her face, thoroughly enjoyed it. "You really don't know the man you're dating, do you? Believe me, he plays a good game, but he's only after one thing."

She looked me up and down.

"And you're not it."

My chest felt like it was caving in.

"Now, get out of my office."

I couldn't stop staring at her, one stupid thought circling over and over in my mind. What did she mean that he was only after *one thing*?

She shoved my camera bag at me, annunciating every word. "I said, Get. Out."

Gladly. I didn't want to have a full-on meltdown in front of this snake. I stumbled out of the room, down the hallway, and onto the elevator in a daze.

Her words swirled around my mind like a vortex, and all I wanted to do was curl up in a ball and never move again.

Downstairs, I stumbled out of the elevator, too numb to do anything but put one foot in front of the other.

Her words hounded me all the way to my apartment.

CHAPTER THIRTY-NINE

I spent the rest of the day, and the entire night, staring at my ceiling, tears leaking out of my eyes, my chest hurting too much to make a sound.

Now I was pacing madly, my last encounter with Stan, with Lola, everything echoing over and over in my head as birds began chirping their morning song outside. How had I messed everything up so badly?

I needed to leave. Get out, go somewhere…and just walk.

I thought about changing, looked down at my pajamas—no one I knew would see me anyway—and headed for the door. I opened my apartment door and froze, my deer-in-headlights look on full display.

Gavin stood there, a steaming coffee and folded brown bag in hand, grinning at me. "Surprise!"

I tried to smile. "What are you doing here?"

He gave a significant look to the side—right! Nosy neighbor. I opened the door wider, and he stepped in, still grinning.

He waited till I locked the door to speak. "I'm here to escort you to work today, milady." He offered me a gallant bow, then straightened and winked. "It's not every day you get to go to Paris for the first time."

A thousand waves crashed into my chest, almost taking me under. I faltered under the onslaught of emotions, too heartbroken to deal with them all.

He frowned and glanced around. "Where are your bags?"

I pointed, unable to say anything. I'd tossed my jacket and other cold weather things on them last night so I wouldn't have to look at them.

He pulled them out from under the pile, then ushered me toward my room. "Hurry and get ready. You're going to Paris!"

I didn't and I wouldn't, but he didn't know that. And for some reason, I couldn't tell him.

He shut the door behind me with a wink, and shame washed over me all over again.

I had to tell him. I had *so much* to tell him. But how?

I got ready in a daze, throwing on the clothes Stan had given me just yesterday, trying to figure out what to say, trying to pump myself up to be brave enough to say it.

I was just going to go out there, tell him I wasn't going to Paris after all…I swallowed. But how could I tell him I'd gotten fired? That I'd been kidnapped again? That I'd willingly sought them out? Twice now, after I told him I wouldn't?

I was so embarrassed, so ashamed.

And…and…Lola…

He rapped on my bedroom door. "Lass, we've got to leave soon."

Attempting a smile for his sake, I opened the door and my mouth at the same time. His eyes met mine, and there was so much excitement, so much joy for me, I faltered.

He handed me the brown bag. "Your favorite. Croissant, egg, and cheese breakfast sandwich."

An ache filled me, so I ducked my head and blinked my eyes so tears wouldn't give me away. Sandwiches were one of my love languages, and I so did not deserve one right now.

"Hey, you okay?" He lifted my chin and searched my eyes.

And I was going to tell him. I really was. But I chickened out, like the scaredy-cat I was.

I gave him a wobbly smile. "Super emotional, I guess."

The first sign that he wasn't as happy as he let on smarted through his eyes. Something that looked like a smidgeon of the regret I was feeling.

"We'll go back, Candace. Just the two of us. I promise."

And here came the waterworks.

I gave a watery laugh and evaded his grasp to dig for a tissue box on the entry table. I swore I'd put one on here.

"I'm counting on it" was all I managed to say.

I turned to find him holding one out to me, so I took it and wiped my eyes and blew my nose. Then I tossed it, sanitized my hands, and grabbed my already-packed bags.

"Well, I'm off!" I gave Gavin a too-bright smile and tried desperately not to lose it. But the smile was staying on my face or else, dang it.

Gavin came over and kissed me, his smile genuine. "Call me when you get there?"

I pulled away and juggled my purse, duffle, and rolling suitcase. Something told me I could've packed better.

My camera was still on my bed, where I'd held it and cried myself to sleep—well, to nap—a few times. I definitely didn't need to grab that either, so why bother?

I gave a fake-ish laugh. "I'll try, but you know how busy they keep me." Or they used to keep me.

I gave him another quick kiss at his look of disappointment, then Lola's face flashed in my mind. Him. And her. What had happened, exactly?

No. No, I just couldn't. Not right now. Everything hurt too much.

I tried to back away, but he held on a little longer.

He stroked my arms. "I can't help but feel we're always missing each other. Too busy with too much work."

I shied away. *Dear God, please not a breaking-up talk on top of everything else!*

My words stuck in my throat. "Don't I know it."

"Candace, wait."

It was the third time I'd attempted to get out my door to the elevator. The one I sincerely hoped was working this time.

He tugged off my bags and set them on the floor. "I'm serious."

He wouldn't let me look away. But I was tired, drained, and didn't want him to see me cry.

"When you get back, let's plan a long weekend at my Hampton beach house. It'll still be cold this early spring, but we can curl up in blankets by the fireplace."

My eyes were huge. "But, but, what about your shoot? Your film? The location and everything?" I still wasn't up on all the movie-set lingo. No matter how many times he'd told me, I just kept getting it all mixed up. "Wait. You have a Hampton beach house?"

"I do." He smiled. "I'll be done by then. In fact, I'll finish filming about three days before you get back." A frown flickered over his face. "As long as everything goes according to schedule."

I knew he was thinking of the movie's diva, who'd only made life more miserable for them since she'd been shot. I mean, I didn't blame her, but she was milking it for all she was worth, costing the studio thousands in delays and special accommodations.

Gavin had told me in confidence that the studio was considering blacklisting her after they'd finished filming.

She was good, but not that good. There was plenty of other talent who'd be a pleasure to work with. Or at least not as horrible.

If only the last few shows she'd been in hadn't made her so popular.

"Does that sound good to you?"

And my mind had wandered off again. "Um, what?"

He laughed and kissed my forehead. "Did I lose you there for a second?"

I blushed, my face burning volcano hot.

He just laughed. The man was a saint. "That's okay. I just asked if I could pick you up after you get back and we can head up then? I know you have some days off coming to you after Paris Fashion Week."

I didn't know how to answer that. "Won't you want to go straight up? I mean, do you really want to wait for me for three whole days?"

"Believe me, I'll be sleeping hard for all three of those days. I'll probably only come out to get you and leave."

I smiled, though it was crazy strained. "That sounds great."

I started to turn away, but he pulled me back. "What am I missing here? Are you concerned it'll just be the two of us. Alone. In my house?"

Now my face was broiling-sun hot. "To be honest, I hadn't even thought of that, but yeah, that might not be so good."

We'd only had a few discussions about that, and he knew I was saving serious physical stuff for marriage, and he said he totally respected that and me.

But we hadn't talked about it past that horribly embarrassing bit.

Although I was sure I'd be freaking out about that later, right now I was freaking out about my job. As in, how to tell him I didn't have one.

He rubbed my arms reassuringly. "Don't worry. I already asked Jodi and Dave to come with us. We can all have separate rooms, but Jodi's willing to room with you, if that makes you feel better."

I tilted my head. "Jodi?"

He looked a little uncomfortable. "Um, my cousin, Jodi. My assistant."

I swallowed hard. Oh. I should've known that. The one who hated my guts.

I hated asking the next question, but I had to. "And Dave?"

I should probably know this one too.

He didn't look concerned about my forgetting who Dave was, at least. "My driver. He and Jodi kind of have a thing going on. Well, I think they'd like to, and I'd like to encourage them. What better way than a relaxing weekend or two where they can get to know each other?"

I couldn't help my genuine smile. "Why, I do believe you're a matchmaker at heart, Gavin Bailey."

"What can I say?" He pulled me closer. "I want everyone to be as happy as I am."

Gotta admit, that kiss may have stretched on for a little while. I didn't mind. I was busy melting at his sweetness.

He pulled back gently. My eyes were still closed, and I smiled. "Mmmmm."

"That good, huh?"

My eyes flew open. He was laughing at me.

"Hey! Don't ruin the moment." I jabbed him, and that led to a tickle fight, which led to more kissing, which led to…Gavin's phone ringing.

"Argh! Seriously?" I threw my hands into the air.

I was a very expressive speaker. All hand gestures, no real words—it was an art form.

He chuckled and pulled his phone free. "I promise to turn off my phone the whole weekend. Will you come?"

His finger hovered over the answer button, not pressing it while he waited for my answer. I started to sweat a little. What if he didn't answer and the person blamed me? What if the studio demanded I stop dating him because I was a distraction?

"Fine! Yes, I'll go. Just answer it."

He grinned. "There's my lass."

And I was a mushy pile of goo, almost forgetting about what wasn't waiting for me at work. Almost.

I scarfed down my breakfast sandwich while Gavin talked, then attempted to haul all my bags toward the door.

He ended the call and grabbed my bags from me. "Hey, let me get that."

I handed everything over quite willingly.

He saw me downstairs, then outside, where I tried to take everything back from him. He just threw it in his waiting vehicle.

I looked at the giant SUV, mouth open. "But…don't you need to get to the studio? I can take the subway."

He kissed me—several people pulled out their phones and took pictures. Had to be tourists. Real New Yorkers wouldn't have noticed. Then he handed me into the car and shut my door, walking around to get in his side.

I really didn't mind scooting over and letting him get in the safe side, this was New York after all, but he insisted on doing everything a gentleman ought.

He was like, every woman's dream guy. And he'd somehow ended up with me.

But Lola had said…

To distract myself from me, I turned to Gavin. "You seriously don't have to do this, you know. I'm used to public transport."

He smiled and linked my hand with his. "I know, but this is your big shot. Your big break. Paris Fashion Week."

He grinned. "You've always wanted to go to Paris, you know."

Tears filled my eyes, and I looked out the window before he could see.

He didn't know it, but I wouldn't be on that plane.

I'd gotten a passport and everything. My dream, in ashes.

I lifted my chin. I just had to get to work, hide for a little while, then head back home. Without breaking down.

He bounced our hands in the space between us. "You know, I'm a little jealous."

I spun on him. "Jealous? Jackson and I are just friends! I'm not interested in him in the least."

He looked completely blindsided. "Jackson?"

I bobbed my head. "Oh yeah, he goes by Jack now. I keep forgetting. We went to college together? Well, not together, together. I maybe talked to him twice. Anyway, he was the one in charge of your photo shoot."

Now Gavin was looking out his window. "That explains all the scowling. I just assumed he was one of the serious-about-their-work types."

I waved my hand. "Oh, he is. Much more so than in college. Um, actually, I guess that's not true. I don't know what he was like in college. Just that one of the girls in my dorm had the biggest crush on him."

Gavin turned and looked at me.

The look was like a slap. "And that's not what you were talking about at all, was it?"

He shook his head, still looking a bit off-kilter.

I smacked my forehead. "Oh, Gavin, I'm so sorry. I can be so stupid." I decided to get real honest, fast. "You see… Peter was furious I'd even talked to him. Twice. He didn't want me talking to other guys. Any other guys. So I immediately assumed…especially after the pictures…"

I shrugged, not knowing what else to say. Because I'd

almost blurted the rest of it, then everything else would've come tumbling out. Which I needed to do. I just couldn't yet. Not right now. Later. Much later.

His jaw dropped. "Candace, do you really think I'm as immature as your ex? Not let you have other friends, no matter their sex?"

I blushed hotly and shrugged again. "No, that isn't you, I know that. I just—sometimes I think my ex messed me up…and I let him." I looked deep into his eyes. "I promise you there is nothing between me and Jackson and there never will be. I just freaked out."

I could give him that much. But I seriously needed to tell him. Everything.

He smiled, but it was the slightest bit wobbly. "I know. I trust you, Candace. You don't have to explain yourself to me. Though I have to admit, that scared the sh—the crap out of me."

He knew how I felt about curse words. And now I felt even guiltier. I covered my face with my free hand. He still hadn't let go of the other one, thank goodness.

"I'm so sorry, my love." I peeked at him between my fingers. "You wouldn't want to risk trying to tell me what you were going to say again, would you?"

He pulled me close. Well, as close as our seatbelts would allow.

"I was just going to say, I'm jealous I'm not going to be the first one to take you to Paris. I admit I'd hoped to. One day."

And I almost died. Because how wonderful was he?

"Huh." I barked a laugh that wasn't. "You just might get that chance."

He pulled back and looked into my eyes. "What does that mean?"

But we were there, at my work, and his driver was

waiting to take him to work, which he was surely late for after taking time to come get me. For no reason.

I wasn't about to explain everything and become a blubbering mess when he had somewhere he needed to be. Unlike me.

I waved it off. "Just that I can't believe this is real. I'm expecting them to tell me they've made a mistake and send me home."

More like I'd made a mistake. One I couldn't come back from.

He shook me a little. Gently. Kindly. "Candace, stop it. You're good. Stop doubting yourself. I wish I could tell you it's the people with inherent talent who make it big, but that's not always the case. It's hard work. Lots and lots of hard work. And you have the talent to back it up. I believe in you. Now *you* just need to believe in you."

I couldn't help it. The tears I'd been holding back all day came to the surface. I tried to smile through them. "Thank you, Gavin. You have no idea how much that means to me."

He gently wiped my cheeks with his thumbs, then kissed my eyelids and my lips. "Go get 'em, tiger."

I gave him a wobbly smile and got out. Mr. Driver Dude —Dave, right?—was waiting for me with my bags, giving us a moment alone and freezing his patootie off.

It was freaking cold in winter-infested New York. Spring had not yet made itself known, no matter what the forecasters said.

I thanked him and hauled my stuff to the towering glass front doors of my work, hoping against hope they wouldn't throw me out while he was watching.

I turned at the door, waved, and went in.

Now to find a place to hide.

✕

Handsome security guard—his name never had stuck in my mind—saw me coming and touched the front desk worker's shoulder.

The guy nodded at him and moved aside.

"Candace Marshall," handsome security guy said with a slight smile and a wary look in his eye. "What can I do for you?"

I was a little breathless from hauling luggage in a frenzy, and I let it all fall around me in a haphazard lump.

"Hey…you." I made myself not squint at his nametag, though I really wanted to. Then I said in a rush, "Look, I know I don't work here anymore, but I was wondering if you could do me a solid."

He looked even more skeptical.

I glanced behind me at Gavin's SUV. Yep, still there. He was either taking care of something or waiting till I disappeared in the bank of elevators. Not good.

When I looked back at the security guard, he'd gone into alert mode. "Are you in danger, Miss Marshall?"

Oh, dear goodness. I didn't want to sic him on some unsuspecting person right now, or even Gavin, were he to follow me into the building.

I shook my head emphatically. "Oh no! Nothing like that. I just, um, I was supposed to leave for Paris today, and…" I eyed my luggage a bit helplessly. Then I met his eyes. "A well-meaning friend dropped me off. I didn't have the heart to tell him I'm not going. Can I please check them in for a few hours? Just for appearances? I promise I'll be back to get them…soon."

He didn't say anything.

After a moment, I realized how bad that sounded in security-conscious New York City. "Oh! I mean, you can totally go through them. Inspect everything. I just want a few hours before I haul everything back to my apartment without being seen."

I bit my lip. *Way to make him think you have a bomb, Candace.*

His eyes tracked the departing SUV, then he gave me a nod. "Just a moment, please."

He walked away, talked into his radio, and came back after every person in the building had walked by and given me the stink eye.

At least, that's how it felt.

His smile was kind. "I would be happy to do that for you, Miss Marshall."

He walked me over to concierge, efficiently went through my luggage, and waited while I scribbled my info on the check-in form. I added Gavin's number as my backup without even thinking.

Then handsome security guard handed me the ticket the lady there held out. "May I ask when to expect you back?"

I blushed, trying not to think of all the wadded panties and bras he'd just seen. Yeah, definitely could've packed better. I had trouble meeting his eyes.

"I'm not sure. I just need to walk, you know? I'll probably get lunch, sit in the park…" My voice trailed off, and I shrugged.

He rested one massive hand on my shoulder. Guy was excessively tall, lean, and way too young for such a serious expression. "When I heard what happened, I was sorry for it. You've been a bright spot in my day, smiling at everyone who catches your eye or stopping to help anyone in need. The world needs more people like you, and I'm sorry you won't be in mine any longer."

I stared up at him, at a loss for words.

He chucked me under the chin. "Be back before closing. And I truly wish you the best."

Tears found my eyes then, but I was determined not to let them fall…or to throw myself at this guy I barely knew and sob all over his pressed uniform.

"Thank you. That was so kind…thank you."

He turned me toward the door. "I've got a double shift today. Come say goodbye when you pick up your luggage."

I offered him a wobbly smile. Then I'd be deep into my sunglasses after crying for hours and my voice would be thick and I'd be a hot mess. Not a good idea.

"Sure. I'll do that."

After one more kind smile that was just too much, he headed for his post, and I headed toward the front doors.

I stumbled out of the building into bright sunshine, air with just a hint of warmth—spring raising its head slowly, deciding if it wanted to come out—loud New York noises, and birds chirping in the park across the street. What a beautiful day to go to Paris.

My shoulders slumped, and I started walking.

I didn't know where I was going, just that I was fragile, tired, and needed to distract myself from the oncoming spiral ASAP.

CHAPTER FORTY

I stood on the street corner, staring into traffic whizzing by. The city never slept, especially at this ungodly early hour. I thought I didn't have to sleep either. I couldn't have been more wrong.

A taxi screeched to a halt. The driver waved me over.

I shook my head and turned away.

I wouldn't know where to tell him to take me. I needed to walk. To think.

I blindly made my way down the sidewalk as I beat myself up.

I didn't have a job anymore. I wasn't going to Paris. I wasn't going to become a famous photographer. I'd messed up one time too many.

As I walked away, numb, I clutched all my earthly possessions in my bag over my shoulder.

Okay, most of my stuff was back in my apartment, and I did have luggage checked into concierge, but I was being dramatic here.

While I strolled the city, part of me wanted to head home, but nothing was waiting for me there. Gavin thought I was in Paris. Well, on my way, anyway. And something told me I'd only hole up and cry for two weeks, so why rush that blissful event?

Just when my legs started telling me they hurt, I stopped in front of an alley. A familiar one. The same one where Gavin and I had first discovered the body and the vampire and all the blood.

The crux that had started this whole misadventure.

I ambled down the alley and stopped right about where we'd found the body, staring down at the spot and having a lovely little pity party for one.

As I stood there, I shoved my hands deep in my pockets and let the infernal freaking cold NYC air whip over my hunched shoulders. So much for the little warmth from earlier. The tall buildings here blocked any sun.

Why had I insisted what I saw was real?

Why hadn't I let the NYPD handle it, like everyone and their cousin twice removed had told me to do?

Why had I thought I could blow off my job so many times and still keep it?

Why hadn't I just told Gavin the truth, for heaven's sake?

He was *right there*.

But I was hurting, he was finishing his shoot, and I didn't want to bother him.

Just how upset would he be when he found out I'd kept this from him?

After my mind spun and whirled and obsessed over questions I couldn't answer, after the cold let me know I was insane for standing still for so long, I turned to go.

Bang.

I spun back around.

A door near the back of the alley had slammed open, and a little old man, a familiar old man, was running toward me, away from two thugs.

One of whom also looked familiar.

"Mr. Withers, please, sir, I need you to calm down."

He stopped and cowered against a trash bin, gasping for air and trembling. "You—you stay away from me, young man. I'm through with your lot. Do you hear me? Through!"

Both men advanced, hands raised, trying to look nonthreatening.

As if anything about them could look nonthreatening.

"Mr. Withers, you need to come with us, sir. It isn't good for you to be out here."

They still hadn't seen me. I startled, realizing it wouldn't take much for them to glance my way. I darted behind two reeking trash bins and peeked behind me, looking for escape.

Dang! I hadn't realized how far into the alley I'd wandered.

I mean, that wasn't safe all on its own, but going where a murder had taken place not that long ago? *Come on, Candace, think!*

I dug in my bag for my phone.

Detective Sawyer was now on speed dial, and I intended to use this superpower I wasn't supposed to have.

The men were within grabbing distance. A few more steps and they'd be able to see me. Old man Withers looked close to tears.

I know the feeling, buddy. I'd been grabbed by linebacker number one over there, and it wasn't my fondest memory.

Detective Sawyer picked up. "Miss Marshall, need I remind you—"

I spoke, low, breathlessly, and a bit unintelligibly. I didn't want the thugs to hear me, for pity's sake! "Detective, I found him. I found old man Withers!"

He was quiet a moment. "This isn't—"

"No, listen, they're about to find me. It's the same alley where I first met you. When he was a body? You know, dead but not really? Anyway, two thugs are trying to drag him back in some dank hole and I—"

"Hey! What're you doing here?"

I shrieked and threw my phone at his face, spinning to flee. He grabbed me and hauled me back as my phone bounced away under the trash bin Mr. Withers was now using to hold himself up, the one I'd just been hiding behind.

He dumped me next to the old man, and I wedged myself between Mr. Withers and the two men on steroids.

I pointed at both of them in turn, my other hand making a stop motion. "You both need to leave this guy alone. Right now. I mean it. How dare you! Beating up an old man? If he wants to leave, let him go, for heaven's sake."

The second thug gave me a strange look but spoke to his companion. "Hey, who is this chick?"

The one I recognized laughed. "The wannabe vampire hunter. Boss says to ignore her. No one believes a thing she says." The other guy joined in sneering, as the first now spoke to me. "This has nothing to do with you, Miss Marshall." He jerked his chin. "Just go, and we'll forget this whole thing."

Like I was taking that option.

I reached behind me and grabbed the man's—still velvet? Seriously?—jacket. I'd been expecting tweed, for some reason. It just kinda came with old man status.

Apparently he'd bought into this whole vampire thing hook, line, and sinker.

"Look, we're just going to go. Okay? No harm, no foul."

Believe me, I did *not* know sports terms, so I had no idea if what I'd just said applied. But it sounded like it.

The first thug pushed me back, and I stumbled. "This is none of your concern. Stay out of it."

Oh no he *didn't*.

Glaring at the thugs, I dragged the old man behind me and started to nudge him toward the alley's exit.

They looked at each other and then, simultaneously, stepped around me toward Mr. Withers, pushing me out of the way. As I squeaked, they both grabbed his arms, lifted him off the ground, and carried him away.

I shot after them. "Hey! You leave him alone this instant."

They ignored me, the old man sobbing and whimpering between them, dangling there like a rag doll.

"Hey! Put him down! I'm warning you!"

Throwing all caution and good sense to the wind, I ran at them. I mean, how many times were they going to make this guy disappear? Enough was enough!

They apparently didn't see me as a threat, cause they kept going.

I grabbed a two-by-four left rotting in the alley and slammed it on the back of linebacker number two's neck, the one I didn't know, and he dropped.

I mean, like, straight down.

It would've been totally cool if linebacker number one hadn't turned on me like he was about to murder me into oblivion. But he tossed the old man down, which I was counting as a positive.

"Run!" I settled into a batter's pose—I think—and got ready to use it again.

The old man ran back toward the door where anyone could just pop out and grab him.

"Not that way! The other way."

He switched directions as the thug advanced.

I waited for the perfect moment and swung.

He ducked under it, reached up and grabbed it, and shook me off in one swift, smooth motion.

I fell on my butt. He reached for me. I rolled away, through something wet and nasty, and sprang to my feet. I took a split second to look for the old guy.

Still running, definitely wheezing and stumbling and struggling…he wasn't going to make it.

Unless I could do something about this guy.

Linebacker came at me. I started grabbing bags of trash from heaping piles and flinging them in his path. Apparently no one around here knew how to make it *in* the trash bins.

Definitely spilled trash juice on my brand-new name-brand clothes that I now couldn't replace. Yuck.

The first bag tripped him, but he dodged the others.

"Go, go, go," I yelled.

Linebacker picked up his own bag of trash, swung it at me, and my head connected with the brick wall.

Goodnight, New York City.

CHAPTER FORTY-ONE

My head ached. My hands were twisted behind me, pulling my shoulders into a super uncomfortable position. Something smelled horrible, and I was sitting upright, in a cold metal chair...

My eyes snapped open.

Metal?

I looked around the room frantically, the dark recesses not receiving any light from the few candles burning in the room. Candles?

As I struggled to place where I was, memories flooded me. The alley—the old man being chased—all real. I fought harder, but the—handcuffs?—clamped to the metal chair wouldn't let go. Oh no. Not again.

I was so over the role of damsel in distress.

And whatever that smell was.

"Ugh. What is that? Smells terrible." I gagged a little.

I swear it didn't smell this bad last time.

I sniffed my shirt. Oh. It was me. Guess that's what I got for rolling around in trash.

Anyway. Needed to focus on escape.

My fingers scrabbled for my pockets and my phone. Not

there. Then I frantically searched for my bag. Also not on me. Of course.

That's okay, I told myself. *Once Gavin doesn't hear from me…*

My shoulders slumped. Never mind. Gavin thought I was leaving on an extended business trip to Paris with a side of photography at my new un-position and wouldn't be back for two weeks.

And I *still* couldn't call him. How could I never remember that when he was around?

What about that thing with Lola?

Nope, I refused to believe it. We may both be crazy busy, he may be crazy for being with me, and he may have secrets in his closet, but surely the gentleman I knew and loved wouldn't do anything behind my back while we were still dating. Would he? And the past was in the past, no matter how much it might bother me right now.

But I should at least ask him, right? Or no?

Of course, if I died in this place, wasting precious time obsessing wouldn't matter in the least.

I tugged some more at my bonds. Maybe if I just…

"Ah, she's awake."

I jumped as several richly dressed and rather vampiric-looking people came into the room. The one who'd spoken was the gentleman in the purple suit at the vampire club card game.

Although he had a smile on his face, he didn't seem quite so fatherly or quite so friendly anymore. And now his suit was royal blue and made of one of the richest fabrics I'd ever had the pleasure of working with. What was it called again?

The Asian guy in the crushed-silk suit stood smiling next to him. He too was wearing something else entirely, but it was no less exquisite. Or expensive.

Several others stood behind them. As my eyes adjusted,

I stared in awe at their luxurious clothing, the brocade furniture. Candlestick holders that towered over my head. Tapestries on the walls. All very lavish. All very Victorian. Steampunk, maybe?

After all, Mr. Withers had been obsessed with all things steampunk and vampire, according to his boss.

Whatever it was, the occupants were dressed to match the décor, and I immediately started placing everyone where I'd want them to stand if this were a photo shoot.

In my head, of course.

Gotta admit, I was slightly distracted admiring the way this scene was set up—another reason Stan and I had worked so well together. We admired beauty in all its forms, and it was a rare session we weren't *oohing* and *aahing* over the models, the clothing, the materials, the sets, the flowers, the props—just everything.

But when I shifted, my handcuffs rattled against the metal, and my predicament came crashing down over me once more. Like a bucket of ice water.

I had to get out of here.

"What am I doing here? What do you want from me?" I demanded. "And where on earth did Mr. Withers go?"

Okay, it came out more like a whimper, but I *meant* to be strong and firm and somewhat in control of myself.

"All in good time, Miss Marshall," the man with the deep voice and blue suit rumbled. "All in good time."

All in good time, my left eyeball. I wanted answers *now*. I opened my mouth to try again.

A shout from outside the room interrupted me. "Where is she? I want to see that meddlesome chit *right now*."

My eyes widened with every syllable of the tirade coming my way, approaching footsteps getting louder.

The cool-as-a-cucumber vampire smiled. "Ah. The All-Father approaches."

"The all-what now?" Let's face it. I was deep in cray-cray town right now.

"The father of all covens. Well, he was, until his brother betrayed him and the covens fractured into factions and this endless feud began. But as the first and eldest and most powerful among us, he deserves our honor and respect."

I didn't have a chance to respond to the guy I'd played cards with, because the All-Father was upon us.

In other words, Horatius, still in that awful velvet suit with all the lace. Did he not get the memo that his entire coven had upgraded to non-embarrassing clothing?

"You!"

I tried to scramble back, but the chair and chains held me fast.

The vampire came flying at me, finger pointing, protruding teeth bared. He stopped inches from me and slapped me. Hard.

I gasped and rocked in my tied-up position, captive, nowhere to escape.

"It's because of *you* we've had all this trouble! No one came poking around, no one came looking for the corpses that disappeared, no one bothered us…until you!"

He screamed in my face, spittle flying.

My knees shook, and I slouched against my bonds, too scared to stay upright.

"Well"—his face grew deathly calm, the sudden change absolutely terrifying—"I suppose you'll get to witness first-hand what happens to those who meddle in things they ought not."

Ought not. Ought not! Was this the guy who'd threatened me the first time? Of course, did that really matter since this was the third time he'd blatantly kidnapped me?

"You have messed with us for the last time, Miss Marshall. Have you ever wondered what it would be like to die?"

My mind just kinda went blank and shut down as we stared at each other.

He swept his hand at the burly guy standing behind him. The one I hadn't knocked out in the alleyway. "See to it that she's disposed of, every drop drained. It's been a while since my children have had an entire person at once."

I would've given anything to react, to fight, to do anything other than shake like a frightened animal. Fear paralyzed my mind, dread clenched my stomach, and stupor overtook my vision.

Stupid me was going to pass out.

I was going to spend my last moments on earth lying bound in a helpless, huddled heap while I *died*. Pathetic.

He turned his back on me in disgust. "Get rid of her."

No, he couldn't. I wouldn't let him. I had to do something, fast.

"But—I wrote that article, just like you wanted me to!" I said it all in a rush. I had to keep him talking. I had to. I was too young to die.

He spun back at me, his teeth bared, fangs long and glistening and…well…kinda gross, if I were being honest here. "That so-called article has backfired. Our coven is getting more attention than ever, police are crawling everywhere they shouldn't, and, thanks to you, we now have to move our entire base of operations!"

Okay, so not good. But at least I was keeping him talking. Yay, me?

He continued. "I should have known you were associating with our sworn enemies…"

I rolled my eyes. "Oh, for heaven's sake. I'm not *associating* with anyone. I just want to be left alone. And your brother made me write that stupid article in the first place. And you made me write the second!"

Spittle went flying as he sputtered. "Well, you didn't have to be so specific. And if you recall, *you* convinced *me*. I should have never let you talk me into another article. You should have left well enough alone!"

I desperately wanted to wipe my cheek. And maybe slide through the floor without his noticing? "I only did what you asked—"

"What you fail to understand, my dear, is that every vampire who wishes our downfall will come clamoring to find us, to finish us off—thanks to you!"

He was shouting again, and it was seriously damaging my calm.

Not that I had any to begin with.

"What about Mr. Withers? Is he okay?" I asked.

"Mr. Withers will receive his due punishment, as will you."

I gritted my teeth. I. Would. Not. Cry! "For heaven's sake, leave him alone! What did he ever do to you?"

"He gave me his word, Miss Marshall, as did you, if you recall. I do not take kindly to those who break such. It has devasting consequences, as you will soon discover."

Another linebacker shot through the door, rushed up to Mr. Velvet Vamp—did they seriously hire a retired football team as bodyguards?—and whispered in Horatius's ear. "You need to come see this. Immediately."

Dude was trying his best, but he was one of those guys who didn't know what an inside voice was. Luckily for me.

"Can't you see I'm clearly busy here?" the All-Father all but seethed.

Something didn't sit right with me.

I squinted at the guys pretending to be vampires. "I don't understand why you hire bodyguards to do all your dirty work when you have a coven full of immortal, impossibly strong vampires."

Horatius smiled. "Who said they are not vampires themselves?"

"Um, daylight? Please. Also, I wouldn't have been able

to knock out that other guy if he were." Um, maybe not the best thing to remind him? "Uh, how is he, by the way? I didn't want to hurt anyone, just get away."

Another smile, though this one looked more genuine. "He is very much looking forward to returning the favor."

I swallowed hard and closed my eyes, trying to push down the fear. I could cry later. When I was home. I couldn't fall apart now.

The giant, hulking, beefy dude wrangled back the conversation, once again trying to whisper. "It's urgent! We've been invaded. They're gathering on the lower levels—"

"Fine," Horatius snapped, cutting off the guard and casting me a disgruntled look. "As for you, I want you to sit here and think about what you should've done differently, young lady."

I hardly dared to breathe. This just might be the chance I needed to escape.

Before hope could rise in my eyes and give myself away, I averted my gaze as he snapped his fingers a bunch of times at his people. "My children, to me. If this really is as important as you claim…"

His voice trailed off as he stared daggers at the security dude who'd dared interrupt him from killing me—*Thank you, Lord*—and the guard audibly swallowed.

Then Horatius turned that dagger-stare on me.

His eyes were cold, hard, and very, very angry. "Our troubles started because of you, and I swear by the great Dracul, you shall not cause my coven another. You will be yet another victim this city has swallowed into its underbelly, only to turn up later as nothing more than a corpse."

My head shot up. "You can't do that. My boyfriend is Gavin Bailey, world-famous movie star! I work at a prestigious fashion company, and I called the cops, a detective I know personally, right before I was grabbed. This will be all over the news, and you won't be able to find another place to hide!"

Why have connections if you can't use them at least once?

"Oh, the company you were fired from for chasing vampires?"

"That wasn't—"

"The detective who hung up on you because he thinks you're crazy?"

"He wouldn't—"

"The boyfriend who thinks you're out of town for two weeks, off to Paris, whom we plan to have our people leave messages you've left him before so he thinks you're fine and has missed every single one of your calls?"

"You can't—"

"Oh, wait just a moment." He tapped his chin as if thinking. "You mean the boyfriend who's going to find a suicide note after you've supposedly returned? A note your detective saw coming a mile away?"

"They wouldn't—he won't—how could you?"

Now I was blubbering all over the place.

Way to hold it together, Candace, way to hold it together.

He just smiled, though it was full of hate. "I shall leave you to your thoughts."

The entire group clustered out of the room as they'd come in, leaving me with fang-filled parting smiles. The heavy metal door screeched closed, its rattle ricocheting throughout the room.

I wasn't sobbing hard enough, apparently. Now I started to dry heave and hiccup.

My body would be decomposing before Gavin even knew to look for me.

I dropped my head and cried as the strong feeling that I needed to pray came over me. Maybe I should, since, you know, I hadn't really done that this whole time?

Maybe I wouldn't be in this mess if I had. Or if I'd listened to all the people God put in my life.

I prayed in earnest. "Lord, please forgive me for not listening to anyone. For not telling Gavin the full truth. For chasing after this when literally everyone in the entire world told me not to."

The words didn't sit right on my tongue. I *had* to do this. I *had* to find out if Mr. Withers was okay.

I stopped, then burst out with: "But I couldn't just let him die! Everyone said he was dead, and he wasn't, and you can see him just over there—well, somewhere down here—I know you can."

I paused, searching for the right words, wondering if anyone else in this nasty place was listening. Didn't care. I needed guidance, and I needed it ASAP.

"I guess I'm just asking for help. Please, God. Get me out of here. Me and Mr. Withers. Help the cops find us. Oh, and please don't let Gavin be *too* mad when he finds out what I've done. In Jesus's name, amen."

I started tugging on my bonds in earnest.

I was getting out, somehow, and I had to do it fast.

The door shifted open, with only the slightest grating noise.

I lifted my head, fire in my blood, ready to get out of here and *do* this. Whatever this was.

CHAPTER FORTY-TWO

Old man Withers burst into the room, his sparse hair sticking straight up and his eyes wild.

I gasped. "You're not dead!"

Cause that was totally what I was expecting after he'd tried to get away from this place.

He rushed over and slipped a key into the handcuffs, shaking so hard he could barely unlock them.

"It's okay," I soothed. "You've got this. Just slowly turn and…there you are."

Apparently it takes someone more freaked out than I am to calm me down. Who knew? At least we weren't feeding off each other.

Ugh. And now I needed non-vampiric-sounding phrases.

The handcuff popped free, and he shuffled to the other side.

"How did you get in here?" I asked.

"Knocked out the guard. Stole his keys."

"And how did you get away from wherever they were keeping you?"

"I convinced them I still want to be here. They p-put me under light g-guard, but I knocked him out too."

"Wait. You don't? Want to be here?" I had to make sure.

He shook his head, his eyes going all watery. He didn't seem like he could say anything else.

I grabbed his arm and shook him out of his trance. "Hey, don't forget the second handcuff."

Look at me, being the voice of reason for once.

My other hand came free. His wide, frightened eyes met mine. "We need to go. Now. I don't know how long we have till they wake up and sound the alarm."

"Don't have to ask me twice."

On our way out, I saw my purse lying on the desk and seized it with joy. I took a few precious seconds to rifle through it—everything was accounted for, even my cash—except the phone I'd thrown at Scary Linebacker's head.

I sighed. What I wouldn't give to be able to call for help right now.

We eased open the door, stepped over the guard slumped there, and crept down a long and sparsely lit hallway. After about a million twists and turns, ducking into hidden nooks and crannies any time we heard a noise, he led me into what seemed to be an old service network for the subway, because we soon came upon an old, empty, cobwebby subway track. It was broken in places, and grates above let in some light.

So we weren't as deep as I thought we were.

But the smell was so much worse. Water dripped somewhere, and I was pretty sure there had to be a pile of rat corpses nearby, the air was so rank.

Hey, at least it wasn't just me, right?

I turned to him. "Where do we go now?"

I hadn't realized he was clutching my arm until that very moment. I almost squealed. Gavin would be so proud of me! Being the brave one for once.

Then I noticed I was clutching his arm right back.

And…Gavin. Oh. Oh no. He would kill me. Maybe hug me, though that was debatable. Then probably kill me again.

Before old man Withers could answer, we heard a shout echo from somewhere behind us.

"She's gone! The old man too!"

We apparently hadn't gone far enough.

"Run!" I squeaked.

We ran opposite ways, and I finally gave in to the old man trying to drag me his way. Fine. Now wasn't the time to lose my head.

Though I desperately wanted to go *toward* the light, not away from it.

Thankfully another light-giving grate came into view right when I thought we'd never be able to see again. Thankfully neither of us tripped. Thankfully our pursuers went in the other direction.

When I thought it might be safe to talk, I asked in a low voice, "So you guys aren't really vampires, right?"

He shook his head, sparse gray hair waving every which way. "No, they only like to pretend they are. At least, they don't *act* like vampires in any lore. Sure had me fooled. I don't know if it's a front or if they really think they are, but I don't care. I just want out."

"You and me both, sir. You and me both."

Most of me was elated to be right, but a teeny-tiny part of me wilted in embarrassment. What on earth was *wrong* with me? If I knew they weren't real, why was I chasing after them so hard? And why had Mr. Withers?

I just couldn't wrap my mind around it. I faced him. "But why, Mr. Withers? You had a job, an apartment, a comfortable living. Why would you give it all up to live, well, here." I gestured all around at the dark, dank space.

Mr. Withers shuffled at my side, looking miserable. "I've always been a little, well, odd."

My heart gave a pang. Boy, did I know what that felt like.

He shrugged, his sharp shoulder blades standing out against his shirt. "I found a place where I belonged. Where I was accepted, just the way I am." His Adam's apple bobbed, a watery sheen coating his eyes. "I thought I was home."

I was a sucker for sob stories, plus I could so relate.

I draped my arm around his too thin shoulders. "I am so sorry."

"So am I." He not-unkindly stepped just far enough away that I had to drop my arm. His eyes got a faraway look. "I would've given anything for it to be real."

My stomach clenched. I would've given anything for my life in New York City to be real too. But it was just an unattainable dream, wasn't it?

I hadn't prioritized it or Gavin.

And now I'd probably lost both.

His voice pulled me out of my pity party. "Come on. This way."

I followed Mr. Withers deeper into NYC's underbelly.

✗

Hours later, we were hopelessly lost.

"Think it's safe…to take…a rest?" I tried not to wheeze.

In answer, Mr. Withers sank against the nearest wall, a dry spot just out of the light, tucked behind a few aging crates. I plopped in front of the nearest crate, trying to keep a lookout in both directions.

"So if you guys aren't real vampires, what are you?" I asked a little too loudly.

He clamped his grimy hand over my mouth. "Will you hush?" His eyes darted feverishly around our hiding place. "I'll tell you everything if you just…hush."

I jerked away, swiping my mouth with the back of my hand. Gross! Would I ever be free of those germs? I glanced at my own dirt-encrusted hands.

They weren't much cleaner, come to think of it…

"Deal," I said.

He nodded. "Okay, here's the thing. The covens are more of a…society."

I raised an eyebrow.

"You know. An association. Institution. Organization?"

I just looked at him.

He paused. "A vampire club?"

I rolled my eyes. "Yes, I know."

He spluttered. "Y-you do? H-h-how?"

"What else could it be? Vampires aren't real."

I said that with far more confidence than I was feeling. At the moment, I could believe just about anything lived in these shadows. Being lost in the deep, dark, dank underbelly of NYC would do that to a person.

But I knew that. Really. I'd just spent most of my time here in New York trying to prove that very thing while believing the opposite. Not that I was about to admit it.

"But there's more."

"I can't wait to hear this," I muttered, intensely curious about what I'd thrown my entire life, career, and relationship away for.

"Just…let me explain." He scrubbed a hand through his sparse hair. "You have to understand. I had no one. Nothing. Well, besides money. I was shy, kept to myself, and enjoyed my book worlds far more than real life."

Didn't everyone? I hoped so, because he was describing me to perfection.

"So when they approached me about becoming a real vampire"—his eyes gleamed in the half light—"how could I say no? It was everything I'd always wanted and more."

And there's where the resemblance crashed to a sudden halt. Like a record scratch.

I just stared at him. "You wanted to drink blood?"

The very tops of his withered cheeks colored slightly. "You have to understand, I didn't think of the moral implications. I just wanted out. Of my life. Of my job. And I was too stuck to do anything about it on my own. To be offered immortality—I had to do something, don't you see? Dracula was my hero."

I glanced around, hoping our very human captors weren't anywhere near us. "Yeah, Bram Stoker's book or the multiple retellings or the many movies since?"

Which, by the way, were all *fiction*, I almost said.

"Any of it. All of it. I don't care the take, I don't care how poorly done, I am fascinated by vampires and always have been. I had to see if it were real."

I looked at him. "And now?"

Again, high color on his cheekbones. "I'm an old man. Living in a dank, musty underground lair isn't good on my bones. I just want to go home. Sit in my chair. Read a book. Have a bracing cup of tea."

"But you have nothing. You gave it all to them."

He looked defeated. Shrugged. "I'll have to start over again, I know. I hope my job will take me back. That's what I get for believing in something that isn't true. For chasing my dreams."

I elbowed him. Gently. I didn't want to be responsible for the old geezer keeling over on my watch. "Hey, don't talk like that. Granted, not everyone's dreams lead to living in a sewer—"

His face colored. "Abandoned subway section."

I smiled and patted his arm. Hey, my nose was working just fine, and I wasn't living in denial. I knew where we were. "But at least you went for them, right? Now you get to choose how you live the rest of your life. Besides, once we get out of here, it'll be a great story. I might even interview you for my blog."

If I even kept the darn thing. I probably wouldn't.

But some resolution would be nice. For both of us.

And my viral vampire-loving following, probably.

I turned to study the deserted subway tunnels once more. We needed to keep moving. I just didn't know where we were going, or if we were moving toward the vampires or away. I wished I'd paid more attention.

But, you know, trying not to die here?

I added, somewhat distractedly, "Detective Lawson said there are some great vampire clubs in the city. Some hardcore and some fun. Maybe you can check those out."

He held up both hands. "No, thank you. I'm going to live the rest of my life vampire free."

I couldn't blame him. I was vowing the very same thing.

I nodded toward the tunnels. "It still looks clear, but I don't know how much longer it'll stay that way. Do you know which way we should go?"

He shook his head.

I bit my lip. "Well, we can't just stay here. We've got to get to the surface. Do you care if I choose a way? Even if I'm wrong?"

He didn't look too confident in my abilities. That made two of us.

"Well, just don't get us *too* lost," he said with a whole lot of doubt in his voice. "It was all very exciting to play undead, at first, but I don't want to do it again. And I don't want to go back to the coven, alive or in a body bag."

Again, that made two of us.

I laid my hand on his arm to comfort him. "I promise I will do everything in my power to get you out of here. I called Detective Sawyer before I came after you, so we should have backup as soon as we get out."

He nodded.

I let out a nervous laugh. "You wouldn't happen to know how to get back to that alley, would you?"

He started to answer, but our cozy little getaway scheme went to pot in an instant. (What? I have no idea what that meant, just that my grandma used to say it all the time.)

It happened so fast, in fact, I did nothing. Literally nothing.

Mr. Withers looked over my shoulder and froze, eyes wide, jaw slack, fear suffusing his face. The bottom plunged out of my stomach, like I was on one of those drop zones I refused to ride because they felt like sudden death, and a hand covered my mouth.

Like I said, I did nothing but sit there like a frozen dummy.

"Hunting vampires, are we, miss?" came a deep, drawling voice, right next to my ear.

I thought about jerking away, I really did.

"Promise you won't scream, and I'll let you go."

I wasn't sure what the right answer was here. Thankfully, Mr. Withers poked me, breaking my trance, and I jumped. Then nodded a bunch of times.

Dude let me go, and I scrambled next to Mr. Withers, my back to the same wall. Except I sat in something wet. Gross.

Scary guy from the bus was squatting there, staring at me with a smirk on his face but confusion in his eyes. "Thought you didn't hunt vamps."

I shook my head enthusiastically. "Don't. Wouldn't ever." I hooked a thumb over my shoulder. "Escaping them, actually."

His eyes lit up. "Really. Hear that, A.C.? Escaping them."

I spared the briefest glance for the other dude I was just now noticing standing in the shadows, keeping watch. Then

I decided bus guy was the bigger threat and kept my gaze firmly planted on him.

"Think you can show me where these vamps are, miss?"

Objections exploded out of both of our mouths at the same time—mine and Mr. Withers—and we shook our heads and objected and tried to save our necks with everything we had. In whispers, of course.

We were still somewhat trying to hide over here, thank you very much.

He eyed us both in turn. "If I promise to get you both out safely, can you at least show us where you came from?"

The guy behind him made his own objection deep in his throat, but bus dude waved him off.

I tried to figure out what *that* meant. Like, was he going to feed us to a pack of fake vamps or use us as bait or what?

Mr. Withers spoke up in a low tone. "We just escaped that den of iniquity, after being held against our will. How do we know you'll let us leave?"

I nodded my head, once again enthusiastically, and hooked my thumb in Mr. Wither's direction. "What he said."

The guy stood tall and pushed his hat back on his head. He looked like a scary Indiana Jones, but with the dark knee-length overcoat and midnight-colored hat, perfect for hunting vamps instead of relics.

That's when I noticed a third guy stood deeper in shadow, clutching the box I'd heedlessly given this dude after paying five hundred freaking bucks for it.

I could've at least sold it to him.

Though, not important right now.

But what was important: Was this guy friend or foe? Should we trust him or not?

I looked to Mr. Withers, and we made some kind of silent agreement. I mean, we were hopelessly lost, hadn't come across a way out yet, and if these guys accidentally found us, then freaking vampires supposedly hunting for our blood would *definitely* find us.

"We'll show you," I squeaked, then cleared my throat. "But," I said, with a clear effort to deepen my voice a few notches, and shook my finger at him like a stern little old lady, "then you are getting us out of here, young man."

Vampire hunter blinked, probably because he was a great deal older than me, like in his forties or fifties or something, and touched his hat in a respectful, old-western move.

"Ma'am."

I took that for agreement and helped Mr. Withers to his feet. We were both still shaking, so I almost dropped him a few times—and probably would've landed on him if I had—but we finally stood timidly before the three vampire crazies. I mean, hunters.

"One more thing." I clutched Mr. Wither's arm and swallowed. "You should know they're not real vamps. More like a club or something. But they like to pretend they are."

I flicked another glance at the gilded chest the third dude carried. I didn't want anyone's heart carved out because I'd failed to mention that little tidbit, even if they'd kidnapped us and threatened to kill us both.

A half smile played around bus dude's mouth. "Ah, I see. The thing is, they have a way of disguising what they truly are from those who aren't true believers. Of course they would make themselves seem like they weren't real vamps to you both."

Mr. Withers and I exchanged a glance, but as I opened my mouth, Mr. Withers shook his head.

Oh well. At least I'd tried.

"Lead the way." Bus guy swept his hand to the side.

I mimicked the move to Mr. Withers—I had no idea where we were—and with a roll of his eyes, the little old guy toddled off. I smirked and glanced at scary Indiana Jones.

I tilted my head. Perhaps mixed with a little Wolverine, from that first X-Men movie.

Scary bus guy gave me a solid, weighty look, as if asking why I wasn't moving yet, and I scrambled after Mr. Withers to "help."

Besides, better the weirdo I somewhat knew than the creepy guy I didn't.

CHAPTER FORTY-THREE

"Are you sure this is the right way?" I hissed, trying to stay as quiet as possible.

Mr. Withers was shaking harder than a leaf in a tornado, but now he also looked worried. "I think so?"

That did not bolster my confidence. Or bus guy's from the weight of his silence behind us.

"Okay." I nodded and smiled. Hey, I was trying to stay positive here, all right? "You're doing great."

He nodded in return, so I took his arm and helped him over a rough patch into a darkened tunnel.

There was just enough light on the other side that we didn't trip over the old tracks or fall and break something, thank goodness, but as soon as we entered the giant room, I knew we'd made a mistake.

They were waiting for us.

These vampires were not dressed in ridiculous velvet with capes. Oh no. These dudes and gals were drenched in black leather, had stringy dark hair and bloodred lips, and were hissing.

I immediately turned and pulled Mr. Withers back toward the tunnel. The three vamp hunters had scattered, hugging the walls of the tunnels, weapons drawn. Looked like stakes and machete-type short swords, but that wasn't what caught my attention.

Glowing eyes stopped me cold.

Coming at us from the other end of the tunnel.

Up until this point, I'd still been holding on to the hope that this was all a prank. Another movie trick. Someone wanting to scare the crap out of me, like my brother.

Though, okay, fair—he wouldn't be able to pull off something this elaborate.

But the glowing eyes, glistening fangs, and sheer numbers surrounding us made me seriously doubt myself.

Oh my gosh, *were* vampires real?

But Mr. Withers has said they were fake! That this was just a club! And then the vampire hunters had immediately countered that. Then again, they *would* if this were another movie set.

Those in the tunnels crept forward, pushing us into the lighter room, and they looked just as scary as the guys at our backs. Except these guys were decked out in velvet. They hissed too, just trying to make me curl into a ball and start sobbing.

Hey, it was close to happening, okay?

Mr. Withers started whimpering, so I put my arm around his shoulders.

"It's okay, Mr. Withers. We'll get out of this." Somehow. *Dear God, please help us get out of this!*

The vampire hunters clustered around us, all five of us facing out, though two of us were clearly going to be no help whatsoever.

Bus guy tried to hand me his machete, but I gave him a look. "Forget it. I'm not cutting off anyone's head. Or staking them."

He grunted, unlooped a large silver cross from around

his neck, and tried to hand that to me instead. "At least take this."

I rolled my eyes. "Let me guess. It will burn them, or they'll fall down in terror or something?"

He gave me a dark look. "I don't think you appreciate the severity of our situation."

I showed him my little blessed silver cross, somewhat embarrassed. "I think I do. I just think we're experiencing completely different situations here."

"I don't have time for this." He turned back to his group. "I want the leader's heart in that box." He pointed at it with the silver cross, then looped it back around his neck.

On second thought, I should've accepted the cross, so on days I second-guessed this ever happened, I could pull it out and say to myself, "See!"

If I lived through this, of course.

"But there are five leaders!" I blurted.

I instantly had their attention. "What?" said the main vampire hunter succinctly.

I pointed at the advancing horde. "Five covens means five leaders. Unless you're talking about that All-Father guy." My mind went blank. "Horticus? Horatio?"

"Horatius," said Mr. Withers softly.

"Yeah, him," I said, but the others were already huddled and discussing something madly.

But then I noticed something strange.

Vampires weren't just walking our way. Oh-ho-ho no. That would've been too easy. They were dropping from the ceiling, landing in a crouch and hissing, and more and more perched on the walls or ceiling. A few upside down.

Then I noticed a familiar face.

Anders came up next to me, and I tried to sound nonchalant. "So, um, either you guys have amazing ropes, or you really can climb walls."

He gave me a look that said I should know which one without having to guess.

Really, Miss Marshall? After all you've seen? he said inside my head.

Okay fine. Ropes then. And I was sticking to it.

Although it was stupid dark down here, dim lighting streamed in from somewhere. Grates above? Recessed lighting? So the movie cameras could get better shots of our faces?

As I turned a little, trying to keep my eyes on all of them, another group of vamps came up, then another. And finally one more.

Each group had something just a little distinctive that made them stand apart from each other. That and they were actually, physically standing apart. Hissing. Glaring.

Making it pretty clear they weren't from the same coven.

What Vampire Bob told me flashed through my head on fast forward.

Those over there, in dark clothing, were fit and younger. What I thought was leather now looked like a cheap imitation, like a Halloween costume, quite possibly plastic. Must be the ones who tried to fit in with the above world.

The Dark Coven?

The ones walking up just now all had bits of brown leather on wrists or hanging from their hair, all with moonlit landscapes etched into them, and dressed like, well, how to say this nicely? Upper-class hippies.

Must be the Moonlit Coven.

And those chasing us out of the tunnel were obviously from the Midnight Coven, who liked to kidnap with abandon and wear velvet like they were stuck in the '60s—I wouldn't mind one bit if I never saw those guys again.

Vampire Bob, leader of the Blood Coven, came up just then, speak of the devil, followed by a group of well-dressed, healthy-looking individuals.

Out of them all, they were the most unbelievable as vampires. Until they smiled or hissed. With the fangs, yep, definitely vamps.

I sooo wished I had all the vampire gear I'd insisted I didn't need. Stakes, garlic, holy water—I'd try it all right about now.

A fifth and final group came up, clutching elaborate daggers with realistic hearts worked into the pommels. It was just light enough to make them out. Tattoos of daggers stabbed through hearts were stamped all over themselves, on arms or ankles or necks.

They all wore leather, but high-quality fighting leathers, molded to fit each person—vamp—exactly. And they stared daggers at the group that looked like a cheap imitation of themselves.

Pretty sure I heard a few mutters of "You'll never be one of us, so stop trying," but I was not getting involved in that particular drama.

Yep, guessed it. The Stabbed Heart Coven.

Mirvas stood at the head of this group, as if she were their leader.

That's when I noticed the players from the card game stood or crouched before each group.

I turned to Anders. "Wait. Why are these guys fighting when they were playing cards so peacefully before?"

He kept a wary eye on the players of a completely different game now. "Sometimes, not always, the Convergence is used to conduct business between the covens and induct new members. They play cards to keep it civil. I was not invited, so you helped me get in." He flashed me a fang-filled smile. "And for that I thank you."

I grumbled a little. "You are most definitely not welcome."

He laughed. "Believe me, this business was a long time coming. They need to stop stealing our initiates."

Of which I was not one, and Mr. Withers no longer wanted to be. I looked around for backup. The vampire hunters had gotten separated from us when Anders had walked up, focusing on the velvet group. So it was up to me.

I tried to be the voice of reason. "You guys don't need us. We're just gonna walk away, and you guys do whatever it is you do down here. Without us."

A diplomat I was not. Nor eloquent.

Horatius, who was clearly unhinged, sneered. "You've already seen too much, Miss Marshall. And Mr. Withers here has lived among us. I'm afraid I can't let either of you go."

Main vampire hunter guy zeroed in on him and grinned, clutching his machete a little too happily. I did *not* want to see this.

A woman spoke up. I recognized her voice immediately. Mirvas. "The old man was stolen from our brother coven. But I am willing to overlook it as long as it never happens again. As he is now of your coven, he is your prerogative. But the girl is under my protection."

"Mine too," Anders cut in. "But as you stole him from *my* coven, I am not willing to overlook your indiscretion. You must answer for your crimes."

The velvet vampires hissed, which now included that Irish guy I'd seen at the card game, as did those behind the crushed-silk and blue-suit vamp leaders.

Mirvas kept going without a pause. "And as such, I cannot let you harm the human girl."

"Neither can I," Anders added helpfully.

A piece of me thawed, letting a trickle of hope soothe my rattled self. To be stood up for—overwhelming relief. I frowned. But who would stand up for Mr. Withers?

I eyed him. He trembled beside me, looking terrified and somewhat resigned.

"I honor your claim over the girl, but we've given her

chance after chance to stop seeking us out." Horatius's cold gaze found mine. "She hasn't taken them. And I fear she is of the disposition that she won't stop searching for the old man, even if we hide him in the deepest, darkest part of our city, not until she's unearthed all our secrets."

Well, I mean, he wasn't wrong.

He turned back to Mirvas. "I'm afraid I cannot let her go."

Growling, hissing, mewling sounds filled the tunnel, sounding like a bunch of angry cats about to tear into each other, and I started shaking just as much as Mr. Withers.

Horatius held up his hand for silence. "If she relinquishes her hold on a life above, if she promises to join your coven and leave the world of men, then I will allow this breech to slide."

Mirvas growled. "You *dare* tell me what you will and will not allow with *my* charge?"

The old vamp kept going as if she hadn't spoken. "But if she returns to her former life, if she once again comes after us in any way, not even you can protect her."

I threw my hands up, interrupting Mirvas's comeback, whatever it was. "Oh, for heaven's sake! The old man just wants to leave, and so do I! It doesn't have to be a whole thing. Just let us go, leave us both alone, and we'll leave all of you alone. Deal?"

I eyed the leaders and Anders and Mr. Withers.

"We don't even have to fight. Seriously. No mess, no fuss. Just let me have him, and leave us alone."

I couldn't read anything from Anders's expression, but Mirvas shrugged. "I'm not opposed," she said.

Horatius's face went all blotchy. "Unacceptable."

Mirvas grinned and formed claws out of her long fingers and sharp nails, crouching down like she was about to attack. "Then we are at an impasse."

And I was ready to pass out. *Not* a good idea.

"You forget one thing, brother." Vampire Bob spoke up for the first time. "You are *far* outnumbered."

Horatius sneered. "You mean my three covens to your measly two?"

Even as he spoke, more vampires crowded around Vampire Bob, Anders, and Mirvas, as well as the fifth player at the card game.

Horatius's eyes widened, and he glanced behind him, as if expecting more on his side to show up, but no one else did.

Vampire Bob's side far outnumbered his brother's, but I didn't care. I just wanted *out*.

There was a pregnant pause, full of heavy breathing, ever-increasing hissing, and vamps straining forward on all sides. And above us. Couldn't forget that part.

And then they charged.

I shrieked and shielded Mr. Withers the best I could with my body, and Mirvas's leather-clad vamps reached us first.

I raised my arms—because that was going to be effective—and they just streamed around me. I blinked, but Anders had me by the arm and was dragging me out of the mess. I reached back and pulled Mr. Withers after me just in time.

The vampire hunters went nuts, slashing and hacking like this whole thing was real.

Something warm and wet splashed across my cheek, and I blinked. My fingers came away dark red and putrid, almost like the blood was rotten, and I stopped and just stared at my fingers.

Anders came back for me at the same time as bus guy and Vampire Bob.

Right there, in the middle of that horrible battle, enemies on all sides, they stopped and eyed each other.

Bus guy spoke first, to Vampire Bob. "Are you the All-Father, Horatius?"

He shook his head once. "His brother, Vlad."

That stole my attention away from my blood-speckled fingers, and I blinked. Vlad? Now why couldn't he have used *that* name from the beginning? Vlad was an *awesome* name, and Bob was just…ridiculous.

Something in scary Indiana Jones slash Wolverine eased, but only a little. "And does your coven still feud with his?"

Vlad gave a single swift nod. "Always."

Anders gave a reckless grin, fangs on full display. "Team up?"

Scary overcoat dude nodded, they gave each other a fist bump, and apparently Anders gave some mind instructions he didn't bother sharing with me, because part of his group and Mirvas's leather-clad group sheared off and started protecting the hunters, fighting with them against the other three covens.

Anders put his arm around me and hustled me away.

Vampires clashed on all sides, hissing, biting, punching, but soon we were free of them.

"Watch our backs!" he called out.

Another vamp nodded, and a team formed into a half circle, shielding us from those trying to get to us.

"Get the humans out of here!" Vampire Bob—I mean, Vlad—called. "Their blood is too much for us to handle."

You know what? The new name did nothing for him.

I couldn't help it. I rolled my eyes. He took a terrifying situation and made it a little too fake with a side of corny. Maybe I was back to thinking they weren't real.

But I also didn't want to end up dead, so I happily followed Anders out.

"Up there!" one of them at our backs called.

I looked ahead to a beam of light, coming from a manhole above our heads. I brightened. That meant we had a way out!

I started to run toward it, Mr. Withers still in tow—he was huffing and puffing up a storm—but Anders grabbed my arm. I swung around to look at him.

"Can you make it from here?" he asked, deadly serious.

I looked the twenty feet or so I had to run, then back at him. "Um, yes?"

He nodded and kissed my forehead. "Good answer. Hurry."

Sweaty, smelly, breath-like-death vampire is not attractive, let me tell you.

He ran off to join his friends in the fight, and I put my arm around Mr. Withers. "Almost there, sir. Just a few steps more."

He was stumbling and shaking big time. Every instinct in me screamed to flee, to get out of there ASAP and let nature run its course, but I set my jaw and trudged along at a snail's pace.

I was *not* leaving him down here alone again. Even if I didn't have a choice last time.

We were so close, but old man Withers was slowing. And I was trying to stay between him and the vampires chasing us, trying to break through our protective ring, which meant I was slowing too.

Which meant I would be the first one to die.

This is why I didn't watch horror movies! My real life was bad enough as it was.

The ladder was right there. If we could just reach the manhole letting in blessed sunlight and fresh air and…hope.

"Run, Mr. Withers, run! You can make it." I bounced a little. We were *so close*.

Just as we reached the ladder under the manhole, a head popped in. "Miss Marshall? Is that you?"

I nearly fainted from relief. "Detective Sawyer!"

Gun drawn, he aimed it at the vamps chasing us. "NYPD, freeze!"

A few of their footsteps faltered, but they kept coming.

I hiccuped a sob as I gasped for air.

Officer Sawyer aimed, called out another warning, which wasn't heeded, and fired. And suddenly all those footsteps were heading the other way.

I helped Mr. Withers onto the first rung. "You've got this."

He was shaking so badly, he couldn't grip the rebar stuffed into concrete.

"Mr. Withers?" Detective Sawyer asked.

"Yes? Yes, that's me. Thank God!"

"Stay there, sir. I'm coming down for you."

He and two more officers climbed down the ladder, followed by a team of paramedics. They looked the old guy over while the officers kept watch.

Although muffled fighting and running footsteps came from the darkness, the officers didn't leave our side.

Detective Sawyer constantly scanned the barely lit tunnels. "Are you all right, Miss Marshall?"

I was still gasping for air, but now the shakes had set in and I was embarrassingly close to tears. "Yes, sir. Thank you, sir. For everything."

He nodded once, not looking at me.

The paramedics finished with Mr. Withers, and Detective Sawyer took over.

"Mr. Withers, this is the closest way out of these tunnels. Do you feel strong enough to climb? We can find a staircase or active tunnel system, if you need us to, but that might take us a while."

Mr. Withers still looked frail and helpless and shaken, but he shook his head. "No, sir, I want to get out of here right this very moment."

"Understood." After some squawking back on forth on the radios, a harness came down the hole, and they strapped Mr. Withers in.

After he and the paramedics disappeared through the hole, Detective Sawyer eyed me, then the two policemen standing guard at our backs. The sounds of an epic struggle still echoed down the tunnel.

"You need me to radio the harness in for you, Miss Marshall?" He eyed my shaking hands.

"Nah. I'm good. But thank you." I tried to step on the first rung but missed.

His expression didn't change, but he raised the radio to his lips and called for it anyway. Smart man.

They strapped me in and instructed me to climb like normal. I put a little too much faith in the harness somehow keeping itself taut and scrambled up the ladder with no fear of plunging back down to my death.

Detective Sawyer came up close behind.

Had to admit, it was *not* fun to be one of the last ones leaving that awful place. Sounds still bounced down the tunnel from the epic fight scene currently taking place, and my skin crawled at the thought of having my back to bloodsucking vamps—and a detective who might accidentally shoot me.

Detective best-buds-with-Gavin Lawson helped me out of the manhole, and I stumbled a little, weary beyond belief. All those late, sleepless, stressed-out nights had caught up with me. Plus the emotional exhaustion of—everything, including getting involved with stupid vampire covens in the first place.

And I still didn't know if they were real or fake.

That looked pretty darn real to me.

As Detective Lawson unhooked me, Detective Sawyer paused for a second next to me, and I nodded at him.

I was okay.

He took me in from head to foot, his gaze detached, clinical, before he headed underground with a team. I was ushered toward flashing lights around the perimeter of our exit from the underground labyrinth while Mr. Withers was hurried off to an ambulance and surrounded by paramedics.

Paramedics checked me over as well and wiped blood from my face. I'd forgotten about it, but thank goodness. I didn't want to wear anyone else's blood. Or my own, for that matter.

Once Detective Sawyer's attention was no longer on me, I wrapped my arms around myself and shivered. I was glad Mr. Withers wasn't dead.

I was also glad I wasn't dead.

He was glad he didn't have to spend his retirement years living in a sewer. Drinking blood. Wearing velvet suits and red-and-black capes. And doing other vampire-y things.

Nope, couldn't have gotten the cool vamps of NYC. Just the cheesy, loser-y ones.

And Detective Sawyer had finally broken his not-being-able-to-close-a-case streak. Mostly thanks to me. (And, bonus, we saved a life!)

But as I stood there, unnoticed and forgotten in the sea of blue and red, I couldn't help but feel empty.

I'd lost my job. All of my connections in New York. Jackson wasn't speaking to me. And Gavin probably wouldn't either once he learned I'd broken my word, gone behind his back, and almost gotten killed anyway.

As an actor, he was used to people getting close to him for what he could do for them. He was used to being used. Trust was important to him, and I'd broken that trust.

This conversation was going to be fun.

Not.

CHAPTER FORTY-FOUR

Detective Sawyer came back my way as they loaded Mr. Withers in an ambulance and hauled him away, probably to get some good nutrition in him—I would've opted for pumping his stomach, myself—and to make sure he hadn't caught anything from living underground for so long.

Those were the reasons I told myself, anyway.

I noticed Detective Sawyer and his officers had returned emptyhanded. "Find anything?"

He shook his head. "Got away."

I sighed, and Detective Sawyer handed me my phone. I stared at it, mouth open. Not a crack, chip, or dent in sight. And I'd thrown this thing at some guy's face.

"Where...what...how on earth did this survive?"

He just smiled. It wasn't a bad look on him. He should try smiling more often.

He gave me his steely cop face. "You gonna tell us what you know about this?"

Lawson glanced between us but stayed back, letting his partner take the lead.

I crossed my arms and leaned against the unmarked cop

car. "What's the point? You're just going to ridicule me and scribble SpongeBob's face all over your notepad."

He grimaced, and Lawson grinned wide and winked at me. Bolstered my confidence, not gonna lie. Nice cop was actually being nice to me! With*out* Gavin here.

I swallowed. I couldn't think about Gavin right now.

"About that, Miss Marshall," Detective Sawyer said begrudgingly. "I do apologize. And I'd appreciate if you'd do me a solid and overlook that, just this once, and let me know what you found out about these…" He looked like he was struggling to find the right words. Or maybe just to say them? "Vampire covens."

I sighed again. "Okay, but you're not going to like it."

He pulled out his flip notepad, poised his pen above the paper, and waited, a purely professional look on his face.

Now this I could get used to.

⁂

Detective Sawyer put his notepad away after filling it with copious notes. I was on cloud nine. Even the pucker between his brows couldn't deflate me.

He'd actually listened, taken notes, and remained interested in all the info I'd learned over the course of my misadventure.

"Thank you for your statement, Miss Marshall."

I shrugged, trying to play off all the preening I was doing on the inside. It felt *good* to be treated like a real, actual, live human being. "Like I said. It's what they think, not me."

Because I refused to believe in real vamps until my dying breath. Besides, too many of the things they did could be explained away. Maybe not all, but most.

Both detectives started to move away, but I had more questions. And I wanted at least *some* answers.

"How did you find us, anyway? That was amazing how you just found the exact right manhole."

Detective Sawyer crossed his arms and leaned against his unmarked car. "After you called me, we traced your phone to that alley." He gave me a solid nod. "Quick thinking, calling me the moment you saw Mr. Withers."

A warm glow filled me, and I couldn't help my smile. After all the hate he'd thrown my way for so long, it was so nice to hear him say something positive for once.

"We couldn't find anything, other than signs of a struggle, and all the entrances were a dead end." He frowned. "Then someone called your phone. I answered, just in case, and someone told me to come here."

He raised an eyebrow, and realization swept over me.

Anders. Had to be. I really did owe him a lot.

"You know anything about that?" he asked.

I shook my head. "I can only guess, but I think that guy I first saw in the alley, the one who said he didn't have anything to do with the murder slash kidnapping slash disappearance, was making good on his promise to get me out of this mess. That and clearing his name, of course."

Detective Sawyer eyed me. "Anything you can tell me about him? Name? Description? Where I might find him?"

I shook my head with a smile. "I'm not sure what you mean, Officer."

He grunted but didn't press.

I was just grateful he was letting me have that one.

I waved my hand to where more police officers had disappeared into the manhole and come up emptyhanded. "So what are you guys going to do about those guys who think they're vampires?" I swallowed hard. "They're not really vampires, are they?"

He snorted. "Miss Marshall. Please."

I shrugged. "They seem to think they are."

Plus they were climbing on the walls and ceiling and

biting each other and blood was flying…*shudder*. I wanted to move away from that subject ASAP.

"How are you going to stop those guys?"

He shrugged. "Not much we can do, I guess."

My mouth fell open. "Are you serious? Those guys make a living kidnapping people and convincing them they'll be turned into vampires, then sucking them dry of their money and disposing of them when they're no longer a valuable resource. How could you not want to stop that?"

His eyes had gone steely. "See, the thing is, even if we did put a handful of these perps behind bars, next week they'll be up and running again. There are far too many places to hide underground and far too few of us to go after them—if we even wanted to."

"But people are giving everything they have to these, these…fake vampire organizations."

"And that is truly regrettable. But the fact of the matter is, these people have signed their rights away. As long as they're not breaking any laws or harming others, there's nothing I can do. They live in relative harmony, even if their methods are unorthodox. No one has died"—he raised a hand to stall my argument—"including Mr. Withers. And he has decided not to press charges."

That must mean they hadn't found any bodies below. Who on earth *were* these guys?

I spluttered. "But it could happen again!"

His smile was slightly friendly—well, friendlier than anything I'd seen on him yet. "You helped solve the case, Miss Marshall, thanks to your tenacity and verve."

My jaw dropped. I didn't know he even knew what verve meant. *I* didn't even know what verve meant.

"And for that I thank you."

He extended his hand. I stared at it. Did he really want me to shake it? For real?

I extended my hand slowly, hesitantly, and his broad, meaty hand engulfed my own.

His eyes twinkled briefly. "Will you be joining us while we attempt to track down the rest of these guys?"

I held up both hands and backed up a little. "No sir. Not me. I have wholeheartedly learned my lesson—they're all yours."

Now his grin broke free, the one I'd only seen one other time—when he was arresting me. "Good girl."

I was still having trouble peeling my jaw off the ground as he saw me to the passenger side of a car for Lawson to take me home.

He'd said thank you? He'd shaken my hand? He'd said *thank you*?

Although I was certain I wouldn't make a great detective, at least I'd gotten justice for that not-dead dude. And discovered that somehow, somewhere, on this very planet even, some people actually thought they were vampires.

I snorted. As if.

Now to scrub the image of their climbing the walls from my brain.

✗

Once I got home, I showered, changed out my purse for one *not* covered in sewer gunk, and set out immediately. I had somewhere else I needed to be. Something else I needed to do. Before I lost my nerve.

I didn't have it in me to fight NYC public transport and crowds right then, so I called a rideshare.

As I headed toward the curb, marveling that I'd somehow survived the vampire underworld of New York City, a hand reached out and pulled me around the corner, out of view of traffic. I slammed into a firm (albeit scrawny compared to Gavin's) chest.

Oh my gosh, not again.

Before I could fight him off, my brain registered a familiar pale face with stringy dark hair framing it. Anders grinned. "Hi."

"Oh, uh, um…hi?" I couldn't make my mind work after that.

Once he made sure I was steady on my feet, he crossed his arms and leaned against the brick wall. "So you discovered I was telling the truth, eh?"

"Uh…" That was me, Miss Eloquent. And also fortunately for me, all these handsome men in my life didn't seem to mind.

Ugh. When had my life become a soap opera all of a sudden?

I couldn't get a date all through high school and most of college—might have had something to do with all the tripping and stuttering and hiding and speechlessness—and now all these gorgeous guys were flirting with me like nobody's business.

Of course, Gavin and the other actors in my film *Zombie Takeover* had been paid to do so…and I was halfway convinced the same thing was happening for a coming-soon feature called *Vampire Feud*…but what did I know?

It didn't matter. It. Was. Ridiculous.

He gave me some space to think, then said, "I told you Mr. Withers wasn't really dead."

I shuddered. "Yeah, but he almost died. So many times! If you hadn't made me play that stupid game…" I looked up at him. "That's what it was, right? You knew I was getting in too deep and needed protection."

"You're welcome, love."

I blushed a little at that and shook my head. "How did you know I needed it just then? And that it would work?"

"Ah, I can't give you all my secrets. But I hear things. I keep my finger on the pulse of the underground. And I was especially motivated not to be accused of murder." He grinned. "It makes my job harder if I'm being hunted by your mortal police."

I nodded, wanting to ask so many questions, not sure where to begin.

He should come back a few weeks from now at midnight, when I sat straight up in bed and everything I wanted to say right now in this moment came flooding in, denying me sleep. For hours.

On second thought, he'd better not. I'd probably scream and throat-punch him.

"I guess I just want to say thank you. For clearing my name."

My mouth may have fallen open. Okay, it did.

His grin widened. "And for ensuring I got my revenge."

Okay, I was with him till that point.

"Um, you're welcome?" I shook off my tongue-tied-ness. "And thank you for calling the detective. And for coming after me. We wouldn't have made it out of there if not for you."

He looked pleased, but he just tapped my chin and said, "Who knew little Miss Nancy Drew here would be so helpful after all?"

We stood there a moment, awkward silence filling the space between us.

Then Anders leaned close, and I panicked that he might be trying to kiss me.

Um, nope. I didn't know where Gavin and I stood—or more accurately, where we *would* stand once I talked to him—but getting more pictures of me kissing some other dude wouldn't help. Not happening.

"That can't be healthy," I blurted. "Drinking all that blood."

"What?" He pulled back and looked at me, startled.

"You look terrible."

"I beg your—"

"Do you vamps have a shortened lifespan? Hair falling out? Teeth coming loose?"

He rubbed the back of his head with a quick, furtive motion. "No, we—"

"Seriously, no sun, terrible nutrition—it's no wonder you guys look so awful." Believe me, I'd spent a million years researching what drinking blood did to a human body.

Like it was even possible, but I swear the handsome pirate vampire blanched. But he was definitely at a loss for words. His breath wafted past me, and I gagged a little.

"Look, I don't want to tell you what to do, but you've *got* to get some sunlight and eat something other than blood. It's not good for you. Take some green pills to detox or something. I mean, it's not like you're a real vampire."

I chuckled at my own joke.

His grin was far too charming. *Or am I?*

Yep. He said it inside my head again.

That wiped the grin right off my face.

"How on *earth* do you even *do* that?" I demanded.

He smiled and kissed my forehead, quickly, before I could do anything about it.

Now that I wasn't terrified he was going to bite my neck and suck my blood or throw me over his shoulder and make me his vampire princess, I noticed it was a little wet and a little sloppy. Um, ew?

I started to back up. "So, um, see…you. Around. Probably. I mean, hopefully not. But thanks for everything! And getting me out of there. I seriously want nothing more to do with vamps for the rest of my life. Which I hope will me a very long time. Vamp free. I—"

He interrupted me. Huh. Guess he *and* Gavin knew what they had to do once I started rambling.

"It's been a pleasure, Miss Marshall. I wish you a long,

full life, entirely vamp free." He gave me an elaborate bow, then turned and strode away.

As I watched him walk away, out of my life and back to the underworld of New York City, hopefully never to bother me—or anyone else—ever again, he said, *We could've never made it work, my darling,* with a decidedly pirate flair.

Ugh. How on earth did he *do* that? It wasn't even a little fair that he was leaving me with yet another unsolved mystery. Besides, I swear I'd heard that before…delivered much better, I might add.

"Uh, thank you!" I called after him. Then winced.

I could tell by the hitch in his gait that he'd heard me—who hadn't?—and it wasn't the response he'd been expecting. It wasn't the response I'd been expecting either.

It never was with me, darling, it never was, I said to myself, but it didn't look like he'd heard me.

I watched him go, a little sad for some reason, then glanced up at the sky. It was overcast, but it was still daytime.

"Hey! How are you out"—I looked toward him, to where he'd been, but the street and sidewalk were empty—"in the daylight?" I said to no one.

I sighed. I still didn't think they were real vamps, probably, and they sure didn't match any lore I'd dug up. But I was sincerely happy to leave all that behind.

I faced the street and took a deep breath. Now to talk to Gavin and tell him everything.

And I did mean everything. Nothing held back, no lies by admission, no secrets between us.

It was time for me to come clean.

And I'd take the consequences like an adult. Even if snot and tears and ugly crying would most definitely be involved.

A car pulled up, jarring me from my thoughts, and I ran for my rideshare.

CHAPTER FORTY-FIVE

The rideshare took me straight to Gavin's. The doorman recognized me and let me in, and I made my way to Gavin's door. He didn't answer, so I shot off a text I knew he wouldn't get and slumped to the floor, my back to the wall and head in my hands.

"Candace?"

I jerked awake.

Gavin was staring at me with wide eyes, concern all over his face and a duffle bag over his shoulder. He immediately came over and helped me to my feet.

"Candace, what are you doing here? Aren't you supposed to be in Paris?"

Groggy, I was ushered into his apartment before I could even begin to come up with an answer.

My eyes riveted on all my luggage piled just inside. Where—how had that gotten there? I looked to Gavin with wide eyes.

"Concierge called, so Jodi had it delivered, though honestly"—he eyed the luggage he apparently hadn't seen yet—"I thought you may have forgotten one bag, not all of them. Care to explain why you and your bags aren't in Paris?"

He looked more curious, more concerned, than angry, but boy howdy was that look going to change soon.

I opened my mouth, but it all caught up to me. All of it. Right then. When I least wanted it to.

I was exhausted. I was heartsore. I'd spent the entire day—I checked the closest window, yep, sun was going down—first thinking I was going to die, then fleeing for my life.

That after losing my job, being kicked off the Paris team, disappointing Jackson, and now standing in front of Gavin, who was my safe place. Who might not *want* to be my safe place any longer. After I told him.

I burst into tears. Dang it.

Gavin handled my emotions really well—better than any guy I'd ever known—but now he fell all over himself to hold me, to drop his duffle, to close the door, and to keep his arms around me, all at the same time.

"Candace, lass, please. Tell me what's wrong."

I couldn't talk past all the blubbering, so he gave up on trying to lock the door and just held me.

I mean, I was supposed to be on my way to Paris, now here I was, with my suitcases as evidence against me, a hot mess from being held underground and fighting for my life.

"I j-j-just need to s-s-sleep…" I wailed, too tired to even attempt to control my out-of-control emotions.

He pulled me into the guest bedroom, kissed my temple, and cradled me against his chest. "I hate to leave you like this. You're really scaring me."

I nodded and tried to explain, but nothing I said sounded like real human words.

He kissed me again. "Shower's in there if you need it. Get some rest, love. And if you need me, I'll be right out there."

I nodded again, he left, and I crawled my hot-mess self into the pristine guest bed and immediately felt guilty for whoever would have to clean up the snot- and tear-soaked pillow after me.

And then I cried myself to sleep.

※

The next morning, I showered, got dressed in something out of one of my suitcases, which were now neatly stacked inside my room, and stumbled my way to the kitchen.

I stopped cold.

Gavin sat at the kitchen island, drinking coffee and typing away at his laptop.

I just stood there, staring at him, wondering what on earth he was even doing here.

He glanced up, then immediately stood, that worried look on his face. "Candace, are you—did you sleep well?"

I gave him a ghost of a smile. "I did. Thank you. Really. I needed that." I frowned. "Why aren't you at work?" I blanched. "It's not because of me…is it?"

My heart plummeted to my feet. Of course it was.

He came over and took me into his arms. "There's nowhere else I'd rather be. Can you tell me what happened?"

Yeah, but this was the last week or so of filming. His studio had to be losing their minds.

I hesitated, but he gave one shake of his head. "Non-negotiable."

I leaned into him and breathed deep of his wonderful scent. "Maybe over coffee?"

He got me a cup, and not only that, he made me a gourmet breakfast of eggs, cheese, arugula, and sprouts on an open English muffin. I was as melty as the gooey cheese over his thoughtfulness, but I knew I couldn't eat a bite until

I told him everything. Of course, we might not be having breakfast together after that…

He placed it in front of me, and I warmed my hands on my mug and took a deep breath.

And I told him everything, start to finish.

How I couldn't let it go like he'd asked me to. How I'd been fired, kidnapped, and had finally found and helped free Mr. Withers. How Detective Sawyer considered the case closed, thanks to me.

When I finished, we were both silent. Okay, he was silent. I was internally freaking out.

I hadn't listened to him, or anyone else, and I thought I could handle it all when I couldn't. I'd let everything important slip away—my job, my relationship, my sanity—all because I couldn't let things go. I had to be right.

At the cost of everything.

I took a deep breath. "Are you mad at me?"

"Mad?" He laughed wryly and shook his head. "No. Disappointed? Yes."

I groaned and rubbed my face. "That's worse! But…I know. Me too."

Gavin came around the island and took my hands in his. "What I don't understand is why you didn't tell me. Why you felt you needed to keep it from me."

Tears, stupid, stupid tears filled my eyes. "You were so busy, I didn't want to bother you. I also didn't call you because I *couldn't*. Stan got me a new phone, and none of my calls or texts would go through. Not only that, I wanted to make it on my own, do it all on my own. I didn't want to be a needy, whining, complaining, crying girlfriend." I waved to my mess of a self. "Like now. I wanted to be good enough for you."

I snapped my mouth closed. Oops. I hadn't meant for that to come out.

He shook his head. "Candace. You *are* enough for me.

Just by being you. I don't need you to be some famous fashion guru or photographer or journalist for me to want you. I only want those things for you because *you* want them."

Now tears were dripping onto my shirt. Ugh.

"Oh, Candace. I'm so sorry you felt you had to be someone else for me. And please know you can always call the studio. Or come down and see me. Jodi knows you're on my most-important list, and she'd be happy to set up your new phone."

I stared at him in amazement. "How are we not breaking up right now?"

"I'd be a hypocrite if the very thing I love about you — that tenacity when you're determined to do the right thing — makes me give up on us when it's hard."

I covered my face, overcome, and he wrapped me in those perfectly muscled arms, and I cried all over his shirt like a baby.

"Besides, I've done some things I'm not proud of."

And that made me think of Lola.

I stiffened. I had to do this while I wasn't looking at him. I had to know. "What — what about — Lola?"

He pulled back, frowning. "Lola? Lola who? Your assistant?"

I nodded, and as much as I wanted to hide, I couldn't look away. "She said that you and her…she and you…she said…"

My face crumpled.

And a look I'd never seen before came over his face. Quite anger. Rage, even.

I wilted.

"What did she say, exactly." His voice was calm, tightly controlled, but a storm danced in his eyes.

I looked away and told him word for word. Because it had been spiraling in my head since she'd said it.

He cursed and ran his hand through his hair, and a sudden realization hit me: he was angry at himself, not me. My mouth fell open. It was *true*, then?

He tugged me over to sit on his barstools, facing each other. "Candace, before I met you, I...wasn't in a good place. Women, drugs, drinking until I passed out..."

My eyes widened. What? I had no idea! He'd been my favorite actor. Still was. But I'd read everything about him I could get my hands on, and no tabloid had ever reported something like this.

And they knew how to dig up dirt like no one's business. (It wasn't theirs either, but that didn't stop them.) Anyway.

I kinda shriveled up inside.

He rubbed the backs of my hands with his thumbs. I hadn't even realized he was still holding them.

"I was good at pretending. Keeping it quiet. Only drinking with those I trusted." He barked a laugh. I knew how he felt about trust. "I was in a bad place before filming *Zombie*. Sure, I clean up for every movie—didn't want that affecting my roles or word getting around—but I couldn't be alone with myself."

Oh my gosh, neither could I, but for different reasons. Should I...ask? Or save delving into his past for another time? *If* there was another time.

He looked as though every word pained him. "I don't remember...much...from that time in my life. After I became famous. If she said I dated her, that I...slept...with her, then there's a distinct possibility I did."

My heart shattered into dust, and I couldn't breathe.

I mean, I knew with my head that people slept together before they got married. And he was a famous movie star who could get any woman he wanted, after all. But I'd been raised with the "wait for marriage" mantra embedded so deep, I hadn't known until this moment how much my heart had hoped he'd waited for me, too.

He dropped his head. "Candace, I'm so sorry."

"What about—what about…?"

He held my hands just a little tighter, looking wrung out but meeting my eyes. "Go ahead. Ask. I'll answer as honestly as I can." He sighed. "If I remember."

Oh my gosh. I didn't remember things because my brain hated me. I couldn't imagine having chunks of my past gone because I'd drowned them in legal and illegal substances.

No wonder he'd gotten so good at remembering everyone's names.

I tucked myself close to his side, needing the physical contact to be brave enough to ask. "What about your film? The current one? Hard-R and strippers and bikinis and drugs and strippers and bikinis? Are you…okay with that?"

He flinched a little. "Honestly, I hadn't even thought about it until that day you showed up on set."

I started to apologize, but he held a finger over my lips. "Don't. I needed to think about it."

I nodded, and he traced my lips before cupping my cheek and giving me a sweet kiss.

Not to sound too pathetic, but I almost started weeping again. We were having this horribly serious conversation, and he wasn't about to throw me out? We were still talking?

Maybe I could do this adulting stuff.

He sighed. "When I'm preparing for a role, it's like I go to a different place. I become someone else, the person I need to be for that role."

I stiffened, and he held me just a little tighter.

"I've never fallen in love on or off set before you, Candace. They told me to be as close to myself as possible for our film, and you were so real and genuine and cared about everyone and everything so deeply—you don't have to worry that was an act."

But I still did worry, no matter how many times he told me this.

I didn't say anything, but I started to relax by degrees.

He took that as a sign to keep going. "I'd signed for this film before *Zombie*, and it was just another role for me until I saw your face. Then I started noticing everything. How…*wrong*…it all was. It doesn't even have a redemptive arc—it glories in the deepest debauchery the writers could think up—and ends with the main character, my character, killing as many of his enemies as he can, in a bloodbath, while he's dying from his own wounds."

I squinted up at him. Was he serious?

And oh my gosh, I never wanted to see this film.

He rubbed the gooseflesh off my arm, his other arm still around me. "After I met you, then hurt you so badly deceiving you about the film, I started taking a deep, long look at my life. I thought I'd lost you, and it was no one's fault but mine—"

"And the studio's," I muttered.

That got a half smile out of him, but he kept going. "And I just couldn't live like that anymore. You were so genuine about your faith…"

I sat up abruptly. "But I was too shy to talk about it! I wanted to sink into the ground every time I prayed or said something about Jesus."

I flushed even now. Geez-Louise. I cared waaay too much what people thought. I needed to get over that ASAP.

"But you still did. And you cared. You loved deeply. You put everyone above yourself, *even if you didn't like them*. That stood out to me the most. You were willing to sacrifice yourself for others, because you saw that they had value, no matter how messed up they were. I craved that."

Wow. I mean, just, wow. I had no idea.

"At the risk of sounding too cheesy, you showed me Jesus for the first time in my life."

I couldn't help it. I burst into tears. I literally had *no idea*.

He wrapped me in his arms again, rested his chin on my head, and spoke softly. "I know this doesn't happen to everyone, but when I gave my life to God, even when I thought I'd never see you again, he delivered me. Wholly. Completely. Never had another craving or was even tempted. It was miraculous, and it was exactly what I needed."

I started hiccuping, my sobs doing their best to interrupt him.

"Then when I saw you at that coffee shop...it was like God handed me the present I wanted most in the world and didn't think I was good enough to have. I've been trying to do all in my power since then to treat you like the precious gift you are. Because you are, Candace. There is no one like you, and I am honored and privileged to be a part of your life. That is, if you still want me."

Oh, sheesh. Now I was soaking his shirt, hoping I'd get a breath sometime soon, and was moving dangerously close to wailing.

But I'd never been told anything like this in my life.

I nodded yes as hard as I could, since I couldn't speak at the moment.

When my torrent of tears had subsided just enough for other sounds to be heard, Gavin started praying for me. Softly.

My eyes flew open. Since when did movie star Gavin Bailey *pray*?

I was pretty sure I was the last person on earth to be a good influence on anybody.

But there he was, his rich, smooth voice filling the space around us and bringing with it peace.

"God, you see how much Candace is hurting right now. Please heal her heart, comfort her when I can't, and show her just how wonderful she is. Thank you for forgiving me for my past, and please show her how abundantly you hand out second chances, and that nothing she or I could ever do can separate us from your love. Amen."

My mouth was hanging open at this point. Simple, direct, and oh so very Gavin—and God answered it. That peace Gavin asked for flooded me, and now I was crying for another reason. But at least I was crying softly this time.

My boyfriend still loved me! Had prayed for me! Wasn't going to leave me in some ditch somewhere with a "you have too much crazy for me" speech!

Joy hit me so hard, I ached with it.

He rubbed my back as I sob-laughed.

Gavin chuckled. "That bad, huh?"

I looked up at him with shining eyes and a tear-streaked face. "Bad? It was perfect! Thank you, Gavin. That means the world."

He kissed my lips with a brush of his. "And you mean the world to me. I hope you know that."

I grinned like a fool. "I do now."

He held me, and I was content to rest in his arms. He played with my fingers, and I marveled at this guy God had placed in my life.

He'd used me to help someone when I didn't even know it was happening. How awesome was that?

And suddenly, worrying about every little thing I said or did didn't seem quite so important anymore.

I played with his fingers right back, for the first time in a long time at peace and still and quiet on the inside. "So… where do we go from here?"

He kissed me. "Always forward, looking to the author of our lives and finisher of our faith, stronger together, with him."

I smiled. I could get behind that.

EPILOGUE

I stared out the window at the brightly lit Christmas tree in the square below. A great huff of air blew past my lips, sending hair strands blasting away only to settle over my eye once more.

This is ridiculous, I groused to myself.

Any more sitting around like this, and I would go stark-raving mad.

I glanced over my shoulder into the kitchen and at the precariously stacked plates and bowls. Nope. Not interested. The dishes would have to wait for another day.

I returned my gaze to the happy scene below. Families paused in front of the tree, pointing excitedly and snapping pictures. New Yorkers rushed by, seemingly heedless, but many sent a lingering, peace-filled glance toward the towering beauty before returning to their hectic pace.

I rested my forehead against the cool glass and craned my neck to see a particularly excited little girl, curls bouncing crazily as she danced around the tree, shouting something unintelligible from my perch above.

Bang. Bang. Bang.

I sat up and rubbed my forehead. It was official. Going

crazy most definitely started with banging one's head against any surface. I had to get out.

Jumping away from the Hallmark-worthy level of happiness below, I paced. And paced. I had nowhere to go. Nothing to do.

Wander through Macy's? Nope. Did that yesterday. Go admire the tree in Times Square with all those annoyingly happy people? Nope. Too cold.

Plus, their glorious mood was the last thing I wanted to be around right now. I liked my miserable mood. I wanted to wallow in it for a while.

Beg Gavin to take me to another Broadway play? No, I was bothering the poor man too much as it was. It wasn't his fault he had a life and I didn't. Nope, it was my fault entirely.

Check my emails?

I stopped. Turning slowly, I eyed my phone, sitting harmlessly on the breakfast nook that separated the kitchen from the living room and my many bookshelves. Should I…? No. I promised Gavin I wouldn't, and I wasn't going to. Not at all.

Maybe…just one peek?

I dove for my phone, cradling it in my palm.

Please, Lord…

I bit off the desperate prayer and flicked open the home screen. My thumb hovered over my email. I'd promised…

With a groan, I tossed my phone on the red beanbag under my reading lamp and slouched on the even redder couch.

Most people's couches faced a TV. Not mine. Mine faced a bookshelf, filled with far too many books to be fashionable. Books I never had time to read. Until now. Except, now I couldn't sit still or concentrate long enough to read much of anything.

My eyes drifted over the spacious apartment, lightly

sprinkled with modern furniture, all artistically placed by Gavin's designer around the brightly lit room. Almost an entire wall of windows helped with that.

I wouldn't be able to afford this place much longer if I didn't get a job. Fast. My savings were starting to run out. At least I'd paid for the furniture as I could afford it. Furniture I might have to sell to keep living here.

I groaned, threw myself sideways on the couch, and smacked my forehead.

"Stupid, stupid, stupid! You had to go chasing vampires, didn't you? 'Don't do it' Gavin said. 'Don't do it' your boss said. 'Don't do it' just about every reasonable person you talked to said. But did you listen? Did you? Of course not!"

I grabbed a pillow and shoved it over my face.

"Mphm…mehiekjdnfientbgid…"

"Talking to yourself?"

I shrieked and jumped off the couch. My foot caught on the coffee table, and I sprawled on the floor, inches from catching my face on the oh-so-elegant Tiffany lamp Gavin's personal designer said I just "couldn't live without."

Gavin chuckled as he helped me off the floor, then kissed the tip of my bright-red nose. "You all right, my bonnie lass?"

"Oh, you know, fine. Just bruised and humbled, like every second of my life lately."

"Stop it." Gavin sternly tapped my chin. "No more of that talk. We agreed. You'll find something, soon, and then you won't have time to remember pacing the floor worrying about your next position. Remember, 'take no thought for tomorrow.' God will provide." His tone lightened. "I brought takeout and a movie. You game? It's your favorite —Chinese."

Gavin threw the last part over his shoulder as he strode toward the kitchen. I realized where he was going about three seconds later.

"Don't! Stop! Don't go in there!" I ran after him, but I was too late.

"Candace!"

I cringed as he stared openmouthed into my disaster of a kitchen. Maybe I should've harnessed some of that pacing energy into cleaning…

"Are those the same dishes from last weekend?"

"Um, well…maybe?"

Gavin marched toward me, and I backed up a step.

"Don't be mad, but I just…"

Gavin's arms went around me in a tight hug. The silence lengthened, and I relaxed in Gavin's strong arms. "You're really worried about this, aren't you?"

I deflated. Unwelcome tears stung my eyes. I blinked rapidly. "It's been nine months, Gavin. Almost ten! None of my applications have turned into interviews, and any follow-up I've done has been met with a stony, 'I'm sorry, but *we* will contact *you*.' It's like I've got a giant 'do not hire' symbol sewn in red on my shirt."

"Don't give up. If you just…"

"I can't, Gavin! I don't know how much longer I can afford to live here! And people usually move here for jobs—they don't come searching for them. I screwed myself over completely by getting fired. Now nobody wants me."

Gavin pulled back and shook me slightly. "Don't say that. I want you."

He chewed on his lip. I knew what he was going to say before he opened his mouth.

"I can help…"

"No, Gavin! I don't want your money." I held up a finger. "Or your connections. I'm *not* using you."

"You know, you started as a reporter and enjoyed it. What if you went back into journalism?"

Technically, I was a copy editor and only whipped up stories when there was a gap, but close enough.

"I have a few connections…" He held up his hands. "Just to get you an interview, nothing else. Promise." A delicious smile spread across his face, a streak of mischievousness in his eyes. "Why have connections if you can't use them?"

He was never going to stop offering, was he?

I jabbed his firm stomach. "Hey now. None of that. I need to do this on my own."

He kissed my nose again. "I thought you might say that. Just remember not to be too proud to accept help when the Lord sends it."

My jaw dropped.

Seriously, who was this guy? He'd changed so much since I'd met him.

And not because I'd asked him to. Nope, he was making changes because *he* wanted them. So why couldn't I do that with my obsessive self?

I tugged away from his grasp and went back to pacing. "I appreciate it, I really do, but if I can't make it on my own, well…" I swallowed and forced myself to meet his gaze. "Maybe it's time for me to move back home. With my parents." An involuntary shudder passed through me. "Get a job in my hometown, where the cost of living isn't so outrageous. Maybe then I can regroup and decide my next steps. What I want to do with my life."

Gavin stared at me, long and hard, considering, thinking. I could see it in his eyes. He slowly walked forward, taking my hand and leading me to the couch. We sank onto the plush sofa, the wall of silent books eavesdropping on our conversation.

"Candace, I know you don't want to accept my help. Shh. Just listen."

The warmth of Gavin's finger on my lips stilled my protest. For the moment, anyway.

"I know you don't want to accept my help, and that's one

thing I love about you. You are so strong, independent. A fighter. But God also puts people in our lives to help each other in times of need, and that's what I want to do for you. I know how you feel about taking my money, but you're not. I'm giving it. Freely, no strings attached."

He gently took my hands in his and kissed my palms, one at a time.

My palms tingled as his lips came into contact with bare skin. *Excuse me while I melt into a pile of goo over here that will never come out of this sofa.*

He kept going, his softly accented voice doing all kinds of delightful things to my stomach. "You have such talent, and I want you to have as many opportunities as possible to do what you love." He grinned. "And I have to admit I selfishly want you to stay here. With me."

I groaned and leaned forward, burying my face in Gavin's expensive shirt and broad and firm and muscular chest. I loved that chest a little too much. "But I'm the pariah of the fashion world right now. No one wants to hire someone who's been fired from *Voilà Magazine*."

He pulled me to face him. "Then don't give them a chance to back down. Take your portfolio—show them your work. Use me as a reference. Use that tenacity I love about you and don't back down. You've got this. Okay?" He waited for my response too long before giving me another little shake. "Okay?"

"Okay," I grumbled. Then panicked. "But Gavin! Everyone and their cousin in the whole entire world wants to use you. You don't understand. I can't do that to you. I *can't*."

"You can if I'm giving you my full permission." He grinned, his lips entirely too delicious. I may have stared at them. "Go on. Use me. I'm begging you."

I flushed bright red, then burst into laughter, and he joined me, chuckling in his deep, intoxicating voice.

"All joking aside," he said, "I'm being completely serious. I hope you know that."

Another huff blew strands of hair away from my face, and I relented. "Okay, *fine*. But only because you insist."

Gavin smiled and leaned forward, but I held up a finger. He paused.

"But if it gets weird, even once, even if it's entirely my fault, I'm done. You're more important than your connections."

His smile shifted into a tender look that had me melting into goo, and he gently rested his lips on mine. I let him kiss me a moment, then threw my arms around his neck, kissing him passionately in return.

His firm shoulders under my arms, his strong arms holding me gently to him, his perfectly fit, toned, and muscular body against mine—I started to forget what we'd been talking about.

Gavin pulled back breathlessly. "Whoa, whoa, whoa, any more kissing like that and I may forget how to be a gentleman. Maybe we should eat out."

I grinned wickedly. "No, I'll be good."

"Sure you will," Gavin mumbled, staring at my lips. "Oh! I almost forgot. I got you a little something. An early Christmas present."

I brightened as soon as he said it. I loved presents.

He slipped off the couch and walked over to his jacket hanging neatly by the front door. He retrieved something from his coat pocket and padded back to me.

He handed me the brightly wrapped box, lavishly draped with a giant blue bow.

"Oh, Gavin, you shouldn't have!" I squealed, bouncing excitedly. Could I act any more like a child? Hopefully neither of us found out.

Gavin quirked a grin. "Go on. Open it." He sat next to me. "I know it's a little early, but…" He shrugged.

In other words, he knew I'd tear into a present, any present, no matter how many days before Christmas or my birthday or whatever other occasion it was.

Which was why he usually waited until day of.

I tugged at the bow, trying to get it out of my way so I could get to the paper. My mind raced. The package was big enough to hold a necklace or a small book. Maybe that scarf I'd been drooling over?

Not that I *needed* a scarf right now until I had a job to wear it to…unless it gave me the confidence to nail the next interview…

The bow finally fell away, dropping to the ground, the blue and silver paper not far behind. I paused at the matching blue and silver box, taking a moment to close my eyes and savor the suspense. Enough of that. The lid bounced and skittered across the floor.

Everything froze. I stared into the box.

Silence.

I didn't know what to do.

A giant, glittering, gorgeous diamond and ruby ring was positioned artfully in the oversized box, little mementos of our time together surrounding it, each one labeled neatly.

A blank, for the time he'd taught me how to shoot. A coffee cup wrapper, from the time we'd first found each other in New York. A Broadway ticket stub, for the first real date we'd had after our movie together. A perfectly preserved rose petal, vibrant red and coated with something to keep it looking like it had just been plucked, from the first red rose he'd given me. And more.

I had no idea all that blue on the box meant something. Hey, I didn't drool over my wedding like most other girls, okay? This scenario had never even occurred to me.

Except to shove it deep down, afraid to hope for it.

He pulled me close to his side. He wrapped one arm

around my waist while he traced my fingers holding the box with his other hand.

"Candace, I can think of no one I'd rather grow old with. In this crazy world of not knowing whom to trust, you've always had my back, and you've proven that to me time and time again. Now I'd like to do that for you. I want you to know I will always be there for you, no matter what. What do you say? Will you marry me?"

I sat very still. A part of me shriveled up and cringed away from what I was about to say.

I slowly peeked at him. "Gavin…this isn't your way of solving my money problems, is it? I'd rather have a loan than marry you if you aren't ready for this."

My heart plummeted as the words left my mouth, but I wouldn't be able to respect myself if I didn't ask.

His face lost all color. "What? No! I was going to ask after you got back from Paris—well, I wanted to surprise you and ask *in* Paris—but then you lost your job. I kept waiting for the perfect moment, but…" He shrugged. "Well, I can't wait any longer."

We'd also postponed our Hampton beach house trip. Jodi and Dave were still polite around each other and not responding to anything Gavin did to match them up. Just one more thing to feel guilty about.

And I couldn't believe *that* was where my mind went while being faced with this question.

We stared at each other. I felt a prick of guilt when worry creased his forehead.

"Really?" I whispered.

He lifted the sparkling heart-shaped ruby with tiny diamonds outlining it, the ring nestled in sheer white fabric. "Really."

He slipped it on my finger.

I stared at it in a daze, then looked between him and the

sparkling heart on my finger. It was *perfect*. "Are you serious?"

He relaxed, and the grin eased back across his face. "I'm serious."

I dove for him, wrapping him tight in a hug. He started to say something, but I cut him off with a thousand kisses. He returned them, his arms sliding around me.

He pulled back, his breathing ragged. "Is that a yes?"

"Yes! Oh, yes, yes, yes!"

There was no one else in the entire world I wanted to do life with.

I dove in for another kiss.

After several of the most blissful moments on earth, Gavin set me away from him with a wide grin, his eyes dancing with joy. "Now we are most definitely eating out."

THE END

Don't miss Candace's final misadventure in:

Mummy Resurrection

Book Three of the Candace Marshall Chronicles.

Coming Soon from L2L2 Publishing.

THANK YOU!

Thank you for reading this book!
Did you enjoy *Vampire Feud*?
Please leave a review!
It helps more than you can possibly know.
Thank you so much!

~Michele Israel Harper

ACKNOWLEDGMENTS

A huge thank you to everyone who helped make this book better!

To Alicia: Your feedback was invaluable. Thank you for being my first reader! I can't tell you how much I love your insight and how your mind works. So many good calls.

To my beta readers: Thank you for letting me know what worked for you, what didn't, and what you wanted more of.

To Bethany: Oh my goodness, I'm so embarrassed you saw this manuscript when it was such a mess! Thank you for helping me wrangle it into shape. You are an *incredible* editor. Also, your gifs and memes are life.

To Jessica "Faestock" Truscott: Thank you again for the use of your lovely image! You are just the sweetest.

To Sara: this cover is gorgeous! I can't get over the drippy font or how you took my idea for a vampire feud and made it look glorious. I love working with you so very much, thank you!

To my family: Ben, Blaze, Maverick, and Gwenivere. I love you all. Thank you for your patience when I disappear into my writing cave once more. Let's take that vacation!

ACKNOWLEDGMENTS

To everyone who shared my cover, about this release, or absolutely anything else about this book: I am so grateful for you. Thank you for spreading the word!

And to my readers: I am so thankful for each one of you. Thank you for reading this story, for encouraging me, for asking for more, and for being the best readers an author can have. Here's to many more books in the future!

(And a HUGE thank you to those few specific readers—you know who you are—who emailed me, messaged me, texted me, or straight-up asked on SM, "Where on earth is the next Candace Marshall book??" I hope you had a good laugh with our girl.)

And last but certainly not least, thank you to the Creator of words, who writes these stories with me and for whom I write all my stories. Any glory is yours. I love you.

In Him,
Michele Israel Harper

ABOUT THE AUTHOR

Michele Israel Harper spends her days as a freelance editor, her afternoons guzzling coffee, and her nights spinning her own tales. Sleep? Sometimes . . .

She has her master's degree in publishing, is slightly obsessed with all things French—including Jeanne d'Arc and *La Belle et la Bête*—and loves curling up with a good book more than just about anything else.

Author of multiple published novels (and more on the way), Michele prays her involvement in writing, editing, and publishing will touch many lives in the years to come.

Visit MicheleIsraelHarper.com to keep in touch or to learn about future books!

ABOUT THE AUTHOR

Michele loves to hear from her readers! Follow her on social media, check out her website, or drop her a line to let her know what you thought of Vampire Feud. *Happy reading!*

www.MicheleIsraelHarper.com
Facebook: @MicheleIsraelHarper
Twitter: @MicheleIHarper
Instagram: @Michele_Israel_Harper

Join her newsletter for bookish news and an ebook copy of
The Lost Slipper!
MicheleIsraelHarper.com/My-Newsletter

More from L2L2 Publishing
Read the Whole Series so far!

Meet the world's biggest scaredy-cat, Candace Marshall. She doesn't do scary, but after being locked in a haunted mansion, surviving the zombie apocalypse, being chased by every vampire in New York City, and going on the worst assignment of her life in Egypt, she has to face her biggest fears again and again. Not only does she grow a little along the way, she just might find a smidgeon of courage. Not to mention that she learns to run faster with each encounter of the stupid-scary kind.

More from L2L2 Publishing
Read the Whole Series so far!

French huntress Ro LeFèvre chases fairy tale creatures across France, Angleterre, Prussia, the Caribbean, and more, to protect those she loves. Join her as she's hired to kill beasts, hunt sirens, break curses, depose queens, and negotiate peace, all to end the fey's destruction across the human realm. The Beast Hunters series is sprinkled with many beloved fairy tales, full of frightful creatures, and complete at seven books. Stop the Snow Queen and End the Fey coming soon!

WHERE WILL WE TAKE YOU NEXT?

Shiver with *Ghostly Vendetta*,
Feast on *Zombie Takeover*,
Revisit *Vampire Feud*,
Devour *Mummy Resurrection*,
or check out the Beast Hunters Series.

All at
www.love2readlove2writepublishing.com/bookstore
or your local or online retailer.

Happy Reading!
~The L2L2 Publishing Team

Milton Keynes UK
Ingram Content Group UK Ltd.
UKHW031301251024
450245UK00004B/371